ALSO BY CHARLIE SMITH

FICTION

Canaan
Shine Hawk
The Lives of the Dead
Crystal River (novellas)

POETRY

Red Roads
Indistinguishable from the Darkness
The Palms

CHIMNEY ROCK

CHARLIE SMITH

HENRY HOLT AND COMPANY

NEW YORK

*A portion of the novel, in an earlier version,
appeared in the Tenth Anniversary Edition
of the magazine* Conjunctions.

Henry Holt and Company, Inc.
Publishers since 1866
115 West 18th Street
New York, New York 10011

Henry Holt® is a registered trademark
of Henry Holt and Company, Inc.

Published in Canada by Fitzhenry & Whiteside Limited,
91 Granton Drive, Richmond Hill, Ontario L4B 2N5.

Library of Congress Cataloging-in-Publication Data
Smith, Charlie.
Chimney rock : a novel / Charlie Smith.
    p. cm.
  I. Title.
PS3569.M5163C47   1993
813'.54—dc20   92-39377
                                                   CIP

ISBN 0-8050-2244-9

First Edition—1993

Designed by Katy Riegel
Printed in the United States of America
All first editions are printed on acid-free paper.⊗

10 9 8 7 6 5 4 3 2 1

To Allen Peacock

There is no faithfulness in their mouth,
and their inner parts are destruction;
and their throat is an open grave,
and all their tongues are smooth.

—Fifth Psalm

"Say good night to the bad guy . . ."

—Al Pacino in *Scarface*

CHIMNEY ROCK

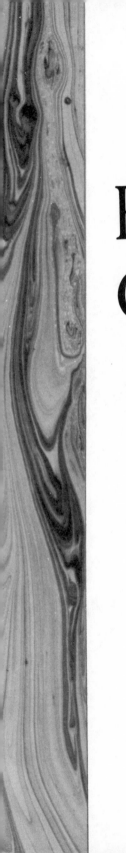

BOOK
ONE

A S WE ROSE between walls of flowers into the terrible city I was speaking of Kate's death and of death in general when the driver said he could show me a place where six people died. I said six people are not so many, thinking of her, of Kate, the famous Zebra Dunn, my wife, of her death that was and wasn't, thinking of the one-legged shadow waiting for me on the beach north of Mazatlán, of the fork-tailed birds flying out of the camphor trees, and of the wild cats crying.

The driver, whose head was small and square, whose jaw looked as if he had pushed his face into soot, swiveled in the seat and said It's a lot when they're your family. I said, Yes that is a lot. He said, You're Will Blake, aren't you? I said, You can call me Bobby. Why is that? he said. I like the name Bobby, I said. That's fine, he said, you all change your names, don't you, you movie stars; you all have these regular names that you change so they'll sound good to the public, I know. Not me, I said, I was born a Blake, Bobby or Will, or Tony sometimes, maybe Constable when I'm feeling dignified and effete, but Blake is what came through the generations to me—how about you? Arnold Pescadoro, he said, as if he was making it up on the spot.

And there, shaken down to the edge of the drift, off the ramble, I was returned to LA, come home now in time for the Academy Awards. Everything was dusty and vague. The palm trees and the eucalyptus trees and the paloverde bushes beside the little Mexican urban rancheros were dusty, and the hookers on Soledad were dusty, and the pale linen and chrome buildings were dusty, and if you lifted in a balloon or a rocket ship you would see that the continent all the way to the isthmus was dusty, even the skin of your loved ones dusty, the jacaranda blossoms and the surface of your drink sprinkled with dust, like a world where nothing could shake off its sense of abandonment. I said, Where are these six people, and he said, They're all gone, dead like I said, but I can show you where it happened.

I said, Is this what you do, take your fares around to show them this site?

No, he said, only the ones who talk about this kind of thing.

Death?

Yeah. It was already six months ago but I can't shake it, I don't think I'm ever going to get over it.

I don't see why you should. I haven't gotten over anything that's ever happened to me.

Yeah, he said, it's like that isn't it?

Thinking, as we momentarily paused for traffic by a set of benches where old women with gnawed-out eyes stared into the bougainvillea across the street, that I wanted to remember it all, the beach of saffron sand under the ochre cliffs and the scrawl of rose bushes by the long stairs leading down to the water and the cats and the figure of her, mutilated woman standing at the edge of the surf, where the waves slipped back, leaving a sheen on the sand like varnish. Thinking it didn't matter whether I wanted to or not—I was going to remember it, carry it the rest of my life.

I said, All right, let's go there, I have time.

Yeah, he said, you got time, the ceremonies don't start for a couple of hours, isn't that right?

Yes.

You're up for best actor, huh?

That's right. .

You going to win?

Yes.

My third nomination, the charm, I figured, I would win for sure. Thinking of the puckered, sunken stump—that blushed, she said, like an embarrassed, punched-in face—my new receptor, she said, a new method for feeling my way into the world.

Uplifted now, off the plain, behind us the whale-colored Pacific, through town and out into the meager Mexican streets; there, up a rough red dirty ridge, a line of royal palms, their ragged tops tethered to slender trunks like wigs on stiff rope; little roughed-up houses nearby; the road curving downhill past stores locked up behind brocades of steel; a couple of kids pedaling furiously toward what looked like a sheer drop into space. Swing right past bushy cypresses, past a used-record store, a store selling movie posters—one of my posters in which I am luridly, handsomely, firing a pistol at a lurching madman (*Point Diablo*)—tacked

4

to a white wall; the smell of brass and rancid cooking oil, frying corn.

How far is it? I said.

Not far, just down here. Pointing off to the right, downhill where the terrain flattened out toward the railroad tracks, a dusty place between a warehouse and a string of wooden shotgun houses, hibiscus blossoming in front yards, stacks of rusted used equipment leaning against the side of a busted car, these terrible brokenhearted attempts to build life no matter what, life like a radio playing a single foreign language station thrusting gritty repetitive music without interruption toward you.

Here, he said—there.

It's an empty lot.

Yeah, but it didn't use to be.

It was an empty lot grown up in yellow grass, ashy fire scars showing, and a set of concrete front porch steps and a portion of concrete walk leading to weeds.

What happened here?

My family burned up.

Jesus. That's terrible.

Yeah. It was the gangs. Kids in a car shooting off guns. Late at night. They came down the street shooting guns. Hit a can full of gas I had on the front porch. The fire blew into the house. Everybody burned up—my wife, my mother, my kids.

Where were you?

I was driving the limo.

I leaned over the front seat. At the rear of the property a low wall showed scorch marks in one corner, but most of it was covered in a fresh mural depicting children playing ball. The mural was painted in fierce primitive colors, bright like the paintings in the basements of the pyramids in the Yucatán.

Let's get out, he said.

Okay.

We got out and stood on the sidewalk in the merciless sunlight looking at the vacancy.

He said, What are you talking about, your wife is dead? Your wife is Zebra Dunn isn't she?

Yes, I said, she is.

It would be in the papers, he said, if she was dead.

She's strangely dead, I said.

5

What's that mean?

Zebra Dunn is no more, yet who was Zebra lives yet.

I don't understand what you are saying.

I'm being purposely obscure.

I don't know, he said, I don't have to tell no lies. This happened—he swept his brown arm out—and it's real. I can't step away from it.

I don't see how you could.

Yeah. I come here every day.

You think about it at night?

Yeah. And I dream about it. It's strange, dreaming. I see us all lying on a beach in some foreign place, all of us, except everybody is lying under a blanket like we were sleeping. There're sounds too. You ever have dreams with sounds in them?

Not much.

Well, there're sounds in this one—gnawing, crunching sounds like some big beast behind things is eating lumber. That's what it sounds like, some big animal is eating boards or a house or something.

That's terrifying.

Yeah, I wake up in a sweat. I wake up crying.

I'm glad you could tell me about it.

Hell, I tell everybody about it. I talk about it all the time. I got to. You're the third customer this week I took here. I'd take everybody here if I could. It's going to get me fired.

You can't help it.

No, I can't.

Or me either, I figured. Everyone says *That's his nature,* and some mean it. They're talking, I've decided, about fate. Which is everything piled up and enchained in your life and all past lives and actions that led up to this. I could very easily wander away down this street, I could turn in a fury and tear this man's eyes out. We push on through the outskirts of meaning. Trying to get somewhere. Even Kate, who has already been everywhere.

The man, a very short man in baggy clothes, had begun to cry. I put my arm around his shoulders, two troopers toughing it out. He leaned into me, I thought he wanted to hug my neck, but he was scuffling in his pocket for something.

Here, he said, let me show you.

What?

The fire burned everything up, he said, nobody could get out, it burned the house to the ground, burned it to ashes. They wouldn't let me go in there even after it was over because the police wanted to look at things, but I sneaked back in later, at night, after everybody was gone.

You found something.

Yeah. He leaned away as if against a wind. He smelled of sweet floral perfume and vaguely of shit. He said, I dug through the ashes. I had to find something, something I could keep. They were all burned up, but I couldn't be satisfied until I found something.

Thinking of the flight up from Mexico, of the clouds in unbroken array stretching from the Gulf of California to the LA basin, someone looking up in Sonora at the same clouds someone was looking up at in San Berdoo. Thinking of Kate leaning back into the darkness, stepping away from the car.

Here, he said, look.

It was a clean white handkerchief wrapped around small objects. He carefully unfolded it. They were three black links, little burned sticks.

What are they?

Finger bones. I dug around in the ashes until I found them. It's one of my kids, I think. They're so small it has to be.

Ah, you poor guy.

Nah, he said, these make me happy. I got something. I got something I can keep.

The handkerchief looked like the crumpled white body of a bird. The bones had stained it slightly. He must pick out a new one every day, I thought.

I carry them with me everywhere, he said. I'm not going to ever let them get away from me.

That's a good idea, I said. Something to keep, something you can't help keeping.

He stared at the handkerchief, this dumbfounded, ruined guy staring into what was left. To the south two helicopters, painted white, followed each other above a ridge. Westward the sun headed, like a failed liberator, toward the Pacific and Japan.

YOU STARE AT *the sun, and soon—it takes almost no time—you can see the dark inside it.* That was from Kate's first video—or the first one in a couple of years—arrived three weeks ago, wrapped in white paper, stamped in Mexico. From the silence, from the desert coast of Sinaloa, straight from her face and her body, from her blue eyes aimed straight at me, they flew, her proofs and messages, stirred alive again out of horror and mad glee, out of the blasted ruin she was left with, reports from hell. Every few days another arrived at my doorstep, and not only mine.

We swung in through the back gate into the Pavilion lot. The guards recognized me, waved us through. I was who I was, famous local boy and son of the man producing the show. We zipped up to the loading dock. My friend had stopped talking; he hummed to himself, pressing a little tune against his demons. There were animal pens in the parking lot, cages for elephants, giraffes, and other African creatures. The cages were empty; the animals apparently had been called to the set. Under the deck's metal hood you could smell the funky, rank circus odors. There were women in silver sequined bathing suits. Guys carrying big baskets of fruit wrapped in cellophane. I was tipped and muddled; even in this clamorous moment I rode a drifting daze, like someone who had lain all day in a rusted patch of desert shade.

I got out, leaned in, kissed Arnold Pescadoro on the cheek, and turned into the zip and bluster, into the arms of one of my father Clement's ADs. He is a man on his way up, tacked by the Academy like an identifying tag to my father's wing so the board of governors will know at all times just what rough flights Clement has taken. He led me through the tumble and shine of the backstage clamor to my father's dressing room.

I knew this world, knew the handlers and service people, knew the long blue corridors with their photographs of stars passed on to the heavenly soundstage, and the ease, the grease of familiarity, moved me on. I had flown eight hundred miles and it seemed, rolling down the corridors smelling of Max Factor and roses, that I had traveled not by plane but by cannon shot. On a long table were gifts, like gifts for a wedding, and in a lounge nearby, fresh fruit was piled high like the proof of harvest. Dancers, actors, and sycophants milled. The workers and overseers had arrived with the products of their labor, and these products were worthy. In the distance an elephant trumpeted. Horses whinnied, calling their paramours. There were no kings in Hollywood, but there were numerous chieftains, and as producer of the Awards, my father was supposed to make sure the praise spilled on the best was of the sweetest variety.

We round a corner, pass a bank of mirrors into which dancers throw their reflections, and come on them, on my father and mother, in my father's dressing room. My father, sitting naked to the waist on his dressing table, leans into my mother as she kneads the fat muscles across his shoulders. He welcomes me, this man who intends to kill me, as if I have been lost.

"Will," he says, throwing up his hands as if to strike, "son of sons."

My mother, Jennie White, the great actress, slides free of him, and embraces me. I can smell the perfume, Chanel No. 5, that she has worn all her Hollywood life. Her full, bloodless lips press hard against my neck. She has been retired for twenty years or more, since, or almost since my brother Bobby died, but she still moves with the aggressively supplicant grace of her character. From the corner, sprawled on a chaise among baskets of chrysanthemums, Max Stein, one of my father's cronies, an old-line producer like himself, hails me. He starts to crank his fat body up. "Stay where you are, Max," I say, laughing. I am oddly delighted to see them both. It's like looking at lions.

"You're inevitable," Max says with a damp fondness, flesh pleating around a broad grin with almost audible clicks. He chuckles, riding the bumper car of his bonhomie. From the doorway, ADs chirp questions—this is my father's project, this is what they have given him to do after too many dreadnought movies went to the bottom—and my father, the producer, snaps answers like a man firing a pistol.

"We were sitting here talking about this picture you're going to do for us," Max says, grinning.

"We don't have to talk about it," Clement says.

I am looking at my mother, who drifts between my father and me, shimmering, who has us all locked onto the set of the role she is playing. Her pale blue eyes, eyes in which irreducible chips of crystal sparkle, are on my face. She smiles, but in her eyes felons flee. I cross the room, bend down and kiss my father on the cheek, bend into the florid, Homeric scent of father smell, and kiss his cheek, which is bristly and hard.

He grasps my wrist. "I am so overjoyed," he says, lying openly. "I am so happy to see you."

There are tears in the corners of his eyes. It is his side of the street, this spendthrift emotion. Everyone knows this about him. All Hollywood has seen Clement Blake roar, rage, sob on a movie set and in his life in the world. He has used his own flowing tears, dipped up by his own hand, to supply tears to a reluctant actress, smearing her face with his salt. He is vicious as well, one of the old-line boys, a tormentor and manipulator, liable to kick down the scenery, to assault the halt and fearful; more than once he has expressed his dedication with his fists. He knows the world is here to run you over and is committed to not allowing this to happen without a fight.

My mother, at the long dressing table, pours herself a glass of champagne. She drinks it slowly, her beautiful head tilted back slightly, showing the yellowing marble column of her neck. I watch fascinated, and I can see the champagne, like a fizzing jism, sliding down her throat, her tongue striking deftly at the taste and bubbles, her full lips just slightly reaching for more. The fingers of her free hand are spread, tense, ready to grasp, the carpal bone protrudes like the stub of a weapon above the soft hollow of melting flesh at her wrist; her back is arched. I am not at all appalled, I am drawn by this, by my mother's sensual, insistent nature; she licks the rim of the glass and sets it down on the speckled counter as if it is a precious and failed thing. My father smacks his lips. Max turns his head away, smirking, proposing through his tiny eyes visions of another universe, someplace where he is in charge of women like this.

My father sighs, sets his shoulders. He would tear my flesh from my bones if he could, eat it unsalted and raw.

"What is it you wanted, Pop?" I say, taking a chair. I am agitated, I can only stay a couple of minutes, a few seconds maybe before I will have to wing away from here. I want to press my body through something irresistible. I have rehearsed the whole award business already, this ceremony, my lift toward the gold statuette. It is not only my speech I have in hand—that will be extemporaneous (my preparation is not to think about it ahead of time)—but I have already selected my route, checked my seat—weeks ago—walked the path from seat to aisle, to stage, moved off left to the wings, handled the curtain fabric, placed in my mind the scaffolding, the sets, the stagehands, the cables writhing like snakes at my feet, the mikes, my cohorts, the smells, the webs of steel in the flies: left nothing to chance. I always do this, always walk the route, always rehearse.

My father hacks his thigh with the flat of his hand. "It's this deal I've been putting together for months," he says, "this wonder deal. I told you about it. Earl"—my agent—"knows all about it." He speaks as if he is crunching stones between his teeth. I know what he is talking about. He will not let the horror between us stand in his way. He has found a way to use it to crush me. "Max and I have been talking about it—the picture is ready to go and we can't make it without you."

I lift a calculated eyebrow. "You and Max are in on this deal together?"

"Hoo," Max cries, writhing on the chaise, "I told you he wouldn't believe it." He hurls himself forward over his knees like a man going for the sit-up record. "Nobody's going to believe it," he chortles, his laughter high in his throat, like water spilling back into a well.

"It's going to be great," my father says, slapping his thigh, "this picture. It's about conquistadores, the New World, desperate acts."

"An *extravaganze,*" Max says. He is beaming, in his version, fleshy lips stretched like thin gray inner tubes across his large teeth, eyebrows cranked into his forehead.

"We're going to actually build a new world, a whole city."

"And blow it up," Max cries, "blow it to smithereens, hurl it down a mountain."

"That's right," my father says, smacking his sides, "this is going to be what they call a real moving picture."

I can tell by my mother's eyes that she is practicing another life. It has been twenty years since her last picture. She was unwilling, so the interviews said, to sully her beauty with age on the screen, but actually unable, if the truth were known, to concentrate on the reality of film anymore. She became dreamy, strange, unable to learn her lines, adjusting herself in the feathery way she does now, mind and body drifting in the imperatives of other realms, a princess somewhere else, Scottish sorceress perhaps, floating in the Highland world of green mountain slabs and brokenhearted streams. So I would have it, if I were making up her life. So I would tell Kate, if she asked. I spin here in the middle of my life, brushing greatness and the future. The world slithers and yawns wide.

"What is it you want me to do, Pop?"

"He's going for it," Max cries. "He wants to do it."

"Wait a minute, Max," my father says. He looks at me, his black eyes filling with light. "I haven't even told you about the deal. You want to do it?"

"What is it you want me to do?"

"See," Max crows. "He wouldn't ask if he wasn't going to do it. You'll love it, Willie. This is something you've waited for. This is going to be prodigious."

"Shut up, Max," my mother says, braking.

My father thanks her, reaches for her hand, misses, rights himself. My mother elegantly fills her glass again, looking at us. She sways toward my father—a movie motion I have seen on the screen many times; as if her bones have melted and she is about to fall—drifts and fetches up against his body where she retakes the battlements of his flesh. She picks up a bottle of gold oil, pours a drop or two into her hands, and begins to work her fingers into my father's shiny shoulders. He preens like a seal.

"This is what I've wanted to talk to you about, Will," my father says. He cocks his head to the side, heavy bird, eyeing his prey.

"Tell me."

"You were off there in Mexico and I couldn't get hold of you."

"Yes."

"This is going to be a real picture. Your part is shaping up. We've got it now. You're this renegade priest, a kind of bandito priest combo, it's right up your alley."

"Up my alley?"

"Sure. This guy, he's a priest and a murderer too. He kills— for a good cause, sure—he's a friend to the Indians—"

"We're on the side of the Indians now," Max puts in.

"Right—but he's in agony—you know what I mean?—he's walking a fine line he can't stay on—got to fall . . ."

"Yeah," Max cries, "trouble ahead . . ."

"Right—he falls . . ."

I'm looking at my mother's fingers, how strong they are. She could make a new man—a new body at least—right here in front of us. "You got a script?"

"Yeah, yeah"—my father shakes his shoulders, leans forward like an executioner— "that's the best part."

"We've got a script," Max cries, "you ought to see it—it's great."

"You got anybody to direct?"

"Yeah, that's the best part too," Max says, shaking his head from side to side.

"Bobby Baum," my father says.

"Bobby will work with you?"

"He's great. He loves it. He's got the script, Max has talked to his people, he's going to do it. Billy Dangelo is going to finance."

"Circus time, huh?"

"Ain't nothing better."

My mother told me a story once about the time her father got sick when she was a little girl. He was taken ill suddenly and rushed to the hospital. On the way to visit him with her mother, Jennie saw a small white bird drawn in chalk on the side of a building near the hospital. She remembered she had drawn the bird one morning on her way to school. She decided that each morning, before she went to school, she would draw a bird, and this would be her bargain with God—as long as she drew a bird each day, her father would live. She felt very good about this, because, she said, she knew she wouldn't forget, she would draw every morning. But five days later her father died. She had not missed a day's drawing, but he died anyway. This was a lesson to her, she said. No matter how prettily we play, she said, no matter what we offer, no matter how deeply we bow, the world has its own ideas. What we get is what's given to us.

I say, "I'll do this."

My father's scarred fists swing around his head. "He says he'll do it, Max," he cries.

"I heard him, Clem. This is going to be great."

I say, "Call Earl. Draw up the papers. I'll do it."

My father heaves to his feet, a wrestler coming up out of a crouch. "Son, son," he says, his voice tangled in his throat, "this is a miracle of our time, a wonderful thing." There are fresh tears in his eyes, little sparks gleaming at the corners. He lays his forearms on my chest, billets he's stacking, he's stroking my head between his hands, leans his stony head in and kisses me on the mouth. I feel a warm prickling, as if I am kissing the prince who still smells of the frog he was. My father has found his way to murder me.

AS I LEFT the room, my father handed me a small package wrapped in butcher paper. He gripped the flat box hard, his fat thumb pressing into the center of it, the blank nail digging, as if to hurt it, to scar it, but in his eyes, amid the fierce attacking glance he gave me, like an unburnt place in a fire, was a look of soft, sustained, miseried appeal. It was a package from Mexico, brightly stamped, a package from Kate. The cancellation date was last week, before I went down there again. Our eyes met, glances ricocheted, didn't engage; I took the box and hurried from the room. From the door I caught a glimpse of my mother. Her wild, dreamy eyes searched my own for a second, looking, as always, for a place to light, a place to curl up and rest. A tumbling, irrepressible wave of love surged through me. There was something, like a terrible memory I couldn't quite call to mind, that I wanted to save her from, but I was moving too quickly, I was around the corner and gone before I could take action, before I could think what it was.

The bluster and yaw of this scene is incredible. Colors move, you can feel the momentum. Speed is what this world is about. I rip open the package: it's another videotape. I stop, lean against the wall. Half of Hollywood surges past, tumbling in the wave. I think I am about to start whimpering. I am whimpering.

Eustace, one of the ADs, spots me. "Will," he calls, "are you coming around from the front?"

No. Wait a minute. I lift my face out of an acid trough. "Eustace. Have you got a video player?"

"There's one in the green room, but I think it's broken." Eustace's puce shirt is wet with his sweat. His creamy yellow hair is plastered to his skull. He looks as if he has taken blows. "Are you coming down from the front? We need you to go on around there."

"Yeah, all right. Just a minute." I come alive a second, return to this universe. I smile. "I need to do this, but then I'm going right out." Several elephants trumpet in unison. Down the corridor, a woman laughs; it is a tinny, loud, actorish, maniacal laugh, like a laugh in the lonely desert.

"Well, hurry please, if you will." He passes a small hand over his gleaming forehead. "Jeez, everything is going haywire."

"Clement wouldn't have it any other way, Eustace."

"That crazy man. Everybody—the whole world's going to hate us for this."

"Ah, Eustace." I slip him a small sharp kiss on the cheek. For one second he leans his thin body against me. He pats my shoulder. "Thank you, Will. You're . . ."

I hold up my hand. "See you, Bud."

Now I am on track again. My father diverted me with his talk of a new picture, but now I have my eye on things again. The best way to hide is to show everything, express everything. That's what's going on around me. There is drama, a wild force pursuing its objects, its completions. A woman over there is singing at the top of her lungs. A bolt of yellow hair spills down her back. A man in a resort suit speaks intimately into a walkie-talkie, his eyes focused as if on the face of his true love. A thin young man in a brush cut is fiddling with a line of potted palms that snake down the corridor. He rubs a frond between his fingers, he leans into the trunk as if he will embrace it. I am moving all this time. Get out of my way. I love the daring intimacy induces in us. It's the secret of pictures, this intimacy the group of like-minded souls induces, the daring that is its consequence. *You are among friends. Yes, yes: cry your heart out, take your shirt off, fall on your ass.*

I spring through a doorway: the green room. Barney Gold and Bevo King, tandem masters of the forthcoming ceremony, with Bevo's agent Trembly Mozon, are in there.

Barney, spry, yellow-haired, leans against the counter sipping a soda. "Hey, Will," he says, glad to see me, "what are you doing here?"

Bevo and Trembly are hunched in straight-backed chairs in a corner facing each other, rehearsing. Trembly's snapping his fingers, keeping a tempo that Bevo follows. Bevo's hard, dark face, mulish under a burst of bright black hair, peers at his agent, leaning forward. The intensity between them is startling and palpable, like a large bird they are plucking. Trembly's finger snaps a sound like small bones breaking.

I say hello to Barney, whom I have known for years. We cuff

15

each other, grin, bob and weave like the old friends we are not exactly. There's a monitor and video machine on the counter between baskets of fruit. I indicate it with the cartridge. "I need to use that."

"Sure. Take it away," Barney says.

"Here's fine," I say, though I would rather cart it off somewhere private, someplace I can close the door of and lock.

Bevo doesn't notice me, but Trembly, whom I have heard used to sit in his car outside Marilyn Monroe's bungalow in Brentwood like a demented fan waiting to get a glimpse of her, flicks me a nod. Bevo is in the middle of a joke, one of the ones he'll tell tonight. "I didn't realize I had my clothes on until I got in the shower," he says, his face as somber as if he is confessing infidelity.

"You coming to the party tonight?" Barney says. I ignore him. I am so excited, I am so scared, I can't speak.

I swing to the monitor, push the black tablet into the VCR on top of it, punch buttons, and stand back. The screen crackles, fizzes, clears. I look around a second to see if they're watching. Bevo's netted in his routine, speaking the double-jointed words as if they are the only words in the world. Trembly stares raptly into his narrow, seamed face, his own face filled with the humility, cunning, and cupidity of an agent's love. Barney looks over blandly, wondering what I'm up to, not really interested, letting the time pass. He's not really alive except when he's onstage. He never thinks a routine through or plans one at all; he steps directly from his idling, wayward drift into the hard shadow of his medium, inside him the accelerant combusting. Tonight he'll be reading most of his lines, which will make it even easier, but there will be fine moments when he soars out on his own.

The screen comes to life: a dark room a camera pans through. It's a warehouse, a storage room: piles of furniture, wooden boxes, what look like coils of wire, bundles of soft material on a concrete floor, light standing whitely in cracks along a metal wall.

"What's this?" Barney says. I ignore him, move closer to the counter, between him and the screen.

The camera tracks in slowly, toward a wooden box on the arm of a green brocade armchair. The camera moves in close to the box, a woman's treasure box, pearl enameled around the corners, a shell rose inlaid in the center of the lid. The camera stands before the box. There is no sound track. Then a hand, a man's hand, reaches in and begins to raise the lid. The hand is covered with wiry black hairs, the finger joints are enlarged, the nails are white. Light glints off a gold ring with a black stone. There are scratchings, carvings on the stone I can't make out. The lid lifts slowly, the arched fingers drawing it back. Inside is a face, a face in the box: it is Kate's face. The skin is painted white, the lips are blue, the white-blond hair is pulled back off her high forehead. Her eyes are closed. The camera sits back on its haunches, watching. It watches for what seems a long time.

Barney sidles up behind me. I hold my arm out to prevent him. "Is this your movie . . ." he says; I raise my hand.

Kate's eyes open. They look directly into the camera, directly at me. Her tongue slides out of her mouth—it's black, the tongue—and licks the blue lips. She smiles, the smile gradually opening as if her face is being cut with a scalpel. The smile is a leer; her large white teeth gleam. She opens her mouth wide, closes it. Her eyes narrow, the thick black lashes tangling; I can see the glint between them. Then they open wide.

"You put me in the box," she says. "You said you could bring me out, but you can't. I have to live here now and I can't. You put me in the box." The tongue slips out, retreats. The eyes blink. "Listen to me," she says. "Discipline and abandonment are the same thing. They both induce flight. A retreat into the dark quiet place. That's the place I'm in. This box. You put me here. You can't bring me out." The eyes close. There is a humming, a faint tinkling, then a small clatter. The hand reappears. It holds a small brass pot. The pot tilts, a thick pearly liquid brims and falls, steam rising. The liquid spills onto Kate's face. The hand slowly upends the pot, pouring the liquid over the face until it disappears under the pale surface. The box fills to the edges, a smooth surface. Through the liquid, which seems to be hardening, I can see the shadow of Kate's face. The eyes are open, looking straight out. The tape goes blank.

"That's good," Barney says, leaning over my shoulder. "Who was that? Was that Kate?"

I watch the screen to see if there's more. There isn't. My eyes fill with tears, but they are not just for Kate, not just for Kate and me, they are for all of us, all of us for whom life becomes so quickly redundant, for those of us who try the quick, resolving moves only to find they are too late, too little to change anything. She made this tape before I arrived there, before I returned to the desert coast looking for her, before I found her at Pedro's hacienda, before everything was already decided, before I saw what we had become, and what would become of us, before she stood me against the ocean and pushed a pistol into my face, and set me straight.

I press my hand flat on my chest: my heart knocks. I look about wildly, as they say. Bevo, anchored in a comedian's dementia, is still practicing his routine. They say his success is ruining him, but right now, staring into his agent's rapt face, he is giving the moment everything he has. Barney, on the other hand, floats in his means, not a drifter like me exactly, but sure of the gift that will lift him soon, and provide. He's interested in what I am doing, in what Kate was doing, but only in his normal lazy, passing way.

There's nothing more on the tape. I'm sure it's true that life is a circle, but this portion of it here, collected on tape, appears to be running out. It's gone.

"Was that Kate?" Barney says. "She's pretty good."

"Yes," I said. "She's better than I thought."

"Where was that taped? Was it a rehearsal?"

These days rehearsals—if there are rehearsals—and sometimes the working scenes themselves, are taped. Cheap and reusable, it's a good way to get a sense of things without the commitment of film.

"Rehearsal of the dead," I say. I give him a grin, a fierce rictus, the grin of a humiliated freedom fighter, something I have been practicing, an actor's grin. He tilts his head and lets a feathery smile flutter across his thin lips, as if he knows things.

I look around. Now, where is the necessary large object? There it is: a steel chair. I hoist the chair, a well-made, sturdy seat, swing it, my hips rotating like a slugger's, and smash the screen. Like a king renouncing his throne. The gray glass shatters with a huge cough, sizzles, an array of white and yellow sparks surges out. Barney jumps back. Trembly, alert agent, as if he has expected this, leaps to his feet. I punch buttons on the VCR, catch the cartridge as it ejects.

Trembly waves his arms as if he's trying to stop a car. "Nix this," he cries, "nix—cut—stop this!" His fleshy face seems to bounce as he speaks.

I grimace at him. Barney looks at me, his gray eyes dancing. "Let's start here," he says, "and wreck the whole place."

"Fine," I say. "You take the left, I'll take the right."

"You take the top, I'll take the bottom," Barney crows.

"You get the quick, I'll get the dead."

"Hey," Trembly cries, dragging Bevo up by the wrist. "We got a show to put on here. You freaks ever heard of the Academy Awards?"

Barney and I turn on him. "The *what* awards?" Barney cries.

"Idiots," Trembly wheezes, shuddering. "Where's the damn security?"

"He's calling the cops," Barney says.

"What is it, Trembly?" Bevo says, coming to. He's just realized I am here.

"It's okay, Bevo," I say. "We're just adding a couple of lines."

"What lines?" he cries. "You're changing the script?"

"Get out of here," Trembly shouts. He's fumbling in his jacket as if he's got a gun in there.

"I'm going," I say. "I was just passing through."

"Was that Kate?" Barney says. "She sure is a pretty woman."

"That was her stand-in," I say.

I am moving, pricked by love's accelerant. Call it love. Trembly takes a step toward me, thinks better of it, brakes. I am gone. It is true that I have let my marriage, let my wild flight around the body of this woman, break my life into pieces—I was there, I watched it happen—but isn't that just like life?

I NEVER WANTED to stop drifting. Bobby, my brother who died, put me on to it, the amble and drift, the light touch, the passing glance, the slow retreat that would get us through the American bedlam without trouble. He hated life here, in this place and time, but he was just a kid when he died, good at everything, without perhaps any real cause for remorse or pain, but a boy who nonetheless understood the danger we were in and wanted to slip away from it, even out of this world if he had to. I learned from him, and what I learned I carried with me like a pet. I brought it home, and later brought it into the lives of my friends, and later still onto the screen, where I can be seen, in tight focus or at a distance, moving across a beautiful and carefully decorated landscape, moving like a man who is telling himself some other story than the one he is playing.

But I was not, I am not—as my brother Bobby is—a shade. I am instead this man alive: William Wheeler Blake—named not for the fire-toothed poet, but for an ancient uncle—thirty-eight years old, five feet eleven inches tall, muddy blond hair short as a Marine's two weeks after discharge, pale Celtic skin, a build like a tennis player's, strong legs, narrow but powerful shoulders, a slouch, a walk like the attraction of opposites, a sort of jumpy complacency sliding toward panic or rage in the gaze, a slight overbite a little like Joe DiMaggio's, strong, bony chin, the wide hands of my Arkansas and Lowland Scot ancestors. I was born here, in Beverly Hills, in a flower-strewn movie star's house, a tear not in every room but in certain corners and on the patio and certainly in the pool house, where my father conducted his love affairs, and where my mother, following, sniffing the air like a bird dog, retreated to weep and rage—my father, son of an Arkie farmer who was driven westward by home troubles he couldn't fix. My grandfather was a wily and mercurial man, determined, hopeless, built for the culture he found himself in, with an immigrant's tenacity, who became a minor character actor in Jack Warner's employ, drinking companion of Bogart and Bill Powell, himself nominated for a supporting actor award in the late forties, sire of my father, who, in local parlance, *hit the ground running,* a vandalous hometown boy, quick-witted, strong-bodied, a traditionalist and, as many a one is within the purlieus, ungovernable, briefly an actor and then, ferociously and with total dedication and the blessing of his godfather, Lou Martin, a producer of small *film noir* gangster movies, then of increasingly larger extravaganzas, a kind of nihilist Cecil B. DeMille, an exalter, if you looked closely, of suffering as spectacle, whose time arrived, crested, and passed and who now mostly fills his life with extravagant plans he can find no one to finance. I came along in 1953, second and final child, so blue and battered by the passage through my mother's narrow hips that the doc had to shape my skull in his hands, molding the clayey head plates into compact human form. My mother, swimming out of the ether with her head throbbing, feeling, as she told it, as if she had been folded until she cracked, said, That is the ugliest baby I have ever seen, and took me in her arms, so I am told, and laughed, right through her pain and permanent damage.

I grew up on the soundstages and in the backlots of Hollywood, at home among painted characters, in the make-believe world that was the world, neither pampered nor pressured, but allowed, as many were in those days of excellence and opportunity, the run of the place. It was a world of light in those days, to me, a world whose dangers glittered nakedly, whose darknesses were slight and parochial, a world of movement, built by men who believed in energy and dash, men washed up here on the far shore who were in no way dismayed or slowed down by reaching the end of a wild race across the continent, but who, naturally and exuberantly, pressed forth into the new worlds and dimensions of the movies. At home, at the beach, in Hollywood, in the dusty, fragrant hills and piney mountains, and in the desert behind the mountains, I didn't seek much beyond the world I lived in, the world that reinvented itself every morning. I attended local schools, mostly out in the Pima Valley, and then traveled east for four years and a philosophy degree at Columbia, but I was not seduced by the iron energies of Manhattan or by the smelly, aging towns of the East, nor by the tamed fields or the compliant, reseeded woods, not by any of the life there. I don't want to be too self-righteous, but I didn't get it, this big country business, American sublime, terrain and the hope of brotherhood et cetera, didn't get the purposive bustle of the East— I didn't see the South—and the Midwest seemed a nation of grim-lipped farmers and factory workers towing snowmobiles, and everywhere the same claims were being made about how it was all—the stumblebum America—somebody else's fault.

A graduate of four lazy years spent mostly in libraries and downtown bars listening to rock and roll, I returned across the country with Esther Miller, a blond, green-eyed Jewish girl whose father was the largest orange grove owner south of Encinitas and whose mother, Elizabeth Hadrian, had been a slow-curve beauty in fifties Westerns, loved and abandoned by Randolph Scott and Rory Calhoun and even once or twice by that fine wooden cowboy Johnny Mack Brown. On a butte in the Kansas grasslands, Esther, whom I had known since childhood, a graduate of Sarah

Lawrence, took all her clothes off, tearing them from her body as if they were an ugly life she was getting rid of, and made love to me under the abundant stars. We were neither's first lover, but as I clutched her ample, springy buttocks under a dry wind carrying the smell of breakfast from the cereal mill in Cuttawee, I seemed to find a sense of proportion and economy, a rightness, that I attributed to the pleasure of lovemaking and to our journey toward the gritty pastel country we were born in.

I punked around, driving fast cars, living at my father's place, the spread up in the Pima where he gentleman-farmed a thousand acres of orange and avocado groves, keeping an apartment in Hollywood for weekends or loose nights, wasting as much time as I could. There wasn't anything I wanted to do. Content to lean back in the long, warm bath of my homeland, to attend parties, spend weeks in friends' houses in Malibu, talking late and walking on the beach in the early morning, riding the supple bodies of girls who were always passing through on their way to glory or nothing, I drifted, lazing like a seal in the glittery shallows. It didn't seem to matter. The war had finally wound down, there was no place to get to, nobody to be, nothing to defend. I did a few drugs, hallucinogenics mostly, drank my share of wine, snorted a couple lines of what was then the new wonder powder, but none of it took; I wasn't interested in that cloistral world. Occasionally I would speak a couple of brief lines in some picture one of my father's friends was making, and I went to the company parties, but there was no purpose to any of it, no one in those places had anything I wanted much; they were all just people I knew, people I had grown up with.

It was fun to watch the outsiders come in, the new actors breathless with obedience or defiance, all of them rocking with energy and opinions, the actresses creating their safety nets and their explanations for what they were doing, the kids with their pure skin and infantile affections. They were all breathless with the promise of their lives, mad for acting or mad for fame, on their way. It's a small world out here, and you can soon know everyone in it, or every kind of person in it, and you don't have to think much to get along or do much if you come from here; you can put it on glide and stop paying attention. I had no theory of what I was doing, no metaphysic to guide me, I did not take a position as I leaned against a flowered trellis beside some upland pool watching beautiful animated faces press themselves into my world, and I did not think of myself as discontented; I was not particularly argumentative or arrogant, I think, not political, a cipher really; though well dressed and wholly at ease, I was neither the hero nor the hero's friend but an old acquaintance without means to affect the drama beyond casually providing an effective transition from one scene to the next.

Some might say seven years is forever, some might say it is no time at all, but that is how long I drifted. I'd wake early, just trailing the sun, fix my toast, peel an orange, and go out on my balcony, if I was in Hollywood, or out on the terrace if in Malibu, or out on the viney porch in the Pima, and I'd settle in, prop my feet up, and let the day approach, wagging its sunny tail. I loved the repetition, the continuity of the world I lived in. Out here the sky, blue as always, hung up its whitewashing. The fields, dusty and green, lifted their broad backs toward the mountains. From Malibu the sea stepped off its distances toward the Orient. LA boomed and wallowed among its brown airs. What I didn't know—I was this ignorant—was that you couldn't make things stand still. And you couldn't make them repeat. The world's not a graven image. And people—you can't even slow them down. This was something Kate knew, something she taught me. Right then, on one of those fair, dumb mornings, as I broke an orange in my hands, out in the wheat fields of Nebraska my girl Katie was starting her car, pointing it west. I wish I could have seen her then; she must have looked like an angel, a blond-haired angel. She was on her way to bust up everything.

I FOUND GEORGE Boudreau, my father's driver, and had him take me around to the front of the pavilion. We pulled in behind Spec Martini and his wife and I watched through the front windshield as they exited their limo, Spec in a gold lamé jacket and Kazie, his wife, in a spangled parrot outfit with tiny triangular panels cut out back and front so her crepey skin could breathe. I told George to hit the horn, but he said he couldn't do that. My father's man, he didn't want to do anything that might reflect poorly on my father's car. So I leaned over his shoulder and hit the horn for him. Spec flinched as if a cat had leapt on his back, and Kazie, one ruby-shod foot just lifted to make the blue-carpeted curb, stumbled and went down on one knee. Some TV announcer helped her up. Her stocking had burst at the knee. Spec swiveled to catch a glimpse of the culprit, and I was delighted to see that if it hadn't been the ceremony, he would have stepped back to throw a few punches. I could see it in his greedy little eyes. The limo had some horn.

The white porches reached out for me; the crowd was a party-colored millipede leading to apotheosis; I was alone with all of it.

George swung in, stopped; an attendant, a boy in a blue tuxedo, leaned down to open the door; he wished me luck, his wide, mustachioed face carrying a look almost of reverence. I patted George's shoulder—"No second thoughts, George"—and sprang forth, resolute as a king, never forgetting for one second the video in my jacket pocket, grinning broadly, affectionately, at the screaming crowd. Beyond their heads, the bright air sparkled with dust. A line of dying royal palms lifted their touseled tops against the side of a building. Here, inside this circle, force, lust, desperation were concentrated, brought to bear at the epicenter of desire; the illusion that we call our lives became real for a moment, palpable—for a moment we shed our miseries, those of us who could get here, for a moment the city, dry as tinder, torch poised at the heart, the city and the exfoliate, crowded world beyond it, fell back into dream, as the dream became the world.

A slip and a dip, and I was inside, parked like a potentate in my seat. I looked around at the sunshined faces near me, the gaudy uniforms of success protecting the feeble mortal bodies. Next to me Jack Whitaker, the director, called across his wife's plump bodice at friends in other rows. Actors, directors, producers straining their jackets, rose and fell like brilliant flares, subsiding into the din. Up for best picture, Jack was wearing makeup, powder a shade or two darker than his skin; the faint line where it ended on his neck looked like a thin scar, where maybe his head had been reattached. His wife, a power in the local clubs, drew in long rattly breaths, her broad chest heaving.

One row back, William Lenz, another actor up for my award, leaned like a collapsed beach chair over the row in front talking to Shirley Baker, the teen pic actress. His long arms, like spider legs, encircled her neck, his hands clutching his own forearms, the fingers patting his own skin, smoothing the hairs, reassuring himself, letting himself know how much he loved himself. I could tell by the taut vein in Shirley's white neck that she was enduring rather than admitting him, and I could tell by the flat blank side of William's face, by the unshifting profiled gaze, that Shirley and what she felt didn't matter to him, that he was acting, that he could sense, as I could, the distant cameras aimed at him from the darkness, the eyes of millions looking at him. For William, I could tell, there was plenty to go around, because nothing was offered. His nut brown hair gleamed under the high lights, and his long, knobby hands with a new wedding ring, worn like a Japanese on the ring finger of his right hand, were perfectly capable of encircling the neck of the small, beautiful woman trapped under him and throttling her, of killing her, if that was what was required, of killing her and in one lanky stride stepping on past to whatever the director said came next. For a second I thought of getting up, of making my way past the polished knees and simply bashing his face in. I mean, he was dead already.

Somebody tapped me on the shoulder and said, "Don't turn around." A thrill of panic shot through me; I swiveled, teeth already bared, but it was only Tommy Sholeen, an old pal, one of those character actors who's brought with him to the screen about a pound of dirt and country sass that he dishes over everything. He's popular now and you can hear casting directors saying Get me a Tommy Sholeen, yelling it on the phone, if Tommy himself is not available. His long horse face, with its shock of black hair sprung back as if the wind had just stopped blowing, leaned toward me. A couple of miniature searchlights swept the crowd, veering down like hawks to touch the ravenous faces and soaring off.

"I'm working on this picture that's just like my own life's story," he said without intro, a grin plowing through his face. "I can't believe it. We were filming in Memphis. I've told you about how I grew up there. I walk out onto a corner where twenty years ago I was trying to talk some little girl out of her pants, and there I am again, trying to talk some little girl out of her pants."

"Yeah," I said, "they think it's make-believe, but it's not."

"What are you doing here? I thought you were too proud for these functions."

"I got cast against type."

"I'm so jittery I can feel every hair on my legs."

His wife, Delia Spence, propped a forearm on his thigh and leaned toward me. "He was so tense I had to give him a massage before he could get in the car." She was a full-bodied midwestern woman, copious in her affections, known for her frankness.

"Shit, Dee," I said, "I wish I had gotten to you in time. My body's full of sticks."

"Well, hand me your foot; I'll help you."

"Dee, he doesn't want to take his shoes off here," Tommy said, squinting at the crowd with one eye closed. He seemed to be taking aim.

"Of course I do." The guy sitting next to them was a stranger. He had bright red hair, dyed, and a throat like a chicken neck. I said, "Excuse me, my name's Will Blake. Would you mind changing seats with me?"

He looked at me with cloudy blue eyes, hardly seeing me. "Why should I do that?"

"So I can sit next to Tommy and Dee. She wants to get her hands on my feet."

The man leaned away from us and looked at my friends. His body seemed to be pulled on a string. "I'm David Benn," he said, licking his thin lips.

"How do you do, Mr. Benn. What do you think?"

Mr. Benn thought the idea was acceptable. As I got up, the room seemed to rumble and sweep away from me. The long hillside of seats poured down toward the stage captured in its scaffolding, the tall blue curtain rippling like a waterfall. The air above us was denser; it seemed to groan with a sea sound, the voices of the sea rolling against an island shore, muddle and cry of voices calling for rescue as the generations drowned. Tommy grasped my hand. "You all right, Will?"

"I'm fine, what is it?"

"You were leaning there—looked like you might fall over."

"I just flew up from Mexico."

David Benn and I exchanged places, dipping and nodding as we shifted past each other. My hands outlined his shoulders as he came around me, I touched him lightly for a moment and would, I thought, have been delighted to clasp him in my arms, to hold for one second his human body against my own, just for the sweet rest of it. I dropped in beside Tommy.

"You look terribly tired, Will," Delia said, leaning across her husband. Her buckeye hair, cut short around her ears, was thick as fur.

"Mexico'll wear you out," I said.

I stripped my shoes and socks, turned my body and lay my foot across Tommy's lap into Delia's soft hands. Her hands were soft and then they were hard. She kneaded my feet, first the right, then the left, driving her thumbs deep into the arches, pressing out the toes between her strong, short fingers, as if there was too much juice in them. Something far up in my body toppled and softly fell.

Tommy, I said, gesturing fondly, speaking in my head, Let me tell you a story. I once saw a woman leap from a bridge. A beautiful woman, a high bridge. Outside Oconee, Washington, as I crossed the Blue Salt River. A child was with her, a girl in a pleated blue dress, perhaps five or six. I watched, seated in my car, on a rainy day stalled, as she took off her yellow slicker, gave it to the little girl, who carefully folded it—I don't know anymore if I am making this up—climbed onto the rail, balanced there just long enough to give her little girl one long look, and jumped. She fell into a coal barge, whack on her back in the coal. She was dead. Anybody could see that. I got out of the car, approached the rail, and watched with the little girl as the barge slid downriver, traveling on silently with not a soul stepping out to see the dead woman, whose body in a pale yellow dress sprawled on the coal. I put the little girl in my car—she said her name was Nancy—and drove her into Oconee and let her off at the police station. I watched her climb the steps and go in the door, and then I put the car in gear and drove away. Except for her name, we hadn't spoken a word.

Delia lightly slapped my left sole and then pushed my feet off her lap.

"I feel much better," I said.

She smiled a soft, comprehensive smile, the smile of a woman who lives in a world better than the one she was passing through at this moment. I thought about the little girl, I guess the dead woman's daughter, and about us not speaking as I drove her to the station. The world is deeply penetrated by something; there is a current so far down inside that we never see it, never hear it, never even think about it. The little girl and I didn't say a word to each other. The current rose silently into our lives and carried us on, to the police station, to the next bright breath.

AND SO THE festivities soared and clamored. One winner after another climbed the four broad steps to the stage and grabbed his prize. The screens in the corners showed scenes from movies that were pictures of strange worlds we might get up out of our seats and walk away into. Arguments, fights, confessions, raged on screen. There are professions in which the practitioners don't want to know what their colleagues are up to. How many lawyers sit as spectators in court watching their peers try cases? How many fishermen watch other fishermen fish? But in this trade everyone's interested. Everyone wants to go to the movies. We go, like children getting out of the rain, to watch the moving pictures. We criticize, we hoot, we suffer with out friends, we believe. I remembered when my father began to film his epics on soundstages. He had filmed this way in the beginning, then moved outdoors, onto location, but in the last few years—when they had let him work—he'd come back inside. All his buddies wanted to see what the controlled interior light would do to his style; they all had remarks to make, suggestions even, but they all still took the pictures seriously, as moving stories that moved them—as pictures. I loved that. I loved how gullible we all were, how ready we were to sink back into dark rooms and believe in the light that flashed before us.

Down the row Bill Lenz craned forward in his seat. I watched the crooked smile shift and stabilize on his smooth face. The long straight tendons in his neck seemed to be holding his head on. His pale left eye, profiled to me, twitched slightly, and for a second in the play of that tiny pulse, I could see his humanness, the scared, attentive humanness of the worker who waits to hear if his work is acceptable. His arm lay across his wife's back, a small woman in a pale blue dress spangled in gold, dragging her slightly forward with him as he breasted the wind of occasion and hope; his long, lean hand worked her shoulder, pumping it, probing the crease between chest and arm, the fingers like small bodies seeking refuge. As I looked at his combustible face, which was highly colored by robust health and the knowledge of accomplishment, I began to think of the lives that were thrust like knives into the heart of the world, and how there were many like that and many more who wished they were, and how there had been in this country, since the beginning, a kind of psychopathy, a tendency, acknowledged by a few in their writings, and by crazy men on street corners, a tendency to press ruthlessly forward, without remorse, climbing over the splayed bodies and the broken embankments toward some ever-receding conception of glory, and how the earth seemed not even to notice this, as if it were helpless or unconcerned. This thought seemed tremendous and transforming to me as the lights billowed and swayed, invoking applause. I pressed my body into my seat, afraid for a second that my back was about to catch fire, or that something irredeemable was about to spring forth from me, as it had from Kate, and I could feel the creep of disaster, like the Tingler, begin to finger my spine, and I wished I had a newspaper column or a radio show so I could get the words that would explain this out; I wished more than ever that my turn would come, that now, any second, Greta Drake would speak my name so I could go forth before millions and say some small speech about this situation.

I leaned hard against my friend Tommy's shoulder, and as I did so I felt the edge of the tape—one of many she had made since the beginning of our marriage—pressing against my side, and I saw again my wife's face drowned by wax in a box, and heard again her words of accusation and blame, and I saw again the wide beach below Pedro Manglona's house, and the scrawny, starving cats tearing at the fish the ocean had washed up, and saw the rose bushes with their rumpled, wild blossoms by the steps, and saw Kate of the indelible gesture, woman of my heart and my hate, leaning against the greasy sea wind, and I saw myself descending the long flight of steps from the cliff that if I could I would have flown down from like a bat or an eagle to rip and tear her body for my food.

I was thinking about this and about the fighting bulls bellowing in their corrals by Pedro's house as the grand Hollywood calamity surged around me, thinking how easy, in my own corrida, it had been to go to my knees, how, after all the posturing and the tough-guy business that is the place we want to come to, thinking of how I loved the humiliation and frankness of it. I was thinking of her muscular body, of the eerie whiteness of her skin, of the smell of the desert behind us, when Greta Drake, in a blue gown flaked with lapis lazuli, stiff at the podium like a stake driven into the stage, tore open the envelope with William Lenz's name in it. I was on my feet at *William* . . . , which was a good thing, because as he edged his way in front of me to get out to the aisle, swiveling his lanky, handsome body to reach for my hand in triumph, I was able, on my feet, crouched, to get exactly the leverage I needed to lace one quick right-handed punch into his grinning blue eyes and lay him like a gaudy trophy across the knees of the redheaded man who had given me his seat.

WELL, I WINGED out of there. My face was my badge, no cop stopped me. What happened was too bad, but the truth is, acts of imagination can't be helped. They wanted me out, they let me go. George drove me to the Beverly Monarch, where I'd had Earl Moss, my agent, book me a room. On the way there, my mind vivid with possibilities, I had George stop so I could get a soda. It was a little store in Hollywood, off Sunset. As I crossed the sidewalk I noticed a guy on his knees near the front door, doing something on the concrete. I didn't pay much attention, but when I came out I looked to see what it was. He had on a battered tux and patent leather pumps with no socks. He was bent over close to the sidewalk. He was erasing. He had a big school eraser, red as a brick, and he was erasing the sidewalk. There was no picture, nothing that called for removing, but he was working away with long sweeps that ate up the big eraser, wiping out the traces of error. I guess he figured you could get the surface clean and still it was all wrong. Up the long street rising toward the bristly hills, the lights kept putting a stop to traffic and starting it up again, and somewhere off beyond the oleanders, a radio accused the country of murderous intent. You are under arrest, I said, but not to the man on his knees.

Sometimes you don't want to go home, sometimes you don't want to come close to the old familiar neighborhood. Actually, the hotel was as familiar as my living room. More so, actually, since I had known it longer. I had my sixth birthday party in the Beverly Monarch Hotel, a little prince with fifty other kids around my feet, sitting on a stool while Dipp Mongloon, the great comedian, told jokes insulting our parents. Later he asked me to put my hand in his pocket. There was a toy mouse in there, and next door to the mouse, a frank, hard penis. It was like touching the stake they drove through Dracula's heart. I reeled back and fainted. And then I remember the yellow-white light streaming through the tall windows in the back lobby and the smell of bacon and mayonnaise and the shiftless rustle of areca palms and the buzzing of small insects, bees maybe, and my mother's cool hand touching my forehead and my father's laughter, coarse and appalled, and a stretch of marble floor that looked softly blue, muddled like a sea surface, so cool and smooth that when they let me up, I laid myself down on it, stretched myself out like a little Odysseus, washed up before the daughter of a king.

George didn't know anything about what happened at the ceremony, and I didn't inform him, but everybody at the hotel knew. Burke Wills, the bell captain, who had been a cowboy in his youth, leaned out from his desk as I came through the lobby and asked me what in the hell I thought I was doing, punching Bill Lenz.

"That's going to cost you a few points," he said, running his hand over his powdered bald head.

"Sometimes I can't help myself, Burke," I said.

Burke grinned. We'd known each other for thirty years. "Your dad used to be like that," he said, "he was always springing around doing something crazy."

"You see," I said, speaking like an Okie, "we got it in our blood."

"They had it on the TV. You could see his eyes roll up when you hit him."

"Sometimes I surprise myself."

"You sure surprised him."

But I had nothing against Bill Lenz, other than that he breathed, walked around, took parts, won my award—I didn't want to keep thinking about him. There was nothing to say.

"It wasn't personal, Burke," I said. "No—yes it was."

"Effective—that's what it was."

The lobby was nearly empty, none of the revelers back yet. Shadows hung like gross webs in the corners of the high ceiling, and men in green uniforms stitched with gold mutely glided by. Through the tall back windows I could see the pool sparkling like shaved ice. I went over to the desk and asked David Pearl to send a VCR to my room. David looked at me in the attentive, shy, energetic way of desk clerks in expensive hotels. I loved it here, loved the eleemosynary kindness practiced by the well paid. It was the only kind of charity worth having. Behind David's head, the slotted message rack shone like Chinese lacquered boxes, keys winking dully from a few, folded notes and envelopes stuck into the nooks between here and there, between coming and going— and arriving—like little proofs of existence, or of the hope of it.

"David," I said, "did you see the Awards?"

"No sir," he said, "not really. I've been here."

"Did you hear that I punched Bill Lenz in the face?"

"Yes sir, I did hear that."

"There was a brief commotion; I'm not quite sure what happened to him afterwards."

"His agent, I believe, accepted the award for him."

"Was my name mentioned?"

"No sir, not directly."

"Indirectly?"

"Barney Gold . . ."

". . . the emcee . . ."

". . . yes—Barney Gold made a comment about the passion of actors."

Many things that suffer don't know they're suffering. Flowers, those gorgeous, rain-battered poppies I saw by the road, don't know it, as some children, slapped down and hauled upright by a grinning interlocutor, don't know it. And some have given everything to their suffering, as old people sometimes give everything to the church. What abides?

"Any messages from my father?" I said.

David said there were none.

I moved down the counter, unable for a second to remember my lines, feeling for the path. A few well-turned movie folk were sauntering through the gilded front door. I recognized a couple of actresses I knew, a producer. The main parties were elsewhere, so these were folks who would soon have to begin making loud claims as they anesthetized their bitterness—a good idea to stay out of range.

I thanked David, crossed the lobby to the bar, took a table in back, and ordered a cup of coffee. The waiter, who knew me, ignored my past and all of my present except for my status and my order. This left him with a neat look of concern on his face, like a thin dusting of powder. I took the tape out of my pocket and put it on the table in front of me. I touched its rough black surface, letting my fingers slide lightly over it. A picture flared in my mind, but I veered away from it, thinking about heroism, the movies' version of it, or their fixation on it, of how the gigantic, godly proportions of being, the fundamental drama, got reduced to human size, made habitable, hospitable, possible, and thinking of how much mercy we all need to survive in a world in which this was necessary.

Across the room, consorts and hopheads recognized me. Fake gentlemen in flashy suits, losers who would never understand themselves. The waiter drifted near, stooped like a hawk, and refilled my cup. I have long loved sitting in the dark corners of bars and cafés. I love the room spreading away from me like an opened fan. These moments, these places, are for those in between. In here happens what happens between here and there. In here are cracks into which lives fall.

And out of a crack one now approaches. Flouncing toward the last border of youth, earnest and delighted in a slivery dress, she struggles toward me. I see the craven figure limping across her soul. It is the one she follows, though she doesn't know it: she thinks she is going somewhere; she doesn't know that the plain she crosses is endless. What can I do for you my darling? She smiles, that dangerous smile of the incidentally shy. "Would you . . . ?" She thrusts a book toward me, opened to a blank page. A black pen waggles between us; I take it. "Of course," I say, smiling, showing off my inexpensive teeth. I look into her eyes, which are a common blue, at her chin, which is a little sharp under a short full bottom lip like a sucked round candy, and because I don't know anything about her and haven't asked her anything, I begin to imagine that her husband and firstborn son have been killed in a highway accident, that this happened recently, on the outskirts of the town they lived in, and that she has come to Hollywood with her unmarried brother-in-law, with whom she is having a depressed affair, an affair she is tired of but doesn't yet know how to end; I imagine that she and her selfish lover were among those outside the auditorium, that back among the tailings of the crowd they watched the festivities on a battery-powered television, bucking themselves up with the projected glamor and intrigue of a Hollywood night with its smells of citrus and methane.

She says, her voice rasping slightly in her throat, "I thought you should have won." It's a border accent, Oklahoma or Missouri, probably Oklahoma, farm country. I ask her to sit down for a minute. She hesitates, flushes, glances back at the table where her brother-in-law is watching us with a bitter, angry look on his country face. He's probably important in the world he comes from.

"Sit down," I say, "I'll get a crick in my neck with you towering over me." She does me the favor.

"What's your name?"

"Susan . . . Susan Tyree."

"Where are you from?"

"Illinois."

"You don't sound like you're from Illinois."

"I'm from the southern part, down in the Triangle. The Little Egypt section."

"Oh yes, I know where you're talking about. I made a movie about some people from that region."

"I know. I saw it four times."

"You must have liked it."

"You were good, but they didn't get the place quite right."

"They never do."

I bend to the page, write her name. She is sitting at a table in a hotel in California with a stranger writing her name. Grace—it has to be that—is the only thing in this world that keeps us alive. I write my piece, hold it up to look at it, close the book, and hand it to her. Her fingers are long, roughed on the knuckles, and in the sallow barroom light, the skin looks puckered and bleached, as if she has just raised her hands from a day underwater. They scare me a little—actually I want to jump up and run for my life—but I stay put. The movie she saw four times is the only movie Kate and I made together.

She starts to open the book, but I place my hand on hers, stopping her. I want her to feel the touch of my flesh; I want to feel her flesh. She says, "I think that guy deserved what you gave him."

"That's a Little Egypt attitude, isn't it?"

"Well, it's true. I never liked him. He's so superior."

"I showed my ass."

"That's all right."

"I think so too. You show your ass and what do they see: an ass, that's all. Pink, plump flesh. There's no mystery in that."

Without the rollers she uses—orange juice cans probably—her dark hair, coarse as a horse's mane, would be straight. Her forehead is troubled, but not by me. She sucks her breath sharply. I say, "I would love to see you naked."

She gives me a crooked, narcissistic smirk. "But you can't." Her slim tongue darts over her candy lip.

"Would you like to see *me* naked?"

"Sure."

She's a partially bold girl.

"Come up to my room."

"I can't do that."

This—as delightful as it is—is a return to an earlier life. I am not as thrilled as I once was by taking my clothes off in front of strangers. My cock is attentive nonetheless.

"We have a conundrum then," I say.

"What do you mean?"

"I can't take my clothes off here."

I see the slyness click its way into her eyes. "You could if you wanted to."

I look at the notebook, which is still open before me. What abides?

"What do you believe in," I say, "what holds you together?"

"You mean like religion?"

"If that's it, yes. When the worst happened, what saved you from dying from it?"

"I don't know," she says, "I prayed a lot."

She looks around the room, looks at the open doorway, where in the bright world beyond, boulevardiers drift like angels toward the fair revelries. She looks at the door as if something from another, more familiar place is about to appear. There are deep hollows along her neck.

"What was the worst thing?" I say.

She looks at me. "When my little girl got sick and nearly died."

For a second I want to slide down the chute of my life and come out in hers, but only for a second. Earl says that if it wasn't for women, none of this world we've built up would exist, no buildings, no autos, no civilization, no nothing. We'd hunt, gorge, fight, sleep, and that would be it, Earl says. I think we would forever be strangers in this world too.

If I give this woman any more of my time, she will write me letters. She will not be able to stop herself from trying to enter my life. Well, Guenevere, time to hit the road. I lean toward her.

"The truth is," I say, "I'm not really Will Blake."

She looks at me a little goggle-eyed. "Yes, you are."

"No. I wish I was, but I'm not."

She flushes. Streaks of color appear in her neck, her eyes dart back and forth. She taps her forefinger on the autograph book. She's embarrassed, not because she's made a mistake, but because I'm lying, which cheapens what has gone before. She shoves out her bottom lip. "I know who you are," she says. "I can tell. I wouldn't ever make a mistake like that."

Once, down in Mexico, at a street carnival, behind some tents, I watched a clown beat his child. The clown, in orange wig, white face paint, and a polka-dotted, baggy suit, beat the small boy with his big fists. I stopped, watched, didn't interfere. A father, his boy, I guess, some kind of due punishment. I thought: if you want to save one, why don't you want to save them all? At church, in therapy, they tell you to do your little bit, clean your own house, and then with what strength you have left over, help out a little in the world. Let your light shine, they say. But—they must know this—some darkness is impenetrable.

"No," I say coldly, "you've got the wrong person."

For one instant she looks at me; for one instant we look at each other. I know the blankness in my face; I could be in her face looking at it. Something in her eyes crumples. "Well then, I beg your pardon," she says, "I have to go." I can taste the hollowness in her voice as if she has thrust her tongue into my mouth. That other one, my father, might insist—coarsely, energetically—that she come out to the house. He would take her on a walk through the groves, he would pick an orange for her and break it open and squeeze the juice into her mouth. We all have our ways of being a hero.

Now, silently, I watch as she jerks to her feet, as she stomps away, moving out of range. Maybe her husband, if that's who it is, or her brother-in-law, if that's who it is, will come over here to knock a little sense into this Mr. Big Shot Actor. Come on, boyo. I may not be ready for everything, but I'm ready for you.

A coolness radiates off the polished tiles. Through the tall, open windows of the back lobby a soft breeze blows, lighting, trembling in the thin fronds of the potted palms. A stairway with a banister polished black by the hands of Mexicans, stolen a hundred years ago from the Museum of History in Mexico City, rides like the ladder of dreams into the heights of the citadel. I hear the festive cries. If no one died, I think, there'd be no need for resurrections.

U PSTAIRS, IN THE cool peach and green room I have retired to, I shove the tape in the machine, switch the TV on, call Veronica. "Yes, yes," I say, "right now."

Then I press the play button, lie down on the bed, and watch my wife's face again. It hasn't changed, it goes through the same routine, the eyes open, she speaks, the eyes close, the hand tips steaming liquid, the box fills. As in a movie, the scene fades to black. I run it back and play it again. Nothing changes. I play it again. Nothing . . . changes.

In a clear glass vase by the bed, the management has placed an arrangement of desert flowers: rock daisy, bird of paradise, and lupine, called bluebonnet in Texas. I call room service, order champagne for Veronica, soda and cheeseburgers for myself. I go to the window. Beyond the descendant rough hills I can see the lights of LA to the south. Beyond them—I cannot see it—the Pacific pearls and flashes darkly.

I punch the phone again, get Earl in his car. He's on his way to another party. We discuss my father's movie deal. I tell him to sign us on. Earl, who's quick and intuitive, says he doesn't trust the deal. It's my father, I tell him, I'm going to do it anyway. Earl is sad. He watched my performance on television. He thinks capers like that can hurt me. You of all people, he says, ought to know how it is in this town. It couldn't be helped, Earl, I say. Maybe you ought to apologize, he says. Maybe I ought not to. Come on, Will, says Earl sadly.

But I won't come on. I'm incorrigible. I didn't tell Earl that my father, who is a man who always does what's necessary, now wants to kill me. That he would probably understand.

Earl thinks I'm just being contrary.

"Earl," I say, "Kate sent me another video."

"Don't look at it."

"I've already looked at it. It's on the VCR right now."

"You're free of all that, Will; don't go back to it."

"I went down to Mexico looking for her, but I couldn't find her," I lie.

"Is that what you were doing? I thought that was what you were doing. Jesus. I'm going to send somebody over there to lock you up. Don't go looking for Kate, man. She'll leave you in your shirtsleeves, she'll leave you in the ditch." There's a moment of silence. I hear what must be traffic sounds. Maybe Earl has the window down. Maybe he is waving like a prince at the crowds.

The discovery I made, after seven years of drifting, of being no one, was that I could become anyone. I could slip into their lives like a phantom, and take the shape of their lives and speak in their voices and believe what they believed, and rise and fall as their lives rose and fell. It was my gift. "Earl," I say, "I'm still interested. I still want to see what's next."

"No you don't," he says, "you just think you want to see what's next. Kate is yesterday's dolce vita, man. She was fine, but she's gone sour. She's an annual, man"—he was a gardener— "you have to dig her up and replant. It's time for the next thing, a new variety—wait . . ." There's a small tapping, a crackle in the line. "Can you hear me?" he says.

"Yes."

"I can't hear you very well. Where are you—I'll call you back."

"I'm at the Monarch."

"You still don't want to go home?"

"No. It's too spooky."

His voice sharpens. "What are you up to?"

"I called Veronica—she's coming over."

"Oh. How's she doing? I thought you were taking her to the—I don't even want to talk about it." I think I can hear him grinding his teeth. The phone crackles, spits. "Listen," he says, "I have to hang up. I'll call you from Sally's—okay?" A little silence. "Okay, Will?"

I slide the phone into its cradle and lie back on the bed. I see Kate leaning against a dark green Mexican wall. She is grinning at me, ordering me to do strange things.

WHEN I WAS a kid—there were several of us, we were boys— we'd wander into the hills looking for adventure. We had pellet rifles that we used to shoot at songbirds or rabbits. The long blond hills were smooth and seemed to us the introduction into a wilderness that no one had explored fully, a wilderness, ranging east beyond streams and oak woods, that might run on forever—into the desert, we'd heard—into a world where you might found your own country, discover magical life, mysteries never imagined. We'd talk about everything as we walked, explaining the world to ourselves, stacking the parts of it like boxes on a shelf, arranging it in taller and taller configurations until it toppled before us, delighting us. Billy Dangelo was one of us, and Freddy Blaine and Tooly Glick, and a couple of other boys whose names I've forgotten now. We all grew up and went on into the conniption of the world, all except Freddy Blaine, who was killed in a construction cave-in the summer he was seventeen, and I think most of us are successful in our ways—Billy and Tooly I know are—most of us sprightly, capable fellows who found plenty to do here in America.

I remember an afternoon in summer, the summer we were twelve, when we climbed into the hills behind the Pima and came on a sight that none of us has ever forgotten. My brother Bobby was with us that time. He did not usually go with us on our explorations. He was not aloof, was in fact a star among us all, but he was so self-contained that the company of others was oppressive to him. I don't know why he came with us—the day would have been remarkable for that fact alone—but he did, appearing at the edge of the orange grove in the white clothes he wore continually that summer, accompanying us—trailing us really—as we climbed into the hills. I say he went with us, but he was not really a part of what happened. As we walked—boys willing to trek miles—he fell farther and farther back. He wanted to look at things he found, and we, itching for the drama that would define us, could not wait.

We had been following the bed of a dried-up stream, stepping from rock to rock, heading uphill through intermittent groves of live oak and mountain ash, plinking our guns now and again at flickers of bird movement in the trees, when Billy suggested we climb to the top of the ridge and make a signal fire to let Bobby know where we were. We climbed up through a narrow defile, wading through a patch of flowering yarrow. Climbing, I looked back and saw the softly rounded backs of hills to the east, and through gaps in the hills, the road that came and went heading toward my father's farm. The air smelled piney and sweet, faintly tinged with the dry scent of the grasses that the wind had pressed down in places as if large beasts had lain in them. Far back, as he moved along the edge of a small grove of sycamore trees, I could see Bobby. He was not part of us anymore, and I didn't hail him, but for a moment only watched as he drifted, like an egret or a gull, in the far grassy distance.

Up ahead, Billy tapped a sprig of sourweed against his leg. He was the only one of us who'd gotten his growth, and though it didn't make him a leader, it made him more fascinating to us, this boy who had been so recently just like us, but who now sported a froth of wiry black hairs curling out of his groin, a cracked voice, and the ability to shoot a string of jism. He made the top and immediately dropped to his knees. The rest of us started to run up, but he waved us down. We crouched in the grass like commandos, quick to suspect foul play. Billy came scurrying back, brown eyes snapping. He said there were men on the other side of the hill and a couple of girls in sundresses. What are they doing—let's see, we said. It looks funny, Billy said. Funny what? Tooly asked. I don't know, Billy said. We followed him back up the hill, crouching, crawling on our knees, finally sliding on our bellies until we came to a stand of serviceberry bushes. We strung out along the ridge among the bushes and took a look. There were three men down there in a little cut below some rocks. They had two girls with them. The girls wore flimsy patterned dresses and white ankle socks. The men were drinking from bottles, and there were a couple of guns leaned against the trunk of a big oak. The ashes and charred timbers of an old campfire were scattered about, and the whole place was littered with paper and other trash. I was snuggled up against Billy's shoulder, and I could smell this strange new smell, a dense odor, weighty and a little sour, like the smell of a horse in sunshine. The hairs on his wrist were thick and black, like the hairs on a man's wrist, and the veins stood out on the back of his hand like a man's. The change that had come over him, that he himself seemed baffled by and a little embarrassed to be the victim of, not only fascinated me but repelled me. There was a coarseness to it, a clumsiness, as if weights had been added to his bones, and he moved through the world like a boy losing his way in deepening water but making claims as he went, pulled onward by a bully. I was still a child, but I could see that Billy was not; like a boy showing up at a birthday party in the clothes of an adult, he had begun to visit another world, and I was unsettled by this.

Down below us, the strange thing we did not know we had come to see began to happen. It was not a party or an outing; the men were not friends of the two girls. The girls had short blond, lank hair, and they were thin; their dresses hung slackly on their skinny frames. A tall balding man wearing a gray suit coat and jeans sat down on a patch of grass near the large oak tree and pulled one of the girls down beside him. He wrapped his long arms around the girl and held her close as another of the men, a short guy with a wide belly, wearing the khakis of a farmer, pushed the other girl against a tree. What is he doing? I whispered, but Billy didn't answer. A thin line of sweat ran down his jaw. The short man made the girl press her hands flat against the tree trunk. He spoke to the girl, but we couldn't hear what he was saying. He kicked the girl's feet wide, roughly, then delicately, positioning her. The girl reached behind her, covering her buttocks with the flat of her hand, but the man slapped her hand away. With his knuckles he rapped the girl on the back of the head. She cried out, and we could hear the cry, faint and thin, snatched away by the breeze. Then he flipped the girl's dress up over her back. From his belt he took a knife, and pressing his knee in against her legs, cut her panties off. I could see the girl's small skinny buttocks; they were pale and dented in on the sides, like the buttocks of children. I thought of the refugee children I'd seen in pictures in *Life* magazine, standing beside roads in Asia or Africa, of how they must look under their ragged clothes. The girl tried to cover her buttocks again, but the man slapped her hand away. He leaned over her back, wrenched her head around, and forced a kiss into her face. I could see her face, and the terror in it. The girl slid to her knees. The man undid his trousers and pushed the girl forward, mashing her face and upper body against the tree trunk. His companions watched from a few feet away, the tall one fiddling with the girl in his lap. I could hear the girl crying, sobs like small wings flapping. Then the man had his penis out. It was short and red; he held it in his fist like a handle. With his left hand he pressed into the center of the girl's back and leaned over her. As he came down on her, the girl twisted to her side, then onto her buttocks, pulling herself away from him. She thrust her legs out, pulling herself sharply with her heels out from under him. When her legs opened I saw that she wasn't a girl. The sight struck me like cold water. There was a sudden, sharp pain in my chest. Billy looked at me and his eyes were wide and amazed. The man grabbed the girl—the boy—but he scrambled away, rolled to his feet, and began to run. He ran straight up the hill toward us. The other boys—my buddies—scrambled back

through the bushes down the hill, but Billy and I didn't move. I
don't know why Billy didn't run, but I couldn't. I watched the
girl, the boy now, come on toward me, running up the hill, his
legs pumping in the long matted grass, the dress swirling and
flickering on his body, and I could see in his narrow blond face
the red splotches of color, the oil of tears; his teeth were bared.
He slipped, fell, bounced up and ran, scrambling on hands and
knees up the steep slope, drawing closer to us with the man running behind, gaining on him. Billy gripped my wrist; maybe I had
started to pull away—I don't remember—but he held me. And
then the boy saw us. I saw his eyes, saw the recognition. For an
instant he and I looked nakedly into each other's face. There was
no surprise in his eyes, no hope, only the recognition. We looked
at each other like two terrible brothers, discovered in horror. Billy
pulled my arm, we scurried backwards, crabbing down the slope,
sprang to our feet, and ran. Without looking back, we ran down
the long hill to the stream and down the stream—catching up
with the others—to the bottom and the road and our bikes, and
we leapt on our bikes and pedaled out of that place.

Billy and I said nothing to each other for a long time, and I
said nothing at home, but some of the other boys told their parents. The next day it was all in the paper. The men had kidnapped
the boys, planning, so the authorities said, to hold them for ran-
som. They shot and stabbed both of them, stuck the bodies under
some cut brush and left them for dead, but one of the boys survived. When my mother learned that I had been up there, that I
had seen the murderers, she called my father. He was shooting a
movie up in Montana, but on the next Sunday he caught a plane
home. He took me for a ride in the car, out through the orange
groves and along the levee by one of the drainage canals. We
stopped and got out and sat on the hood sharing a candy bar. The
mountains in the distance were the color of palominos. He put
the candy bar down on the hot hood and grabbed me into his
arms; I could feel his heart beating against the side of my chest.
He breathed hard as he hugged me, panting, stroking my head
and back as if he wanted to press his hand into my body. And
then he held me out from him, straight-armed, as a man would
hold a baby, and asked me why I hadn't told my mother about
the terrible tragedy. That's what he called it, the terrible tragedy.
I said I didn't know. Those are things you have to let us know

about, he said. All we want to do here is protect you from trouble and pain, he said. Please, son, you need to tell us. You don't know what it means to us to know you are all right, and how it scares us to think something might happen to you. I didn't mean to scare him, and I could see that he was right; I could see that it would relieve him for me to come to him. I knew this before he found out. But in my family, no matter what was said, it was clear that everyone was on his own. I wouldn't have told him, or my mother, or anyone except Bobby. I had seen the boy's face, and I had seen into his eyes as he sprawled not twenty feet in front of me, pulled backwards by a madman. And what I saw was secret. It was my secret—it might have been everyone else's as well—and it couldn't—shouldn't—be spoken. When they catch you, the eyes said, no one can help. They weren't pretending.

I didn't talk to Bobby about it, but I tried to. I started to tell him later, one night when we were cleaning a pan of fish by the back steps. The fish were red snappers, caught by one of my father's actors, and their bright pink skins shone in the porch light as we slit their bellies and spilled the glossy guts onto the ground. I started to say something, to tell Bobby what it had felt like to see the boy running up the hill toward me, to tell what I saw in his eyes as the man dragged him down the hill, but he stopped me. "I already know," he said, without explanation. He smiled at me, very gently, pulling a shiny gray string of intestine out of the fish's belly. His eyes were bright, and though there was a tenderness in them, there was also fear. In a quick motion he spun the guts around his wrists and held them up, to divert my gaze, I know now. He didn't want me to see what was in his eyes. He knew—I know now—that I would see in his eyes what I had seen in the boy's. He was not the boy, he had not been raped and shot, but maybe, even then, that far back, a madman was pulling him down the hill. He held his crossed wrists up. The guts hung from them like rope.

And here's a funny thing: I saw that boy again, years later. From the paper, from what came out, I couldn't tell which one survived. The boys were from a little town down near Escondido, from another world, so I never saw what happened in his life. But one day—this was about ten years ago, not too long after I'd begun to make my way as an actor—I was on a movie set outside Monterey when I ran into him again. He was a camera operator working for Bennie Steele, the DP. The shoot had just begun, we were filming a scene up on the cliffs inside a small grove of pines, and when I walked through the equipment to my mark, I noticed this guy looking around the side of a camera. He was thin, about my age, his colorless hair was lank and receding off a narrow forehead, he was bony about the face, nothing special, but something kicked inside me and I recognized him. It was the boy. I made the shot and then afterwards, when everybody was wearily leaving, went up to him and took him aside. He didn't know me. I asked him if he was the one, if he was the man who had been the boy up in the hills. He said he was, he said it happened a long time ago, he said he didn't think about that shit anymore. I said, I saw you; I was there. He looked at me then, raising his eyes as if he were raising a weight off the ground, he looked me straight in the face. I don't remember anybody being there, he said. But don't you . . . I started to say and stopped. That's all gone, he said, don't worry about it. I let him go then and we both went on about our business. For the next six weeks I saw him almost every day, and I saw him sometimes at night drinking, partying with the crew. He laughed, he passed drinks around, he shouted out lines from old movies, mimicking poorly the voices of the stars who had said them, he looked as if he was having a good time, as if his life was okay, as if he didn't wake up in the night thinking of his dead buddy or of the man who held him down and then shot him. He went on, the world went on and so what, so what? I never spoke to him again.

IT IS LATE now, the spring constellations are falling into the ocean. From my balcony, through the ruined air, I pick out Betelgeuse, the diminished North Star. Veronica, friend of my youth, my best friend, has come and gone. She was exasperated with me, as usual, vexed that I would make such a scene in public, but as usual, as has become usual again after a break of years, we made love, in the big bed, in the dark. We both like the dark, like the possibility and the dreams it contains, the protection it offers. In the dark I ran my hands over her body, I pressed my fingers into the crevices, I swung down the long slopes, the rises and outcroppings, exploring, launching voyages of discovery that moved toward the interior, losing myself in the wilderness of flesh, losing my mind, losing for a minute what was in my mind, rubbing the stink of Kate's body off me, grinding out the marks of her hands, obliterating her.

Like me, Veronica fears the unknown; like me, she is at home only in a familiar world; like me, she believes in portents, in the dark shapes that move among us; like me, she believes change is impossible.

Her body is long and slender and pale, though not as pale as Kate's, and as we made love, we spoke of our lives in Los Angeles, we drew the threads of time into a rope in our hands and we tugged on the rope, just hard enough to believe it would hold us. We let ourselves down its length, talking of walks in the mountains, of a party we went to in an almond grove outside Pasadena, of the year Bobby died, of my mother, Jennie White, who has been Veronica's lover since she was a teenager, since the summer Bobby was shot. As we talked, as our voices rose into the dark that in my mind was almost the same dark that the first men here, Indians and the trailing Spaniards, experienced on the shores of this desert; I thought how quickly life had begun to move now, how what was murky and tumultuous had taken on direction, how this last five years of my marriage had gathered into the events streaking by me now, how the momentum of my life had snatched me up, how what I found in Mexico, what I left there and found again mutilated and incorrigible, had not brought this version, these years, to an end, how the long caper continued on, accelerated now, how I had seen in my father's black eyes the news of my death flash like the titles of a movie, and how this day and its events, which seemed as they occurred so random, looked now, from the dark, to be part of a design—Arnold Pescadoro's dead family, Clement burly and avid and dangerous in his lair, Bill Lenz, the clucking admirer, even Veronica herself earnest and judgmental above me, even Kate's new video, her obliterated face—part of a design for a conclusion that was already inevitable, rolling seamlessly, like a movie, like the three thousand feet of film that make a feature, toward resolution.

Down there, down where the hill slips away from Sunset, is a newsstand that stays open all night. The magazines and papers are racked against a long outdoor wall running down the street. A bank of fluorescent tubes illuminates the stand along its length. Men come out at night—insomniacs, night workers, the demented—

and read the papers, standing in the grainy, acidic light. I watch them carefully turn the pages of newspapers in which my story, my name is printed. They hold a version of my life in their hands, a life that has become, is becoming as I watch them, a part of their lives. It is what I always wanted; it is everything I wanted. It is what turned me, ten years ago, from the pale, sunny rooms of wastrels toward the soundstages of my birthright. It is what brought Kate into my life. It is what drove her out. In a minute, secretly, as a man who has lived to the other side of his fame, as a man who has returned to his lost home, I will go down and join them.

―――――――

B RIGHT MORNING. I swam, ate breakfast by the pool, watched a workman roll the white legs of his coveralls to his knees and wade down the pool steps to retrieve a flotsam of bird feathers his scoop couldn't gather. The feathers were bright red and red streaked with black and dunnish brown, a cardinal's feathers probably; there was no sign of the bird or of what put the bird there. The workman fastidiously picked them off the surface, one by one, and put them in his shirt pocket. The early sun stung the tall palms. Hibiscus flowers, bright red and bright yellow, lay in limp scatterings on the white pool tiles.

I swam to slow my heart down—it helped—but by the time I was back in the room everything inside me was moving fast again. I ran the tape again, sat on the edge of the bed holding my foot in my hands, watching the drowned face, listening to Kate's blunt speech. She said the same things over and over. It was like watching whales from up at Point Diablo. Massive, brilliant, destructible, they didn't know a thing about us. Which was too bad for the whales. We were, after all, rulers of the earth.

―――――――

I DID NOT see the woman at first, did not pay attention to her, at first, when I saw her. The day was bright with dust like ground-up quartz. Dust glittered in the palms and in the sycamores lining San Carlos. I wanted to race somewhere without purpose and so had come out and gotten into a small blue rental car and headed on Sunset toward Malibu. Clouds over the Pacific were piling up like loose white clothes. I began to see people I knew, an actor jogging, a producer in a red Ferrari talking earnestly to a young girl seated beside him dressed in a pirate costume. Someone honked and hailed me, I waved without looking; a voice called my name but I was past, shooting down Celia under the flowering jacarandas. The yards were green and immaculate, prim.

Next to me, leaned against the door, was a small doll I had carried both times to Mexico and back, an image of Kate that had been a prop in her last movie. It was a movie she made with my father in Italy, a picture financed by Italians for the international market, a crazy picture in which every character in it had these small effigies that appeared leering in public places. The doll's mouth was daubed with lipstick; its eyes were painted. I was thinking of Kate holding it as we drove south through the mountains toward our messy rendezvous with the ape of Hollywood, thinking of the delight in her eyes when she saw him sitting on the hood of the wrecked car, thinking of the Indian village and the ruins of the big tourist hotel and the parrots flickering like patches of fire among the banana groves.

Stopped for a light, headed on my regular route toward the ocean, aimed downhill, I reached for the doll, cooing to it, and just then saw a woman in a white dress slashed with red step from behind a bank of yuccas. She started toward the street, stopped, turned, and shouted back toward a house among tall bushes. There was a scarlet building back there, an apartment building of some kind. As she shouted she swayed, not drunkenly, but like a fighter taking measure. I was thinking of the clattery roar of the car engines on the beach beyond the Indian village, of Clement and I staring at each other like gladiators. The woman shouted and I looked straight at her. "Can't come," she cried, "—can't." And then she reached into her madras handbag and pulled out a small silver pistol and fired three shots at the building.

I ducked, quick as a seal going under. What the hell was this? I raised my head. The light changed, but the street was empty. The woman whirled, the bright red slashes flashing against her legs, and strode off down the street. She got into a black Corvette and sped off. I thought to go and see what she was shooting at, but the scene back there around the scarlet building was peaceful, nothing moved, and the woman, the quick, fierce power of her, maybe the way the sunlight snapped across her straight black hair as she spun around, maybe the change of heart that Kate had hammered into my life, stirred me; I began to follow her.

At the next corner she turned, heading north on Mt. Silver. She moved along at speed. My body seemed to accelerate; I felt the brisk, creepy fear that I felt sometimes walking onto a movie set. Dust hung in the eucalyptus trees like spider webs.

On the slim little phone that came with the car, I punched Earl's private number. I said, "I just saw a woman fire three shots into a building."

"Get out of there," Earl said. His voice was raspy, weak.

"I'm in the car. I'm following her."

"Where'd this happen, I'll call the cops. Or you call the cops. Hang up and call the cops."

"Did I call you back last night?"

"Not that I know of. Where are you?"

"Hollywood. One of these streets off Sunset."

She was two cars ahead, driving in stately fashion down the sun-spanked street. Around us low, roughed-up buildings glittered. She had slipped the gun back into her bag, turned without looking around, and walked away down the sidewalk, casually, without hesitation, as if nothing important had happened, or something final had. I said, "I think I'm going to follow this woman for a while. See what's next."

"Don't do that, Will. Vickie just called to tell me she's got the contracts."

"From Clement?"

"Yeah. Apparently this project's set to go. We need to talk about it."

"I don't know where I'll be. Kate sent me another tape."

"Kate didn't send you a tape, Will. That's just bullshit. Where were you last night?"

"In the hotel. Veronica came over. I showed her the tape."

"Jesus—Veronica. You guys are going to get each other so stupefied you're going to fall off a building. Or drown yourselves trying to drink water. Why don't you come down to the office?"

The woman turned on Valencia and accelerated along the wide boulevard. "I don't want to come to your office."

"You want to have lunch? I can put Vinnie off."

Vinnie was another of Earl's clients, an actor getting more famous by the minute.

"I don't know—maybe. She's just turned onto Valencia, I want to see where she's going. Where do you go after you shoot at someone?"

"Are you kidding me about this woman?"

"No. She pulled this little gun about the size of a frog out of her purse and fired three shots at a red building, or at somebody in a red building. I couldn't see for the bushes."

"Was she firing at a person, or just shooting?"

"I don't know, I'll ask her."

"Don't get close to it, Will, I'm telling you. You made your twenty-four-hour quota last night."

I swung in behind a baby blue Rolls, one car back. "Was there anything in the paper?"

"Yeah, it was in the paper. But don't worry; they're treating it as a joke."

"I wasn't joking."

"I know, but it was entertainment—I think it'll do you good."

"It'll probably be worse when I punch him again."

"Don't punch him again, Will. Let the fish go." Earl coughed, said something to someone nearby, I heard my name.

"Is that Connie?"

"No—it's nobody."

"Oh, you rascal."

"I know. Do you want to have lunch?"

"I think I'll go away for a while."

"That's a good idea. Go up to Vegas. Spend some money."

"Not Vegas. I don't want to go there. Maybe out to the desert, that place in Death Valley where you can rent a cottage."

"Good. Go there, but don't stay too long. You've got work to do."

The woman was not traveling fast. Her black hair swung lightly when she turned her head to look at traffic. She slipped on a pair of shades.

"I'm looking at Kate's face right now," I said.

"What do you mean?"

"There's a billboard up on a roof. There she is: Kate in a blue dress, falling."

"Oh yeah—*Murder by One*; that's an old picture. I'm surprised the billboard's still around."

Her hair in the eroded billboard picture was long and wheaty blond. It flew behind her as she fell through space, her dress tangled around her waist. In the movie she fell from a plane, tumbled fighting a killer for three miles—before she cut his throat—and crashed, parachuteless, through the leafy green canopy of the Amazon rain forest. In her face, falling, as in all her pictures, was the sad, smiling loneliness, the exhausted, knowing, hopeless smile she brought home like a draggled bird every night of our lives. If I hadn't been following a shooter I would have stopped, right there in the middle of Valencia, to look at it.

But now I had somewhere to get to, something to do. I didn't know where or what, but there she was, my lure, bobbing and skipping along ahead of me. The trees lining the street, the junipers and the jacarandas, were eaten along the bottoms, and the crowns of the date palms picketing the median looked exhausted above their shabby gray skirts. The green world is dying everywhere, but out here in the desert death has its own quality. The trees are dying, not like the trees in the East that die, from the top down, rained on by acid, but savagely, from the bottom up, like trees bitten by dogs. And the scarifying, brutal climate that everyone not from here seems to envy—it's harsh, not the opposite, but the ascetic twin of the East, just as deadly with its sun like radar, its air stinking of eucalyptus and napalm, its demented, gritty wind. Just over the mountains, in the world of the Joshua trees, you can sit down beside your car and be dead by the end of the day. The sun will kill you. The sun and the heat and the dry, corrosive wind will kill you. On the roofs of the meanest bungalows, sumps work full time, leaching the tinny moisture from the air, vaporing the rooms so the inhabitants won't dry up, won't bake today to skeletons inside.

Earl was speaking to his companion, a beautiful young woman as I imagined her, limber, tall, a certain angularity about the hips, a boniness around the eyes, a small, clever, parochially witty mind, every door in herself locked against the truth of her condition. "Earl," I said, "is Billy D. really funding the picture?"

"That's right. It's strange isn't it? Three years ago they were done with Clement."

"Maybe Billy's been up to something and Pop caught him."

"That's probably it. Listen, I have to go. You want to have lunch?"

"You bet."

"Let's get snails, I've got a craving for snails."

"Earl," I said, "did you know that the snails on your plate are the same snails you see sliming around your garden every morning?" Earl, I didn't say, did you know Clement is planning to kill me?

"I didn't know that. Is that true?"

"Honest injun."

"Hell, that's good news. I'll start picking them up before I go to work. You want to go to Sonny's?"

"Okay."

"I'll see you at . . . one?"

I didn't say anything.

"Will? I'll bring the contracts. You want me to call Billy, see if he can meet us?"

"Whatever. If you can get him, fine."

"Stop following that woman."

I was about to answer, but the woman, two cars ahead, accelerated. I hung up the phone, swung out into the free lane, and followed. She was driving fast now, maybe the daze wearing off, coming to her senses on a Wednesday morning, sun bright under a pale brown sky, LA bedlamic and triumphant around her.

I kept a car between us at first and then I dropped back, unsure of how to go about this business. My life had become secret. The Mexican boys on the street corners selling oranges and star maps couldn't understand it, and the slim woman walking from her house toward a car the color of a blue whale didn't know what I was up to, nor did the old man in tennis whites standing on a streetside balcony as a young woman—his daughter perhaps—berated him, couldn't know that I had become the bearer of a secret, indecipherable life, momentary consort to violent beauty here in the obvious, flowery streets.

She sped swiftly along, turning corners, heading north and west, never hesitating, as if she were following a route she knew intimately. They say there's no perfection in the world, they say we have to settle—yearning still—for the crabbed, frayed articles we find here around us, but I think they're wrong. Everything teaches us about perfection, everything shows us where it is. The petals of a flower show us about perfect skin, the sea breeze teaches us perfectly the salt taste of our own bodies, a look shows us the perfection of bitterness, and the movies—rich, buttery film—teach us about the perfection of our lives. No wonder Kate worked so hard at getting into them. She who was built for the life of a figurehead wanted to become one. And this woman, tossed elegantly into the raw space before my eyes, was perfection, the sunny, sleek Los Angeles version.

But maybe not perfection, maybe only someone I could save. As I had not been able to save others, as I had not been able to save Bobby, or Kate. What do we do when the wounded one steps into the room? It was a question I had pondered. It was a dilemma I had lived. I had missed chances—chosen to save myself, to flee—and the missed chances haunted me. I spoke of them to those near me. And now, as I drifted, but drifted on my regular route toward the beach, toward Veronica's and my mother's houses in Malibu, another panicked, damaged creature had crossed my path. What had sprung this on me—or who had sprung this on me? It was easy to figure: Clement. But how could it be possible? What elegant woman could he charm or blackmail into doing this? And if he did it, what did he have in mind?

For an instant, as we rolled along past the jacarandas and the palms, the world shifted, tilted, the focus whirled, and I was driving through a monstrous and ungovernable creation without reason or substance. It seemed to me that a dark claw poked through into the sunny world and ripped it, tore it loose from itself. There were circumstances, arrangements I knew nothing about. They were as elaborate as cities, as countries. For an instant it seemed I was driving into another world, a world that sped along in shapely pageantry beside the familiar, but which had nothing to do with it. If my father, whose life had nearly been taken from him in a sea village in Mexico, who had risen from a fire to seek my death, had constructed this caper, then there were possibilities here I knew nothing about.

These thoughts cut through my mind as I followed her. If someone I knew had arranged this, it was someone who knew me well. It was someone who knew I would follow such unruly caprice. Someone who knew what I couldn't resist. But so what, I thought, so what? I had long ago stepped out onto this road. I wasn't going to get off it now.

I followed her up into the hills and down again, onto the freeway heading north and out into the ranges overlooking the Pasquale Valley. She stopped once to make a phone call—to Clement?—and again to run into a convenience store. She came out of the store with a can of soda that she sipped from a straw.

From across the road, under a flowering poinciana, parked in the half-circle drive of a director I knew, I watched her. Her face under the thick black hair was pale and lean, and her skin shone. She did not seem hampered by what she had done, she did not betray emotion, she gave away nothing, there was a beautiful blankness about her. She sipped the soda, standing square-legged beside the car, looking into the sky as if there was something up there it was her job to keep an eye on. The sky was clear, the air smelled of frangipani and creosote, the car softly purred, and I was on the other side, beyond the ditch separating one world from the other, looking around. Up here in these hills, beyond every yard, just past the last glittery patch of watered lawn, the desert sprang fiercely to life. There was no transition; the barbarian, untamed world coiled like a snake around the immaculate, coddled fortresses. Drunk at a party, wandering out, if you didn't watch, you would find yourself spinning in thorns, dust in your mouth, pale lizards crawling on your skin.

We cruised up into the hills again, along a road that wound through chaparral and dusty yellow rock outcroppings. The ascending bends were so tight that I could see small tan lizards on the rocks as I slowed to make the curves. We came out on the crest and ran along the ridge, snaking down under the brow and rising, the road following the contours of the range. The valley, patched with green fields of lettuce, opened away toward the east and north. In the plowed portions, the soil was chocolate, the fields fenced, two roads cutting through the floor angling south. Far to the north, up where the valley drew in on itself, above a patch of woods near some farm buildings painted white, a hot-air balloon, striped red and yellow, idled along. It was so far away that it looked pinned to the sky, as if this was a feature of this part of the country, these gauds.

The woman had slowed down, but she still traveled at speed, slinging the Corvette around the curves with a muscularity and verve that delighted me. We were alone on the road, and by now I couldn't believe she didn't know I was following her, but there was nothing I could do about it, or nothing I wanted to do about it. It was easy to make up stories about her, to see some marginal though accomplished life lived up in these hills, back in a canyon in a stucco house with swimming pool and tennis court, a husband who made his money in real estate or medicine, see the table in the foyer where she placed invitations to parties that always disappointed her, see her children out in the garage igniting their dirt bikes, see her alone in her bedroom reading a magazine, attempting to construct for the ten thousandth time a version of her life that she could live with. But now she had made a mistake, she'd started an affair with a guy who turned out to be no good, a guy who used her and now wanted to blackmail her or leave her for someone else more his style. I could see her, see her looking at this guy as he told her, offhandedly, coldly, that he had to move on, and I could see the thoughts rolling like balls of ice into her mind, the sting of humiliation and simple embarrassment, the awareness, slung suddenly across her brain, of what she had gotten herself into, and then the fury that came over her as she saw herself for the chump that she was, in love with a son of a bitch who was cutting her loose and breaking her heart.

Why not pull a gun and fire a couple of shots?

But then—my scenario aside—what face did she fire them into, what shifting form? Who would you kill? And what wrenching tug of your life would bring you to the place where murder was all you had left? It was something I could ask Clement when I saw him. And something I could ask myself, or ask Kate, or my brother Bobby, pale under his heart's blood, if I ever met him again. Maybe, in one of Kate's videos to come, we would discover how someone comes to this—or maybe, under this merciless sunshine, among these dry hills, this woman, soon enough, will explain it to me.

My pistolero, steady at the wheel, drove smoothly, accelerating out of the curves, pushing the big engine on the short straights. She drove as if she was familiar with driving big cars fast; it was only because we were in the mountains that I could keep up. The brake lights blinked like warning lights, but I didn't pay any attention. Her head bobbed from side to side as if she were talking to herself, and occasionally she looked down at something in the seat beside her, as if she was reading. Maybe a map, maybe the contract she had just signed with Paramount, maybe the letter her foul lover had written trying to write her off.

The road rose again, winding through hills the highway department had blasted a way through. The rocks hadn't weathered. They still showed the grooved dynamite tracks, the rough places where the blast had broken them.

I let more space build between us, letting her dangle off the line, following her loosely, like a dog follows his huntsman, bewilderment coming on like a cold, the clues fading as I devised them, the world beginning to spin, bristly Kate, high in my mind, marching back and forth on a bone white road, my father's hairy body turning in my hands, the slow, careful organization of a new scene taking shape, the dazzle all around me, a laziness like sleep, like laziness, coming on. Ten years ago I got up out of a silky bed and drove through the depleted gray dawn to the studio where Billy Dangelo waited to usher me through the initiatory paces of my first movie. A steel door opened and a woman wearing a halo of small white flowers handed me a cup of coffee. The work began, and I moved with it, amiable and attentive; I went along with what they wanted me to do, and it was easy because I knew, as the lights cracked on, and the dry-ice fog began to circulate, that I was moving deeper into the mystery of my life—as this woman up ahead of me was—and I wanted, helplessly, to see what was there, what goon or angel panted behind the door.

She slowed down—I thought maybe to let me catch up—and pulled into a level area overlooking the valley. I pulled in behind her. Neither of us got out of the car. I watched her looking at me in the rearview mirror. Both her hands were on the wheel; I figured she was gathering herself, getting ready for what would come next. Maybe she was letting it all go blank, seeing if it would. My heart beat fast—the vein in my wrist popped a little—but I wasn't afraid of what I might do. I had already done the worst, just two months ago, in a hospital in Mexico, and before that in a hut in an Indian village on the Pacific coast; I had accomplished it.

The side of the woman's face, which I could see in the mirror, was unmarked and still; she was changed now, ruined maybe, but the change didn't show. She was still in that space I had come to, after the worst has happened but before the consequences slide like a mountain onto you. She looked straight ahead, and I would have given anything to see what she saw among the corroded rocks, where some sparrows hopped about and the dry bushes rattled. I wanted to tell her now that I too had looked straight ahead after the horror, and I too had peered into the simple distance where the world shuffled on oblivious, that I too had seen it. Maybe, if we got honest with each other, maybe we could work up a little community of around-the-bend folk, of sports who had gone too far, done the unforgivable, maybe we could hold meetings like the Vietnam vets and hoot and cry about the crazy murders we'd performed, the babies and the wrinkled old women we'd slaughtered, and maybe we could get so straight and ordinary about it that the small-time sinners would be attracted, and the spilled milk crew, the boys who talked back to their mamas, the tardy and the flakes, the women who overshopped, and the men of the simple faux pas, maybe we could spread this thing around, lower the threshold of error until everyone could step over it.

It was time to let her know about this, and as she swung the black door open, I swung my door open and got out to tell her. I was putting the words together, the ones you gather when you are ready to talk about what you do when you have gone past the end. I was about to say, Listen, maybe then it's all right to just let things drift, to sit down somewhere in the shade and let the big world rumble by. I was thinking of Kate and of what she claimed about being able to ride the chaos, and I wanted now to step aside with this lovely lady and chat about this a while, get a few things straight about how humble we would have to be if we were going to get along, but I guess she wasn't ready for it, because as she straightened up I saw that she had the little silver gun in her hand.

"Whoa, wait a minute," I cried, "I am with you."

She looked at me in terror and fury, as if she were looking at a snake.

I thought, Jesus, I am sorry, I have gotten it wrong again. I should have known, I thought, but I thought it in the midst of wondering surprise.

She grasped the gun two-handed and she pointed it at my face. This was my cue. It was no time for speeches and truths. Or it was time for others than I had handy. Her face was cold and beautiful, there were black tear lines on her cheeks, there was lipstick on her bared teeth. I raised my hand, but only for diversion, because I was going down behind it, I was diving for safety. I didn't hear the shot, but I felt it hit me, or I felt my head explode. For an instant the world turned scarlet, surging, covering everything, but it wasn't the world, it was me, and I snapped out into the black behind it, skidding at the speed of light into the void.

A WHITE SHADOW moved before me, not dancing but lurking and darting, and I was thinking of the two of them, of Kate and Clement sitting in the big kitchen out at my father's farm playing blackjack with thousand-dollar bills as Clement created a movie in front of her eyes, the movie she would make in Italy with him, and Kate laughing, pushing back in her chair, throwing her handsome head back to laugh, her eyes never leaving his face, which was filled with joy and menace and greed. There's a tenderness in the center of every disaster, like a sweet taste on a bitter day, there's a humility that softens, and I raised my hand, almost touching her, and watched it float like a white bird to light . . . on a large, pale face looking down at me.

It was the face of my momentary saviour, a Samaritan, a hunter, so he told me, from Arno passing by with his partner on their way to check the deer population in the Refuge Hills. The partner had gone on down the mountain to get help. They had wanted me to stay on my back, but I wouldn't, I forced myself up and got into the car. Now I looked out through blur at the bright day. The phone rang, but I didn't answer it. We both waited until it stopped ringing.

My mind went *ah, ah,* and the tenderness slipped through me like a thief.

The man's face was large and round and sucked in when he smiled and he recognized me.

"You're Will Blake, aren't you?" he said.

The words seemed to fall one by one and hit me softly. "Almost Will," I said.

"What is that?"

"Bobby?"

"I'm Dretty Johnson."

I seemed to be missing half my head. "No, me."

"You're Bobby?"

"Will's brother."

His eyes were a pale, rainy gray. His hands were large, trenched between the knuckles; they held me up. I'd taken a blow to the head, glancing but sharp. "You certainly look like Will Blake. Who is someone I've seen. The movies I mean. I've seen him in the movies."

"Me too."

I slumped down. He pulled me up, held me steady. My blood had splashed on his wrists.

Gray, powdery rocks rose in piles against a climbing hillside; there were gray, dusty bushes in clefts; the air smelled dryly of sage. A light wing of sadness brushed my body. That was some woman, some shootist, some tough soul.

"Did you see anyone else?" I said.

"There wasn't anybody around here."

"How about on the road?"

"We didn't see a soul."

I placed my hands on the wheel, made a little grinding sound in my throat. I squinted, hunched forward, aimed for the finish line. I looked at the hunter, grinned. "I think I can do it."

He shook his head. "I don't think you should go driving off just yet, Mr. Blake."

"Call me Jack," I said.

"I thought it was Bobby."

"Call me Jack."

"Jack . . . you look too beat up to travel."

Then he reached in and hooked the keys out of the ignition.

"Well, *shit,*" I said, "*goddamn.*"

"I can't let you go harming yourself," he said, "and others who might be on the road."

"It isn't a request," I said. "I must be going."

Sometimes you fly, sometimes you crawl. I was an actor after all. I began to force tears out, like blood from a lash. "But I've got to go," I said, "you don't understand."

"I think the blow hurt your mind," the man said. He leaned against the car hood looking at me, the keys wrapped in a loose fist. His forearms were pelted with stiff red hairs.

"Ah, Jesus," I said, "it's my daughter—she's sick. She's got meningitis. I drove up here to get away from the house for a while. Her condition is driving me crazy. It's killing my wife."

He looked at me, his eyes sympathetic and apprehensive both. "Your daughter?"

"Yeah. She's twelve, a little redheaded thing. She was staying with her aunt in southern Illinois when she woke up sick, running a fever like an engine, raving out of her mind. My wife's sister got her on a plane and they flew her to LA." I shook my head, wiped my face with a slow hand. "It's meningitis; she's dying."

"They flew her all the way across the country?"

"Yes. My sister-in-law was frightened to death."

"If that's true, I'm sorry to hear it. But how come you're up here? How come you're lying on the ground with your head busted open? How come you're shot?"

"It didn't happen up here; it happened down in the valley."

I liked this, this whining and crying.

"It happened down in the valley—how is that?"

"My sister-in-law did it. She's gone crazy. She took a pistol after me."

"Your sister-in-law from Illinois?"

"No. My brother's wife."

"Will Blake's wife? The actor's wife? Zebra Dunn?"

"Yeah, that's her. She shot me with a little silver pistol. Christ, man, it was like a movie."

"Zebra Dunn the actress? Oh yeah? I love her."

"We all do, we're all helpless before her beauty."

"Man, she's something."

"At times she's everything."

"Yeah. I'm a fan of hers. I've seen her movies. She's wonderful."

"Yes, she is, but very volatile, very volatile. Sally getting sick has driven her crazy."

"And you drove all the way up here after a blow like that?"

"I was in a daze. It didn't hurt much at first. I pulled over and must have passed out."

"There's blood everywhere."

"Scalp wounds bleed."

Kate would say, What you make up you have to live with. She would ask me if I could do that and I would say no. Are you buying this, Bub? He looked at me, almost weak eyed.

"The ambulance is bound to be here in a minute."

"I can't wait for that. My wife's so crazy I don't know what she'll do next. And I can't stay away from my daughter any longer. She doesn't have much time."

"Maybe I can drive you."

"No, no, man, you go on about your business."

"I can't just let you go in the condition you're in."

I've been in this condition all my life, sportivo. I said, "Give me the fucking keys, asshole."

His eyes popped as if I'd hit him. You've got to give it a more subtle take than that, pal. "Whoa," he said, "Jesus."

"Yeah. Give me the goddamn keys."

"Well, all right."

His arm swung up, but he didn't let go of the keys. "I don't know," he said, "this isn't right; I've got an obligation here."

"You've got—ow—an obligation to hand me the keys to my car."

"But you're a hurt man. I can't let something happen to you."

"Listen," I said. "I'm all right. I'm just going down to the valley, to our farm." And to the colored lights that were flashing out over the valley, and to the flying shape of a woman in a white dress blown along by hurricane. I thought, all right let's see what this does.

I slid out of the car on my back, turned onto my side, my arms going loose and floppy, anguish in my face, and puddled at his feet. I waved up at him. "Please, mister," I whined, "you've got to give me my keys. You've got to let me go. I'm so broken up and beat I can't take any more of this. Please let me go. I'm just going home, I'm just going home to my baby. Oh please, please, please let me go, please give me my keys, I'm not going to make it if you don't, I'm just not going . . ."

He tossed the keys onto my body. "Here, jeez," he said, "come on, man, cut that out."

"Oh thank you, thank you." I shoved up to my knees. Dust stuck to blood patches on my shirt and I could taste it at the corners of my mouth. "God bless you, sir, you are a kind gentleman and good will come to you."

"It's okay, it's okay," he said and took a step away as one would from a maniac. "I don't know, you're . . ."

"That's fine, don't think anything about it," I said, my voice half-strong again as I raised myself to my feet. The blood drained from the upper parts of my body, but I forced myself up anyway, wouldn't give in to the weight and the tremendous fatigue that lay like a column of lead inside my bones. "You have done a good and worthy job here, my friend. Maybe I could repay you."

"No, no, nothing like that. I just hope you're okay."

I looked around. The black tar road seemed to turn with my head. The scent of roses drifted by. "Which way did you come from?"

"That way," he said, pointing, "up from Arno."

So she'd continued on in the same direction.

I fumbled the key in, started the car, backed and wheeled it around. The guy stood there in the middle of the level place, surrounded by rocks on the top of a mountain, and looked at me. I had made a picture like this, one of the last Westerns, where a wagon train, beaten by Indians, starving, abandoned one by one its wounded and dying members. I leaned from the car and waved. "Look out for yourself, old Scout," I said, which is what Dalton Cummins, who played the hero in the picture, said to me as he leaned down from his horse bidding me good-bye. The man waved back, somewhat as I had waved as I lay in a cleft raising a hand out of weariness and resignation, out of the real jollity that comes sometimes in the fading wake of loss, and then I swung the rental car onto the pavement and gunned it down the mountain.

The valley—here in California—stank of the raw life of the world. The pale green coagulated lettuce stupidly prospered in wide rows that were as long as runways. The ground was the color of cocoa. I caught the main road, ran south down the valley, climbed again through brief dry hills, and came through a grove of mountain pines into the valley I was raised in. Here, instead of plowed fields, were pastures and orange groves, vineyards scrawled on the hillsides, stone houses set back among live oaks, windmills turning their papery sails in the light, crossing breeze. My head throbbed, singing its jumbled song. I thought I might see my pistolero princess again, but she had vanished. Well, easy come easy go. Each time the blood surged in my head, my mind barreled out of my body into configurations that were ornate and disheartening. A confusion of parts played themselves out, rearing like clowns, parading across the green pastures like a string of painted horses.

I stopped the car, got out, and sat down in the grass on the road shoulder. Around me crickets and small green grasshoppers jumped. I lay back and looked up into the broad blue sky. It was cobalt, like the edges of the ocean in winter, in the highest reaches. A summer sky paying a spring visit. I raised my hand to look at myself, to make sure I was alive, and I saw my hand tremble. I wanted to look at the videos again, to see Kate. Maybe if I looked hard enough I could stop looking.

The Spanish troopers and priests who settled this country were not the same exuberant killers who stomped the Indians in Mexico and South America. They were second-generation colonizers, and like all those of the second generation, bent on preserving and extending what their fathers had already died for. Early corporate men, they wanted to build establishments that would last for generations. I could almost see them out there under the oaks at the edge of the field, standing by their houses in gaucho trousers and short black jackets giving their overseers instructions. No foul-ups, get it right—that was the idea.

Kate, oddly hostile, seemed nearby, watching. My mind raced, caught up with itself in Mexico. We were bumping along the rocky drive under cedar trees approaching the monastery. The big event had happened by then; we were exhaustedly returning from it. She was sick with pregnancy, I was sick with anger and shame. The cut on her leg gleamed. Ahead, the monastery rose from among its low protective trees, the color of biscuits. There was a church, two churches, a row of cottages, a front of plain wooden doors, a corral, sheds, behind it all a river among willows. The river was dry, a white sandy alley disappearing into brush. Beyond the river was a grove of pecans shaking up green again with the spring, and beyond the trees the mesquite scrub rising toward the whitish, stony mountains.

We got out and wandered around awhile by ourselves, looking at the ruined artifacts the monks had collected, the paintings with their flaked gold leaf and the swords and tools the monks had used to subdue the place, until Kate got tired and went back to the car. I went into a small half-built chapel in back, tried to connect with something larger and couldn't, and wound up later in a walled garden beside the main building. My thoughts seemed as weathered as the rocky place. I napped a little, and waked and napped and let my thoughts run to ruins and how much I loved them and how I wished there were more in America, real broken places that had mysteriously survived, and I remembered the few Indian places I'd seen, some of the Anasazi settlements in Arizona, and a couple of wind-melted adobe forts in New Mexico, but they weren't really much, you had to go all the way down into Mexico to find the big-time stuff.

Around me in the little garden, the monks had planted a mingled array of fruits and vegetables, native plants and European varieties they had brought over from Spain. Pinot grape thrived near ocotillo; small barrel cactuses bloomed near rosebushes. I thought of how a man starts out with an idea of things, some hope or intention of affecting the world, how he's got some plan and a method, he thinks, and how life snatches him up like a robber and carries him away. What we hoped to accomplish was rarely what we accomplished, but somehow—this came to me as I got to my feet then and moved absently among the tulips and the bristly pricklepoppies—what we have for the world gets passed on anyway, though so often in a shape completely foreign to what we had in mind or what we thought we knew, and the world ambles on. What had it been like, I wondered, for these monks in their cheap dyed robes and their ornate faith, stranded here with God in the Sonoran Desert? What had happened when they began to tire, when the dust and the heat and the obstinate Indians became too much? There are some in the world who can find the faith to continue no matter what, some who don't back off, but they are rare. The rest of us, even the adventurers and the entrepreneurs, even the guys who rove through, bludgeoning everything in the way, tire, build themselves a little perch they might sing and spit from, and fall back. But sometimes there is nothing to fall back to. For the monks, this berth was a sentence. Spain was out of sight; it didn't exist anymore. Cortés, Pizarro, those meaty boys, could count on a return voyage eventually, a hope for recognition, a flag painted in their colors, fame and gratitude of a queen, but these fellows, these bit players here eating their dusty bread, had to go on with it, no respite. Did they come out here, some evening after the hot wind had died down, did they shuffle along through these plants, or through these plants' great-grandparents, and take a little look at the damask rosebush that had once thrived in the plaza of the house where they grew up in Castile? What did they think then? Where was God and vocation then? Did they think that their hearts, not so long ago muscled and pumping resolutely, had crumbled to dust, and did they ask themselves what they could do about it? Did they care? Now that's a question. Did they care? What if the love of God, what if its realization, fully blossomed in the hearts of men, was simply the realization that we are not supposed to care?

From the garden I looked out at the river, at the willows sagged down on their knees above the absent stream, and I could picture the monks walking out there, picture them by the river in the dusk. They had seen it through, these believer boys—there was a graveyard out back, shabby as the rest of the place—and here is what was left: a monastery converted into a museum, the crumbling architecture, ghosts in the eaves perhaps, this garden in which a few flowers thrived. A hard future to hoe toward. I didn't like any of it, and I couldn't agree with the motivation or the outcome, but just then I began to feel a little better. It hadn't been that long since my days of drift, I could remember when my decision to let the world pass by was lived *outside* and inside. The monks may have gotten tired, and they may have wept for their home, but they had succeeded after all; the country was Catholic. But here in the garden it was as simple as the dusty desert flowers. They leaved, bloomed, withered in their shabby irresistible way season by season. Let me not say too much.

I plucked a sprig of plum and carried it out to the car, feeling a little better about myself, a little resigned to my life, a little less defiant about marriage and oncoming child. Kate sat in the car with the door open, one leg swung out. There was blood in the center of her dress. She was dabbing at the blood with a handkerchief and crying. I knew instantly what it was.

"Will," she cried, "you have to make this stop."

I started to get up, but then I thought crawling was a better idea, so I crawled back to the car to get something that had escaped me by the time I got there. I crawled across the road ditch and up the other side and sat against a fence post. Behind me was McKinney land; they were another Arkie family who'd done well, old man McKinney had come up as a roustabout and gone on to minor speculating and now raised Santa Gertrudis cattle on five thousand acres. He had a son who hanged himself, a schizophrenic who had stopped eating because his voices told him to, who had attacked his mother with pruning shears, who had been institutionalized, who on a weekend pass had stolen his father's pickup truck, driven to the mountain cabin, and hanged himself from a rafter. His father, frantically tracking him, had been the one who found him, a strung-up bundle swinging like a pendulum. Now the McKinneys told everyone that the son had a brain tumor, that the tumor had twisted the son's mind, driven him to kill himself. It was an awkward, human way of avoiding culpability. Last year old man McKinney told me that he still, six years later, waked up in the night from dreams of the death scene, from dreams of the door flung open on his son's hanging body, he couldn't shake them. I knew all about the stories we make up when the little god dies; I knew about them and I had told them myself, after Bobby went.

Kate, the sky was pale the first time we made love, there was a slip of moon, fog coming in off the ocean. Do you remember it that way? Or are there a hundred other versions, each one slightly different from the next? You told me about living in a small coastal city in a warm climate, about buying a book from among a pile of dusty books in a dusty shop near the docks, about carrying the book home through the hot streets to the boarding house you lived in with cripples and women who worked in the night trade, about passing through the house and glancing into the dining room, where the boarders and the woman who owned the house, a woman with legs like oak stumps, were at dinner, about hearing as you passed the meager, bitter conversation, the breath of accusation in every word, about toting the book upstairs to your single room overlooking a paved alleyway across which cats in heat called each other in the night from your neighbor's roof, about sitting with the book at the table and reading about the deep mystery in ordinary things, about looking up to see out the window a woman standing alone under a streetlight, hours later you said, watching her until a car whispering by on fallen leaves stopped and the woman got in, and it seemed to you there in the night in your single room with the book open on the table before you speaking of majesty in the drabbest life, that the woman was getting into the car of the dead, the boat car that would carry her across the river of darkness into the black territory of death.

In one of your versions, Kate, you told me you were born in a country hospital in Maine on a sunny, cool morning in June. You said you learned to read when you were four and a half, from a book about monkeys that your mother had saved from her own childhood. The house you were raised in was gray clapboard with white shutters, you said, there was a garden in back with a flagpole in the middle of it, stone steps leading down through balsam firs to the estuary. Across the estuary was a golf course and a swimming pool that sometimes you rode across to in a small blue boat piloted by your mother. The boat had a five-horsepower motor that sounded like your mother's sewing machine. The grass at the club was springy, thick as moss, and in places flowers sprouted through. The pool was filled with sea water, a vague, dream-soaked green; it was cold, so cold that your legs ached when you stepped into it. You said you had the body of a butterfly, spindly and shiny, and on summer days you wore a frilly yellow bathing suit that you have remembered all your life. Your hair was white blond and your skin was as white as Devonshire cream, nearly translucent. You were the daughter, you said, of ancient aristocrats, of the blond-haired Italian nobility, your father was an aristocrat and a killer, your mother was imperious, demanding, frail. You said you would never forget the northern lights, you told me of a bus trip you took to New Brunswick to see your aunts, of buying lobsters on the docks, of the smell of the fishing nets flaking iridescent scales—you told me this elaborate version of childhood one morning when we waked to high clouds and cool weather that you said reminded you of mornings in New England, and the story, Kate, was finely phrased and textured, but it was only one of many stories you told, only one of the many versions you told of who you were and where you came from.

Dreamily, without emotion, as the Texans must have watched Santa Anna's troops begin their final charge toward the Alamo, I watched a cop car, a state trooper, slow down, pull over, and stop behind the blue rental. Causey Clark, an old friend of my father's, got out. He was square, rough as a blasted stump, black-haired, carrying his hat in his hand. He hailed me.

I swayed, watching fire streaks take shape behind him. "What is it, Causey?"

"What's happened to you, Will? You sick?"

Causey, hard of hearing but unwilling to wear a hearing aid, a trooper near retirement, always spoke loudly. He lumbered around the car, crossed the road, and looked at me across the ditch. "You know there's blood in your car? You okay?"

"I hit my head," I said. A flock of gulls soared over the road, swung up high, descended, and lighted in the field.

"Did your dad tell you he and I were racing last week?"

"He didn't say anything about it."

I got to my feet, a little unsteady, forcing myself to cohere. I didn't want more than a couple minutes socializing with Causey.

"Yeah," Causey said, running his thumb around the sweatband of his hat, "it was on this stretch of road, heading out to his house. I came up behind him and flipped my lights, and he took off." He looked at his thumb, wiped it on his pants leg. "I had to hit a hundred and five to keep up with him. He was in that Jaguar of his. You need any help?"

"I may need a little."

I stepped gingerly down into the ditch, seeing myself years from now as an old man, surprised but not alarmed, like someone who, expecting to see himself in a full-length mirror, sees instead the piles of drab clothes in the closet behind it. My feet were smaller than normal and itchy around the edges.

"Is that a cut on your head?"

"Wait," I said.

He wiped his palms on his thighs and extended one to me. I grasped it and pulled myself up, slowly, feeling the gravity pull of the earth, something wanting me to fall back. For a second I saw myself lying in the ditch, eyes open, flies crawling on my face. I lurched forward and spilled to my knees beside him. "Damn, Will," he said, "you're in a bad way."

"Nah," I said, looking down at the crushed grasshopper by his boot, "I just celebrated too hard last night."

"Oh sure." He helped me to his car. I leaned against the side. I could see right through this country, through the grasslands and the rounded tan hills with their proprietary rock mountains lifted behind, straight through the valleys and the mountain ranges, through California, all the way to Mexico and the raw beach north of Mazatlán, where we'd gotten the final business straight, where like a queen come down through a war, she stood among the snarling cats, speaking, above the sound of them and above the sound of the surf, the last empty words. There had been a time when I thought I could put her in my pocket and walk around with her next to me, like some talisman I had found in the woods. But she had taught me the lie and the wishful thinking of all that. She had taught me and my father had taught me.

"Just a minute," I said, speaking to shapes, and leaned away one-handed, as a man would lean out over a gorge, and vomited. Causey caught me around the waist.

"You need to go to a hospital, Will," he said. "That's a nasty cut on your head."

"No," I said. "Just take me up here to the farm."

I got in the cruiser and Causey drove me, at speed, his meaty hands casual on the wheel, as he carried on conversation.

"Causey," I said, "how well do you know Clement?"

He cocked his head. "Well enough to ask for money, I guess."

"You need money?"

"Yeah. I'm about to retire and I want to open a tackle shop. I think maybe I can get old Clement to go in on it with me."

Was that a lesser kudu running along beside the car? That was, yes, that was a herd of buffalo over there under some trees on the Baziotes property. Paul Baziotes collected buffalo, American bison, he had a herd of a hundred animals. They are very dumb, buffalo, dumber than cattle, almost as dumb as chickens.

I stuck my head out the window, I may have barked like a dog.

"You starting a new picture?" Causey said.

"I'm going to make one with Clement."

"That's good. I know he'll be pleased."

I looked past Causey's thick jaw at the speeding landscape. "What did you think when he tried to outrun you?"

"I thought he was the same madman I knew when he was in high school."

I didn't think that was it. My father was probably scared to death. Or maybe there was nothing at all in him but the instinct to hit the pedal.

"Those Jaguars'll fly," Causey said.

The double rows of tall cypresses lining the driveway of the farm I had been raised on appeared, swinging out toward us beyond the curve. The fields, planted in Bahia grass on either side, were a pale spring green. A half mile in, where the drive curved toward the south, the groves began, running in fulsome rows past the house. Behind all reared the pale fronts of the Cordoba range, grassy slopes giving way to pines and rock outcroppings, to thickets of myrtle and toyon.

"I was out here to a barbecue last week," Causey said as he turned into the drive. "I was glad to see your mom and dad have gotten back together."

"I heard that," I said. "It's surprising."

Blackbirds chattered in the tops of the cypresses. They rose as we passed under, like crickets from a lawn. "It makes me feel good to see folks working things out," Causey said.

"I know what you mean."

There was something missing, something essential. You could take me down to the police station and grill me, and I would give up and confess and I would say yes it's this woman, yes, she's the missing number, she's gone, vanished back into the mad world she came out of; I could describe her, describe the bony face, the blue, pale eyes, the snap of bone at her hip, her pinched toes, but after I finished, after I sat with the sketch artist putting her together, after I made a model out of clay and dressed it in the clothes she wore to accept an Academy Award, after I pressed my flesh against the clay, breathing life into the shape and mimicry of her, still, still there would be something missing. What I couldn't say to the police, or to anyone else, was that it had been missing all along.

I began to laugh.

"What's the joke?" said Causey.

"Tides of memory," I said.

"Good you can laugh."

Yes, good that I could. What had been stolen from me, this marriage, this presence, this shape that yelled at me from the corners of my life, that cavorted on a television screen through the antics of expertly produced video scenes, had been only a figment. The thief had stolen a shadow. I knew this, it was as plain as the bright day, but why didn't the knowledge free me? Why did knowing this only open a vaster space, one into which I seemed to be falling?

My head throbbed and burned. Thin streaks of yellowish vivid light shot by, headed somewhere they had to get to in a hurry. A yawning female voice spoke a few words and subsided.

The cypress lane opened onto a wide turnaround in the center of which were planted four traveler palms. Bougainvillea vines climbed a pine by the drive, a drizzle of purple flowers hung from the lowest branches. The low stucco house, several winged, its wide porches open to the midday sunlight, ranged away in colonialist sprawl; we could have been in Mexico, somewhere up on the central plateau, in one of those provincial states where the Spanish had thrown up compounds that looked like fortresses, where the aging governors sipped the dregs of Castillian wine, going slowly crazy in the heat and the loneliness, even in their dreams forgetting Spain and the loved ones they'd left behind.

My father in a white suit and a torn panama hat stood at the top of the steps. He had a gray pigeon in his hand that he released as we pulled to a stop beneath him. The bird wobbled into the air, slipped sideways, caught itself, and flew off between two sycamores. My father came down the steps washing his hands. His black eyes glittered. "Well, Causey," he said. "What have you got here?"

"I ran up on old Willie out on the road," Causey said getting out of the car with the deliberation of an aged badger, "and I thought I'd bring him by for a visit."

"Isn't that fine," my father said, his thick hands squeezing fists.

To me, floating in haze, powdered with dust from the high roads, a man flown just twenty-four hours ago out of Mexico, out of the presence of the falsely magisterial Zebra Kate Dunn, a man who had come up with a few ideas about the end of things, an actor pressing toward the end of the scene, my father reared like an enfolding shadow, a dark space charged with crackling sparks. As I raised myself, as a man might raise himself out of the dry ditch he had floundered into, raised myself in greeting and took a tottering step forward toward the blankness on the other side of things—or toward the singing glory; I didn't know—my mind, and its trailing body, flew. Already, as if some greater season had come, as if a white corner had been turned, I seemed to fly into a world in which the old commonplaces had fallen to dust; I could see her, see Kate, abandoned by her production values, by her directors, by everyone, standing at the edge of the rattling surf, speaking words to me that she could have been speaking as well to the ocean itself, and I saw Arnold Pescadoro stepping out of his limo into the ashes that had been the flesh he gripped most closely to him, and I saw the figures of past and future moving across a screen, shifting as they moved, and I saw my own life, the sweet enterprise of it, arrived here in dust and blood—what abides?—and it seemed to me that everything I thought I knew had changed.

"Hey, Pop," I said. "I was out this way, so I thought I'd come over."

Then I pitched on, almost gladly, into darkness.

BOOK
TWO

M Y BROTHER BOBBY, dead and gone, tapped along the edges of my life. He had been dead for twenty-five years, but now on the shore of the dream sea, out here in the piney farmland of the Pima, he returned to me. They would tell me later that I rose from the bed they had laid me in and tried to escape the house, that I fell through a window, that I was discovered after midnight, covered with dust, crawling in the rough grass among the orange trees, that I fought them—with my eyes shut, Earl told me later—crying out my brother's name, crying out Kate's name, and the names of people no one had ever heard of. I was weak, unbalanced, dizzy, I was easy to subdue, they said, but not so easy to convince to stay put. In my mind, in the pictures that came in flashes, I was riding horses with Bobby down a long grassy valley, I was climbing in trees that seemed to go on thick as jungle into a huge sky, I was running beside him into a great torn surf, falling behind, always falling behind.

Bobby shot himself with a .22 rifle in his bedroom in my mother's house in Malibu. It was the summer the world became too dangerous to live in, the summer I watched the ruined boys raped and shot, the summer my parents reeled back from their marriage like exhausted boxers, a summer without rain, a corrosive and battering season that my brother Bobby, behind his knowing and tender smile, drifted through, like a man dazed at a wreck, toward a bullet. I was out at the farm, but I have believed all my life that I heard him cry out my mother's name, cry out for her to come to him because he'd been shot. My mother, who heard him, who ran to him through the summery house reeking of gardenias, and flung herself down onto his bloody body, did not get over his dying.

Bobby was fourteen, blond, strong faced like a country preacher; he had the supple, quick body of an athlete and gray eyes the color of rain. In our family he became a kind of small, perfect god, fixed in memory, a figure from the clattery, indigent past who maintained great and uplifting powers. I believe my mother prayed to him in the night, and I had seen my father, that brutal man, dash tears from his eyes open-handed, like a rube, as he recollected my brave dead brother. Nobody knew for sure whether his death was intended or accidental, but it broke my family to pieces. Rage and grief—they were too much for us. At least it was convenient, and easiest, to think so.

My mother tried suicide a few times afterwards, after she had been lifted screaming off my brother's body and after she had beaten the minister with a switch she tore off an alder bush as we walked behind the coffin to the grave up in the little cemetery in the hills he was buried in; for a while she got the wayward, purposeful look in her eyes of those who have branched out beyond what this world has to offer, and she would perform the suicide tricks, the magic acts of walking into winter surf, of pill taking, of trying, if no one had caught her, to fly off high balconies. She was always stopped. And who knows if she meant it or if the acts were only gestures performed to draw others close, because I too, because none of us—even Veronica, who stayed beside me as I wobbled through the woods behind the farm and walked the beach trying to explain how the empty place inside me seemed to be proof against all the world's idiot claims of felicity—believed we would get over what had happened.

My parents, tossed back together, tried to have another child. My father lurched about the world swinging wildly, dragging my mother behind him like a prisoner on a rope. Inside Jennie no child budded, or none that lived, and my father, king only of his own rough passage, bashed on down his thorny path leaving wreckage in his wake. They broke up shouting, broke up amid stinging threats and the inarticulations of sorrow, and the seasons and life rushed on, no consoling message left for them in the dust, nothing to understand but their own agitated grief.

The old-timers, the ones who believe time teaches us something, all say you never know what's going to show up in life, but this is not really true. Much of life's quirkiness, it seems to me, is that often we know exactly what's coming. The difficulty's in how we take it, what we do with it when the doorbell rings and some cross-eyed man in a purple suit hands us the shabby package that is exactly what we ordered last winter when things got too rough to stand. What we do with the clawed, smelly creature that climbs out of the box is what gives our lives their sense of variety. And even that, for some, is only fate, character's child.

Bobby came to me, softly and insistently in my dementia, he came out of a prison or off a movie set, he stepped out of heaven for a minute to be with me. In the dreams that came during the ten days I was out, he and I were lovers, it seemed to me, not in some scurrilous, greasy way, but chastely and permanently; maybe we were married, because there seemed to be the complicated, hard-won understanding that comes in marriage. This state made a heaven of its own in me. I could see us, dressed in movie costumes, at the edge of a scene, moving from the dark of a sound-stage into the lighted halls of playacting, into the arranged, immaculate arena where we would live. We spoke lines that seemed crafted by a genius. Great, eloquent speeches poured from our mouths. But in the words, and accompanying them, like wolves trailing the herds, other phrases, other speeches played. Mingling with the sweet talk, I heard snatches of warning, cries, sudden garbled shouted accusations, all edged against the clarity of our talk, all about to come clear, about to break free from the shadows that seemed to grow around us; and then I saw his face, the clean, handsome face of my brother begin to turn away from me toward the other voices; and then it seemed that the words came not from distant pursuers, but from Bobby himself, and though I could not make out what he was saying, what he was warning me of—they were warnings—I knew he was telling me what he had known all along, what he had known in the dusty days of our youth lived in the houses of lust and empire our parents built; and it seemed then that there was something in my life that was as large as my life, something brought forth now in these manic passages that was wholly familiar to me though I had never looked at it before, and it seemed to fill the world, to *be* the world; but then, with no corner turned, the voice became Kate's, and my brother's face became Kate's face, and I was standing in a windy place before my wife listening to words that had just now seemed ancient and revealing, but that were only the words of fierce love, of need and desire, and I could see in brilliant establishing shots the scenes of our marriage, and I could hear her clearly, in a hard, anxious voice, telling a simple, terrifying story of loss and pursuit, the story of a man coming from a long way away, a man who hated me, who crossed mountains and desert to find me, a man who sowed, from hands as hard as rocks, the seeds of destruction and death, a man who bashed his fists through life to get to what was behind it. And Kate, risen now fully before me, her pale, smooth, muscular body standing before me, grinned as she told me her story, and I could see that she did not fear this man, she did not shirk from his violence or his pursuit, and it seemed, though I didn't move, that I became a child running through a darkened house, a boy frantically fleeing this murderous entity, fleeing through rooms that turned back on themselves like folds in paper, like fever thoughts, returning me again and again to the presence of this creature, this deadly, unappeasable thing that would not let me be.

It was all a dream, but it was very clear. I heard the words, I saw the faces, I felt the raucous pursuit. I believed everything. But there is no truth in dreams. What truth there is for us, I think, is only in life itself, in what we live and breathe, out here among our fellows in the lunatic world. From these imitations of life, these imposturings, we learn only the pale or fancy modes of a world that cannot help or harm us. These knobby shapes, these dark forms, cannot hurt. We are safe from them, no matter how they frighten us. We are safe, that is, until they step from dream into the world.

I WAKED TO the smell of apples, to the smell of apples and to oblongs of light lying like fresh yellow pelts on the floor, to the sound of voices, to the sound of Veronica's voice, rippling and slipping, the delicate tones merging with the sounds of the spring day. I heard her speaking as I careened through crushed mansions, down prickly hillsides, and into and out of one of the long-gone restaurants on Hollywood Boulevard that Clement used to take us to when we were children. Her voice seemed to be coming from the kitchen of that place, or behind it, in the alley where once my father had beaten with his fists a producer he thought had betrayed him. I could see the producer, a stout man with black shiny hair, fall backwards into his wife, knocking her to the ground, and I saw the blood on his lips like lipstick and the look of hollow surprise in his eyes. I cried out as I had not but wanted to then, weakly as it turned out, cried out for someone, someone to come here and lift me wholly from this place. Had that man, a skinny producer, been killed? Had I wondered then if my father's fists killed him?

A clear-skinned man wearing a flat black hat poked his head into the room and said, "What's up, Willie? You coming around?" He was eating an orange, cupping his hand under it to catch the juice.

"Where are the honey biscuits?" I said, lost in taste, loopy and feeling friendly, feeling a little rosy despite bad dreams, now that I was awake. I could tell it was the world, it seemed hugely familiar, almost amiable; bright sun streamed in through open windows, I could smell, besides the apples, the scent of citrus and cut grass.

"We've got anything you want out here," the man said. "The whole place is set up as your kingdom."

He slid into the room on slippered feet, and as he approached, his name came along with him. "Earl," I said.

"Yes," he said. "You've got it. You're back on earth."

But who exactly was Earl? I said, "Have you ever worn a blond wig, or a black one?"

"Only in the privacy of my own home," he said grinning. He turned, leaned toward the doorway, and shouted, "He's come to."

I knew I'd been out, but it didn't seem for long. In my mind I was still traveling, still following—following someone, some—I couldn't tell. An emptiness, the size of a mystery, opened slightly; I tottered, I thought I might fall through.

"Are you okay?" Earl said. "The color just went out of your face."

A woman—Veronica, yes Veronica—stuck her head in the door. She whirled in, and smiling she kissed me on the mouth. "Don't go anywhere," she said. "I'll be right back."

I twisted on the pillow, reached for something that wasn't there. I was the victim—or the perpetrator, I couldn't tell—of an elaborate pretense, something like a movie I had once seen in which a man who wants a woman's money pretends to love her and marries her, intending to kill her. But then, yes, he fell in love with her, and she fell in love with someone else, and the two of them, the wife and the lover, plotted to kill the parvenu. But was it—"Earl, wait a minute," I said—"I'm not going anywhere," he said—was it a movie, or had something like this happened in my own life? Was I recovering from an attempt on my life?

I winked at Earl—or tried to; both eyes closed—and said, "Has anything unusual happened around here lately?"

"You mean besides the police bringing you home covered with blood?"

"Well, yes, maybe that. Or maybe something to do with that."

"Don't worry about it. It's already taken care of."

Had someone been murdered? Was the fix in?

"Bill Lenz called," he said.

"Ah yeah, old Bill—how's he doing?" Who was Bill Lenz, an accomplice?

"Earl," I said, "are the police here?"

"They came and went."

"Am I charged with a crime?"

"None that I know of."

Maybe I had gotten away with something. Then it began to come back to me, or the hotel came back to me, the tiny orange fruit of palm trees scattered on a terrace, a woman sliding an autograph book across a table toward me, cats screaming on a beach. But the cats weren't at the hotel, the cats were on a beach north of Mazatlán, and the hotel was in Hollywood; I had a room there. I said, "What is the date exactly?"

"It's exactly May first."

"We have all been dancing and cavorting?"

"Only you. You were a real character. We couldn't leave you alone for a minute. If we took our eyes off you, you were crawling for the open spaces. Jesus"—he passed his hand over his pale face—"you had me worried, Willie."

"How did I get here?"

"You took a blow to the head."

"I think it must have been a pretty strong blow."

A woman, a woman once ravishing but now ruined, her beauty like fine lamps shining in the windows of a broken fort, came in carrying a tray. She was dressed in black that gleamed vagrantly as she moved, and she had wound a purple-and-red scarf around her head; the long ends trailed down her back. Her arms were spangled with tarnished silver bracelets. "Ho, delight," I said, totally baffled. "What now?"

"Lunch," this woman in black carrying a tray, said.

"Bill said he's not going to press charges," Earl said, "but he wants to meet with you."

"Have we got anything to talk about?"

"You said it—I'm not sure that you do. He might just want some publicity. I told him we'd get back to him; told him also that you were under a lot of strain, what with the Mexico business and all."

"You told him about Mexico?"

"No details."

"That's good."

The country wobbled and shimmered in my head like a mirage, a mirage, however, that I had visited. There was a sorry tailing fever in my head, a slippage that smelled of garbage and frightened sweat, and it seemed somehow attached to Mexico, like the refuse of a party swept under tables at El Polito in Puerto Vallarta the next morning when you come out from a terrible argument you can hardly remember and stare like a fakir straight into the hard white sunshine—but I knew that wasn't it. Pictures reared in my mind, and they were vivid and precise, but they did not seem attached to anything, anything more than the memory of Kate leaning against me as she made smart, grave talk above the rustling noise of the surf. Sprinklers in the yard shedding frills of fresh water over the grass made a sound like the surf on that beach, but I was not there any longer, I was not there, I knew that, and an ache like a rock was wedged in my chest.

The woman looked solemnly at me, studying my face. "You, Earl, tread lightly," she said, turning to him.

Earl took a step back. "I will, Miss Jennie."

The dishes were covered with the silver hemispheres they use in hotels. I wondered if the woman was trying to confuse me. "Smells good," I said.

She flung a white napkin open, leaned in and fixed it to the neck of my pajamas, which were purple-and-white striped and confused me further, because I didn't remember wearing pajamas as a rule. She smelled of chicory flowers.

"It's red beans and rice," the woman said, "your favorite."

"I remember that."

"And banana pudding."

"I remember that, too."

I beamed at her or what I hoped was beaming. She smiled, a beautiful woman, a little thin, creases in her long neck, but the skin on her face was clear and tight, rosy. "Are you English?" I said, blushing.

"No, darling, I'm Scottish. And that's a cruel thing to say."

"I didn't mean it. I think I am slightly confused."

"Actually you're getting better," Earl said. He was a large man, slightly stooped, wearing white trousers. I am an . . . a . . . She was my mother, Jennie White, the actress. I had seen her pictures. I had grown up, either here or somewhere near the ocean, and I had sat in a darkened room in the house I was raised in watching my mother prosper and fail, fall in love, fall out of love, live happily ever after and die on a movie screen. A large rush of gratitude filled me. I felt like inviting everyone over to my house, which was, yes, I remembered, a large wooden house behind tall stone walls in the Hollywood Hills—yes, I'm an actor too, a very good one, known far and wide. Wasn't it time for me to be going home? No, not yet; let me be polite.

"This is very good," I said.

"He is enjoying it," Earl said with grave awe, as if I were an ape doing arithmetic.

"You want some?"

"I've already eaten, thanks."

He sat down on the edge of the bed, rubbed my foot through the chenille coverlet.

"The police want to talk to you," he said, "but don't worry about anything."

"I'm not worried." The beans burned the roof of my mouth. It was good to be eating. I was ravenous. "Why do they want to talk to me? What did I do?"

"I don't know. Don't you remember?"

"I'm a little confused."

"We'll tell them that. You've taken a blow on the head, or a shot. You're a lucky guy, so the doctor says. Somebody nearly killed you."

"Don't badger him," Jennie White said as she went out the door.

"I can imagine that somebody tried to kill me," I said.

Earl looked out the window. The sprinklers turned slowly on the lawn. "Can you remember anything?'

"Vague shapes, huge forms. They move at the edges of my life, indifferent to me."

"Ha ha—actors. The police don't have anything to go on, as far as we know—did this have anything to do with that woman you were following?"

"Oh, yes." I remembered now: the woman in the Corvette. "She shot me."

"Damn, I knew it. I told you not to follow that woman."

"I couldn't help it."

"Did you have dealings with her?"

"Dealings?"

"Did you get involved?"

"No."

"What—did she shoot you from her car?"

"Where's Veronica?"

"I don't know—Ronnie," he called, craning to look into the other room. "She's in there."

Veronica stuck her head around the door. Her black hair swung over her smooth face. "Hello," she said, smiling.

"I thought you were here before. I thought you were coming back."

"I was. I am. And run a restaurant at the same time."

"Well, you've done a good job on this particular meal."

"Just a natural gift," she said, breezing in in a flowered summer dress. She glanced at Earl, who looked away out the window, his mouth turning down. In the distance gulls shrieked. The soft, sweet scent of orange flowers blew in.

"Lean down here a second, would you," I said. I was very pleased to see her.

She put her face close to mine, kissed me on the cheek, started to draw back. "No, keep your face close." I wanted to smell her, I wanted the human, transfigured smell of a woman near me. Her perfume was musky, almost sweet; through it I could smell her body and the astringent, washed smell of beans. I touched her face lightly with an open hand. She kissed me again. "Ah, good," I sighed.

She drew back. "You're smiling like an idiot."

"He took a blow to the head," Earl said sharply, as if I needed defending.

"You look drunk," she said, not paying attention to Earl.

"I'm going out to the kitchen," Earl said, hoisting himself up, his heavy body moving as if he had a pain inside. "You want anything?"

"No thanks. This is enough."

When he was gone I put the tray on the table. Veronica got up, heading for the corduroy armchair in the corner. "No," I said, "come lie down with me."

"Okay."

"Get under the covers."

She slid in. Her feet were bare—like me, she didn't wear shoes in the house—the long toes crooked and smooth. They were cold. She snuggled against me.

"This is good," I said. "We can play our tempestuous games right here in the house I was raised in."

"They're pretty mild, mostly."

"You're jaded."

"I wish I was."

I was thinking of a scene, a movie scene I watched in which a sun-haired woman was lowered from a tree in a chair. The tree was a huge redwood, the chair was ornate, carved, gold, and the woman sat in it with a regal and undisturbed dignity as men worked ropes to bring her down, and then I was thinking of Barbara Stanwyck, who never left her house except to work, and of King Vidor, that fine old man who was a friend of my grandfather's, and of Jimmy Cocoran, the director, who taught me that a natural gift for acting was not the same as acting, and I knew, though I couldn't quite place myself, that they were all in some way part of the world I lived in, remembered—this came through suddenly—they were all dead. I said, "I know there has to be a heaven."

Veronica dipped her head and kissed me again on the cheek. "I know it, too, sweetie, but what's it got to do with the present moment?"

"There are a lot of people who must be in it."

"So many, yes. Too many."

My life flared in front of me, like a gasoline fire. "Has anyone heard from Kate?"

"Clement got a couple of things I think."

"She sent some more stuff to Pop?" It hurt to think it.

"He didn't say what it was."

I had thought the videos would stop now, but maybe she still had more to say to my father. There was a plan that had settled like dew onto my life, a plan cast into the world by Clement—something brutal that would break what it set out to break—and though I could feel its clammy damp touching me, I couldn't see it yet. He was a man who didn't step out of lives he stepped into, who could only move forward, snapping and biting, toward what he wanted.

Veronica raised her long arms, opened her hands. Her fingers were slender, waxy, the squared nails buffed to a shine like the polish on jewels. "When I was a girl," she said, "I swore I would never shave a single hair on my body. I hated the idea."

"You hated growing up. Why do you mention it?"

"This house."

"The flowering plum," I said. "That's what does it to me."

"What?"

"I don't know. Every year when I see a plum tree in flower, it starts something in me, a memory or something, a feeling. I know it comes from long ago, but I don't know what it is; I can never place it."

"Déjà vu."

"Or worse. I'm not even sure it occurred in this lifetime. It's a good feeling, though."

She pressed herself against me, curling into my hollows. Her ass was bony, the ass of a woman aging toward gauntness. I felt a twinge of sadness, remembering her years ago, the ruddy endless youth we both shared.

She said, "I try to prepare myself for the day, but my preparations never work. Something unforeseen always shows up."

"Is that why the producers rage?"

"Probably." She worked a ridge of cloth between her fingers. There was a shout from workmen in the distance, some business out in the groves. The thin, wheat-colored curtains soughed into the room.

"I was dreaming of Bobby."

"I was thinking of Bobby the other day. I was remembering how he used to jump off his horse into the stream."

"He broke his ankle."

"Jumping into the stream?"

"Yes, that's how he did it." But I pictured my brother in a tree somewhere, at the edge of a plain, looking down at me. There was a beautiful tenderness in his face. And then I could hear the voice in my dream again, the voice filled with rubble, warning me. "I haven't dreamed of him in a long time. After he died I would dream that he was in heaven, that I visited him there. He said it was a great place. He said he was having a wonderful time."

"I used to dream about him too. He would undress me."

"He used to do that in real life."

"Yes. When he was twelve years old and I was ten, he took me into the bathroom, right in there"—she indicated the door with her thumb—"and asked me if I wanted to make love. He said *fuck;* it was the first time I heard the word."

"What did you say?"

"I told him no."

"That's the girl I love."

"I wasn't against it really, I just didn't know what it was; the experience was all too new. We took our clothes off and touched each other. It was funny: talking his way to it, he went so fast I could hardly follow—I wasn't sure what he wanted to do—but when he touched me, touched this little hollow between my breasts, he slowed down. His fingers were cold and soft, and they touched me everywhere, moving so slowly—he said it was as if I was coming out of him, out of his body, or his mind, coming to life from the touch."

"Most probably it was the other way around."

"Yes. There were times he was an awfully dead-eyed fellow. As if he had no life at all. He was beautiful, though, to look at. His body was slender—like half a body—and white; you could see his ribs. His hips were very narrow, and his legs were long; the muscles were just beginning to sprout all over him. He touched me all the way down; he put his finger in me—a little way—and then he brought it to my mouth and had me taste of myself." She touched her mouth lightly with the tips of her fingers, as if remembering. "He would have done everything if I had said yes."

"I wish you had."

"I do too. It would have been a wonderful secret."

"Bobby had a lot of secrets."

"He never told me one of them."

"Nor me. But you could see them, you could see them in his face. Just now, when I woke up, I was thinking about the time my father punched this guy—I don't remember his name, a producer—knocked him down in the parking lot outside Chasen's. Bobby was there. I don't know what happened. It was terrifying—have you ever seen what apes do . . . when they're threatened?"

"Yes."

"They scream and rush at it—it was like that. Bobby was there. Mother, I think, swept me away, but he watched. That man went down. Blood spurted from his face. I don't know if he got up. I don't know if he ever got up."

"Clement could have killed him."

"He could have."

I thought of what I couldn't remember: of Bobby's face, of my brother's face as the two of them, father and son, came around the corner—maybe, maybe there was some new terrible knowledge in my brother's face—I couldn't remember—and maybe what he had seen wasn't the first time he'd seen it, or the last.

"Who was that woman?" Veronica said.

"What woman? Oh. I don't know. I can barely remember her."

"She shot you?"

"Half shot me."

"You saw her shoot at someone, and you followed her, and then she shot you?"

"That's how it went."

"What was it about?"

"Nothing I know of." But then, I thought, it could be about everything I knew. It could be the only thing strange about it was my own ignorance.

The telephone rang somewhere else in the house. The one by the bed didn't ring; it was turned off to protect the sick person. I heard my mother speaking into the receiver. I picked it up and heard Bill Lenz's voice. "I thought we could meet for lunch," he was saying to my mother.

"What is it, Bill?" I said.

"Will, is that you?"

It's Lenz, I silently mouthed to Veronica. "It's me. What's up?"

"I was sorry to hear about your accident. Are you feeling better?"

"It was just a knock on the head. What can I do for you, Bill?"

"Are you mad at me?"

"No, I'm not mad. It wasn't personal, Bill."

"Oh, I'm glad. I thought I had done something to you."

"Nothing like that. And don't worry—I'll make public reparations."

"Public what?"

"Apologies, Bill. Earl'll put out a statement. It was my fault, I was envious of your great success."

"Well, thanks. It was pretty good, wasn't it?"

"You did well."

"I was calling to see if you wanted to have lunch. I thought maybe we could meet."

"Okay."

As Lenz spoke, recounting his triumph, I began to think of the time I met Kate—one of the times—at a party in the Hills, at a house down the street from my own. It was at Jack Dayton's, an actor who was known fifteen years ago for his blond beauty, for his gentle blue eyes, his wistful way with women, and for a kind of steadfastness that usually got him in trouble. Kate had arrived from Nebraska a couple of weeks before, and like a dreamer had already met men of influence, been invited to parties, had been signed up for tests on three pictures, and here she was at the fancy jamboree at a house owned by one of the major stars of Hollywood's late-middle period, out on the pool terrace in a soft white dress, surrounded by half a dozen fawning players. She was telling a story about applying for a job in a carnival. As Lenz droned on, her voice came to me, clearly, out of the desert or from whatever world she had tumbled from, and I was again leaning against a piece of marble, a statue painted, as the Greeks had done, to look human, a figure with a pink face and bright blue eyes that looked over my shoulder at her, along with me, as she spoke. She said she had come out of her wanderings onto the carnival at the edge of a little town out in the West and gone straight in to apply for a job. She said, I applied for a job with a man who did an act with an ape. He had a small silver house trailer that he pulled behind a pickup truck. It was that time in the fall, down in Oklahoma, when the maple wings are shimmering in the trees and the air smells of wood smoke. The man liked me, she said, I thought he was going to hire me. He was a little fellow, puck faced with tiny dancing eyes shiny as seeds. He invited me into his trailer, I thought he had something else on his mind—you never know—but that wasn't it. He wanted me to meet the ape. The ape was wearing a pair of loose blue trousers, sailor pants, no shirt, and he was sitting at a table. The man introduced us, deferentially, earnestly, as if we were two he hoped would be friends. The ape shook my hand. His palm was black, heavily creased, thick and soft. The man poured cups of tea and set them before us, before the ape and me. And then he said, I'll leave you two together, so you can talk, and left. I was surprised, a little frightened, but then I thought it was lovely. The ape picked up the cup with both hands and drank from it noisily, slurping the tea down. He made smacking noises with his lips. I asked him how he was, told him a little bit about myself. His eyes were large and brown, the irises ringed with black, very sad eyes, liquid, pleading almost, as if the ape had known sorrow. He had coarse black fur, like horse hair. I liked him very much. He wanted my tea, so I gave it to him and he drank that too, smacking his lips after every swallow. Then we sat there looking at each other, not much to say, since we had just met, like two strangers on a bus who can't quite work up a conversation. The man came back and asked me to go outside—he wanted to discuss me with the ape—and I did, walked around the trailer that was parked under some large crab apple trees. I picked an apple and ate it; it tasted just like an apple from the store, only it was smaller. Then the man came out and told me he was sorry but he couldn't offer me the job. I asked why. He said, You make Clancy nervous. Clancy was the ape's name. He said, He's afraid you wouldn't stay with the job. He thinks you're just passing through. I glanced up and saw the ape looking at me from the window. He'd put on a hat, a tiny white sailor hat, and he was staring at me with a very wise look in his eyes. I waved to him, thanked the man, and left . . .

I said, as if I was the one who thought it up, "Bill, I think we ought to have lunch. Let's go out to this place I know in Santa Monica. They make a really good abalone salad, we'll talk about things."

"Sure, that's good," Bill said. "What's the name of the place?"

I told him and we made the date. I hung up the phone and looked at Veronica, whose bony body sprawled at my feet, and I began to think about Kate, about the story just come to mind, about how I was dazzled by her on the terrace there at Jack's, how the men around her seemed to sway like the stems of flowers swaying in a breeze.

Sometimes your future walks right up to you and introduces itself. Sometimes you turn the corner, step out of a summer squall, and there it is, gleaming like a new car, ready for you to ride. She was very beautiful sitting there among the bobbing men, her white-yellow hair trimmed short, chopped off, her eyes flashing as if she was telling a story about battle, and I was delighted.

I asked Veronica if she remembered the party. "Do you remember Kate that night?"

"Yes," she said, "I do. I told Jennie about her the next day."

"You told Mother?"

"Yes. Jennie wanted me to invite her over, but I asked her not to."

"Why?"

"She was too vivid. Jennie needed a quiet house."

I asked her to help me up and she did, holding my arm as I wobbled to my feet. She walked me to the chair by the window. "I feel as if I've gotten old all of a sudden."

"You look old. Your face is worn."

"So is yours."

She swatted me lightly on the shoulder. "Honestly, Will, I don't know what makes you worth it to me. I don't look old."

"We both do. Life has worn us down."

"You're kidding. You haven't done anything all life long but drift around. I used to think there was a time when you stopped paying attention, but now I don't; I don't think you ever paid attention. You're the boy who isn't there."

"You're bothered by my character?"

"Well, yes, but I'm commenting on your nature."

I leaned my forearms on the windowsill, slid the curtain aside, and looked out at the green yard over which the sprinklers flung their shattered curtains of clear water, at the plum trees and the cottonwoods in clumps down by the fence, at the mock banana bushes and the patch of wildflowers over by the dark green barn, at the groves beginning beyond the barn, ranging away in glossy green, almost blue rows toward the first rise of tan hills. A white limousine was parked in the shade under a large live oak near the house. Inside, two men—one of them my father—sat talking. The other was Causey, the state trooper. I could see their heads nodding, as one, then the other, spoke. My mind began to drift.

Several years ago my father had cheated me over points in a movie. It was an urban detective epic, filmed in New York over eight weeks of rain and snowy weather. I played a rogue cop who gets killed in the end, shot by his friends. My father had skewed the profits in his direction, raising the incline of the money roll so that it ran downhill toward him only, slipping by too fast for me to catch. It had been necessary, he said, when I confronted him about it, to keep him from going out of business. There was nothing I could do, since he had covered himself legally as well; I could have initiated a lawsuit, but it would have done no good. I raged, accused, swore vengeance, shook my fist in my father's face, but the money was gone. The final round had taken place out here, on a dry fall afternoon. I had arrived alone, leaving Earl and the lawyers in town, making a last attempt to break through to my father, thinking, despite evidence, that if I put the case well, or well enough, he would come around, see his venality, repent, and pay me. It was a way of claiming love, but I didn't think of it like that; I had already disassociated myself from family ties—so I thought—and was concerned with this man as a business partner who had brazenly cheated me. I came in through the back, through the white-and-copper kitchen, along the tiled companionways through the airy house that smelled always of citrus and my mother's delicate French perfume—even after she was gone, as if my father himself sprayed it around—into the largest of the three living rooms.

I had called my father's name, but no one answered. I called again, and then I heard his heavy voice, off down a corridor. I tacked down that way; the voice came from his bedroom. The door was ajar. I knocked, said his name, and pushed inside. He was sprawled naked on top of my mother, making love. They had separated years ago, but never divorced. As I took a single surprised step into the room, he swung off her. His greasy penis flapped against his belly. I saw that. And his thick bear face looked at me, the black eyes small, twisted down to points. Under him, her wrists bound by a black silk scarf, my mother struggled, writhing, frantic with desire. Her body seemed caught in some wild rebound off the earth she had been hurled down on. I flinched, I looked away—not from pain but from privacy—but not before I caught a glimpse of her eyes, not before I saw the wolfish, bleak despair in them. Her body gleamed with sweat, and her hands clutched at my father's shoulders, pulling him down to her, but the eyes that looked up at him, that clicked toward me as if a swivel turned in her head, were the eyes of someone who had long ago seen too much and long ago been changed by what she saw. They were filled with a barren, ecstatic rage, like the eyes of someone forced back from the dead.

A sharp thrill, like a straight, hot wire, pierced me. I shouted, idiotically, yelled, "Stop it," and fled the room. Trembling, I hurried up the hall into the living room. I lost myself in there for a minute. The tall sunny windows seemed filled with fire, and the conch shells on the long table, each painted with the name of one of my father's movies, looked like skulls, mouths grinning. On the polished desk by the windows, the propped family photos looked at me out of their silver frames. There were many more of Bobby than of me or any of us. It struck me as I stared at them that in each photo Bobby was somehow apart, even when it was a picture of all of us together, even when he frisked about among his friends. In none of them did his body touch another body.

This seemed to me to be a fact of fantastic importance, a secret revealed. I had sat down on the sofa to ponder it.

Sunlight poured over my head, it lay on the intricate maroon carpet like the fresh yellow skins of animals. My mind raced, but what it hurtled past I saw clearly. I saw my brother's face, my mother's. And I saw, again, the video Kate sent of herself taking a shower—a video made that year on a movie set in Louisiana—of her turning her white body under spray bristling with sunlight, and I wondered who the cameraman was. She too had stood before the camera alone, untouched by human hands. She too, like Bobby, projected forth a secret life that thrilled and enticed the observer. But what was the difference, I wondered, why did blows bring Kate back grinning when they had forced my brother, the sleek and capable boy, into a bedroom with a gun? I wondered if the cameraman was Clement. Then my father came out roping a white silk kimono around his prosperous belly. I sprang up, and in me I felt my life, I felt the strength and vigor of it. My father advanced on me, grinning sheepishly, but his hands were solid fists. I was young, I was quick, I was filled suddenly—amazingly—with glee: I belted him with one flat right hand into unconsciousness, yelled a hello and good-bye to my mother, strode out of the house into the antic sunshine, got in my car, and drove away.

THAT WAS FOUR years ago. Until last year, I had hardly seen him since, and when I did, he was often playing a meek and frightened guy. He sent me Christmas cards and called on my birthday, but he didn't come around. Not for a while, not until he caught Kate's heavy scent. From a distance I had watched his career grind to a halt. Nobody wanted those big pictures anymore. He was old, stiffening up, it was time, so they said, for him to rest on his laurels, let the younger boars root in the trough.

But he didn't look like an old boar now. Inside the car, he was intensely talking, had been for a while. Causey steadily nodded his head. Clement raised his fist, banged it against the dash. Outside, his chauffeur, George Boudreau, leaning against the hood, jumped. Clement opened his fist, held it up to Causey. There was something in it I couldn't see, something that glittered. He took Causey's hand, held it up as one would a child's, and placed the shiny object into it. And then he cuffed him on the shoulder, a blow affectionately rendered, a blow—I knew—of contract, that made Causey's head jerk.

Veronica massaged my shoulders, her fingers sinking deep. "Don't," I said.

"Oh, I forgot," she said, leaning past me out the window. "You don't like it."

"Not massage. It's too much like abuse. I think it's really just a cover for sadistic impulses, for revenge. All this business is."

"What business?"

"Jogging, exercise, trainers. Only people who hate the body would come up with shit like that. They're just puritans who envy the beauty of the world. They really want themselves and all the rest of us dead."

"That's pretty harsh, but not unexpected."

"Do you remember that night at the party when I first saw Kate?"

"At Jack's? That wasn't the first time you saw Kate."

"It wasn't?"

"I don't know whether you are stupid or you just change everything to suit you. No, that wasn't the first time you saw her. You met her at my house; you had an argument with her; you threatened to throw her date off the deck."

"I did?"

"Will."

"I've taken a blow to the head. There are many things I'm not sure of anymore."

"Actually you've always been this way."

"I'm in the movies, darling; it's a world of dreams."

"Lucky for you."

I touched the bandage on my head gingerly. It was hard as cement. I said, "Try this: We met at your party. It was late at night, after you got off work, after midnight. You were wearing an ice blue dress, you had your hair up. Kate was there with that actor—what's his name—Paul Brand, who was teaching himself to smoke so he could play some gangster who smoked—what an idiot—I was there by myself, dressed in white clothes . . ."

"You had on one of your grandfather's Mexican vests; it was black silk brocaded with gold beads . . ."

"That's right—and cowboy boots, I was wearing cowboy boots—I can't remember why I did that since I hate them—"

"You were showing off—strutting . . ."

"Right, I'm sure I was. You came up to me, I remember—were you drunk or high, or what?"

"Tired . . ."

". . . and said you were fed up with the indistinctness of things—is that what you said?—tired of this feeble world . . ."

"I thought the restaurant was about to go under."

"Music was playing, I grabbed you and whirled you around, off the ground, and your feet struck that guy, that actor Kate was with . . ."

"Paul Brand—he's dead now . . ."

"He is—that's right—he went off a cliff trying to do his own stunts in that movie of Charlie Burke's—what was that called?"

"*Sand Storm* . . ."

"Right—he was really pissed . . ."

"Probably because of the smoking habit he'd picked up . . ."

"Maybe he was stoned too—I remember I turned around to apologize—you could see the lights of the tankers way out, and the lights of houses up the bay—the wind had that crisp, kelp taste to it . . ."

"The seals had arrived . . ."

"Yes, that's right—and I saw Kate, or I heard her—no, I saw her, leaning against the porch rail . . ."

"You always call it a porch."

"That's my Arkie heritage. In Arkansas they have porches."

"Playacting . . ."

"Yes—I saw her; she was leaning against the rail, in black clothes, she was wearing black silk pants and shirt . . ."

"Which was unusual for that particular year . . ."

"But it struck me not as a fashion statement but something else . . ."

"Her clothes?"

"Yes—like someone speaking about her life, or about the way her emotions worked, something directly evolved from life, like a hawk's plumage or a cat's fur—something they've put together over the years to help them get by, do their work . . ."

"I know what you mean . . ."

"She had this incredible nonchalance . . ."

"She looked bored . . ."

"No, it was a kind of exhausted sensuality, like she'd been making love all day in some den close by that she'd just now slunk out of . . ."

"You're romancing it . . ."

"Yes, I was struck by her—I had this feeling, all of a sudden, that Paul Brand was going to offer to sell her to me . . ."

"That tout . . ."

"It was excruciating, the feeling I mean, against all my principles, but I felt it strongly, it was like a taste in my mouth; I thought—it was almost as if he *was* saying it—I thought he was going to say, *Do you want to buy this woman?*—maybe he did say it—no, I'm sure he didn't, but maybe she said it . . ."

"I don't think she did—you're just jazzing it up."

"Sure, that's what I'm doing, but I can't help it, and I don't do that with everybody, I didn't think anybody was asking me to buy Paul Brand, *pour example* . . ."

"No . . ."

"I think she put the thought in my mind . . ."

"That witch . . ."

"No, it was natural, maybe I couldn't help but think it—she had her hair back, not like yours, not up, but pulled back, almost harshly, so thick it looked like a helmet, and held down with a wide silver clasp in the back . . ."

"You have a *good* memory."

"Yes, but where did that other come from—that other story?"

"Maybe she put that in your mind, too."

"Or maybe I met her for the first time more than once . . ."

"That's probably it."

"Sure. I said something to Paul Brand, who didn't take it kindly . . ."

"He was an irascible guy—like you."

"Us artists can be ornery—I remember he was angry, but there was also this odd, defeated look in his eyes, as if he'd just listened to the bad news he'd been trying not to hear all day . . ."

"She'd just turned him down . . ."

"Yeah, maybe that was it."

Veronica shuddered, clasped herself in her arms. Chill bumps made the silvery hairs rise. "That *was* it. He was in love with her, Paul was, and she had just told him to hit the road."

"Is that right? That guy was in love with her? I though she'd just gotten to town."

"Kate was a quick worker."

"Yes, that's true, she worked on me . . ."

"Poor boy . . ."

"And then—I remember this now—it was as if he didn't exist, as if he just dissolved, left the planet—I started to speak to Kate—I didn't know it was Kate—I started to say something smart and Hollywood, something lazy . . ."

"And she said . . ."

"Yeah, she said—what was it?"

"She asked you . . ."

"That's right, she asked me if I didn't believe that emotion and thought were the same thing; she said—she called me Glide—was it Glide or Clyde?"

"Clyde probably . . ."

"—said, Clyde, don't you think emotion and thought are the same thing?"

"I remember."

"I was flabbergasted. I mean maybe that's not an important thought—I don't know, I'm a movie star, we're all dumb as posts—"

"Talking horses."

"Right—but I was struck by it, because that's what I was experiencing, right at that moment."

"There was something else . . ."

"Yes. She started talking about paranoia as the tie that binds. The common response to contemporary life . . ."

"And the honey in the lion's jaw—she mentioned that."

"You remember? She did say that—honey in the lion's jaw—good out of evil, that kind of thing."

"It was unusual for a party in Malibu, at least for my parties in Malibu."

"Unless you were going to invite some of those aging English and German freaks. But they were all dead by that time."

Veronica pressed her face against an upper windowpane, pressing until her features smeared the glass. As she did, she extended her arms out the open bottom half. "Sometimes I could milk the world," she said. She slid her face sideways, looked at me with one clear eye. "She got through to you in a second; she pulled you right in."

"I don't deny it."

My head had begun to hurt. A crinkling light jagged across my eyes, slowly. The cool spring air blowing through the curtains was like a body trying to enter the room. It felt good, like a loving touch after a long journey. The drift began, the slow languorous movement toward dream. Veronica continued to speak, but I couldn't hear her. I was in Mexico, in flooded streets. People bobbed about in boats, small craft. I lay in the bottom of a dugout that an Indian man paddled toward the central square. I raised myself on an elbow to look at the flooded town. From around the corner of a florid building a large boat appeared; it was painted with black enamel, open, with a platform in the stern. There was a helmsman pushing a sweep. Under a canopy amidships someone rode on a scarlet chaise. It was Kate on the chaise, dressed in black. She was queen of the flood. As the boat approached I saw that it was riding low in the water. It was sinking. No one aboard seemed to notice. I wanted to speak, to warn, but I was unable to make any sound. As we approached I watched the elegant boat go under, water washing along its gold gunwales. My heart pounded violently. *Save yourself*, I wanted to cry, but as the words rose into my mouth I saw that it was not Kate's boat sinking but my own. I was underwater, I was sinking, watching the blue sky recede through pale water. I could look up and see the sleek black hull passing over.

NOW I REVIVE to see my father sitting in a white wicker chair beside the bed. It is later, the sun is going down. Have I just now come to this, or have I been awake all along and just now gotten my brains back? The movies didn't stop my drift, but they documented it. I was interested—am interested—in the fashions, the mores, the expressions of time past. The hats men wore in the thirties, the long forties' hemlines, the toaster like a lump of silver on the zinc counter. The clothes and expressions of the sixties seem quaint now. The Sabre jets screaming over Toko-Ri look handmade. My father is speaking of his picture, our picture. It is a story of crime and punishment. Of retribution. Long ago, in a faraway country, a man fell in love with his father's wife. Because of this the wife was exposed, cast out, destroyed. The father chases the son, seeking revenge. The son, who becomes a priest, wishes to revenge himself against his father as well. They meet: death. All this takes place against the backdrop of revolution. The father and the son are on different sides. The son is exemplar of the future, of freedom for the people. The father, a Tory, seeks to preserve the old authoritarian ways. The country itself speaks to this, in the binary contrast of its high desert mountains and lush valleys. My father describes the final scene, its revision, the scene he was telling to Max when I came upon him at the Oscars. There has been a great flood, after days, weeks of rain. Houses have been swept away. The father's great white mansion, which had stood for a hundred years on a rise of ground in the deep green valley, is uprooted; it rides like a great white frigate on the flood-waters. Inside, in the ship of death, the father and son fight their final battle. The house is carried through the town into the wide flood-broadened river and onward into the lake that is as shoreless as a sea: the white house drifts out into the sea.

"Think of this shot," my father says: "The camera pulls back from the house, this tilted mansion riding on the waters, a house as large as a cruise ship, as authentic you know, until we see the house alone riding the lake, and we see the wideness of the lake, its emptiness, and behind it the day going down in oranges and pale scarlets, nothing in the world but this ancient white house and the empty world all around it."

"But Pop," I say, "who wins the fight?"

My father leans forward in his wicker chair, his bottom lip poking out so far I see the purple underlip, and doesn't say. I don't know what I am going to do about him, I don't know yet. He is as massive as a bear, and restless, filling the chair; he smells of the earth like some old druid risen from under the leaves. His hands are streaked with wet black dirt drying to gray. He's been out there in back, in the garden beside the barn, rooting around in his muck of compost and sludge, the material that he hauled here from the sewers of Los Angeles, the strained and weathered shit of millions he'd folded into the limestone valley soil, planting tomatoes. There are specks of dirt on his face.

He looks now as he did the night after my brother died. He came in that night, too, covered with dirt, cuts gleaming on his knuckles, came in, so he said, from a fight he had provoked at a gas station he stopped at on his way home from beating up one of his mistresses. He mentioned his mistress and the fight with her in passing, dwelling, as he ripped the skin off a grapefruit and thrust chunks of it into his mouth, on the three men he had tussled with on the shoulder of Highway 70. "We were covered in grime and dirt and oil," he said, "out there in the weeds with the traffic hurtling by, heaving punches at each other. The thought came to me"—he shook his head—"that I live a mythic life, that I'm some creature from the time of the titans, that everything about me and everything that happens to me is bigger than life, or it's life with more life in it than there is in anything else around me." He smashed the grapefruit down on the table and glared at me. His eyes looked as if the skin had been torn off around them. "I don't understand how anything near me can die. I don't understand it. I've got so much. It just ought to invigorate everything."

And then, muddy streaks of oil matting his hair, grit spinning off him, he made me accompany him into the living room, where my brother, in a white suit and a sky blue casket, was laid out among candles under the east windows. He threw himself down onto his knees, mumbling a prayer that sounded like wet meat in his mouth. He drew me to him, held me with one arm clasped against him. I could smell the liquor and the oil and the grit of earth. He threw his head back and cried out, howled like a dog. And then, rising on his knees, candle flames guttering in his eyes, he pulled himself over the rim of the casket and punched my brother Bobby in the chest. Bone cracked, and what was under the bone made a greasy, pulpy sound. He shouted at my brother, flailing at him. I pulled at his clothes, frantic to stop him, grabbing him, trying to save Bobby, to save someone who was already dead. He struck me a blow with his forearm, flung me across the room, knocked me out. When I came to, I was in bed, and my mother, in a black silk dress, was leaning over me, pressing a cold cloth to my cheek.

Now he raises his arms, holds them straight out, and dips them as if he's flying. "I'm buzzing in on the victor," he says. "I know, but I can't say."

He can't say, but if I let him, he would act out the whole movie here in front of me, taking all parts, including the scenery. When I was a kid he would grab me up and dance with me around the room. He's famous for his ability to make actors do what he wants. The key is his smelly verve, the way he talks to you as if you are the only person in the world and he, this great man, has to share his problems, his truths, with you. Actors, who love to get to the bottom of things, go for it every time.

He stamps his heavy foot. "Yeah," he says, "this thing's got meat on it, all the way through."

"I'll bet it does. But I can't believe they're really going to let you do it."

"Aw, shoot. They can't deny me. I'm a terrible person, I fuck up all the time, I trip over my own feet like a drunk in church, but I make 'em a big goddamn picture."

Beyond the open windows a thin rain is falling in the sycamore trees. The air smells of the sea, and of fresh earth. "We're filming this in Mexico?"

"That's right. We're going to rip Mexico off its goddamn hinges. Max's getting me enough dynamite to blow fucking Guadalajara into the sea."

"Who's playing the father?"

"David St. Vigio."

"St. Vigio? That sleaze?"

"Vigio's good. He's old, but he'll do anything. He'll eat dirt, he'll kiss a man, he'll pull his guts out and use 'em for a lariat. He's exactly right."

"He's a fucking ham."

"That's what I want. This is an overblown guy, this father. He's out there bullfighting without a cape. He's the guy who-charges the enemy without a gun."

He swivels, turning not just his body, but the whole chair as well. I am amazed, in awe of his pretense; we should be trying to strangle each other. His legs bunch and relax, bunch again; he leans over himself; his flabby thick shoulders look as if he is wearing shoulder pads.

"Listen," he says, "this father wants it all, he wants everything. He can't help himself. It's like a disease except he doesn't know it's a disease. He's unreflected, you know, he doesn't think about things, he just goes after them; he eats and drinks and shits like an elephant. He runs over anybody in his way, he doesn't know what the hell he's doing half the time, but he does it, you know, he just rushes out and does it. There's all kinds of background—I've looked into it—all kinds of past where he's left the ruins of smoking villages behind him, dead marriages, brokenhearted children, friends hanging from the wires, you name it. He stinks from the ruin and rot of his life, but that's the smell of life, you know? That's the smell, and he's got it on him, this mortality. He's more alive *and* more dead than anybody around him. Anybody, that is, except his son, who's just like him. That's the rub, see? His son is the same way, peas from the same pod, you know. Sometimes it works this way, you get these two freight trains, running the same track full tilt, dead at each other."

Something terrible has happened between us, between my father and me. For weeks now I have waited to hear the whispery clatterings of his vengeance begin. In Mexico, two months ago, in a burst of my own revenge, I humiliated him. I threw him beyond humiliation. We all betray our fathers, but we do not all destroy them. In my dreams I see him coming for me, coming out of shadows as I sit under a Mexican canopy eating shrimp. I see him stepping into the room where I am sleeping. I see him accosting me on a sunny street. But worse than these images, which tremble and blare, is the knowledge that slinks through the dream like the stink of a corpse, the knowledge that I would not tell to anyone, not even to Veronica, that my father, the man who spit me living into the belly of my mother, wants me dead. Could I be wrong about this? It is, I know, a crazy idea. But in my dream it is true. And in my life it is true, I believe this. I have seen it in his hard black eyes. I know him, I know he is a man who gets his own back, no matter who takes it. I took from him as he took from me. We should be even now, but that is not the way my father sees life. He can't stand to be the last to lose.

I say, "Pop, did Kate send you more stuff for me?"

He stops abruptly, shakes his head. His eyes search my face for a second. We are back in Mexico, struggling in the surf. I see his fury. Inside his head—I swear I can see it—there is a film running. In it he leaps up, swinging his fists, and smashes my body bone by bone. His brow contorts, the muscles in his forearms twitch. He can move toward me, he can move away: it is like watching tectonic plates grind. Perhaps his love of me, or of what I stand for to him, causes hesitation, because he is not a man who thinks things through, who thinks before he acts. But then, I think, yes, there is something sly in his eyes. He has figured a way and doesn't need his fists right now. I see this in his eyes, in the set of his lips, in the way he turns his big head slightly, looking slightly past me, as if what he has called forth is near. And I sense, in this second of time, that what he has devised for me has appeared already in my life, has already touched me. It is with us now. I am amazed, realizing this, that I feel no desire, no instinct to avoid it. Is this what the drift has done to me, or is this only what I have waited for, arrived at last?

He rocks forward and pushes back, as if against weight. "Yeah, yeah, she did. I have it in the bedroom. You want it now?"

"Yes. Go get it."

He scurries out, quick as a young man, though I see he is not quite what he would pretend; he loses his balance slightly as he turns through the open door, bangs his hip against the knob. But the shot doesn't stop him. He rushes away, outrunning blows, hurtling from one pretense into another. I lie back in soft pillows. Sun shines gamely through the rain. The grass sparkles. Many of the worst things have already happened and still life goes rankly on. My father and I could live forever and we will never speak of what is between us. I respect the massivity and relentlessness of his purpose. He is a man it is not hard to bow to. It is the old struggle—give in or don't give in, but then, no, it is nothing like that anymore. We are not father and son duking it out, none of the usual business of two energies banging away at each other.

We struggle, but we are two shadows pitching around in the dark. It is all over a woman, over love you might say, if you believe in that, or over what love represents, the concentration and power, the access it gives. Kate has fucked us both, and we will probably kill each other because of it.

THE HOUSE SOUNDS empty, hollow. Once, as a child alone in the house on a summer evening, I heard a strange noise coming from the rear living room. From back in my bedroom I heard it and thought it was a burglar. I sneaked down the hall into my parents' bedroom, found my father's pistol in his beside drawer, and crept toward the front of the house, prepared to shoot whomever was out there. I wasn't brave, but there didn't seem any other alternative. I didn't think of running away. I was *drawn* toward the noise, toward what intruded. I hid behind the living room door and called out words from the movies. My voice was small and creaked in my throat. I called again, stronger. No one answered. It was then that I fully saw the pistol in my hand. It seemed suddenly to claim a place. I waited, hoping for something else to happen. Then I rushed out from behind the door. I saw movement in the corner, whirled, and fired. A bird flew past me and banged against a closed window. I sat down on the sofa, got up, stiffly opened all the windows, and sat back down, trembling. Gray smoke drifted near the ceiling; there was a small black hole in the wall beside a painting of my mother in a gray silk dress. I listened to the bird fluttering against the glass. Nothing but a bird flew out the window. I had shot a gun off inside the house. It could have been a burglar; I could have killed him. I fired before I could see. I had no idea I was so afraid.

A VOICE—KATE'S voice—says, *I don't know—have we changed, have we crossed a line, or what? Does the ill wind blow? It's hard to think of these things, though everybody claims to think of them all the time.* In the darkened room, behind the door I have just closed to keep my father out—Did you watch this? No, he said, lying—I can hear him in the next room banging things, rummaging, breaking; he would like to have a wasteland ready for me when I step out of here. He leaned close to lie; his breath smelled of compost, of dirt, as if he had dug the tape up out of the earth with his teeth. I look at her on the screen, a figure naked from the waist up, painted white, standing, eyes closed. She appears mummified almost, her lower body wrapped in gauze, her eyes taped, her mouth taped. Her voice speaks from behind her, behind the still form. *We don't really believe something terrible has happened; we say we do, but then we go home, fix supper, take a hot bath, call our friend and talk about the shoes we saw in the window at Saks. But let me tell you, oh yes, let me. Did I tell you this? About the time I was in New York doing that film about the woman stalked by a murderer? The one where the policeman tries to protect me? We were filming in the Bronx, up near the zoo. Have you ever been there? You must have, you went to school up there, didn't you, but I guess not quite in the Bronx. Where is Columbia? Is it in Manhattan? All those jerky little students, each sure she's destined for fame. That's where they had the riots, isn't it? Well, I was on the set, it was morning, mid-morning, I was waiting to be called. I decided to take a walk. Not a good idea maybe, but it was a new location, there were no crowds, the section we were in was pretty, all the old wedding-cake buildings, the little raffish stores. I walked up the street alone, it was a clear day—in May—the sun was shining through the trees, the air was a little chill, but the light was summery, almost tropical; an island light, brand-new. I passed a couple of stores and a small park, heading up a hill into a grove of trees, heavy women out shopping. Across the street a little crowd of actresses were standing around one of the trucks, waiting to go into the scene. They were all clean and perky, delighted. I noticed a man on my side of the street; he was wearing a dark suit and carrying a D'Agostino's shopping bag—there was a store up ahead—I thought he had just come out of it. He was standing beside the car truck. The car, a dark blue BMW, was still on the back of the truck, but nobody was around, and he was leaning against it, supporting himself with one hand. His other hand was at his crotch—this guy in a suit—and I thought, My God, he's peeing. I know this happens all the time, especially in a city like New York, but I wasn't prepared. I'd thought how nice it was to see a man in a suit bringing groceries home from the supermarket. But there he was, leaning against the car trailer, with his hand in his pants. And then I saw he wasn't peeing at all. What I took to be piss wasn't piss. It was jism. He was masturbating. He was looking at the little actresses across the street and masturbating. Coming. His face was white and crazed. His eyes were locked on the actresses. Without thinking, I shouted at him. He didn't look*

around, just shucked his penis, raised his leg, wiped his hand on his sock.
Then he lifted himself back into his pants and zipped up. He turned away
from me and walked on down the street. I started to run after him, but I
couldn't; my legs were too weak. I thought, It's gone too far, we're past
the point of no return. This clean man in a suit carrying groceries stopping
on the street to masturbate. I felt a chill in me, all through my body. Maybe
I should have been angry, but I wasn't. I was exasperated, irritated, and
then sad. I stood there in the bright sunshine that spilled all over me and
all over the street and all over the Bronx and New York City, Feeling—
what? Feeling disappointed. I felt so disappointed.

Absently, I pat the smooth place on the sheets beside me.
Come and lie down here a minute, girl. They talk about all the
chemistry of love, about love's pain, of obsession, but that doesn't
come close to it. Even if you feel those things, the truth is they're
not anywhere near what love is. Love would be easy if it was
some kind of knockout punch, if it swept you away. But love's
no punch. It's this choice you make, this surrender. You decide
to take someone else seriously. It's as simple as that. There are a
million years of learning and needs behind the choice, and it's
always scratched and fretted, run nearly crazy, if you want to
know, by all the heavy training and upset you've dragged your
life out of, your past and raising et cetera, all the folderol, but it's
still a choice you make, and it still means that you back off a little
from time to time on your own sweaty projects, it means you're
on your knees occasionally, grubbing in the dirt after somebody
you don't really understand and don't always think you want to
be next to, and it's this huge risk—anybody can see that—because
after all, no matter who she is, she's going to die, or she's going
to find somebody else who can chime her bell with a cleaner
stroke; you're not going to get it for free, and it wears you out,
and it makes you think the world is some lunatic rig you got
tricked into going along with by mistake, and then you think it's
a joke, that is what it has to be, just a joke, and the joke's on you,
and you wish it had something to do with all this greasy Hollywood heartbreak, this heat in the bones and this chill like breakfast on an iceberg, but you wake up in the morning, in the
morning of sunshine or vague splintering rain, and what it is is
she wants you to take ten minutes and listen to her—she wants
you to pay attention to her; that's what it's about—and you think,
My God, my life and my dreams are going down the drain while

I sit here listening to this idiot go on about the latest discrepancy, and you look up like some old green dinosaur with a mouth full of wet weeds, just dumbly chewing away, and you see yourself and you see her, see the two of you, a couple of old dinosaurs so creaky and worn out you might as well be on the brink of extinction, just the two of you standing there in the antediluvian quiet all by yourselves, nothing happening, man, nothing important going on, but everything going on, the whole razzmatazz as simple as a mouthful of grass, and you say, Yes dear, yes dear, there, there, I know just what you mean.

This blind, white mannequin who is doubling for my wife, and who *is* my wife, stares blindly out at me. She hasn't moved an inch. She says, *I feel a lack of weight not in but on my chest; as if my breasts have been removed. The years between us are ropes across a gorge: my craziness, your world revolving on a point, the way the mind focuses on detail: dust on the water—gray and tan—that reminds you of the powder on your mother's breasts that you saw once long ago, in sunlight, on a morning in spring when you were young.* She chuckles, coughs, a couple of brief guttural chords sound in the background. *Will, I am out here, crossing the rope bridge into the next life. But it isn't a bridge I see, it's simply a path that ends. Sometimes I am very small to myself. So small I think they might not notice me. For a long time I couldn't eat, and then for a long time I could only eat soft green things. I knew a man so vegetarian that he would eat only fallen fruit. Someone told me that. The problem, as you probably know by now, is not that reality is too much, it's that reality is not enough. I remember the shirt I wore, with the small wood buttons, which I unbuttoned slowly, revealing my breasts. I thought it would take your breath away, but it took my breath away, like a fire drawing all the air out. That was a moment I wanted to lead to a greater moment. I have never wanted anything to last forever. I have wanted everything, every moment, to lead to something better. Do you understand this? I want the volume . . . higher. I want the silence deeper. Will, you just wanted to ride along for a while. Then you wanted to get off. It's difficult isn't it? To get off? You thought I had trapped you, then you thought you were free, now you know you can't be free so easily. Did you think you could find me again? I am a switch you have to trip. And fulfillment changes the original purpose doesn't it? Isn't this what we've found out? That what you wanted is different, when you get it, from itself when you first wanted it, and from what you wanted now that you have it?*

I think of the dainty white lace-up shoes she put on one night after we came home late from a party. It was winter, raining, cold, after midnight; the terrace was slick, icy looking under the pale house lights. She took her clothes off and went outside. After a while, through the open bedroom windows I could hear her singing, and then I saw her sliding on the wet marble. She ran and slid, ran and slid, singing some country song they must have told her when they taught it to her was the saddest song in the world. Her white shoes sparkled and shined as she slid. She held her body upright, without effort, as if sliding was the way she usually got places. In her face was a look of delight, of pleasure unmitigated by any sorrows. I was a fool for a look like that. Now she speaks from the other world. *I so wanted the world to be a place where sweet love endured, where tenderness won the day, where what you hoped for and believed in came true. I wanted the happy, dazzled look you saw on people's faces when they came out of a good movie to be something they carried into their lives. I wanted everyone to still believe in all the true things of childhood, I wanted them to believe in melted chocolate and sunny days and cobwebs in which the raindrops were jewels. I wanted a couple, fifty years married, to drag their furniture out into the backyard and sit out there on a spring night when the world smells of cloves and orange flowers, watching a variety program on television. I wanted to lie in bed on a summer morning eating buttered toast with your smell on my body. I wanted to walk down a lane under leafy trees arching over and see horses in a field. I wanted the taste of cherries in my mouth . . .*

I sit here, propped on expensive pillows, with tears in my eyes, watching this. Jesus, if you could only believe what people tell you. You have to say this, Katie, painted white, with your mouth and eyes taped shut. That body there, turning to stone, won't carry the message anymore. You are beyond that now. Somewhere in Mexico, you are beyond that. The truth is we are all going to suffer in ways we never heard of. In ways we never imagined. Why, there, right this minute, standing in the yard under a sunny oak, is my mother, the ruined actress. She's wearing a dress so white that if you weren't prepared, it might blind you. The pains of a lifetime are in her sixty-five-year-old face. They are ineradicable. No wonder we decide to believe in God. There's nothing down here could dissolve pain like that.

THE NEXT DAY, on a morning of bright sunshine when the stellar jays squawked in the sycamores and you could smell the loquat flowers blossoming in the bushes under my window, I got up off my back and moved out to Veronica's. She had to work, she had to keep her restaurant running, but I wanted distance between myself and Clement. A voice did not tell me to do this— Bobby didn't say anything—and no good soul came by to recommend it, but a rattling urgency came on me nonetheless. I waked stark upright and a fear came over me; I didn't want to be in the same room as my father, didn't want to be in the same house, the same part of the country. My parents had broken up years ago, though they had never really divorced, but Malibu had been the part of this world that my mother took for herself; my father was banished from it. He wouldn't show up out there, where my mother lived in a cool, sunny house down the row from Veronica's. He might show up, and did, at my mother's in-town house in Beverly Hills, but the beach was not his zone.

Veronica put me upstairs, in the guest room beside hers. The room looked out over the ocean. I sat in a wicker chair under an umbrella and watched the waves roll in, as Kate, after I abandoned her—so I was informed—had sat in a breezy house watching the Pacific crash in at the foot of the mountain. But unlike Kate—always unlike Kate—I did not lie down among strangers. Veronica left late in the morning and arrived late each night bringing culinary delights her chef had prepared. Friends found out about my case and showed up bringing gifts. Those who thought I could help them called, expressing best wishes and angling for favors. Friends of my youth, men who had once been rascally boys with sun-streaked hair, women who were once laughing, careless girls, called to wish me a speedy recovery and to tell me of their lives in the suburbs and of their children who were all stars on their club soccer teams. There were calls from reporters and industry flacks, but these were routed through Earl's office, and they didn't cause much trouble. For me, they were all hoots and cries flung at me from a great distance. From my wicker chair, in shade, sunk in flowery cushions, I stared into a blankness, into a hollow and senseless space that I could not bring order to. I looked at my body sprawled out in front of me, and it seemed to me that if I could only concentrate hard enough—or no, not concentrate, if I could only let go completely enough—I could be released from it, I could drift out away from it, and like one of the black-backed gulls soaring over the surf line, drift out into the blue. I wished for this, I entertained the hope of it, but it was not real to me; I had no belief in such fey cosmologies. I was here, planted on earth.

And here on earth, I was on call. I say I was trying to do something, I say I was angling toward some release, as if I had power, as if I was the energetic manager of my own life, but the truth is, I was only lying in a chair. I didn't want to get up from it, and I wondered if I *could* get up from it. Veronica came home and she looked at me sitting there surrounded by soft drinks and bowls of fruit, a telephone I occasionally answered on the table beside me, and she scolded me, told me to do something, to at least take a walk, go swimming. I started to tell her about Mexico, about my return to the desert coast north of Mazatlán, but I couldn't bring myself to do it. I wanted everything I had discovered there, I wanted Kate and the years of our marriage for once, for a moment, to keep their distance from me, to be quiet. But what I wanted was not the engine running things. I had work to do. I had a killer to defend myself from, and I had killers to get up and go see.

———

THE LOBBY OF Billy Dangelo's office was done in pale blue with stripes of lavender. Behind a receptionist in a circular desk, a set of double doors with lion's head knobs opened onto a corridor of offices in which you could hear the clatter of copying machines. A set of windows covered in thick green glass turned the lot outside into a story told in deep colors. Beyond the white corner of a soundstage, streets named after the great stars of the twenties and thirties led through pockets and corners of movie-making. A sunset was painted in secondary colors on the side of a building. Beyond a wall, tall palms stood like sentries. You could see the gray, glittery sky beyond, and beneath it, the city that from here looked like an American city anywhere with its tall collapsible buildings. The secretaries buzzed me through.

I was getting 3.7 for the picture, plus gate, points later. It was a good package. There were others who took more up front, but the 3.7 was still a lot for me; in the last couple of years I had begun hooking my work to the gross, betting on the picture—which the producers loved me for—letting others buzzard the front-end cash. I had been rich all my life, but beyond the houses, an occasional car, I didn't need much. I had an accountant for bills and taxes, one of Earl's people handled logistics, I kept a housekeeper-cook and a gardener at the Hollywood Hills house. It was part of the drift, the buzz I moved through, the bee life I had returned to after I made it. In the beginning I took what I could, armored by Earl and my lifelong knowledge of the business—which was simply the fact that everyone knew me and I knew everyone—but once I crossed over, I let that race go on without me and began to cruise. The idea in pictures is to build so many cash generators into each one that no matter what happens, there is always a tap in your yard spewing gold. It's not that hard to do once you're famous. We were pay-for-play on this one, which I hadn't known about until Earl called me at home, and that was why I was here to meet with Billy. He would have to front the salary whether the picture got made or not, and he wanted to make sure I was tight.

Billy was in the kitchen behind the office, wearing a blue baseball cap, cooking omelets. "You want meat in yours, don't you," he said. "I got bacon or sausage."

"Sausage," I told him.

I'd known Billy all my life. We had rambled through the hills as kids—it was Billy who was with me when we watched the boys in dresses get hurt—and we played ball together at Fremont High up in the Valley. Billy's father, David, had been a character actor and won two Oscars for his portrayals of crazed old men. He was specializing in old men by the time he was in his forties, rough irascible types, which if the truth were known, was not far from who he was in real life. He was a drinker, a wife-beater, a murderous blockhead really, and Billy had hated him. His death at fifty-five, in a barn fire that charred him and a dozen quarter horses that he raced out in the Valley, had set Billy free. He'd directed a couple of pictures, then began producing; now he was production chief for Celestial.

Billy had an odd head. In profile it was long, a full sail of a face with a stiff, raked brow, Indian nose, a chin like a door knob, but straight on it was so narrow that you thought it must have been shaved down. "Ax-head," he was called in the Valley, which he never said anything about but I knew he never forgot. He had long-fingered, gentle, monkish hands that he used like an orchestra conductor's, but they always returned to his face, touching it lightly, pressing the chin, the cliff forehead, checking the bars of his cheekbones to see if his face had spread while he wasn't looking. He was a Hollywood killer, the tough guy his father had claimed to be and never was, and he knew it.

He said, "I was thinking of that fall we went bear hunting every weekend and never saw a bear. Do you remember that?"

I said I did.

"It was a strange thing, man, I think about it a lot, all those weekends up in the mountains, finding bear sign everywhere, scut and stripped bark, all that, and no bears. I wanted to see a bear more than anything in the world, I just dreamed about them, especially that big brown you told me about—that you saw with your dad?—I was ready, I was so ready, I had wanted all my life to see a bear and here we were way up there, almost to the snow line, and no bear. How many weekends did we go?"

"It must have been at least half a dozen."

"Why do you think that was? You think that was something spiritual?"

I said, "I thought we were going out to lunch."

"Nah," he said, "we got to do it here. I got all this crap coming down on me. Some fucked-up star who's bolting a picture. I got to talk to him. You know Frank Dallo?"

I said I did.

"Well, he's gone crazy. Jesus, these guys, man. I'll never get it. They just don't know God's plenty when they see it."

He shook the omelet pan, scooped a handful of chopped sausage, and flung it in. "Yeah," he said, "those bears. I wish we'd seen one. I think that experience had meaning in my life. Something I was excluded from like Moses not getting to go to the Promised Land, you know what I mean?"

"What brings it to mind?"

"I got a picture something like that. Guy who wants to see a wolf. The wolf's not the story, but it's an element. Guy up in Alaska, falling out with his wife, with the bank, with all his friends. The guy kills someone by mistake and runs off into the wilderness. He gets to thinking about wolves, how he's always loved them, wants to find one. There's a girl, an Indian, they meet up, go off hunting for wolves." Billy shook the pan. The kitchen smelled of garlic. "The police get the guy in the end," he said.

"It sounds interesting."

He pressed his forehead into place with the tips of two fingers.

"What's this latest with Bill Lenz?"

"He set me up."

"That's what I figured."

I'd met Lenz at Le Poisson Bleu, a fish place in Santa Monica. He was his usual boot-licking self, grown tall now though with his little gold award, ingratiating, oily as a cod. I knew there would be photographers there; I didn't mind. Let him make his play, show the world that he was a big man, capable of forgiveness. It would all work to my benefit too. But Bill had something else in mind. Midway through dessert, an almond flan, he stood up quickly, reached across the table, and lightly tapped me on the cheek. I didn't realize his fist was closed until he touched me. The photographers caught it. In the paper the next day it looked as if he was slugging me. Old Bill Lenz, who takes no shit, paying back the outrageous Will Blake, putting the putz in his place.

Earl had been furious, first at Bill Lenz, then at me. We got to get this back, he said, we got to turn this around. I'd laughed. He should have told me what he wanted, I said; I would have helped him out. Jesus, Earl'd screamed, you're losing your mind too. Who else is losing his mind? I asked him. He hadn't wanted to say. It's Kate, he said finally. What do you mean? She's sending me stuff too. What stuff? Tapes—listen Will, he said, his big voice swelling with sadness, you've got to get this thing off your back. I don't want to know about it, but Jesus, you need to do something. Like what? I said. I don't know—get a divorce, move to New York for six months, let it blow away. Sure, Earl, I said. That Lenz, he said and started to laugh. That guy'd rape his mother if it was in the script. It's life or death for him, I said, you have to take that into account.

"Yeah," I said, my nose twitching at the smell of frying oil, "Lenz made sure he came out ahead."

"It's not a pretty scene," Billy said, "you know that, don't you?"

"I don't mind it."

He cocked his head, looking at me down his cheekbones. We were exactly the same height; Billy was thicker around the waist, but when we were kids there were times when we thought of ourselves as twins. Under the grape arbor one afternoon when we were thirteen, we'd taken a vow never to curse, smoke, lie, or steal. We had considered ourselves knights.

"It's chancy to take on your dad," he said.

"You're making him very happy."

"I wouldn't do it if I didn't think he was a great man, if I didn't think *he* could do it."

"I'm supposed to be the insurance."

With a small silver knife he took from his pocket and un-folded, he cut the omelet in two, slid each half onto a red plate.

"It's very important that you're in the picture," he said.

We carried the plates to a white marble table under a bank of windows that looked out through venetian blinds onto the back lot. A range of small red hills, a pond tucked into the cleft of one of them, a stand of cottonwoods, made the area look like the beginning of open range. I thought of how I loved hunting as a kid, how I loved everything about it, and about how one day I stopped loving it, put down the gun, and never took it up again. Thought of my father, who loved it too, popping the heads of quail against his boot heel. Of Bobby, who hated it, who came out of the fields crying. Billy, who had gone with us often, would shoot anything. We sat down across from each other.

"Now you're worried about me," I said.

"No, I'm not worried. I just want to know what's going on. First it was Kate, then it was Bill Lenz, now you've been shot."

"Actually it's still Kate."

He attacked the omelet with knife and fork, stabbing it, tear-ing it into pieces. He shoved a hunk into his mouth harshly, as if he had to hide it there.

"Is your head all right?"

"It's fine, though I might have to wear a little tuppy, as Grandpa used to call it, on this spot." I touched the waxy scar above my temple.

"You could have been killed."

"I almost was—but then I wasn't."

"Did they find the woman?"

"Not yet."

"Are you through with the cops?"

"Apparently." I took a bite of the omelet; it was greasy and pungent, the sausage hot and garlicky. "What's bugging you?"

"Nothing. I just don't do that stuff anymore and it bothers me to hear about it."

"What stuff?"

"Getting in public trouble. Gunfire, punch-outs."

"Well shit, Billy, you're missing the fun."

A woman's melodious voice whispered from the box on the desk, announcing Frank Dallo. Billy took a zapper from beside his plate, aimed it at the box, and said, "Send him back."

"I don't want to sit in on your Dallo dealings," I said.

"Stay. You'll like this."

"No, I won't."

"Well, keep me company."

I knew Billy. I knew by the way he turned his face away like a dog caught in the garbage what he was going to do. I was thinking about the friend Kate told me about, a woman less than five feet tall who fell in love with a man well over six feet, an athlete, a ballplayer that she had to stand on a chair to kiss. I pictured the woman, redheaded and beautiful, quick-witted, climbing on a chair at the kitchen table, reaching for the face above her, as one would reach to change a lightbulb. The strange places, beyond anything we imagined, that love takes us to.

So I sat there at the marble table eating an omelet as Frankie Dallo scurried in to do his dance. He was a portly fellow, full of energy, with black triangular eyebrows and wet purple lips. He walked in small but flagrant steps, flicking his bulk along as if it were as light as cotton. Billy got up and took him in his arms, pretending he had sorely missed him. Frankie stepped back, acknowledged me with a wave, as if he was tossing me something, and went into a rant. He hated the director, the script, the actress he was supposed to play with. He had better ideas and he had brought some of them with him, a few pages in a canvas portfolio he held up like a sign. Billy leaned against his desk looking at Frank, letting his hard gray eyes rest on the actor's plushy face. Frank had some success two years ago in a picture in which he played a gross, ravenous character who stomped everything in his path. He was merciless and repulsive, but his wild energy, like a fire raging in a refinery, ate up the screen. Everybody could see how good he was. Now he'd gotten smart, he wanted to run things. He flicked a glance at me as an iron pumper might pop a muscle; I could see he figured he would run over Will Blake too if he got in his way. Billy listened, his sharp killer's face cocked to the side, his hands as still as two spiders on the desk. Frank wound down.

"Let me tell you a story," Billy said.

"I don't want a story," Frank said, "I want some goddamn changes here."

"I've listened to you, now listen to me."

"Then you fix this picture, right?"

"Then I fix this picture."

Billy stepped over to the table, forked up a hunk of omelet, and shoved it down. Slowly, as if it were a bloody knife, he wiped the tines of the fork between his fingers. He set the fork down, then licked his fingers clean to the tips.

"You ever been to Oregon?" he said.

Frank said he hadn't.

"You ought to go up there; I go up there a lot. There's a place up on the southern coast, a kind of cape where for years whales have been beaching themselves. Nobody knows why they do it, but every few years a dozen or so whales'll shove themselves right up onto the shore, die there in the sand. I was up there once—this was a long time ago—when it happened. Three or four baby humpbacks—stuck right up on the sand in this little weedy cove. Their skin was blue, almost black, tough like an inner tube; they had barnacles on them, like the pilings get—you know—at the pier."

Frank fidgeted, wanting to speak, but he didn't say anything. Billy didn't take his eyes off him.

"Well," he said, "I wanted to try something, I wanted to see something. I got a knife from the house, a butcher knife, and I went down there. One of the whales was still alive. He was a mess—you know what happens when they get on land, their bodies can't support the weight, their insides collapse, just pull off the bones, they smother from the inside. It must be horrible. This whale was still breathing though, these gross, reluctant breaths, wheezes, like denim curtains ripping. Breathing and groaning. The whale's eye was open, a big round black eye, with lashes—did you know that? They got lashes just like you and me.

I took the knife, and I cut into the whale. You follow me? I cut into the whale, into his living side, and I kept cutting while the whale groaned and sucked air, right through all that red and gray meat for an hour until I got to the heart. It was bigger than your head, glossy purple and scarlet, filled with all this watery blood, and I cut it out, and I stuck it on a pole I found and walked down the street carrying that heart for everyone to see."

Frank Dallo looked at Billy blankly, as if he didn't get it—which he didn't—and then he did. His face drained of color. Billy raised his plate and licked a spot of omelet grease off it.

"You cut his heart out while he was still alive?" Frank said.

"It was bigger than a basketball."

"Well, shit, it was just . . ." he said, trying to be tough, but beginning to sweat. "It was just a whale."

"Yeah," Billy said. "It was just a whale. Jesus."

He lashed the plate right past Frank's head. The plate burst against a shelf, knocking down a silver plaque presented to Billy by the Theater Owners' Association. The plaque rang against the hardwood floor. With Billy there was no way to tell if the story was true. It could be. It could be true, and it could be worse than he said it was. He also tells the story of the barn fire that his father died in. He was there, he says, a teenage boy who hated his father, and knew it, who understood his hatred for what it was and cultivated it like a field of tomatoes. He will tell you that he could have run into the barn and gotten his father out, and he will tell you that he didn't, that he refused to. He could hear his father screaming, he says, screaming above the screams of the horses. He will say, I stood in the yard with the heat on my face hot as the sun, sweating, listening to my father scream. He called out to us, to me, to save him. I didn't do a thing.

Billy swung the rough ax of his face toward Frank Dallo. "Frankie," he said, "this is real life. This isn't Sheboygan—it's Sheboygan, right?—this is Hollywood. Out here nobody cares. You understand me? Nobody gives a shit about what you know, or what you feel. Either do the picture or go home." His thin lip lifted off his large, polished teeth. His ape grin, I knew it. "Go, Frankie," he said.

Frank Dallo swallowed, swiveled on his tiny, light feet, and floated his bulk out of the office.

Well, sometimes it was that easy.

I looked at Billy. He shook his head and laughed his thin, whistly laugh. He knew he had gotten away with something. "It makes it worth it, don't it," he said, "when they fold up like that."

"Somebody's going to catch up with you," I said.

"That's what I think too, but nobody ever does. They're so busy trying to pound the little nail of their lives just a bit higher, they'll go through anything. I had a guy in here last week crawling around on his hands and knees. And the guys with money, the ones who get a little power—all of a sudden they think they've got integrity. They think there are things they won't do."

I got up, took my plate into the kitchen, and washed it. There was a photograph of Billy's mother in a silver frame by the sink. In the shot, his mother, in a flowered summer dress, was swinging in a swing. Big cabbage roses were twined around the swing ropes. When we were kids he would tell me stories about her locking him in a closet. Apparently she would leave him there for hours, until, so she said, he decided to behave. He said he was shocked to his bones when he discovered as a grown man that he wanted to do the same thing to his own kids. His mother was the second woman, after my own mother, I saw naked. She used to invite me in to watch her take a bath. She'd had both breasts removed because of cancer and wore a small green half tunic in the tub. I don't know why she did that; it was as if she didn't want to look. She would ask me to bring her something, a towel or a glass of sherry, and I would, and then I'd sit on the toilet beside the tub watching her. This is how I remember it, though what I remember may have been a dream. Under the clear bathwater Billy's mother stroked her white hips. Her private hair was the color of brass. She asked me to come close. She raised her small, dripping hand and touched me through my pants. My penis hummed like a harmonica. She squeezed gently, firmly, and let me go. Her fingers left wet marks on the cloth.

I said, "Billy, did you go through that so I would get a message?" I touched his mother's photograph. Her long slender legs aimed at the sky.

He came to the door, leaned against it. "Yeah," he said, "I want to bring you back to earth."

"You know I've never had much gumption."

"I know. You always did everything, you were always in on

everything, but you just seemed to be there, like some guy who's passing through the airport when the terrorists attack."

"You're wondering whether I can work with Pop."

"Yeah, I wonder about that. Can you?"

"Why are you asking me now? The deal's done, isn't it?"

"Yeah, it's done, it's locked together, steel solid. But we've covered ourselves."

"I would imagine so, but what do you mean, oh ruthless one?"

"Clement's on deadlines. If he doesn't meet them he's out—and I mean out. If he fucks up, he won't be working again—or if he ever does, he'll be paying us."

"He signed a contract like that?"

"He didn't have any choice. His pictures haven't made money for fifteen years. They've cost money and a couple of them have caused embarrassment. Which is important, you know. These corporate guys don't like to get embarrassed. They're sensitive; they want things to work out, they want to be praised; it's human."

"Which is where I come in, right?"

"That's it."

There were several hats on pegs behind me. Billy plucked one, a flat gray fedora, and put it on. "What do you think?" he said.

"No—not you. Now you're concerned about me going haywire."

He shook his head. "I don't care about that, not really. You're right: Bill Lenz is a fuckhead. He's had his moment and will now fade into mewling obscurity, as they say—what I'm wondering about is if you can work with your dad."

"Why didn't you ask this before?"

"I didn't need to. I know you, I've known you all my life. You don't care about anything, but you do what's before you to do."

"That's my reputation."

"You've earned it, bro." He adjusted the fedora. "I saw one of the tapes Kate sent your dad."

"You saw one of them? You looked at it? Jesus Christ, Billy. You fucks."

Billy took the hat off, hung it on the peg. "It's not like that. The tape was addressed to Clement—he didn't know it was for you. I walked in on it. We stopped watching when we realized what it was."

"But you saw something."

"Yeah, I did." Billy took the plate off the counter and put it in the cabinet. He looked at the photograph of his mother. She swung on, caught in her moment of eternity. Clear sky behind her, the kind of sky you think you could leap into and disappear. What had she thought of as the swing rose, a Hollywood wife with no breasts, married to a man whose bitter envies left a stink behind him, mother to a ten-year-old gangster? She had died in a car wreck, crushed by a truck as it turned off Olympic onto Sepulveda. I saw a picture of it; the truck had flung her runabout against a golden rain tree; the car was covered in blossoms.

I said, "What was it, Billy?"

"It was that shit about Kate and Clement. Is it true?"

"Yes, it is."

"Jesus, man, your dad and your wife?"

"So I'm told."

"Jesus. Where *is* Kate?"

"In Mexico."

"In Mexico? What's she doing there—getting a divorce?"

"She's clearing her head, getting over things, going surfing— I don't know."

"Is that where you were?"

"I went down there, yeah. I came back for the Awards."

"That's why you hit Bill Lenz."

"I hit Bill Lenz because he's the asshole who stole my award."

Billy laughed. "Yeah, well, that would piss me off too."

He opened the black refrigerator door, stooped, brought out two apples. He handed me one. "You ought to come up to Oregon sometime," he said. "That's where these come from. My farm up above the ocean. It's amazing—apple trees covered with sea spray. You'd love it."

"I'm sure I would."

I looked at Billy. He was looking at me the way the dog looks at the rabbit.

But Billy, I am no rabbit.

I shook myself. "Buckeroo," I said, "do I have to reassure you? Is that what you need, my friend?"

Billy tapped the walls with his knuckles. "Yes," he said, "I need reassurance. I want you to tell me you are still able to work with your dad." He smiled the slow easy smile of one who knows how to get his way. "I know if you tell me you'll do it, you'll do it."

"All right. I can work with my dad. I'll do what's necessary to get this job done." And again, as I agreed to work with the man who had slept with my wife, I waited for the warning signal to flash, for, what—revulsion, rage, revolt—to overtake me, but nothing happened.

Billy went up on his toes, came down. He laced the apple at a wastebasket by my leg, hit it. "That's good," he said, "that's good. Now I feel fine. How about you, how do you feel?"

I said, "Why did your mother lock you in the closet?"

"When? Oh. Back when I was a kid. For the same reason your dad made you work all day out in the orange groves. She wanted to break me."

"But she didn't."

"Impossible to do, my friend."

"How come?"

"Only an equal could do me in. She didn't have what it took." He grinned at me. His teeth made a **V**. "Clement's another story. That guy, your dad. You remember the time he shot his own dog? The dog wouldn't hunt right, so he shot him—blam, right there in front of us. It scared me to death. He would have shot us, if we'd fucked up."

"He might have."

Billy laughed. All my troubles, Lord, will soon be over. His gray eyes scanned me, X-rayed me, slid into my bones. The look, my friend's look, said what a fool.

BEFORE I KNEW it I was sailing through the front door of the Monarch trailing three or four tourists stalking my autograph. They were trying to be discreet about it, but they couldn't help themselves; they wanted my name in their books, or on the rims of their buttocks, and they weren't going to let me get away. I slid past Burke Wills, who caught them and, his belly swelling like an umpire's, turned them back. I heard his stern admonitions fall upon them. I had come to gather my stuff; I would chance it,

I'd decided, I would go home, face the empty places, the chairs, the crannies, the bed where Kate no longer was. At the desk a message waited. I unfolded the engraved, stiff gray hotel stationery and read a note from my father. He was in Mexico, he said. Priming locations. A sharp, cold, neatly swung hammer hit me. I leaned against the desk, attempting to absolve everyone of everything. A woman with a hairy white dog in her arms stared at me, tapping her foot, signaling the clerk with one wagging finger. I reached to pet the ratty dog, but he snarled and snapped at me, almost getting my fingers. "He's a fighter," the woman said, "you have to be careful," which I assured her from now on I would be. I looked at the note again. He must have called from Mexico; he was already there. This was a sign, if I wanted signs, that it was time to do something. But I had already done everything.

Someone touched my elbow: a man in a gray summer suit, a slice of a guy with knobby black eyes. "Mr. Blake?" he said.

"No."

"You're Will Blake the actor."

"I'm Bobby Blake," I said, "his brother."

"Ah. I'm Sergeant Kwilecki—from the San Xavier PD. I'd like . . ."

Antic, I spoke from the side of my mouth. "Are you arresting me?"

"I don't know—are you guilty of something?"

The clerk caught my eye; he had something else for me. "I'm the only innocent man you've seen today," I said.

"How's your head?"

I touched the rosy, crescent scar. "It's opened new worlds to me, given me flashbacks, visions. I can see through time."

"Maybe the rest of us ought to get something like that."

The clerk, a black-haired boy who looked like Marcello Mastroianni as a young man, handed me another package from Kate. "Mr. Earl Moss left this for you," he said.

I turned to go, but the detective touched my arm. "I need to talk to you," he said. "Just routine things, but I need to get them out of the way."

Four young women in light summer dresses crossed the lobby, heading toward the glass doors that opened to the terrace and the pool. Their dresses flared and shimmered around their smooth legs. How do you resist the idea, I thought, that things are about to get better? The detective dug with one finger inside his collar. "Can we go somewhere?" he said.

"Sure," I said, "come on up to the room. I'm just checking out."

He accompanied me across the lobby, talking about my pictures, and about Kate's pictures, about his favorites. Outside, the sun seemed to have exploded over the city. The pool shimmered like a bed of blue quartz, a ghastly clarity shone on the trees, on lounges, on the white-and-red-striped bar roof, on the fall and rattle of the city descending into the wide basin, on the distant strip of blue sea pinning Santa Monica to the mainland. My eyes hurt. I took out dark glasses, put them on, but they didn't seem to help, even in the elevator's artificial light. I remembered riding up the elevator four years ago with Tony Wales, a friend from my first pictures who was being sued by his wife for adultery. She'd hired a detective who'd taken photos of Tony and his paramour naked at the beach, and now the man was free-lancing, threatening him with blackmail in his own right, beyond anything his wife was paying for. I remembered how drawn Tony looked, how white his face was, how no comfort seemed to help. "They're going to ruin me," he kept saying, "they're going to ruin me." There was a bleakness in his eyes as in the eyes of a man who's seen too much war, something irredeemable and forlorn.

The skinny detective chatted on, filling my silence with accolades. I looked at him. He was working hard. "You're pulling my leg, right?" I said. "All this praise?"

"Right, right," he said, tapping his wrist with two fingers, "I'm nervous."

"What's there to be nervous about?"

"I'm out of my jurisdiction—I don't like the city."

"Well, we're both just a couple of country boys."

"You from San Xavier?"

"Hell yes," I said, juking, "I was born there. LA's the big town for me too."

"I'm from Utah," he said, "Covis, a little town south of Salt Lake, nothing but grass and dry mountains. I don't know what I'm doing here."

"I can't figure it myself," I said.

The elevator whispered to a stop at ten. The gold doors cracked with the fine, clean sound of a good pocketknife opening. "This is us."

He followed me down the hall, skipping to keep up. I slipped the key in the door and hesitated, standing there a second with my face eighteen inches from the cream-and-gold embossed door thinking. It is moments of perfection that we seek, that's what we are looking for. Moments—we'd rather have eons—when the arc is perfect, Beethoven quartet moments, sun on the lake surface moments, orgasm moments, moments when the curve of her bottom lip is angelic. These are moments of stillness, of empathy, of unhindered sight. We tear up our lives looking for them, attempting to make them appear. Just a minute, we say, I'll be with you in a minute—we mean I have almost got it. I thought of my friend Pedro Manglona, vice-chairman of the Mexican board of Theater and Film, whom I stayed with sometimes at his place north of Mazatlán, his biscuit-colored seaside villa surrounded by bougainvillea, where he raised fighting bulls. We would mix toddies, lie in hammocks out on the terrace listening to the ocean slap itself quietly silly against the wide beach, talking of the moments when everything snapped to, like a field of poppies blooming all at once, holding the moment in our minds like a sweet taste in our mouths, the night passing. It was Pedro who took Kate in. "That's the thing," I said out loud as I pushed the door open onto the rumpled room. "Even as you so delicately wrap these moments time is terribly passing."

"What is that?" Sergeant Kwilecki said. "Um, it looks like you've had a party in here."

Sheets wadded on the floor, a gold bedspread tossed over the back of a chair, clothes scattered about, Veronica's black vest hanging from the open closet door—her smell, scent of patchouli, a perfume I hated, everywhere. I'd left instructions for the maids not to come in. "Yes," I said, "it does look like that doesn't it? Is that suspicious?"

"I guess you can expect it from movie folk."

"That sounds like a slur."

"It does. I'm sorry. I just mean that the way you live your lives is more expansive I guess than the rest of us."

"Well, that's why I got in it," I said. "For the possibility of large gestures. Have a seat."

As long as I felt I was in control I would probably continue to talk in this silly, sportive manner.

"I haven't been here in a couple of weeks," I said.

"You've been out at your father's place."

"That's right—recuperating."

The detective lifted the bedspread off a chair and sat down. He took out a small notebook, made a couple of marks. His snappy hair was close trimmed, like mine; he had the wide, untroubled forehead of a teenager. He was younger than I first thought.

I dialed room service, ordered a pitcher of orange juice, a couple of cheeseburgers. The detective said he didn't want anything. My mind was on the run to Mexico. With the news that my father was there, another picture, one I had heretofore denied myself, took shape. I could see the two of them together, two laughing, *sympathetic* characters, sitting on a long galleria, somewhere near the ocean, see them leaning toward each other, light sparkling in their eyes. It made me feel delicate, and alone.

I set the phone in its cradle; it immediately rang. Veronica's voice said, "It was the way it was when we were kids."

I said, "What was?"

"You on the bed, me sitting there in the sunlight telling you stories."

"No, I thought it was the way it'll be when we're old, me in the damn home for demented actors and you doing your pink lady bit."

"Can you come by here?"

"What for?"

"Kate sent me a tape."

"Jesus, why doesn't she just send them to the networks? Consolidate her damn operation. Clement's in Mexico."

"With Kate?"

"I don't know. He left me a message saying he was looking at locations. My mind's racing."

"Are you on your way back down there?"

"No, there's nothing down there for me."

"If you go, let me know. I'll go with you."

"Then I'll have to do something for you in return, won't I?"

"That's how adult life works, soldier boy."

I looked around at Sergeant Kwilecki. He was writing in his notebook. "There's a policeman in my room—a guy from San Xavier."

"Anybody we know?"

"I don't know, I've never met him before. His name's Kwilecki—he's from Utah."

"Oh."

Kwilecki made a sign asking if he should go out. I nodded no. Outside, in the bright yellow air, a flock of gulls swung by, veering downward. The scent of Veronica's perfume was strong, and I wondered if she had been in the room while I was away. "I'll come by," I said, "when I finish here."

"Okay."

I was about to hang up then, but she said my name.

"What is it?"

"Do you know how angry you are?" she said.

I looked down at the wedding band I still wore, or that I should say I had begun wearing after I found out about Kate and Clement. "I can't tell," I said.

"Well, you are."

"If I don't know, does it matter?"

"Don't act naïve, Will."

"Acting's the only profession where you don't have to take sides."

"Where did that come from?"

"I don't know. Every time the facts approach, something in me skips."

"You'll come to eventually."

"Maybe. Maybe not. I'm not sure it really works that way."

"I'm not either, but it sounds hopeful to say it."

"Well, as long as we can be hopeful we've got a chance."

"If this were Hollywood and we were in a movie."

"Would it were so."

As I hung up, out of the corner where the room bent away from the windows, like dusty, sun-scoured voyagers, the dreams began to approach. I could see them coming, like cars on a desert highway, miles off, zooming my way. There was a large white boat—maybe it was my father's movie boat—a ship, and a grove of trees, water trees like willows or ashes; there was a red beach and a wide sea beyond of blue going to gray to black under a descending sun. My head ached. I could tell you now my mother's story of her uncle's suicide, of how he spent the afternoon teaching Jennie and her cousins how to bake rum cookies, then as the sun was going down through the cottage windows—this was in Skye at the uncle's farm—he excused himself with elaborate courtesy, took his shotgun from the vestibule, went out to the barn, climbed into the loft, and reclining against a pile of timothy hay, placed the twin barrels in his mouth and blew the top of his head off.

When she told me this story, my mother said a curious thing. She said, For some people there is a delicacy in them that they can't stand. The delicacy shows them the truth about themselves, which is the truth that they are helpless. Being helpless is sometimes too much for people.

I remember how she smiled when she said this, her wide mouth opening in a kind of appalled glee that frightened me. I thought she was laughing at me, and maybe she was, but maybe she was only acting, maybe she was playing the game she couldn't help but play, slipping past herself—which, as if she were a dead woman, I remember of her: antic parts played out in the midst of family and everywhere else, claims made, positions taken, all fading with the sunset of each long-ago day.

I lay down on the bed, exhausted suddenly. The detective leaned over his knees. He looked around the room. In his moment of hesitation or preparation I thought I saw his family life, his tract house at the edge of town, his hopes for himself and his kids, the plans for the future like insurance policies locked in a steel box. He said, "My boss wants me to clarify the time frame of the incident."

I turned on my side. "Have you found the woman?"

"Not yet."

"She's disappeared?"

"Except for what you told us, she never appeared *or* disappeared."

"Do you guys think I am making it up?"

He passed his open hand over his hair, wiped it carefully on his pants leg. "It isn't that. We're just having a little trouble following the trail."

"She was a wily woman."

"So it seems." He looked at his notebook. "Would you mind going through it again, from the time you left the hotel?"

I told the story again, trying to remember it clearly. It was like piecing together a dream. They had found the house, or what I described as the house, on Berea, but there was no sign of the woman there, or of any woman who could have been my shooter. There was no sign of bullets being fired. What I remembered was the way she held her head, as if she were balancing plumage, and the tragic and final way her gun hand came up to punch the button that would change everything, and the look on her face of angry sorrow, and the way after the shots went off, she turned and strode on into what was next in her life, what was left or what was coming. I had followed her—I didn't say this—because in that instant it seemed to me I had seen my twin, or one maybe of many twins, one who had cracked the surface of her life and was moving now into the interior. I wanted to tell her about Kate, about my father, about Mexico, about the shift in my own life, about the moment when the world cracks.

I told him she wore a gold belt, gold shoes.

"You didn't get the licence number?" he said.

"No, I wasn't thinking of that."

"We don't think she was local."

"I couldn't tell."

"It's very curious," the man said.

"How so?"

"We don't usually have violent crime that just evaporates into thin air."

"I didn't think of it as a crime."

"She shot you."

"Maybe she thought I was after her. Maybe she was in trouble and thought I was one of the troublers."

"One of the troublers?"

"Yeah, who knows? Maybe she was being blackmailed or something, maybe her kid had been kidnapped and she was trying to get him back—maybe she thought I was a member of the gang who was after her. Maybe she'd finally decided to do something about her sorry lot, to take her life in her hands and run it herself."

"It sounds like you know more than you're telling us."

"I know what I'm making up."

"What do you think—what do you think was going on?"

"I think it was a busted love affair. I think she was shooting at some guy—the first time, I mean—some guy who had turned on her. I think she was coming to herself."

"You got any way of knowing that?"

"I just followed her."

"You should have called us."

"I'm not a cop; I didn't think of it."

He leaned back in the chair. "You left the hotel when?"

"About noon I think—yeah, I'd had a late breakfast by the pool. The staff'll remember it."

He looked toward the door as if he expected someone to come through it. He had a scar on his face, a red worm that crawled up into his hair behind the ear; it looked recent. "You've had some trouble in your marriage, haven't you?" he said. He looked at me straight on.

I laughed. "You know about it too, huh?"

"I'm sorry to bring it up, but we understand your wife has . . . gone away."

"She lit out for the territory."

"Pardon?"

"She's in Mexico, writing her will." Why did I say that? I looked at the package on the table beside me. Its festive stamps were double and triple canceled. Even the package speaks to me, even the tiny rainbow stamps. Whatever exists invigorates the world. We want to be selective, we want to say I accept this, I reject that, I draw the line here—but we can't afford to. What if later we find out what's excluded was the key? I looked at the detective writing fastidiously in his notebook. His hand moved swiftly, and then it was as if I could see his hand move right off the page, and the writing looping and flowing after it, the words getting bigger as the hand moved until they were not words but pictures, lines fashioning a world figures moved through that took on shape and substance, and color, that spoke and acted, all of it alive and vigorous before me, a world made of past and present, spiced with the future maybe, in which Kate rose like an odalisque and my father swung his fists like hammers, and my brother Bobby sang like a beautiful bird at the window, and there was nothing in it I could understand or change or live among.

I said, "Don't you guys usually work in pairs?"

He placed his hand flat on the open notebook page, as if he wanted to hide it from prying eyes. "Yeah, we do. My partner's downstairs."

"You mean he's down there checking up on me?"

"He's doing the detail work about your schedule."

"Damn," I said, "that's the scary thing about the cops."

"What is?"

"You let the police—strangers—into one part of your life and they're liable to rummage their way into areas you don't want uncovered."

"You up to something?"

"Nothing criminal, just embarrassing."

"You mean like your wife. I'm sorry about that—it's none of our business."

"Not just that," I said as I began to feel the Mexican sun roll over my skin. "Everybody needs a secret life—even policemen I think."

"Well, secret and criminal might be different."

"Yes, of course, but maybe not. Sometimes what's secret *is* criminal—we still need to keep it secret."

When I lived mostly out at the beach, before I met Kate, my father would sometimes come visit me. He'd arrive out of nowhere, in the middle of the day, whirling up in his steel gray Jaguar, wandering in to sit on the sofa that looked out toward the Pacific. He'd chat about nothing for half an hour. He'd get a little relief, then he'd push off the sofa and drift away, still the middle of the day, a weekday, no explanation about what he was up to, and disappear. I'd think, Well maybe he's a busy man looking for a break, but then I'd wonder what he was doing. I spoke to Veronica about it. She said he was probably passing by on his way from his mistress's house. It came as a shock to me. Not that he had a mistress, but that he had a secret life, that he had things going on that I had no way of knowing about and would never know about. But I saw how important it was to him. And I saw what a mystery it made of life, all these dusty gold and secret veins we work, that nobody ever knows about, not even our spouses or best friends.

I got up off the bed and began to pack. I had called from the plane to make the reservation, on the way up from Mazatlán, watching as I punched my card number into the phone a man show his little daughter chess moves on a magnetic board. I had called my cook, Carol Brass, and had her pack some things and send them over with the yardman. I didn't think I could go back to the familiar world of home for a while. I wanted strangeness around me.

"You have a lot of gear," the detective said.

"When you're famous, and rich, they expect it of you," I said. "And you begin to expect it of yourself."

"Do you have servants?"

"A couple, I don't like to have too many."

"How come?"

"I talk too much about myself, then I get embarrassed. I have to fire them."

There was a knock on the door. I opened it to let the waiter bring in the burgers. "You sure you don't want some of this?" I said after he'd left.

"No thanks. I ate lunch on the way."

I pulled the table next to the bed, sat down, and began to eat. Everything was covered by heavy silver domes. I felt lightheaded; I thought for a second that I might pass out.

"Mr.," I said, "Mr. Kwilecki, what is it you want from me?"

The detective leaned back in his chair with the expansiveness of a large man, though he was small. "Now that is the big question," he said, clasping his knee. "I'm not sure we know what we want from you." He shook his burry head. "This case is a mystery that so far is beyond our capabilities to solve. You are our only witness." He looked at me sharply—it came to me: they think the whole story is made up.

I said, "Have you got another scenario?"

"Well," he said, "it's hard to put into words exactly, because I didn't know where to start—we really don't have much to go on here—but maybe all this has more to do with your wife than you are telling us."

"You mean you think I was following my wife?"

"No—we don't know—maybe you were just upset about something. I myself know how that can be, having had the same trouble. It's easy to get . . . confused."

"Ah," I said, tiring of this, "maybe you're right."

The detective got to his feet. "We run these things through

various procedures," he said, "until we come up with an answer that fits."

"But nothing fits," I said. "Isn't that the way it usually works?"

"Quite a bit of the time. It's frustrating."

"This is probably one of those things that will eventually get filed away—a slightly strange but not very unusual story, hardly even a crime, of interest because it happened to a celebrity, but what the hell, who knows what really went on?"

"Actually we probably won't get off that easy—you being important and all. The papers have it, so the public has it—we'll have to come up with something."

"Shit, I shouldn't have said anything. I wouldn't have but for Causey, and being a little out of it and all."

"It's all right. Sometimes you just can't help yourself."

Maybe he was a drifter, or maybe this is what we had come to. Unless it was a real knockout deal, nobody wanted to fool with things anymore. Life had become simply too wrenching, too time-consuming to bother with. I understood this, being a movie star and all; it was my job to provide thrills for the jaded.

"I wish I had something more," I said. "I mean, if it wasn't me, I wish there had been a homicide, something really desperate, so everybody could generate a little enthusiasm, you know what I mean?"

"Yeah. That would have probably been better. But we all got our limitations."

He started to slip his notebook into his pocket, hesitated. "Could you give me an autograph?" he said. He extended a blank page toward me.

"Sure." I signed with a flourish.

"Put down two," he said, "so I have one for Jimmy downstairs."

I wrote my name again.

He thanked me and left. Ten minutes later I was out of the room myself.

THE CAB DROPPED me off at my front door, which was standing wide open. Arthur Makasani, the yardman, was washing the window panels with a sponge and bucket. He was a thick-bodied Japanese man with long, sleek hair that he tied behind his head with a colorful scarf. I asked him what he was doing, and he said Veronica had called and told him to prepare the house. Is she on her way over here? I asked, but Arthur didn't know. I went in the house to the kitchen. I was still hungry. Carol Brass was back there watching television. What's up, Carol? I said. She smiled her gappy I-don't-know-you-but-I'm-sure-your-name-will-come-to-me smile and went on watching her program. I said, How about fixing me a corned beef sandwich? With tomato and mustard. Okay, she said, and slid off the stool. She wore a white uniform like a nurse. Anything been going on around here? I asked, and she said not much, only a couple of calls from Miss Veronica, who said to clean the house. Did she say anything else? I wanted to know. Nothing, Carol said, just that I was to get Arthur to wash everything and for me to make sure the upstairs rooms was in shape.

A distance had grown up between me and this place, the house I had earned and bought with the first real money I made. It had several levels, stucco and pine boards that dropped down the hillside, pushing edges against the gritty gray air. I had liked to lie back in it, like a man lying at the bottom of a ship, letting Hollywood spin outside, but now it seemed strange to me, some place I had only been passing through. The sun spilled like gold gravy onto the kitchen floor. The room smelled of gardenias and cherry pie. Carol chattered on, making jokes about how lonely they had been without me, but I was wondering why there were no signs of Kate around in this room we had sat in over breakfast, talking on the occasional days when neither of us was working. We would make biscuits and eat them with syrup and butter at the little table under the back windows I had had Arthur plant morning glories outside of, and I would look up into the tissuey flowers that the sun brought life to thinking about what a good life it was, how easy it was to get by sometimes in this world if you didn't want anything more than a sweet morning licking syrup off your fingers. But there were no signs of her; there was nothing in here that had belonged to her.

"Mr. Clement said you were coming along just fine," Carol said.

"When did he say that?"

"The end of last week, when he came by."

A rasp of anger brushed me. "What did he want here?"

"He didn't say. He just walked around looking at things. He went out on the patio and walked around downstairs, and then he went upstairs to you and Miss Kate's rooms and he stayed up there for a while."

"Jesus. And you didn't say anything to him?"

"Why would I do that? He's been here before. He's your daddy."

Arthur struggled in with the luggage. That goes upstairs, Arthur, I told him. He looked at me as if I had broached an impossibility.

"I thought you might want it," he said.

"I do, but I want it in the bedroom, not in the kitchen."

"Oh," he said, then to Carol, "Pour me a glass of water, please."

"Get your own water," Carol said, "I'm not your servant."

They began to argue, steadily and quietly, calling each other names.

"You're not boss," Arthur said.

He had a way of bugging his eyes when he was standing his ground, like John Wayne, and he did that now. Arthur too had once been in the movies, but he grew tired of the small, self-hating parts he was given to play and quit. His small, square face was glossy with sweat.

"Let's go, Arthur," I said and followed him upstairs thinking of my father, of him banging around in the rooms of my house. I was angry, but inside the anger was a kernel of pity, of sadness that swelled like a seed in wet ground as I pictured him lurching through the rooms, touching things, trying to make his presence give him back what he'd lost, forcing himself into the empty place, trying to fill up space. Kate was gone no matter who was here, no matter who came looking.

While Arthur unpacked the suitcases, I changed into my bathing suit. Carrying the fresh video, I went through the double bathroom with its companion fixtures, Kate's bidet, her yellow towels fluffy as a cheerleader's pompoms, through her dressing room with its library ell packed with a thousand books arranged by size on white shelves, into her bedroom. The bedroom was pale blue, faintly blue, the color of breast milk, bare. No pictures on the walls, no hangings, no plants. There was a bed, large and square, a muddy Afghanistan carpet, a couple of soft armchairs, a sofa against the wall, French doors that let out on a terrace looking toward the city. I pushed the tape into the VCR on the second dresser, punched it up, and lay down on the bed.

Sometimes I don't want to put my foot down onto the earth, sometimes I don't want to touch the planet at all. I don't want to know anything about myself sometimes. Earl, when he came back from his trip to Africa, had pictures of elephants with their faces cut off. Ivory poachers did it, he said, with chainsaws. Don't show me those, I said, I don't want to see them. Be a man, Earl had said, this is what's going on in the world. He was furious. But I didn't want to be a man if that was what it took. This acting, this making movies, this star business, my picture in magazines, my shadow moving across a thousand screens, is a quiet life, an untouchable life, filled with distances. Don't believe what they tell you—it is much, much easier to live an illusion than it is to tell the truth. Polonius was, after all, only an old fool whose meddling brought him a knife in the gut. Be true to myself? Not a chance. There are so many other things I would rather be true to. Any yellow feather, any blue day, any soft call at the end of the long night would be better.

Bang—there she is, my wife. Changing shape before me on the screen. Kate in an ornate blue gown, her short, hacked, white-blond hair, her sapphire eyes wide open. A long, silent moment, Kate staring at me. Then a green wash followed by a blue face, then red, and the screen goes white. Then Kate again, in a white dress standing in a field. Behind her, an olive tree burdened with fruit. Kate looking away into the distance, down a rough, grassy slope. Another long moment; the wind ruffles the long embroidered hem. Then fade to black, rise slowly, grayly, to white, a long silence of white. Now Kate, in the blue gown again, sitting on a veranda. She makes a series of elaborate indecipherable gestures. A red mist rolls over her, passes. The camera closes tightly on her face, which is screaming silently. Cords in her neck stand out, her eyes bulge. She stops screaming, looks into the camera. Nothing but despair in her face. She licks her lips with a tongue as red as cherries, raises her right hand, aims her finger at the camera, fires, falls, the screen fades to white.

I held it on fast forward and watched her at speed. There wasn't any talking, no sound at all. Then I let the video play itself out while I made phone calls. I didn't need the tapes anymore. I felt as if I had been in a hospital, in a locked ward somewhere, and needed to catch up with what was going on in the world. I called Tommy Sholeen, and Gloria Bates out at the beach, called Jack and David and Sissy Markham, and Fred Hall. Some were home, some weren't; I left messages on the machines or with the secretaries of those who weren't around; all the secretaries said my call would be returned very shortly. I wanted to be back in circulation, wanted my feet on the ground here, just some contact. My life was a weave, so dense it looked impermeable, and the cloth it was part of billowed out across this city, out into the world like a bright floating carpet—I had taken this for granted, had been born stitched in, but lately I had noticed the scuff marks and the tears, I had watched the rip begin, or had noticed the rip that had begun a while back, the one, or the several, Kate Dunn had slipped through. Kate danced on air. All of us had been delighted. Something new, a fresh perspective, goodly, jumping times arrived. I had walked out with her into the sunshine where the flowers and the bushes and the ragged palm trees glistened with an exuberant light. In the midst of it, in the midst of the glitter and polish, she had shown me the dark gullet that opens to swallow us all.

The tape wound down, rolled on blankly. I called Earl, asked him to come out; he said he would. Carol came in with my sandwich. I told her to leave it in the bathroom. Then I lay down on Kate's bed. It was as hard as wood under my back.

The phone rang, Kate's phone. It was Clement. He said, without preamble, "I am loose in the world. I am out here in this vast space where they keep the desert and the lions and the rocks the size of spaceships; I am out here in the rocky place where you said God thought his last thoughts before he jumped off into space; I am down on my knees holding a telephone, watching a child fight back against her mother, who is slapping her as she fights; I am swelled up with liquor and terror, and the sun is shining on my bare head and it is burning me like some fire I am being drawn into; there are date palms out here and a little mossy stream, and you can see mountains that look like they are made out of gray paper or ashes pasted against the side of the sky; the sky is blue, and it looks like a hole, some kind of excavation God's been digging at for a million years; it is huge; I'm going now to lie out under it, I'm going to lay my body down under it and look up into it and I'm going to look at it until I come to love it; I'm going to come to love it before I die, I'm going to come to love all that space, all that nothing, and when I do, I'm going to get up and I'm going to rip the living heart out of whatever's between me and you, I'm going to rip it out and I'm going to crush it in my fist like a peach."

His voice broke, and he began to sob. Big, walloping sobs. A sound like some sound from under the ocean.

I said, "Pop—it's me."

And then I lay the phone back into its cradle.

I HADN'T LOVED KATE at first, I hadn't fallen in love. There was too much energy, too much smell of the world on her, she was too quick, too sure of herself; she had the air of someone passing through, another itinerant. Even so, I went home with her the first night, whichever night it was. I asked her if I could. From the first moment we were alone, our lives seemed perched on the brink of chaos. I don't think this is unusual—perhaps it is to feel this in the originating moments—I think any couple, any member of which pulls aside for a moment to look, feels this. The joining that takes place in marriage, the surrender toward love, is that powerful, powerful enough to make anyone feel the whirl of chaos as he pulls back from it. But it was there in the first moment, on the drive to her place in West Hollywood. Her hand lay on the door handle patting it; she felt it too.

She lived in a big old turreted Victorian house set back among dusty oaks. The place had been cut up into apartments, most of which were inhabited by young actresses. I had been there before with Bobby Consolo, when he was in love with Betty James, the singer. She was running around on him, and Bobby was driving himself crazy, lovesick and manic, desperate for some maneuver that would bring the light of her attention to bear on him again. We had stood at her window watching Betty make love to Sammy Stringfellow, the guitarist in Red Poison, a basher group headed for disaster, and the look on Bobby's face as we watched the skeletal Sammy take her naked into his skinny, tattooed arms was one of fascination and horror, a look profound and gouging, so cleanly worked into his face that I thought it might be there for the rest of his life. We had walked away from that place in a stony silence, driven into the mountains, and gotten drunk. Or Bobby did. He raved all night. He wanted to kill himself, he wanted to kill Betty, blow up the world. He wanted to see Sammy strung up in cords, electrocuted alive onstage as he sat in the front row applauding. He was very graphic about this. He wanted him trussed and stretched, bound in a chair, and the juice thrown; he wanted to watch, he said, the crackle and flare of the electricity as it burned out his brain, as it singed his skin black. Drunk, weaving in his seat, he had cackled and sobbed, picturing it. But the fit passed. Eventually it passed. Which was the key, the secret, the fuel of the drift: it will pass. Today Bobby is a director living up on Mulholland, he's married with a family of young boys; Betty is in New York singing in the clubs. They speak of each other with passable affection, neither cares much anymore about what happened years ago. It is an example of what civilization, that charm school, can do.

Kate had a big room in back on the second floor, a room decorated like a hunting lodge, with nappy red velvets and dark wood, stiff sofas and oakwood pews around the walls, tapestries of hunting scenes, a screened-in porch filled with palm trees in washtubs. She had about a dozen pairs of cowboy boots, a saddle on a sawhorse in the corner, dresses in plastic bags hung on hooks around the wall. She had an altar—some kind of Catholic job— next to the bed, colored statues and several rosaries, a painting of the bleeding heart bandoliered in thorns with blood dripping from it propped in the middle; everything set in front of a mirror like some wacky dressing table.

She wouldn't let me make love to her, which was about all I was interested in. When she told me we weren't getting in bed, I wanted to go. She asked me to stay. I said no, then I said yes. There was no deep reason for it, I think I was just tired. She made a bed up for me on the floor. Pretend you're out on the prairie, she said, sleeping under the stars. I stripped to my Jockeys, lay down on the floor in a welter of blankets that smelled like horses, and watched her undress. She didn't mind. Her body was pale, slender but well muscled, an athlete's body, the skin smooth like a bleached, fine-grained wood. Her hands were large, the fingers long and bony, but strong. Her waist was thick, but with strength, the waist of a worker, a bender and a shaper; her legs were muscular, and she moved across the creaking floor with a step like someone who vaulted onto things. She rustled out of her clothes, standing in a pool of light from the bathroom door, her face lifted, like an animal's, I thought, like the face of some wild creature testing the airs of the night. There was in her eyes a look of distance, not of dreaminess or disdain, but of detachment, almost a baleful look, half-musing, half-gestural, a look not piercing but acknowledging without engagement, the look of a priestess who had lived her whole life among grand monuments and procedures in a broken-down country far from the great empires. It was a backwater look.

There was a moment during the procedure when I thought the time had come to touch her. She stood by the bed, between the bed and my pallet. The lamp pressed a gentle radiance around her body. She wasn't looking at me, but she was talking, telling some version of her past—that I only later learned was a version—some story about the Nebraska grasslands that she apparently spent a lot of time alone in. She turned her body slowly toward me, swiveling on the balls of her feet, and stopped, so I could see her completely. My cock began to swell, and I felt the rake of breathlessness beginning as I looked at her. The insides of her thighs were slightly hollowed out, faintly shadowed, there was a small scoop of flesh inside each hip bone that seemed to me as delicate and beautiful as anything I had seen. Her thick pubic hair was pale, nearly white, springy, and it seemed dyed, glossy with a polish that could have been worked into it, like gilt. Underneath it, faintly visible, the swollen split mound of her sex rose: I stared at it, at the slim, infolded lips, the narrow clitoral hood like a clasp fastened, at the drawn edges of it disappearing downward. My body crackled and hummed. Some buffalo, way out on the plains, some big beast, rose from the wallow, and shuddered. But I didn't do anything. There didn't seem to be any need; I was inside already. Inside, and hog-tied.

From under her pillow she drew her long green nightgown, pulling it out so that it unfolded as she withdrew it, letting the soft silk run against her side. She raised it, a soft canopy that she settled over her head, the small waves of cloth floating down through the lamplight onto her slender, muscled body, covering it. Her body was there, richly and eloquently, and then it wasn't.

I was thirty-three, I had seen a hundred women naked, but it was always a mystery, always a delight, every time. There was a click in my chest like a piece of breath breaking away and falling and then something inside made a small shift toward sadness, a rosy palpable sadness that was almost luxurious with promise. I asked her if she would do it again. She asked what again, and I said put on your nightgown. She slid it off and put it on again, just as slowly, but looking at me this time, her eyes shining with the knowledge I had given her, as if I was the one arranged naked before her.

She pulled the edges of the gown against her body. It was even better. I could see the soft, sturdy shape of her under the frail cloth, see the roundness of her small breasts, the curve of bone at her hip, the slight rise of her thigh like a swell on the sea surface.

Do you want me to do it again? she said.

I said yes, do.

She did it again, raising the gown, letting it fall. I watched the hem, the closing line of it, descend down her body, absolving it, ending it, making it vanish from the earth. I looked at the other body, the new soft green silky shape that she held in front of me.

She looked down at herself, pressed the cloth in below her breasts. I've always liked the way I look, she said.

I like it too.

There's some boy in me.

Yes, some boy, and some horse, and some river and some stone and some plum and some—I could go on and on.

You're a sweet talker.

Yes, I said, I am.

I'm from Nebraska; you don't have to charm Nebraska girls.

What do you have to do to them?

Go straight ahead.

I want to make love to you.

Yes, I know. I would like that, but I would rather you didn't for a while.

How long will I have to wait?

I don't know; there's no formula.

She got into bed then, pulled the white sheet around her. She asked me if I wanted the light off and I said yes. Do you go to sleep quickly, she asked, or does it take a long time?

Sometimes it takes a long time.

Me too. Sometimes it takes all night.

It used to frighten me, I said.

Not being able to sleep?

Yes. I would get afraid about the next day, about coming apart in it.

Did you?

Come apart?

Yes.

No, but I did get tired sometimes.

I was lying on my back looking up at the ceiling, which was streaked with paint as if some wheel, or some hand, had repeatedly brushed it.

Actually, it works out all right, I said. Acting in movies is a pretty good profession for an insomniac.

How so?

There's plenty of time to rest.

I would think you might be nervous.

Not if you don't take it seriously.

You don't take it seriously?

No. How could I? It's the family business; I've known it all my life.

In your movies you look like you're having a good time.

I am.

She turned on her side. I could see her shape in the dark, the heaps of her, the long line of her legs. Even under the sheet and in the dark she looked muscular.

That's why I like you, she said. That's why I wanted to meet you.

I thought *I* wanted to meet *you*.

You did, but I thought of it first.

I put my hand out into the darkness, not reaching for her but testing the air.

Why do you have trouble sleeping?

I don't want the day to end.

You mean it's scary?

No. It's too much fun. It's too interesting.

I thought, This is another ambitious one, this is one who is bound to go places. She'll hurl herself right by me.

Human beings are dynamos, that's my experience. There's

nothing else as powerful. I had known this all my life. My father taught it to me; it was the lesson he couldn't help passing on. I had seen my mother, that beautiful Hollywood princess of a woman, get eaten up by it. I had seen friends go under, and enemies, and I had seen friends and enemies triumph, I had seen them win through. People can bust through walls, they can dive to the bottom of the sea, they can hurl themselves so high moon dust powders their hair. This is a world where if it's in the world you can get it.

And here, for me, was the rub. It was in the helplessness, in the powerlessness of the world to resist. You don't have to go through an earthquake to realize that the steadiness, the dependability of the earth, is just an illusion. Out here they can tell you about it at the 7-11. Watch out, they say, as the goof at the end of the counter pulls a gun from his jeans and demands all the money—watch out, everything's going haywire. You could spend ten years of your life working to get a picture made and have it fall apart at the last moment. The stars of yesterday are selling real estate in Pasadena. The world turns toward you, pulls back the flaps of its coat to reveal a city of gold, but then it loses its place, begins to mutter to itself, wanders off down the track stumbling and crying for its mama. Better, I thought, to slip aside, to drift. Better to idle along, touching lightly. Don't get too attached. Don't let on you're really here. If you have to, pretend you're blind, pretend your legs don't work, go mute. When the conquerors come, be the first on your block to kneel before them. When the evil crashes through into your living room, cry out, Hallelujah, Satan, I was yours all along.

I said, That story you told, about the ape—was it true?

She chuckled, a soft sound. I don't know. Sometimes it is, sometimes it's not.

I don't guess it matters. It was a good story.

I like it too.

Do you have others?

Plenty. They're my stock and trade.

Tell me one.

The sheets rustled as she turned toward me. Then her voice began, a new voice, lower, soft and almost silvery, as pale as the ribbons of moonlight that eased through the open windows into the huge room. In the darkness I could see the shapes of her goods, the saddle on its stand that was like a riderless horse in the shadows, the dresses that looked like headless bodies floating on the walls. The story was about a trip to Florida she had taken as a child. She visited Florida or she lived there; I couldn't tell which. She had gone with her family to the Gulf coast south of Tampa, and then to the Ringling Brothers circus museum outside Sarasota. She had a brother, she said, a little older than her, who was her blond-haired hero and champion. He was cruel, she said, a capable, brilliant, loving boy, who got his way in everything, who came home with plums in his pocket and funny stories to tell, who didn't care about other people beyond what bright conniptions they could perform in front of him, and she was beside herself with love for him. It drove me nearly crazy to simply look at him, she said, I wanted to kiss him and make love to him, I wanted to marry him and live with him forever. I was the only one he liked.

Here's another, I thought, in love with one of the impossible ones. I knew about that business.

We toured the circus museum, she said, and toured the clown college, and then we went to the training place, this circus camp; I guess it was where the acts worked out, where they planned their stunts for the coming season. My brother was twelve, he was tall, almost as tall as my father; he wore his hair short, like you do, except he had a cowlick on the crown of his head, where the hair stood up like a little tuft of grass. It was a sunny day, you could smell the animals, all the different smells of them, the camels and the lions in their cages, and the elephants—a wild smell, stronger than the smell of flowers, stronger than the smell of the ocean or of anybody human. We came out from among some tents into this field, a grassy place where they'd set up the circus rings—those painted curbs the acts perform inside of—and there was a guy in blue jeans putting his elephants through their paces. He had six or eight elephants, all of them full-grown except for two babies. One baby was bigger than the other. The little one must have just been born, he was so small, a little hairy gray thing with a sweet mouth. I was so excited. I'd never seen anything like him, like the little elephant.

She stopped talking and the silence slid back between us. I could hear the faint sound of traffic out on the street, the hiss of tires as cars accelerated along the open stretch of pavement before

Monrovia. In Veronica's yard, once when we were kids, the Japanese beetles came and ate all the plums. From the kitchen steps you could see them in the trees, fifty feet away, purple, green, and shining, hear the buzzing of their little metal wings. If you walked out there under the trees, the beetles would get in your hair and cover your shirt, bumping against you clumsily as they flew between the trees and jockeyed among themselves for position. Harmless, blind, it seemed, to humans or threat, they tumbled in the leaves, crawling over the pale fruit. In a couple of days the trees were ruined for the season.

Her lips moved, but she made no sound. I said, What happened then?

She turned toward me. The moonlight glinted faintly in one eye. There was dampness there, tears maybe. I wondered what I had gotten myself into.

She said, I was astounded. I had never suspected there was such a thing on earth. As a creature like a baby elephant. It had hair on its head, faint and fuzzy like a baby's. I ran toward it—I couldn't stop myself—I wanted to touch it. Someone shouted at me—the man, I guess, the trainer—but I didn't stop. As I reached it, as I was almost there, I stumbled and fell. My brother, who had been walking behind me, ran to help me. As he did, one of the grown elephants—the baby's mother—swung around and charged us. David had just reached me—there was nothing wrong, I was all right—he had leaned down, his hand touched my shoulder, I could feel his fingers through the cloth of my T-shirt, but when the elephant charged, he leapt up. He lunged at the elephant, I don't know what he was thinking. He ran at it, yes . . . he ran toward it. Maybe he pushed at the baby elephant, I don't know. I have played the picture of it in my mind one thousand times, but I still can't see it clearly. The mother elephant ran over him, trampled him. He folded up under her like a Japanese paper flower. He didn't cry out. The elephant was trumpeting. I guess she would have come at me, but the baby ran to her. My brother was under her feet. She made these little movements on his body, almost dancelike, mincing almost, like she was trying to tiptoe, and then she backed away, like a show horse.

The elephant trampled your brother?

Yes. The elephant crushed him, crushed his chest and one of his legs and his skull. Some of his hair, the part where the cowlick was, scraped off on the elephant's foot. I saw it, a tuft of blond, bloody hair caught on the elephant's toenail. There was screaming everywhere: I was screaming, the trainer was screaming, my parents were screaming—there were others around—tourists—who were screaming too. The elephant was trumpeting, blowing her trunk. The trainer beat the mother elephant across the face with his stick. The stick made a hollow, thumping sound like hitting a suitcase. I ran.

You ran away? That makes sense.

Yes. I didn't think, just ran. I wasn't scared—or I was beyond scared—I wanted to erase what had happened.

I know about that.

Yes. It's natural. I ran around some tents, past some trailers. There were two clowns sitting at a picnic table by a little silver trailer. They were playing cards. Just as I passed, one of them said, *You fucker, gin*—I remember that; it was the first time I heard that word—and slapped down the cards. The other looked at me, frowning behind his red, painted smile. I ran by them and through the housing area to an open place. The ground, the property, gave out into some marshes, a sort of bay, I don't know what it was, the arm of a bay, a lake or something, not the ocean. The marsh grass was pale green, there was a foam scum at the edge of it, and then empty water beyond, black and oily looking. A white heron, a heron or a crane, was walking around at the edge of the grass. I stopped. There was nowhere to go. I watched the heron. It was so calm and stately, this ridiculous skinny-legged bird; it took these long, slow, rickety steps. Every once in a while it would dip its face into the water. Its whole head would go under, long yellow beak and little white head . . .

Feeding . . .

Yes—all in a kind of slow motion, very carefully, ponderously, except it was such a skinny bird, not aware of anything else, even of me standing there shivering at the edge of the grass. I hated it, I truly hated it, and I wanted it to die, and all of its kin; I wanted all the oblivious, useless, stupid creatures in the world to die. I wanted a fire, or bombs, or some murderous terrible device to come crashing through the sky and trash and wreck everything. I started to cry out, not screaming but yelling, crying in a rage, yelling at the heron and at the marshes and at the water and the terrible world, yelling at myself and my dumb brother . . .

She broke off. A headlight flashed against the wall and disappeared. There was the scent of lemons, some trees probably, down in the yard. You know, she said, I could be a fascist, a killer, just like Hitler. I know that rage. She sat up in the bed. The sheet fell away from her breasts. I know how you can get hurt so badly you just want to hurt everything back. I know something can happen that you didn't expect and how it makes you different from what you were, and there's nothing you can do about it but be the new thing, however terrible and crazy it is.

She stopped talking and fell back on the pillow. The low urban approximations of silence came back. She was quiet a long time and then I saw, her face aimed at the ceiling, that she was still talking; her mouth was moving, but without sound. Her hands moved as she spoke, shaping the silent words, squeezing them, cuffing them. Her eyes didn't blink.

What is it? I said.

She went on noiselessly for a second longer, and then she sighed a long drawn-out sigh that seemed pulled up from deep inside her. Sometimes, she said, I can't fill the silence. I try to, but all the sound just dies out in me.

I can't fill it either, I said. I have to keep moving.

I used to tape myself, she said, I used to tape my own voice and play it as I was going to sleep, turn it on when I became too exhausted to go on speaking, so I could hear the sound of my voice, hear the stories right into sleep. It was the only thing that would soothe me, and I had to hear it, I had to know some of me was going on awake into the dark.

I started to speak, but then I didn't have to. I could see her, out there somewhere in the country, supine in the place she came from, living with an empty space where a brother used to be, living with empty spaces I couldn't imagine yet in the wall of being. And then I could see her, as if it was my gift, in another moving picture, see her, sooty and frantic, throwing buckets of water into the burning void, and I thought, That's what we're all doing, only some of us don't know it's a void, and some of us think it's only a cupful of emptiness out there, but all of us, even those for whom the world seems to work, flicking a little water off their fingers at it as they pass, are trying to fill it, working at it, coming home late in the day and putting on old clothes and going to work at it, riding along under the tall palm trees, working at it, digging down into, or digging up onto the body of love trying to fill it, shoveling in the energy and the love and the catty remarks and the whooping sobs of the bereaved, building something, anything, between us and it. And she was one for whom the work was everything.

She rolled toward me, to the edge of the bed, her hand dropped, not reaching for me, but for the floor. Her fingers spread, tapped the narrow boards, nails clicking. People are always going on about forgiveness, she said.

What people?

Everyone. You hear it everywhere. About forgiveness, about love, all that, but the truth is there isn't enough forgiveness available in the world, not for the world we've got. There's not enough to go around. Some people are going to have to make do without it. Some of the ones who need to give it and some of the ones who need to get it. It's like going out into the winter without a coat. Some just don't get coats. They have to go out anyway, of course, but they don't have coats, so they're going to have to stomp around and raise a ruckus to work up some heat in themselves.

I'm sorry about your brother, I said.

Yes, how could you not be? We have to be sorry about the dead brothers, don't we?

Yes.

When it happened, she said, the world, the one I looked out on, that prairie, began to look to me like a huge expanse that was covered, closed off by panes of glass. The whole world. And I had to walk out on it—what else are you going to do?—walk out onto the glass that breaks with every step you take. I had to just keep walking and stepping through the glass, window after window laid down on the ground, no matter what. My parents, my father and mother, didn't do a thing about my brother dying. He died, they went through the funeral motions, and then they ignored his life; they acted as if he had never lived. They never said another word about him. Mutes. Statues. Idiots. They went silent, and then the whole house went silent, and then the yard, and then the town went silent, the country around it, and the whole state. Nobody said anything.

I looked around the room at the massive ghostly shapes. The saddle rode on, horseless and riderless. Bits of metal on the altar gleamed. I said, You want dramatic action, you want noise—you have come to the right place. The Blakes of Hollywood will give you plenty. We're the guys who suffer out loud, in front of everybody. We're famous for it. If there's any big emotion around, we head straight for it. We've been shouting and firing off pistols as long as anybody can remember.

She laughed—a quick, torn sound. That's what I figured, she said.

I LISTENED. I was willing. I got it, but she didn't stick to her story. Less than a week later I heard her, at a party, both of us still unfucked by the other, tell a story about her brother that was nothing like the story she told me. In the new version, her brother was alive, a government agent chasing pirates in the Caribbean. He had been shot at many times and he had shot at living men many times; he had killed a few.

She told the story clearly, with authority, laughing as she told it, dropping in the vivifying details—the smell of bananas, conch chowder in an open-air kitchen on a cay at the end of the Bahamas chain, a scorpion in a tin can, the black blood of a liver wound—so that her listener, the executive producer of the picture she was about to start work on in two weeks, began to lick his thin killer's lips with the avidity of a stalking carnivore. I thought he was about to do the leg banjo, he looked so struck, but as he gathered himself to leap, she whisked away, sliding out of reach into the circle of another group of reckless men that she began to charm with another version of her life. She had already changed her name by then, to Zebra, Zebra Dunn, the name of the horse in the folk story that kicked out the light of the moon.

I saw what she was doing and I have to say I admired it. She didn't care what she said as long as the story was vivid and alive. She said she had lived on a houseboat on the Mississippi, described the icy winter with the cold coming up through the deck, huge catfish that they cut steaks off of. She described crossing the Sahel by balloon, a season she spent looting Indian ruins in Peru.

She'd been a print model in Paris, secretary for six months to a minor French philosopher. She'd carried messages for a colonel in the Druse militia in Beirut. She'd sat all afternoon in the bright sunshine of a café terrace off the Ponte Vecchio wrestling with suicide. Even this, suicide, a woman all by herself in a foreign city, sweating out the craziness, had a clarity, a felicity and appropriateness in the way she described it. She'd picked grapes in Spain, taught a black-sheep son of the Lubavitcher rebbe to jitterbug in Brooklyn. She had not graduated from high school, she said, had not attended college if you didn't count the time she worked briefly as a call girl specializing in cut-rate sexual acts for students at Cambridge. She'd been a burglar and then a wheelman on a bank job in Pahrump, Nevada. She'd swum the Hellespont. She'd lived in Oregon, in Minnesota, in Florida, on a tobacco farm in western Massachusetts, in Martinique, Tuscany, Nebraska, Rio, a village in Norway; she'd bought her way out of a Venezuelan jail with sexual favors and a gold medallion she'd lifted off a diabetic anthropologist she'd met in a bar in Caracas. She could whistle through her teeth, hit a doorknob with a spit pearl from fifteen feet away. She'd driven a car 140 miles an hour across the Mohave. She knew the major fashion points of three dozen countries. She could quote John Donne, Auden, Eric Hoffer, Lao Tzu, and Paul Harvey. She had sung on the radio, skated across the Neva under January stars that burned like fierce white points of scattered intelligence above her head.

What was funny was how easy it was to see she was lying. An idiot could get it, a boy could get it. In one story her parents were alive, in the next they were dead. She was in two places at the same time. She supported opposing beliefs. I listened avidly, and everyone around her listened too. We were, after all, more comfortable than most with this approach to life. Out here you didn't have to eavesdrop on the next table to hear lies being told, you could turn to your best friend and hear the whoppers, rosy and swollen as a spider's silk stomach. This was a world of dreams and promises, and if you stayed in it long enough, you began to love the dreams better than you loved life. Better than you loved real life. Everybody was into it. It was like a time of myth, the time when gods walked the earth, turning themselves into swans and golden bushes. Movies teetered like twin ends of a plank balanced on the point of their actual making: one side the dream work of invention and proposal, of grand claims and promises, of the tall tale of possibility—like the country itself, a sort of manifest destiny played out on the edge of a dangerous and beautiful unexplored continent that would open itself to each of us and spill riches and acclaim (those symbols of love) into our lives—and the other, the completed light show that brought to the viewer, to the citizen crouched in the dark of a movie theater, this inexplicable, unreal vision of life that keened and pranced before him, unmistakably—no matter how errant—alive.

I took her up into the mountains, to some property I owned in back of the Sierras, and by the little stream that trickled down through the willows, she took off her clothes and ran away up the mountain like a deer. She was gone so quickly, she ran so fast that I couldn't catch her. I called to her, suddenly panicked, and heard her voice small and distant calling to me to let her go, that she would be back, don't worry. I gave up the chase, returned to the slanted, board cabin, and sat on the porch listening for her in the wind that banged around fitfully in the pine trees. The air was drenched with the dry, piney, herbaceous scent of the high desert, and the chuckle of the little clear stream was like some small unappeasable commentary from the place itself that I couldn't put an end to. Eventually I went in and tried to sleep but couldn't and came out again onto the porch, where the crickets had taken up their dry song and the wind rustled in the toyon bushes rattling berries; I called out to her, but there was no answer. I thought of going down the mountain to get someone, but that was impossible; I couldn't bring myself to admit such a ridiculous situation. Toward morning, I leaned back in a rocker on the porch, I slept, fidgeting awake what seemed to me every few seconds, but not often enough to catch her; when the early-morning cries of birds woke me, I went inside and found her asleep in the bed.

Awake at a touch, her skin flushed as if she'd just jumped out of a cold pool; she looked at me with her clear, pale eyes—strange eyes, eyes that you would remember even if you only saw them once—and said, I heard raccoons, and I saw an owl swoop down on some small animal—a rabbit, I think—and at a bend in the path, up near the top of the ridge, I saw a white deer step out of some azaleas and stand in the path looking at me. She got up, and I followed her outside. I knew it wasn't really a deer, she said, but I wasn't afraid. What was it? I asked her. It was a goddess, she said, come out to offer me good fortune if I would go with her. They always do that, she said, the woods are full of them actually. They come out at night to steal naïve girls away into the woods. They are looking for slaves, for living blood. Sometimes they come as deer, sometimes they come as white panthers, sometimes they come as women. They approach in the dark, when you're alone, and they promise that every dream you ever had will come true if you will only follow them. They steal girls away and the girls don't come back. You've probably heard about it, she said. I was surprised to see her, this spirit, shaped like a doe, because I had already met my goddess, years ago in some other woods; I had gone through this ritual already, and come out alive, so I was surprised. She spoke to me, she said, and it was in the same voice the other spirit used, whispery and childlike and intimate. She said she was my special spirit, my protectress, which is what they always say, and she told me that what I desired most in the world would come true if I would come with her. I said, Spirit, I know you, I know you are a liar; you can't fool me. I wouldn't dare try to fool you, the deer said. I want to help you, she said. Then she told me what I wanted, and since it was true, I was confused for a moment. I thought maybe I had misunderstood the procedure, maybe this was the way the thing went, the spirit showing up for a return engagement and all, making beautiful promises, truer ones, maybe I was supposed to go with her. But then I remembered that's how they do it: they confuse you. They are so beautiful and so sincere, and you, after all, are alone, a girl lost at night in the woods, you're happy to have this kind of attention, this consolation that we all need and desire, this pleasure—it really is that—this liveliness come just for you—most can't resist.

She walked over to the porch rail and leaned against it, looking down the mountain. I figured she was talking about me. There was the thin smell of sage. This place was part of property my grandfather bought after his first success as an actor. He never did much more than homestead it, and he soon worked ritzier claims, but it was important to him, the wandering Arkie who had been shoved off the land he was born on. For him, as wild and strange as this country was with its dry tangle of brush on the hillsides, flannel bush, and calico trees in the draws, its streambeds thirsty for eleven months of the year, the cottonwoods with their ratty skirts of dead leaves, its endless blue sky—for him there was essentially no difference between this place and the place he came from. He did not moan about the jumble of piney hills he was born among or sing the old songs, not in any sentimental way; he acknowledged only loss, the real loss of place, of a stake in the world; he couldn't afford to be particular. He was one who had had to get up and go forth into the jarring world and make a new life there, without training or tradition: the place he took for himself was his place. And then I thought—and it seemed somehow that this was what her story evoked—about that long line of pioneers, the Spanish conquistadores and the Forty-Niners and the Okies, all those who'd trekked the prairies, stumbled through the burning desert, crossed the tall stony mountains to discover this place, and thought how you could fool yourself into thinking that time was over and gone, all those days were just history, some mythical world once lived but now gone down the path of the dead gods, and how this, believing this, was a terrible thing, because if you really came to believe it, that the world had been conquered, then you were a dead man, but how it wasn't so, it wasn't—so *clearly,* so *obviously*—so, because just this morning, on the porch of this old board cabin set in a notch of the Santa Dominica Mountains, naked as a jaybird, was this feral, buzzing woman leaning over the porch rail into the sunlight, basalt dust splashed up her legs to her buttocks, her short white hair tangled and wild, her hard hands beating a rhythm on the worn, shellacked rail, her mouth spewing a story retrieved from the Land of Lunacy, a story so silly, so self-serving that it made me cringe, but who couldn't stop telling it, as she couldn't stop telling her new director that she had been the mistress of a mafia capo in New York City, that her hair wasn't actually blond, that she had descended three hundred feet into Florida's Wakulla Springs and there watched as one, then another, of her companions panicked among the limestone tunnels and died, gasping from shock, with air still in their tanks. She brought me back, or she brought me for the first time—Homeboy, Mr. Complacency—to the Age of Discovery, which I am sure now is part of the job we are supposed to do for each other on this earth, whether we are expedition leaders or crazed shouters waving our skinny arms by the side of the road.

Reaching out to stroke her bare, scratched arms I said, Why is it the girls always get that deal? Who comes to steal the boys away?

She laughed, turning half around so the sun shone on the side of her face, and she looked at me, assessing me as if I were a piece of fruit she might pluck. Nobody, she said. You fellows get scared too easy, all the spirits know that. And anyway, unless it's some big-time god charging down to tell you to set his people free, you wouldn't be interested.

What I want to say is that I wasn't charmed. This isn't what it was about. I didn't think, Oh lucky me, isn't this a strange and wonderful girl. Or if I did, it wasn't because she told such wild tales. I lived in a world, as I have said, of tale-tellers, of gamblers and makers of fancy claims. What I liked, what I came to love, I might as well admit, was the wacky authority, the shamelessness, the pure helpless investment of being she brought to her stories and claims. But even this is not what I mean. This doesn't explain it either. What got to me was much smaller. Maybe it was only the wily gleam in her eye that appeared like some delicious interior knowledge, some joke, winging in, as she told another outrageous story; it was what I think we all fall for in the human beings we love: that crafty, cunning glint of intelligence, of access that we see in the eyes of those we have allowed into our secret rooms. It is this, this gleam, that is the key to our hearts, this cunning, this ability to perceive that snags and holds us. When we recognize it, we throw the door open and invite the rascal in—rascal or saint, it doesn't matter—ready to go along with whatever gag's offered.

IT IS LATE spring, the jacarandas are blooming in Beverly Hills, school has ended, the small boy I once was walks out on the lawn and begins to turn slowly in a circle. My mother, her lovely face rinsed clean of makeup, will be home soon. As I follow her through the windy house, she will untie her fantastic straw hat and shake her hair loose so that it swings down her back in a rippling dark fan. A servant will fix a drink and bring it to her in a tall green beaded glass on the western patio, where she lies in a comfortable chair in the shade. I will watch her long, white arm rise to take the drink, see the small smile of blessing and thanks appear on her lips, see the servant bow at the waist and move silently away, and then it will be my turn, I will approach her, my queen, my heart's delight, bringing my gifts of drawings and tiny, talismanic stones. Carefully, as if both of us are fragile, she will draw me down beside her, nestling my body against hers, she will pull me close against her so that her sweet-smelling frail body touches me everywhere. Her hand will drift toward the scarlet oleander blossoms floating in a bowl beside her and linger there. She will pluck a flower and hold it above my face, letting drops of water fall on my cheeks, bringing the flower close, rubbing it lightly across my forehead. The pale, smooth-petaled flower is poison—we both know this; it is a small thing—and this thrills us, there are chill bumps on her smooth arms from which the coarse, dark hairs have been shaved. She begins to speak, her voice low, catching in her throat, I can feel the soft vibrations of sound in the hollow of her throat, a trembling resonance in the thin bones above her breasts. My hand wanders down her body, touching her lightly, pressing lightly into softness and against bone as she begins to tell me a story that is an old story, original with her, that she calls the Drunken Women of Lomond. It is a story that is hilarious and ridiculous and sad, about three women who drink grain liquor and kill their families and flee to the hills, where they establish a country all to themselves. In the mountains they fight and drink and begin to merge themselves with the old gods, thunder and rain and wind, each taking one of the gods for a husband, each dominating the god or natural force until it performs her will, raking and changing the land, making a new country all around them, confusing and overwhelming the people so that they are changed and humiliated, brought to their knees. But the women, whose names are Beth, Patricia, and Morgan, discover they can't enjoy their triumphs, because they have, without meaning to, become trapped in the forces they dominate; they have become thunder, rain, and wind themselves, which was not what they intended; they've become more merciless and cold than they are able to endure, and though the world around them is at their mercy, is changed and leveled and chastened to their will, their will is endless and unappeasable. The story ends with them howling in the darkness of a Highland night as lightning bolts and wind and rain break in torment across the land, storms continuing forever.

MY MOTHER AND Veronica played this dress-up game, they would drive out to one of the guest cottages my grandfather had built up in the hills behind the Pima farm, and my mother would dress her up in her acting clothes and try to teach her a few things about the profession. There was a summer, our thirteenth, when she did this. Every morning Veronica arriving on her spotted horse from her family's farm a couple of miles down the road, and she and my mother would head in the Land Rover up the dirt track into the hills. I was intensely jealous and a little heartbroken. It was the summer after Bobby died, and I was a lost boy, coming on but not yet arrived at the first flush of manhood, feeling every day of my life a growing impatience and a kind of building intemperance of spirit and desire that propelled me out of the house into the fields, where I could run wildly in circles pretending, as if my life depended on it, that I was still a boy playing soldiers, playing the war games that only a summer before we had lost ourselves in completely. Nothing would take, everything I had depended on lost its adhesiveness, even the farm seemed small and spent, the nooks and clefts already investigated. I'd walk down to the irrigation pond with Billy Dangelo or Gilbert Apple trailing along, but that summer usually by myself, looking for something I couldn't name. The fascination I felt in the wild world turned that summer into distemper and rage—a sudden striking rage that hit me like a rabbit punch, so that without speaking to myself of this, I had become frightened of myself, of what I might do.

One day, down by the pond, as I slipped out from the pine grove, I came on a wild duck trailing a line of ducklings, a companion duck, resident of three winters and summers. I crept close while with light nudges and feints the dam herded the chicks to the bank. The broken reeds along the bank were matted and thick, and the ducklings crawled over them clumsily, reaching a bare place near a fallen eucalyptus log. They were brown, streaked with white, and lightly feathered; their slim black bills tested the air, cheeping. In Vietnam, American officers were directing tank attacks against an enemy they couldn't catch or even name; the president was growling in his bath; my father was casting a picture called *Black Lightning* about the wars in the Texas oil fields that would include, so he said, the largest fire ever filmed; my brother, in a white tuxedo, lay face up in a grassy grave dug into the hillside above the house, and my mother, abandoned by the producers, her beauty and usefulness worn to parody, her first-born dead, was up in the hills with my best friend playing acting games.

That day I hung back behind the first line of pines where the ground was covered so thick with tawny needles that you moved noiselessly, like smoke, and crouched down to look at the duck with her chicks. They made it to the muddy bare place near the reeds; the dozen chicks crowded around the mother duck, pressing against her. Across the pond, the water seemed to form itself under the shade of oaks that spread muscular branches over the bank, but on this side, the sun shone brightly, streaking the surface with patches of mercury. The mother duck raised and lowered her dark brown head, ignoring the chicks, and settled her body into the mud. Just as she did so, from off to the left where the reeds lay against the low bank, a weasel, slim and brown, darted out. I saw its black eyes and pointed face, its moment of assessment; it sprang at the chicks, streaking low across the ground, its body fluid as a snake's. It was too quick to stop, but I leapt up yelling, appalled, my heart racing, and burst out from under the trees. The weasel snatched a chick, spun on itself, and darted back the way it had come. It made a low whining noise, a mean, soft, fussy sound, and its body twisted as it ran, veering from side to side as if the bank were an obstacle course. I hit the bank and nearly caught it, coming in at an angle. But the weasel got by me. The chicks scattered, the mother duck quacking, bustling her wings, and then, there in the pond, my feet slipping on the black mud, without a thought in my head as the weasel turned against the bank, its body poised as if in display against the folded and matted reeds, its eye catching me, the torn, bloody duckling in its mouth, something broke in me. A growl rose from my throat, I crouched low, and my legs churning, I sprang at the ducks. It was a fit, a slippage of some kind, another version of myself that I didn't know about, it was me, Will Blake, thirteen rising to fourteen, thrashing on the bank, lunging at the scattering birds, rushing into the water after them. I rode myself like a jockey, watching myself, a curious dispassion holding me as I raged and grasped at the ducks. They slipped through my fingers, they darted out of reach into the dark water though I waded after them, yelling—all but one, a small tan creature, so young its feathers were almost fur, that I caught. I snatched it up, falling into the water as I grasped it, pulling it down with me as if it were my mortal enemy, squeezing the warm breathing creature in my fist. I didn't see it—I went under—but I could feel it in my hand, and I could feel its bony softness and then feel the deeper softness of its insides as its body burst. There was a raging like some shouted song or cry in my head, the pond stank, I raised myself onto my knees in the shallow water, coming up dripping from the water as if from another darker room, coming up out of the ruffled peaty water as if from another country or another zone entirely, coming from another body and person, from someone unknown to me to someone unknown to me, clutching in my hand—upon which, just that hot summer, new thick veins had begun to rise, as if the center of myself were rising to the surface—clutching the limp body of a small duck, duck of the ebony shining beak, of the brown and gray feathering, of the tiny yellow webbed feet.

My hand seemed to move across my vision, as if I were passing an object to be observed before me, there were springs in my legs and I rose on them, shooting out of the water. I threw the duckling away and lunged at the others. They were too scattered, too far away, too quick to catch.

What had risen in me subsided. I sat down in the water. The little duck floated in the thin foam along the bank. I looked around for the weasel; it was gone. Then a voice behind me called my name. It was Veronica. She leaned against a pine tree in a pale gray dress, her black hair pulled back tightly like a dancer's. For a second I didn't know her. She called my name again, but she didn't approach. I looked at her, squinting into the deep shade under the pines. Will, she said, hello.

I pushed to my feet, tromped out of the pond, stopped in the sunny grass, and stared at her.

You look ferocious, she said.

I am ferocious. I looked at my hands. They were bloody, a pale blue string of duck gut wound around my wrist. I thought of Bobby's hands stained by fish guts. I'm a killer.

Come sit down, she said.

For a second I couldn't move. The sun pounded on my head. It was desert sun, sun like a golden hammer.

She stepped out, took me by the hand, and led me under the

trees. She pressed me down beside her. I leaned against her and looked up. The pine branches cut off the sky, locked it away from us. There was a trickling noise of water from the pond spillway. The small breeze slipping into the woods had the faint smell of wet life in it. I thought of my father years ago hitting the horse he used to ride Sunday afternoons, the horse nipping his shoulder and my father punching it in the face, quickly, efficiently, and without a break in the conversation he was having with Bobby, and how Bobby flinched at the blow, just slightly, something blurring in his face a second, and his hand coming up to touch the horse, to caress it, and missing. He hadn't been dead long; his room, everything he owned, still smelled of him.

Veronica pulled my head down against her small new breasts, not minding that I wet and dirtied her dress. I said, What are you and Mama doing?

I don't know exactly. What are you doing?

I was killing ducks.

You ought to let them get bigger; then they'd be worth it.

They would?

Sure. You could pluck them and eat them.

Nearly an adolescent, I wanted to say dark, troubling, great things, but I couldn't think of any. There was a weasel, I said.

I saw him.

The pine we leaned against, a digger pine, forked halfway up the trunk. The separate trunks ran up into the sky carrying the flag of their needles aloft. From here it looked as if the sky itself had split the tree. A small, hot wind felt its way through the woods, found us and touched our faces, passed on. I touched the green and yellow, gold string and cloth bracelet Veronica wore around her ankle. What are you and Jennie doing? I said.

We dress up, and then we undress and she draws pictures of me.

Naked?

Yes. And then we have tea and she gives me a cookie from a green tin. She says the cookies are made from a seed found in the Scottish Highlands and are very rare.

Bennie wafers. They're not from Scotland.

I didn't know what had happened to me, didn't know why I had attacked the ducks, but I sensed something in myself, something startling and uncontrollable, and it frightened me—

frightened and awed me, a terrible thing, but something that seemed to claim and bolster me as well, something about myself I hadn't expected. I said, I'm really jealous of the two of you. It's like you and Bobby.

She stroked the hair off my forehead. You don't have to be.

It looks like I do. My best friend slipped off with my mother, both of them stripping naked in a house in the woods—me not getting to go along.

It's something girls do.

It is? Are you sure?

She scratched her ankle. The soft hairs above the calcaneus bone were unshaven. A few of them were black. She looked toward the pond. The ducks had gathered behind the mother toward the far side under the large oaks. I'm not completely sure, she said, but I like it.

I didn't yet know much about the ridiculous, weighted insistence of the world on its own meaning, on the validity of its momentary version of itself, but I knew about how things could dance off in another direction, how spring came to the mountain fields in an orange cry of poppies, of how in summer the thunderstorms stood out suddenly above the mountains, crackling and glowering, and I knew about how I was still a little kid who couldn't help but hope for the best, and that my brother was dead and that my mother had been changed by this, and changed by the fashion of the times that turned its back on her, and I saw the change, the advancement, the sleek particularizing conjury that was taking place in Veronica's life, and I wanted to shake her, I wanted to run into her life, as I had run among the ducks, and grab her up and force her back. But even at thirteen rising to fourteen I knew the silly futility of this. Here she was, tall already, the muscles in her arms and legs stretched along the bones like stressed silk, the first dark hairs collecting in the secret places of her body, her breasts swelling in the night. Something about growth and change shames us, though there was no way I could separate this out from myself or tell it to her then.

A vigorous new way of being had stepped forth in both of us: a violence in me apparently, a sensual surrender in Veronica. If I was jealous of her—jealous of the attention, of the closeness—I was also fascinated; I wanted to see what they did up there in the hills. Veronica didn't mind telling me; she would even play it out in front of me if I wanted, but I had to see for myself.

The next day, or the next time she came over—it was overcast and windy, there was a smell of sage blown in from the desert—I followed them up into the woods. Billy showed up, riding a small clattering motorcycle he'd stolen from the parking lot of the Tecuma Baptist Church and which belonged, so we found out later, to the juvenile delinquent son of the minister who was conducting the summer revival, an awkward, buck-toothed boy whom Billy beat into silence and submission with a bamboo pole when the boy confronted him about the theft, and who, oddly, did not seem to have the normal recourse of turning to his father to right the wrong. Either the boy didn't say anything to his dad, or his dad, amazed at finding himself among gentleman farmers and movie folk, didn't want to rock the boat. The boy did make a disturbance in church—he tried to set the church on fire—which we only heard about later, since we weren't Baptists and certainly weren't going to revival. Nothing happened much, the fire was put out by the janitor, but it was a terrible thing, I guess, for his father, an embarrassment and humiliation for him and his family, for him in his ambition, since even the Baptists of San Xavier were important people and maybe he was a godly man, or trying to be—Billy got a kick out of it. He came by on the black, choked-up bike and wanted to go with me, but I told him he couldn't—I had a plan in mind—and he got angry. We got in a fight, which was how our friendship for a time expressed itself, a serious fight that boys on the verge of adolescence can get into, a fight in which all the vigorous, murderous feelings of childhood ride briefly on the fresh muscle of arriving manhood. The hitting hurt, and when I stepped under a level left hand, the knuckles of which looked like small white stones coming at my face, and punched him in the ribs and then, twisting away, tripped him into a patch of red phlox, I was happy to get it over with. I'd outlived my usefulness as a boy fighter, and when Billy got up cursing me and rode off on his stolen bike, I wasn't angry and called to him to come back the next day, but I was glad to be free of such dangers; I knew that stuff was finished for me.

Mama and Veronica were a couple of miles into the mountains, up one of the old logging roads that wound a grassy way through pines and toyon bushes, past sycamores and laurel and ash in the draws, like roads through wilderness, the frail country returning to itself hesitantly and then lustily, gone wild beyond the double tracks that were bony white in the sunshine. I ran up the road, I ran the whole way. In the distance, through breaks in the trees, the nappy, lion-colored hills lumbered away toward the peaks of the cordillera.

When you're a boy you think sometimes that you could just shoot your arm out and follow it into flight, soar everywhere. But soon you know you can't, and as soon as you know this, as soon as it sticks in your mind, you begin to build an immense longing that you think is going to drive you crazy. Boys are the ones who at fourteen climb into the scrubby hills after dark and lie on their backs in the grass masturbating and screaming. Boys are the ones who suddenly, for no reason any sane person can figure, turn their bicycles over the edge of the nearest cliff just to see what it feels like to fall. I ran as if I was in a race, pushing myself toward Thermopylae.

The house was set in a notch in a stand of flat-topped sugar pines. The road curved toward it, past the stream that now, in early summer, carried a memorial trickle of bright brown water down from the mountains. The rocks in the stream were white, like skulls. Crickets and grasshoppers twirled among the long grasses. I slipped off the road, made my way through a tangle of myrtle bushes, and sneaked to the house. It was a small square board cottage with a front porch that had been painted white but was now weathered to gray. A short catwalk led to a kitchen in back, separate from the house. Where the pines stepped in toward the back, mountain rose bushes continued a few feet closer, falling on their faces in the rough grass under the back windows. The yard was strewn with fading pink petals and the air smelled of roses.

I came along the bushes, sneaking low, and crossed the short open space to the bedroom window. The windowsill was half-crumbled and slightly pulled away from the frame. This house, along with three or four others my grandfather had built like sentry posts strung along the notches in the high hills, had been used for hunting and for the drinking parties my grandfather liked more and more as he got older. He died at a party, though not up here, knocked from his poker hand by a heart attack that tossed him backwards out of his chair like the kick of a horse. Everyone said it was a fine way to go, fine for a man who had driven a tombstone Chevy truck cross-country in 1935, hauling his family out of the dusty ruin of life in the Ozarks, to Hollywood, where with guile and the country Scots brooding refusal to give up, he'd pounded the nail of his life into the movies. He was holding a pair of fives when he died, bluffing his way, as usual, to the money.

Well, I poked my head over the sill and looked in. The glass was foggy with dust, but I could see them. They were naked in the bed, my mother and Veronica. They lay on their sides, facing each other, on the black iron bed. Jennie was kissing Veronica's breasts. She held them in her hands, kissing them with short, shapely kisses. Veronica's head was thrown back, her long black hair fanned out on the pillow. Her pale face protruded from the hair like a white carving, her long neck was slender.

I dropped down from the window to my knees; I clutched myself in my arms. A bird called from the woods, a short metallic cry like silver striking silver. The sun was breaking through the overcast, throwing down cloaks of yellow silk onto the tops of the pines. Love is brutal, then it's beautiful, then it's brutal again. You can't set your watch by it. I raised my head above the sill; with her fingers, as if by conjury, my mother turned Veronica onto her back. Her long-fingered hand trailed down her belly, touched the narrow strap of dark hair. Like a bird's beak, one long crooked finger dipped in. I started to cry out, but the cry stopped in my throat. My mother's dark head trailed her hand down the white belly. My mother's tongue was bright pink; it darted, licking. Her hand slid down Veronica's thigh, pushing it away from the other, the hand sliding back to its nest in her groin. She pushed her face in.

I sank down onto the ground. I pressed my hands against my face, not trying to stop anything, but touching myself, feeling for the reassurance of my own skin. There was a terrible familiar awkwardness about what they were doing, as if I were watching myself do something natural that I never saw myself do. It was like looking at myself from behind. Not terrible, but for a moment so strange that the sight seemed to come from another world.

I raised myself and looked again. It was as if they had strung a line between themselves and me and were reeling me in. Shock burned on my skin like salt. I swayed, the side of the house reared like a wave, my vision skipped, lighting here and there like a frantic bird. My mother's hair was a shade lighter than Veronica's, a shaft of sunlight streaked it copper. On her right hand she wore three rings that looked like blue and black buttons. The hollow of her back looked cleaved, a place where a heavy blade had driven into her. I expected bleeding, I expected something to burst from the two of them, or something to rise up, the floor itself maybe riven by an underground wave, by the earth snapping, but nothing happened. I whirled away. I had to tear myself away really, but I tore myself away. A huge wobbly desire stumbled through me, and a strange lightness entered my body, as if what held me to the earth were draining away. It seemed then that I could step through things, as if every solid thing were without resistance. I could push my hand through stones if I wanted to, through trees, through the white cottage wall and through their pale bodies; I could reach through them and through the bed and through the floor and the earth underneath it; I could fall.

I spun away, I ran off into the woods. The pine needles covering the ground were the shed hair of lions. Through gaps in the trees, through gaps in the overcast, blue punched through. I ran until I was out of sight, ran noiselessly on the thick needles, and then I stopped, not winded but stunned, and I lay down.

Not stunned, but amazed, not amazed but come to discovery. Do you remember, Kate, down in Mexico, when we crossed out of the cordillera that morning and came out from under the trees and saw the valley spiraling away from us under the white piled clouds, and you said, It's just what I imagined, and more too. Well, that's what it was. Who can stand up to seeing a thing like that, like what I saw my mother and my best friend doing in the mountain bedroom? I'm not saying I could. But in some strange way it was just what I expected, and more. And more. It was a road opening out of familiar territory, worn-out territory I believed I would have to live in, resigned or turbulent, for the rest of my life. Don't let anyone tell you adolescence is a time of discovery; it's a time of shame and loss, a time when you are convinced that you will have to live in the same old ways for the rest of your life. That's where the turmoil comes from. Life's a thing that wears out. That's the truth and everyone, whether they can speak it or not, knows it. And adolescence is the first proof, the first experience of this. It makes you so mad you want to destroy everything around you just to see what it looks like when it's been chopped up—something new—you understand? But then, what happens, you get a crick in your pecker, a girl touches you and you feel a tingle running under your belly and you say, My word, what is this, is this something I hadn't thought of? Well, yes it is, and it is something, Buster, it is really something extraordinary.

You have to understand that what I saw corrupted me, probably in some fatal way—I don't know, I've never been to a therapist—I mean what are you going to do, what is your *system* going to do about catching your mother naked with a girl who has been your best friend since you were five years old—but alongside that, jivvying it, slapping it along like a reluctant steer, was this other, this other fact in a clown suit, that what I saw, that what was going on in that room where, I noticed, my mother had set a vase of mountain poppies beside the bed and made up the bed with fresh yellow sheets, and someone had swept the room and maybe even washed the white board walls, was a new paved road leading out of life as I knew it into another, richer, wilder, tempestuous life, and the road was open. I saw that one thing does lead to another. And I saw that though I had no idea what that other was, would be, it was something I would recognize when I got there. I wanted some of this, I wanted it the way a hawk wants prey, the way the deer wants water. I could feel the chance of it like a shot of speed in my blood. A jolt, a tug, a cry.

These are just words, and it's true that I didn't think them as I lay there on my back under the tall sugar pines in the mountains of Southern California, but words are laggards, they only show up after the fire's been put out. Christ, I had wheels in my body, jets. The wheels spun, the jets roared, and I saw what I hadn't been looking for, saw this without seeing it, you understand, still a child: desire betrays. What you want is who you are. I pressed down flat, lying on my back under the pine tree. I looked straight up, along the shingled trunk; it seemed to be falling on me. The branches were platforms, raceways for takeoffs. They soughed and trembled in breeze, but down here everything was still. Let me say what happened here, because it was clear to me, engraved as it were on my eyes, because it was going to happen again, I was sure, and I wanted to recognize it; I don't want to forget even now, no matter how late it's getting. Through pale yellow dust I saw my mother lean her skillful, aging body over the lean white shape of my best friend, watched her sup from skin, from the hidden well in the center of a world of skin, the old verifiable, find it and lap from it. The muscles on my mother's thighs bulged like straps pulling tight; she was squeezing them together, trapping herself, forcing the energy arcing off Veronica deeper into herself. Her own black patch was small, nearly absorbed by the press of her thighs. Her black, henna-streaked hair rivered along her throat. As she dug in, the small muscles below her mouth working, Veronica's body began to lift off the bed. Her trunk, her neck arched, like someone trying to float. Veronica's hands dived into my mother's hair like two white birds, clutching the hair without hurting her, hiding themselves in the springy mass of it, the Hollywood actress hair that the movies made beautiful. And my mother *was* beautiful. I have never seen a great actress who did not carry what she gives to the screen out into the world. There is a power that shoves right through their bodies into the banal space we inhabit. They tamp themselves down, bank themselves like peat fires, they put on old hats and gray, ragged sweatshirts, but when you see them, from the corner of your eye if you like, see her get up from the old lounge chair to answer the phone and see the swing of her arms that seem even in a casual walk to be reaching for chunks of life, see her face, tilted slightly upward, the expression triggering the corners of her full mouth, the glint in the pale blue crystalline eyes, the power stabs through, pierces everything around her that is still living, and something in you clicks, jostles, sucks in breath, and stands back—it's like that. My mother was beautiful, in the lees of her life still carrying the power, but Veronica, my Veronica, was just a girl. She strained upward, her body rising, her long mouth lifted off her lovely crooked teeth, but even in extremis, as sweat shined in the smooth places under her shoulders, in the hollows of her neck, on her wide forehead, there was a lightness, a vagueness, a lack. I saw it, the way you see a friend trying to do something he can't quite do, the way you see the dumb boy sweating over the problem in geometry, the way you see yourself after the argument lying in bed baffled, confused by yourself and by the strange hunger of the world to break what it makes—I saw, and I was flooded, my whole body was flooded by tenderness, by compassion, and then by the desire to reach through the murky glass and pluck her out of that place. It was not because she was a child, it was not because she was a limber, innocent child grabbed up by an old woman—my mother—and pressed to the service of rampous annihilating need—she would tell me she wanted to be there—but because she was not dragon enough.

That was the key. Dragons project. Like light, the force of dragons shoots around corners. I saw it, and maybe I had never seen it before. My mother held Veronica in her arms as a beast would hold its dying prey. And the prey, the girl, was helpless. I don't know how to say this, because I am not talking about the advantage my mother was taking of Veronica. That was not important. Veronica, as she has told me all her life, wanted to be in the room; she wanted, she has said, to feel the blast of heat and desire that my mother instigated, and I believe her. It was the helplessness itself that stunned me. A layer of the world peeled back, and I saw where desire could lead us, I saw where it *does* lead us.

That was not the only time I climbed to the cabin in the woods. That summer I went there many times. I watched through the window and later, when the windows were cleaned with soapy water that Veronica and my mother splashed on each other, I watched with binoculars from the shadows of the pines. They probably knew I was there, at least my mother must have, but no one said anything about it. I would lie in my cradle of pine needles in the soft cave under the tall, flat-topped trees, my sweat drying in small breeze, watching them move about the four rooms of the cottage. They were like a couple who had run away, a pair on the lam, making a small new life for themselves in the high mountains. They fussed, they cooked, they sang together, they tried on clothes, they walked about naked, admiring each other's bodies, they teased each other, they argued about the things of the world, they shouted, they tossed cake crumbs in the yard for the squirrels, they made long, slow love in the iron bed that my grandfather had trucked up the mountain.

The shock of it all faded and I began to see the ordinariness, I began to see how they were like everyone else, that what they had up in the hills was not a circus, but something simple and human. I envied them still, and I was jealous of Veronica, who knew my mother in a way I never would, but the curiosity banked the more violent feelings, banked them long enough until they became only a whisper among the ordinariness of their lives together.

The day came when I didn't follow them. From the kitchen in the Valley house I watched them get into the truck, and I went on eating my bowl of cereal and didn't rush to put my little stash of day supplies together so I could come along behind them. I walked out onto the back porch and leaned against a post wound with morning glories, and watched the truck make its slow way up the farm road through the cedars and the oaks until it disappeared around the shoulder of the tan hills. It took almost no effort to let them go. I felt the tug in my chest, but it was not very strong; I didn't even have to say no to myself. I finished the cereal, turned the bowl up, and drank the milk from the bottom, went inside, washed the bowl in the sink, set it to dry, and then I called Billy and told him to come over. There were other things to follow than these women.

Later Veronica told me about the things she and my mother did. She told me of the games they played, dressing up in movie outfits, dancing through the rooms to the music of Shostakovich and Elvis Presley. She showed me drawings my mother made of her, and she showed me the photographs she took of my mother. I didn't really want to look at them. Seeing the two of them fixed on paper made something rise in me that was scary. I turned away from it, or half turned away. I told Veronica that I had watched them, and she was not surprised or angry. She said she was glad. I don't want to leave you behind, she said, and she smiled her girl smile, and stroked my arm. She said, If you want to do some of the things we do in the cottage it is all right. She said, I would like to. I don't know how to do those things, I said. I can show you, she said. I don't know if I want to learn, I said. Why not? she asked me. I am afraid, I said. Afraid is all right, she said, I was afraid too. I don't know, I said.

She got her mother to take us to a fortune-teller down on Hollywood Boulevard, and as if she had arranged it, the fortune-teller told me that I would fall in love with a black-haired girl

whom I already knew, but whom I had never looked at as a girlfriend, and we would love each other deeply for our whole lives.

That's me, Veronica said, and the fortune-teller told her to
hush, but she said it again, That's me. The fortune-teller wore a
blue, yellow-speckled turban and had a glass eye that didn't move.
She said she couldn't guarantee her diagnosis, and I told her I was
glad of that. When Veronica's mother, tanned and wasted by the
cancer that would kill her in eight months, honked the horn and
we ran out into the sunshine, up the street past the place in the
sidewalk where I had watched my mother, kneeling on a white
towel, place her hands and feet in wet cement, trapped for a second like a deer, and watched her raise her beautiful head and saw
her smile the famous shy smile that had made the country fall in
love with her, and had known for the first time, as if it was the
truth, that she was not mine, that there were too many others she
belonged to, too many to fight or snatch her away from; and then
later that afternoon, in the Beverly Hills we had all returned to
at the end of the summer, in a small cul-de-sac among bushes
where the desert, pushed back from the small lawns and from the
glittering swimming pools and from the trellises with their heavy
weight of bougainvillea and passion vine, stood its ground, re-
fusing, for a moment yet, to be tampered with, in a little clearing
beyond which the yucca bushes sent up their feathery white flowers like signals from someone dying among the tangle, we took
off all our clothes and made a place for ourselves on the ground
that was the color of and crumbled like saltine crackers, and on
her knees in front of me she showed me her body, showed me
the widening hips, the thin white belly, the tender breasts like
small white muscles raised on her chest, the pink pearly translucent nipples; she opened her legs, pushing them apart with her
hands as if she had to work them that way, and she showed me
the wispy stripe of black hair and the grooved swelling of her
pubis, and she drew my hands to her and made me touch her,
and she touched me, softly as my mother had taught her, pressing
her fingers lightly into my side, caressing flesh and bone, drawing her fingers lightly down the length of my penis, speaking to
me quietly as she leaned over me, speaking as if we were still
children hiding in a closet, here in the Land of Discovery, in the
outback of Beverly Hills, where worthless, crazy people who

earned great sums to portray characters in the eternal struggle between good and evil lived the days of their lives amid servants and drugs and swimming pools in which once and a while a body floated face-down. She had spent a summer learning the ways of love, but now it was different—I could see it in her hazel eyes— because I was not my mother, not the leader, nor a woman, but it amazed me anyway when her breath caught in her throat and a flush spread across her breasts; and it amazed me to feel the rush of blood and desire in my own body, which was different from the shock and desire I felt in the woods outside the cottage, and even stronger. Just before my body penetrated hers we looked at each other, and it was as if we were two woods creatures looking out of darkness across a lighted space, two frightened and naïve creatures; for a second I thought I saw past her left shoulder my mother standing at the edge of the clearing. She was smiling the old familiar smile of one who knows everything, of one who can save you from all danger, and will, always will, and as I reached to pull Veronica toward me, it was as if I was pulling my mother, as if the pale skin of my friend was the paler, rougher, worn skin of my mother, as if the bones were her bones, and the face and the breasts and the soft thighs that shuddered open to accept me were hers; and then I saw, for another second, what was beyond my mother, and beyond all the mothers in the world who do or don't teach and protect their children, I saw the huge gulf, or what seemed to be a gulf, and I saw what swam in it, and what rose from it dripping, and I saw beyond that, and beyond that, saw things I couldn't name or even speak about, things that had nothing to do with me or with what we were doing there in the chaparral, and then Veronica leaned in, and she pulled my body onto hers, and the human, banal joining of flesh took place, and for six minutes what I saw didn't exist.

WELL, WE ALL have the inborn and perpetual desire for an eternal kingdom. So Dante said. *La concreata e perpetua sete, del deiformo regno.* I for one am always on the lookout. Up there in the mountains, on my knees before the dusty window, I was on the lookout. Veronica brought me messages, brought tidbits and trophies from her explorations, my mother showed me her life's turbulent inner chamber, I myself experienced some of that bounty, got its smell and taste on my fingers, and what happened? Nothing happened. That was the secret that was spread at my feet. Nothing happened. Life rambled on in its stumbling, exuberant way. Veronica and Jennie remained lovers for a time, and after they were lovers they were friends, in that joshing, affectionate, intimate way that independent souls can manage. In an odd way, the affair made all of us closer, even though I was not a part of it. I grew up, became a youth and then a man, and all the time I carried the half-secret knowledge of what I had witnessed, and after a while it just seemed to be life. It was no eternal kingdom.

Thus, as we say, my drift began. I had seen what I had seen and I was still alive. The truth is, I was waiting. I read somewhere that genius is the capacity for long-term patience, and if that's true, then I am a genius. It comes with the movie life, I think, this ability to wait, so maybe I would have gotten it anyway, but I was a prodigy; I learned it at home. I stepped back from my life and I began to watch it; I began to watch my life and the lives of everyone around as if they were circus dogs about to do tricks. I was looking for something to happen. I was looking for something to exalt and destroy me.

About a year later my father and mother split up. There were a lot of things that went into it, all the imponderables that go into failed love that we all know about were there, but my father, who had to find something to focus on, to train the camera of his hurt and frustration on, blamed my mother's infidelity. He took me for a ride in his new purple XK-E to tell me about it. We slipped down Sunset onto the PCH and cruised up toward Malibu and then north along the ocean, bashing through the salt air past the scrubby, torn hills. My father whacked the gear shift with the heel of his hand, popping the small black knob as if it were an enemy he was coercing. His ruddy face was ruddier and his bright black eyes shined as he told me how he had one day a few months before found in the mountain cottage shirts and jeans that didn't belong to my mother. It was odd, he said, they were small and they smelled of a perfume that wasn't my mother's; he couldn't figure who the guy could be. I can't picture it, he said—and I don't want to—but who could this guy be? He shook his dark, heavy head and banged the car into fourth. It was the last straw, he said, the last of many straws; he couldn't take any more, he had told his lawyer to draw up a petition for divorce. This is not the only thing, he said, there are years of others, years of misman-agement and mistakes—most of them mine—but this last is too much. I can't get over, he said, how small this guy is. She's in love with some perfumed shorty—Jesus.

We all knew about my father's mistress—a young actress who was biting her way to the top—she was the latest in a string, so he had no ground for complaint. Even so, I felt for him. But I wasn't going to say anything. Maybe, if the lover hadn't been Veronica, I would have. Maybe if it was some guy, someone I could hate and accuse of taking my mother away, I would have told him, but it wasn't, it was this girl, my best friend, so I said nothing. My father raged and swatted the gear shift, and by the time we got to the Thousand Oaks turnoff, he had nearly burned up the engine. A weeper and a shouter, my father was also a sweater; when he hurt he sweated, water gathered on his fore-head and at his temples and in beads across his lip; the more he hurt, the more he pictured himself as alone in the world without a clue, the more he sweated. The steering wheel was slick with sweat, and there were clear drops on the dashboard, flung there as he changed gears. He just couldn't get over it, he said. What kind of guy could this be?

I passed the word to Veronica that my father suspected house-hold crime. I thought, or maybe I didn't, that it would make her laugh, but as we walked on her back lawn near the horse lots where the fall rain streaked the flanks of the horses, her pale face grew paler, her long bottom lip trembled, and she began to cry. I had watched, and life had gone on, but I hadn't learned much, because the truth was I had no idea what all this meant to her, or to my mother. Already, for me, the drift had begun, that turning aside that kept others at a distance, but for Veronica, then or later, there was no such thing. She spoke angrily to me and then the anger broke and the fear came through. She hunched her shoul-ders in the misty rain and shivered, and the look in her hazel eyes was the look of someone who is trying to escape from a harsh and alien terrain. Then she touched me, her long fingers going over me lightly for a second, as if to discover and place me, and she said she would talk to me later but now she had to go. Not long after that she told Jennie, and soon my mother wasn't living with us anymore. She moved down to the beach house and she bought a small palace in Beverly Hills. When she did this, Clement choked up and backed off. He didn't want a divorce as much as he thought. The fit passed. It passed, but they never moved back in together. Jennie discovered she liked living alone, and if the truth were known, Clement liked it too. Or at least he liked not having to explain himself. For a time Veronica walked around in a kind of wan distraction as if she were afraid if she was not careful she would break through the surface into a terrible place. But this too passed. As for myself, I was never called on to say anything; no one looked to me for an explanation or even any facts. If they had, there were a few things I could have told them. Here's one: I don't think we are ruled by rational law. In other words, nature's limits are unknown. In other words, you have to watch out; anything can happen.

IN THE YEARS since all this took place, it has seemed to me that for a time I lived in a dream. It was a dream both horrible and gorgeous, like some glittering, dangerous circus act that I was somehow called to take a small part in. Those early days with Kate, in which we stayed up late, first in her apartment in West Hollywood and then in my house in the Hills, that time of adjustment and exploration, of delight and danger, brought the dream back to life. As she told her wild stories of enchantment and disaster, I began to want her to know all about the chancy, bright activity that had taken place in the last years of my childhood. So I took her to meet Veronica. She had met her before, of course, had, if I could believe myself for a moment, attended a party at her house, but I wanted Kate to meet her in private, for her to see the face of this woman who had done the strange thing of swimming so deeply into the arms of my mother, who had been the unacknowledged corespondent in my parents' near divorce.

I told her the story, filled her with detail, told her of the cottage and the pine tree with the forked trunk that I leaned against, watching them with my father's binoculars. It sounded better and made the story more interesting to say they knew I was there, so I told her that. I told her that they danced in white sheets in the rain for my pleasure. I don't know why I did, since when she talked to Veronica the truth would come out, but I liked the magic whirl of the story as I embellished it, so I kept on. They wore movie costumes and acted out parts from my mother's old movies, I said. They brazenly rode around in a convertible. My father had discovered them and tried to kill them, but the two women had beaten him up. Kate's eyes glittered as she listened. She knew more than she said; she was one who dragged herself through civilization as if civilization were a destroyed country. She picked up shiny things, bits of food, the torn clothes of a child. Tell me everything, she said, I want to know everything. It was easy to lie—or not to lie, to build from the strange, mad details something even stranger. This was why I loved her—I saw it in a flash—because she wanted me to lie to her. By then she had moved in with me up in the Hills, into the old house that had belonged, so I was told, to Eustace Conroy, the old silent-screen star who had been killed in it, stabbed by two male hookers, and though we slept together in the ornate, spacious bed I'd had flown in from the set of a picture I made in Spain, we were practicing a little cha-cha with the sex business, dancing light-footed around it, like vegetarians about to revert, sharpening our teeth for the kill. Oh, she was a beauty then, my Kate. Someone told me once that love includes possession without the need to possess, and if this is true, I was up the wrong road, because I can tell you that I wanted to possess her. In sunlight on the patio, as Carol Brass brought us huge silver trays loaded down with the chopped-up pastel fruits of California and the sausages and thick bacon of Arkansas, the morning sun shone in her spiky hair like the white fire of heaven. It was a fire I wanted to leap into.

We told each other our stories as if we were reporters from separate planets come to interview each other, each digging at the other for more information. Like the iron chairs of wire woven and painted to look like wicker that we sat in, and whose sudden weight surprised you when you picked one up, there was unsuspected heft, a fluky power we kept running up against. I watched her unfold her long, muscular legs and saw the sun catch lightly in the fuzz of hairs at her ankles—that she never, until she went into the movies, shaved—and watched her hands slide up her thighs and come together as in prayer into the delicious cotton-covered V between them, and I felt my spirit gather and throw itself toward her. I wanted to touch her, which is all I had done with women for years, touch her and lick the gloss and sweetness from her body; I wanted to taste her on my tongue, to hold the state of her like the taste of plums in my mouth, but more than that, I wanted to know everything about her. I wanted to hear every story, every adventure, every tale about her life in the far places she claimed for herself. I wanted her to lie to me without stopping.

I told her the Veronica and Jennie story, and then I told her that I wanted the two of them to meet. Veronica knew everything already, but she hadn't spoken to Kate beyond the words they exchanged in passing. Kate was delighted with the idea. The basin fell away from the patio like the earth stepping back from itself, sweeping itself aside to introduce its greater partner, the ocean. I looked past her knowing already that we were going to marry, listening to her talk about the time she had held the head of a dying freedom fighter in her lap, of the words he spoke to her about his mother as his life seeped away, and it seemed to me that not only had the earth, as I saw it from the high fastness of my big house, stepped back, it was speeding away from us, as if we had leapt to just the right vantage point above the hurtling planet and could see it now, in its speed and clamor, rushing along through the cloud chambers and the antimatter toward the end of space.

How I connive and ramble, how I twist my life into a shape I can tell. We drove out to Veronica's beach house, and I found the key in the little clay pot and let us into the house with its big sea room tipped against the wide porch overlooking the ocean. The house was up on pilings, and though Veronica swore it was plumb, the wide, open room with its bare plank floors and wheaty sofas and its slatted windows like gun ports in a Mexican fort seemed to tilt toward the sea. It made me feel as if I were on the back of a large bird just trembling into flight. She had paid one and a half million dollars for the house—a high price in the seventies—but she hadn't bothered to renovate it. She didn't really care, but since people in Southern California treat houses as expressions of the last twitch of manifest destiny—it is their calling and fate to renovate every freshly purchased domicile to the point that no traces of earlier human habitation remain—she was aware of falling short. It was something else she laughed about.

We were grown now, we had filled out, we'd gotten through the ambiguities of youth and the certainties of early adulthood, we knew how to make money and prosper, we cavorted before idiots and sleazy saints, we had found and furnished our little hideouts, we had the routes of our lives mapped in our blood. Veronica had tried it on a movie set and gone under as almost everyone does, the lights and the camera not giving comfort but pain, the instructions of the director, who might be someone she had known all her life, confusing rather than releasing her, the other actors under their painted faces no more than the fools and sufferers she knew from daily life. She didn't like the charade, she didn't like the confusion or the translation of mimicry into story, and she didn't like the stories either. She liked the aftermath and the residue, what remained at the end of the day when the work was over and exhaustion and irritation left everybody spinning; she liked the way, exuberant or defeated, movie people swung in through the doors of her restaurant, their voices high-pitched and patinaed with lies, their eyes unable to hide the secret knowledge of their failures and terror and their human dumbness, and she enjoyed gliding up to them in her fine, soft clothes, inviting them in like an innkeeper in medieval France, or the abbess of a baroque nunnery, calling for drinks, for food to replenish their wasting bodies; she liked to watch them come slowly alive again, the memories of their lives and their work and a terrible century dissolving for a little while into the green shaded quiet of her orderly world. Swank and untouchable, friendly, she was chief of her life.

She and my mother continued to meet—Clement never caught them—and they still played some of the old games, but there was a rich, winey taste to the friendship now, a worn and pliable familiarity that soothed them both. My mother's place was a mile up the beach, near town, and one or the other would often walk the gray slanted strand early in the morning to have tea. I had a house out there too, down in the next pod of houses where the beach slanted up into the cliff face, but more often than not it was rented out to some actor just arrived to riches.

Veronica wasn't there, but then I saw her out on the beach. She was down near the water feeding pigeons. Beyond her the cold, green, cloudy ocean tumbled slowly in. A couple in black jogging outfits chugged by. I waved to Veronica and the couple saw me and waved back. I didn't recognize them. Maybe they were tourists playing at the movie game. Their faces were bright and open as if they had spent hours somewhere buffing themselves into an illusion of natural health, and I was sure that if I called to them they would drop everything, even their clothes, and spring happily into my life. We were on our way, oddly, to the fights, which was where Kate said she wanted to get to know Veronica. I saw it for the put-up job it was, but I didn't care; I too was interested in how other humans adjusted to unusual venues, even my own close friends, so I had said okay. The couple stopped to talk to Veronica. I shouted to her and she waved back, and then she trudged up the strand to the house and climbed the long stone stairs and came in. Who was that? I said. She said they were a new couple, the man an actor from New York who'd made a hit picture in which he played a pilot who flew around the country in a circus biplane murdering people. He's got a lot of new money, she said, and they're both really lonely, so I invited them over to a party next week.

Maybe later you can babysit for them, I said.

Oh, they don't have children.

We looked at each other and then we began to laugh.

I turned around and saw Kate, who even then I thought of as my wife, staring knives at us, and it struck me that maybe this wasn't such a good idea, that maybe I'd been a fool again to think that these two might become friends, and so I began to juke and cavort, to play the small connective games people play when they are out of their depth but have to go on anyway. I offered drinks and quick movie talk, and then Kate and I followed Veronica up to her bedroom and lay on the bed while she changed into one of her black silk rambling outfits. All of a sudden, there on the broad windy bed overlooking the ocean, from which rose now the orange and lilac of sunset, Kate ran the back of her hand up my leg and dragged the tips of her fingers across my crotch. She pressed her face into my neck, making kisses against my skin, or speaking—I couldn't tell which—setting fire to me. Even then I knew what this was about, because I was a guy and we had our own versions of this maneuver; we had our struts and feints that let other guys know whose bread got buttered in this particular configuration, and, noticing this, knowing it for what it was as Veronica twirled among the mirrors and secrets of her dressing room, passing in and out of view in the tall mirror that covered the door, a feeling came over me that I recognized as a feeling that had been inside me for some time now. It was not a feeling exactly, more a sensation, or a sudden knowledge, a falling into place. I saw it as I once saw David Loomis on a soundstage step through his character into the space behind, step right through the movie tears he had been instructed to cry into his own tears, into sobs that were wheezy and whistling in his mouth, and saw for a second or two his life pick him up like a bad man grabbing a lost child, and how for a moment the actors around him continued to play so that there were two or several worlds whirling at once, the dream worlds and the real world, which—this is what I am talking about—I realized was a dream too, no more than that, of no more or less weight than the carefully arranged and elaborate world the production team had created for us to play in. I saw that for Kate, as she picked at me, as she pressed against me, turning up a fire, I saw that for her the dream was no different from the reality—this was the fact I'd been acknowledging for the last few days in an unacknowledgeable way—and saw poking along beyond that, like an old woman poking in the weeds for something to eat, her inevitable humanness, the stupid power-lessness that's our common ground as human beings.

And then quickly, as if I were afraid of being caught, I leaned over and unzipped Kate's pants and pressed my face into the soft cotton of her panties. I could smell the laundry soap she'd washed the pants in, the banal soap, Cheer I think; an immense desire not to protect her but somehow to honor her came over me. For years now I'd been drifting, before the movies and into the movies, wallowing in the boat of my life, coasting the channels, unafraid and unconnected, shambling through movies and my life, not paying attention, not asking for much, at home really everywhere I was, homeboy in the city of dreams, and it came to me now as I picked with my teeth at the elastic, drawing it away from the soft blond hairs, running my tongue lightly along the seam of flesh and hair, that I wanted to give someone—this woman—everything she wanted, that I wanted to be means and vehicle for someone's dreams coming true.

That's what I would do. And that is what I did. It's what I did as much as anyone can for another. Veronica twirled out to discover us tangled in each other's arms, and she laughed her twinkly laugh and leaned over the bed and kissed us both, and then she went downstairs and made potato salad, which she brought up to us half an hour later and which the three of us ate sitting on the torn bed, Kate and I naked as children, the three of us laughing, Veronica making sharp little loving comments about our prowess, about our bodies, and then Kate and I got dressed and the three of us tooled down the highway to LA where from ringside we screamed our lungs and hearts out at the fighters who sprayed their bright blood and sweat in our faces.

Then I stepped forth into the pastel city and with a firm hand opened every door I knew to open. I got Bennie Oxe to do her PR and Belinda Wilson to give her acting lessons and I introduced her to the executives at Paramount and Warner and Disney. I arranged lunches with the packager moguls, with screenwriters and directors. I optioned books for her and hired a couple of new guys to do scripts. I took her to parties and stepped back so she could wing out on her own quick lines, and I backed up whatever she wanted.

She got a smart-talking ingenue part in a big picture Harold Davies was making about a bunch of ruined characters home from Vietnam, and she stole the picture. She went straight on into leads, playing bright, vulnerable women, often women miseried and baffled by the world, but capable in an offhand way of deep Hollywood understanding, capable, remarkably, of action, of finding the beast that tormented the players, and killing it. She was a wonder, gifted, charged with an energy that whirled off her muscular body crackling; she got a couple of good directors who knew enough to let the camera have its way with her—that celibate, yearning lover—and you could see it following her around like a lovesick boy, see the lens pleading with her, see it beg and promise heaven. She gave to it, holding back nothing, as if it were the messiah, arrived at last.

I say I helped her and I did, but she didn't really need my help. If I did anything, I cut the time lag, shortened the leap between her and the places she wanted to get to. The truth was she knew how to get there already, the method was written inside her, like the ability to swim in certain animals. There was nothing she couldn't learn, there was nothing that was too much for her, nothing big enough, or dense enough, or heavy enough to stand in her way. Strolling through my life, an adept myself, a natural perhaps, or not caring enough to be put out by the vagaries and venalities of my milieu, I watched her streaking like a hawk, swimming like a fish. She was a commando, a hotshot, a sweet-tempered conquistadoress. Everyone wanted her, everyone praised her, tried to charm her, promised her riches and fame, promised her heart's love and life like ripe peaches in a basket. Raphael Skortch, the producer, sent her flowers every day for a year. At Hezekiah Rose's party he stripped out of his clothes, dived into the swimming pool, and offered, his long mouth gleaming, to drown himself if she would do his picture. She said yes, of course, she would be glad to do his picture, if the drowning came before shooting began. She was nominated for an Oscar for her first movie, supporting role, and though she didn't win, she won for her third, outright, best actress. At the podium in a white dress streaked with silver beads, wearing a blue cotton rag from Martinique wound around her white hair, she grinned like a kid and did a little stooping, whirling dance, spun back to the microphone, and in her silvery deep voice recited a ditty about an old bachelor who loved a pig named Shirley, thanked us all and then, laughing, her heels flashing, sprinted off the stage.

That night we rode in the polished limo with her agent, Burt Campis, one of Earl's associates, to the mainline party, where she swept in beaming, happy as a queen who has conquered a fashionable country. People rose to applaud her, their envy translated momentarily into an energy directed in sound and accolades toward us. Drifting away, letting her ride the roll of her triumph, I saw in her clear blue eyes the look of passion and wonder, the slightly mocking amazement, and I watched the applause break against her like a silk wave. It seemed to lift her, seemed to shine and transform her face until it was the face of one who believed she could never die; and I saw how her life, risen from Nebraska cornfields or from wherever, lived vividly and anonymously in the cold harbors and hidden places, had twirled free into this place, come to itself for a second or two. Her arms rose, and for a moment she stretched her hands out and clutched the sound, the praise, in her fists, catching it in her strong hands as if it were jewels tossed at her.

That night she didn't want to go to bed. We partied up in the high places of Beverly Hills and Bel Air, flashing from house to house, trailing a growing entourage, sweeping up the curved driveways through rose hedges and past the guest houses and swimming pools of rank sports who had become her peers. From Jake Tillis's balcony she sang songs for half an hour; she made promises she could never keep and would never remember; she cut a lock of her hair and gave it to Phyllis Sabin, an actress who worshipped her; she danced, imitating windmills and dervishes, frightening the caged parrots at the Spellmans'; at Rollie Kingdom's she dipped her hands in a bucket of red lacquer she found in the garage and slapped her prints onto the white tile foyer; she skipped the length of Jack Gerry's driveway—a quarter of a mile at least—on the tops of parked cars, crying out her name to everyone who passed; she tossed full champagne bottles over the retaining walls at Minnie Frank's, laughing like a jackal as they burst on the roofs below; she told more wild tales about her childhood, about a winter above the Arctic Circle, about buying lace underwear from a woman in Paris who claimed to be Lord Byron's illegitimate great-granddaughter, about butterflies in Peru with rainbow wings as large as cabbage leaves, about gunplay in Australia, about cowboy gangs in Madagascar. Each story came alive in her mouth and in her body. She laughed as she told them, her eyes flashing, her silvery dress flicking against her legs as she twirled before the assembled.

And then the spirit of the dark, and of the world that lives behind our world, hating it, came upon us, and it was five in the morning in that black light rimmed at the edges with gray, when just before you can really see you begin to think you can see, and the eucalyptus trees smelling of Vicks VapoRub seem to take a step forward in the scrubby yards, and the traffic lights on Sunset are vivid and begin to blink in unison, and you can smell the sweet flavors of early-morning Mexican cooking and smell the frangipani and the plumeria hidden in yards off the thoroughfares—in that time when your life seems longer than it will ever be again, when you are still young or you are old and don't care anymore about growing old, and, star of stars, you are riding down Hollywood Boulevard in an open convertible, yelling at the tired prostitutes in their sadly glamorous clothes, and in the windows of stores selling totems to tourists you can see yourself in the open car passing, see your white face and your laughter fleeing by, and for a second it is as if you are watching a movie, the one you have been starring in all your life, that is not the movie you make on location or in the high caverns of a soundstage, but only the movie you are living, vivid for a moment in the rising dry-eyed day, and you wonder as you watch yourself leaping from screen to screen just who you are, and where this rush of life is taking you, and you can hardly remember now where you have been and who you met on the way here, and you look across the red leather seat at the one who is riding with you, this woman or this man sporting, in the remnants of evening, the torn armor of heroes, and she is a stranger to you, he is a stranger, so distant, so alien that this one you are speaking to might have flown in from outer space, and my God it is tragic, as tragic as you hoped it would be, tragic and irredeemable; there is no way, you see this now, to find your way back to a place where you are comfortable, where you know everything and everything is in its place, and you see, as if it has hopped down from your shoulder, that everything you feared is true and everything you loved and hoped for is true, and you see it doesn't matter, and see there is nothing you can do to save your life or anyone's life, and this is what tragedy means—because you know it—and there you are, little fellow or fellowess, streaking down the wide avenue in your painted car, and the sun is coming up on your life and on all the lives one after another, the omnivorous, singular sun, and if you begin to scream in terror it is all right, and if you begin to laugh maniacally it is all right, and if you begin to shout at the top of your lungs it is all right, nobody cares.

Heading the other way now, streaking along, yelling like characters after a high school football game, through Hollywood, through Beverly Hills, through Brentwood and Westwood and Topanga, diving down through the gap in the torn hills to the Palisades, rim shot off the flat Pacific wall, heading north on the PCH through the little warped beach settlements, our hair gleaming with spilled champagne, the sycophants and stooges, the asskissers and helots, the pals and ex-lovers fallen behind and all returned to their rich and lonely homes, we swung down onto the beach road past the shuttered stucco chalets that stand there squat and stunned, motionless, empty forever, abandoned in the grayed light like the dead America Gregory Peck listened to tapping its aimless message in *On the Beach*, here and there sprigs of white daisy, mimulus and milky yellow cinquefoil poking out of cracks, like dwarfs wearing hats, reefs of morning glory in the sandy places gathering energy for brutal blossoming, a ripped queen palm given up to its windy shuddering—and so came, descending through speed, through power and drunkenness, through the pliable amplitude of lives in which what is worshipped sprawls helplessly at our feet, to Veronica's cream-and-saffron-colored house, shadows like mold on the smooth walls, and let ourselves in.

And there she was, my compadre, my Veronica, alone in the big room, wearing a girl's tuxedo, leaned back on the wheat sofa, her slender ankles crossed, resting on the blond coffee table, a drink balanced on her chest, looking out the vast windows at the weak, diligent sea out there, at the small winking lights of tankers heading north from San Diego. We spoke, we joshed, we twirled around the room. Aging, aching, fatigued, Veronica watched us. She was disgusted. She was mourning her own losses, I could see that. She was thinking about what might have been, what couldn't have been, about how life grabs you up like a kidnapper and flings you down where it wants you. She was thinking it's more than she can take, this life. She said a few harsh words, she wanted us to come down from the tall trees.

"Come down from there," she said.

Then she apologized, her voice cracking, and began to cry. I went to her and knelt beside her, and she leaned against me and placed her head on my chest.

"Hey there, girl," I said. She smelled of sweat and a gardenia perfume, a young girl's perfume. I touched her smooth hair. "It's a long night for the orphans, isn't it?" She banged her forehead lightly against my chest.

In muffled battlefield voice, she said, "I am sitting here by myself thinking I am thirty-five years old and I don't have the faintest clue who I am. I just don't get it. I am halfway through my life and it is all a lurch from one confusion to the next. Am I out of my head or is this the way it's supposed to be?" I pulled my shirttail out and raised it to her. She wiped her eyes on it, blew her nose, looked at it, and laughed. "I blew my nose on your shirt."

"You Okie."

I looked up to see Kate limping up the stairs. She had gotten a bruise somewhere, I think she fell against a table at Spago. Her glittery dress was open down the back, all the way to the sweet, shadowy crack of her ass. Her back was as smooth and white as church marble. Sometimes I loved her so much I wished I could leap right out of my body, didn't have to take the time to get up and run to her, transmogrify, shoot around corners, like light, to wherever she was. She was limping badly; I hadn't noticed that before. She was singing, too, a mournful Mexican song she picked up in the barrio on her last picture. Ah, querida. I watched her ascend the stairs and it was as if she were ascending to heaven, I was so filled with love for her, so surprised and happy for her, so rosy and entertained. Then she turned on the stairs, swirling in her slow, graceful way, and her white, muscular arm lifted, drifting in my direction, a light, casual wave, as if she were on a ship pulling out from the dock. I was with her on this, and happy with myself because I saw what she was up to, and I thought how good it was to be in love, how good it was to love someone so well you knew what they were going to do next—or you didn't know, and it was delicious not to know—and I was a dumbfounded, drunk man, happy to be in the movies, happy to get a job in his hometown industry where every morning when you came onto the set there was a cup of steaming coffee waiting, and bacon and eggs if you wanted, and someone you had probably known twenty years took your face in her hands and began to prepare it for the day, and men and women swirled around you like fish in an aquarium, taking care of business, and everyone wanted to get the job done.

In a minute Kate came back down the stairs naked. There was a long greenish bruise on the top of her thigh. Her skin from her face down across her breasts was flushed. I leaned back from Veronica and smiled at her. Veronica turned her head. "Ah, empress," she said, but her smile was kind.

Kate sighed and grinned. There were dark smudges under her eyes, but she wasn't giving up yet, she was going on. "You want me to come with you?" I said.

"No."

Veronica pushed herself wearily up off the sofa. "I think I'll fix some breakfast," she said.

There's a famous photograph of an actress sprawled exhausted in a lounge chair beside her pool in the early daylight, her new Oscar beside her. She's beautiful and alone and happy. You can see the glamor and glory of the situation, you can see the revels in her face, and the joy, there at the intersection of desire and accomplishment, as the clear morning light rises around her. For me it's a picture that captures the heart of things out here, captures the pretense and the hard work and silky romance of it all: we would all wish for this moment and wish to look this way when the moment came. But the photographers following Kate had long since fallen by the wayside. She moved too fast, she moved too quickly from place to place, for anyone to follow her for long.

Ready to let go myself, I trailed a little farther, out onto the deck, caught up with her at the stairs, turned her with a touch, and kissed her. Her lipstick had left a faint residue on her mouth that tasted of cherries. She leaned briefly against me; we looked out at the ocean, toward the empty side of things. The ocean was oily, a low swell walking in on its knees, falling clumsily onto the gray sand. A few rocks poked out of the high tide like the heads of seals. A flight of blackbirds passed over, heading off for their day's work. Westward there was still plenty of night, a few stars hanging on. Kate's hand gripped my shoulder, I could feel her strength, something under the skin as if she had done harsh labor all her life, not the smooth, coagulant muscles of the exercisers but something much stonier in her body, a gristle and imperviousness that only time and work could put there. My stevedore.

She let me go, rocked slowly back onto her heels, and swung forward until her face swam past focus and tapped me lightly, forehead to nose. She held my face to hers. "You're silly and earnest and concerned," she said. "It comes naturally to you."

"I guess so. I'm crazy about you."

"I'm crazy about you too. But I'm not a hometown girl."

Her elbows were scuffed and there were scratches on the back of her hands. There was a crust of blood between the toes of her right foot. As she talked to me she beat a soft steady rhythm with her fingers against the porch rail. I caught her eye again, but her gaze slid past me. I said, "You can't slow down at all, can you, ever?"

"No," she said, "I can't."

She opened her mouth wide, bit the air. "Everywhere around me," she said, "I see the girl I was, and life as it was, I see everyone I have loved so far, and every place and everything that happened. And I'm falling through it all, like falling from a tower through sheets of painted glass. I lie awake at night—you lie awake with me sometimes . . ."

"Yes . . ."

". . . and I feel myself falling, and I hear the glass breaking as

I crash through each painted sheet of it, and my whole body is so tense I think I am going to burst out of my skin, because I know any second the glass will cut me, and I know that what I'm falling through, what's about to cut me, is the life of everyone I have ever loved, is everything I've ever seen and loved . . ."

"We're all going down."

"Yes. And I don't understand why everyone doesn't run screaming into the streets. I don't understand why we all don't go mad."

"We don't think about it."

"How can you not? I don't understand that. I don't think about anything else. I'm falling; any minute my body will be ripped open—there's nothing to catch on to."

"We *would* go mad if we thought that way."

"Your father thinks like that."

"I don't believe he does." Clement, from location in Africa, had sent two truckloads of flowers, flowers in dump trucks that dumped their loads in our front driveway. I had to hire help to shovel us out. "He's not falling; he's just hungry."

"That's just another word for it. Every one of those words— hunger, thirst, lust, greed, desire—they're all just words for the same thing. You hear it on the radio, and you hear it in all these helicopters going overhead, and you hear it in the Saturday night gunplay, and you hear it inside the room with you late at night when you can't sleep—this demand, this crying out for what we can't live without, this something to grab hold to that we can't quite catch—you hear the cries of us falling through space."

"I'm tired now."

"Yes. Exhaustion—that's what we hope for. But some of us never get tired."

I knew I was very tired because I had begun to think of Bobby again, I thought of the thin, beautiful boy in his bedroom on a sunny morning out here, leaning into a rifle. I wondered if the fine, black hair he had always worn long had flopped over his face as he bent down to the muzzle.

"Falling," I said. "I'm about to fall down."

"It's good you have me to catch you."

"I thought it was the other way around."

"Ah, Willie," she said, "my little thinker."

"Put it on glide, darling."

"Let it drift. Drift, yes—but that's only your word for the same thing. That's your greed."

"My eyes are crossing."

"Go lie down."

If someone had overheard us then, he would have thought she was a woman of great autonomy and decisiveness, a woman who had looked terror in the face and lived, but if he had looked in *her* face, he would have seen something else. The quick, spasmic smile that jerked across her mouth, the way her eyes narrowed and then opened wide, would have revealed something her words didn't. I saw it as she began to turn away from me. It was something like fear, and in a court of law I would have said it was fear, but it was something else, something generated beyond fear, something that appears after you have lived your whole life scared to death, and it is not the fear itself. It was what I had seen looking back at me over Veronica's shoulder the afternoon she took me out into the chaparral and we made love the first time, after Bobby died, after she became my mother's lover; it was the look, that way of being, that lives like a dark abiding presence in the world that existed before any of us were here, the world of the trees and the animals, who waited for us to show up; it was a look of ravenous, reckless sadness, of such famishment that gazed at, given in to, it would turn us to stone. It was there for less than a second, but it was in her eyes. It must have been the look in the eyes of the Titans as Zeus and the Olympian gods swept them from power, the look in Priam's eyes as he watched from the towers of Troy as Achilles dragged his son by his heels around and around the walls; it was a look I had seen in my mother's eyes, and in my brother's; it was the look at the Gates of Eden that the wild tangle of perfect creation gave us as we glanced back a last time before we stumbled forth into the raw fields of our fate. In that look was everything we once loved and everything that once loved us, everything we were going to have to live without and everything that would live without us, forever.

Come, then gone. She touched my cheek lightly with the heel of her hand, spun on her good leg, and limped away down the long flight of white stone steps.

I leaned over the rail and watched her go, watched her nimbly, briskly limping, make her way to the water. Up toward town porch lights shined silvery in halos of mist. Behind the houses, up the ripped, bushy hills, the songbirds had begun to crackle into life. A truck changed gears up on the highway. Before me, the sea was coming alive, teaching its small morning lesson in the white line of surf, typing out the same story over and over. Down there was a lightness, a thin place in the rubble of waves, something in the mind maybe, or in the mind's tendency to make of the observed world something we can understand and live with, something that seemed to slip out of the bushes each dawn, cross the hard, yellow sand and disappear into the water. I was hanging upright at the edge of sleep, at the edge of hallucination. I thought of our wedding, which had taken place at a truck-stop chapel outside Vegas with Veronica and Earl and two cowboys in spangled chaps witnessing after we fled Clement's rough attempts to produce the affair himself. He had wanted to bulldoze an amphitheater out of a hill behind the Pima house, transform it to an Eden bower and invite all of Hollywood. We'll invite two thousand people, he said; it'll be bigger than *The Ten Commandments.* A ploy it was, a ploy to impress Hollywood with his ability to stage another perfect extravaganza; and a ploy, it struck me now, to impress Kate, the new star. She danced in the waves naked, as she had danced out on the highway after the wedding. In the merciless sunshine, the Mohave zooming away on either side, she had rushed out of the chapel with the preacher's final words in her ears, my kiss on her lips, and danced, her skirts lifted about her hips, in the middle of Highway 86. Cars filled with deadbeats and the tanned riffraff of the retired set, with gamblers and touts, spun past her without stopping. She had waved at them, whirling, shouting good fortune to them as if she were a queen sending off ecstatic, doomed knights to the Crusades. Earl, clasping his hands as if he were squeezing out the life of some bug caught between them as he watched her, had said, leaning against me as if he wanted to push me down, You'd better watch out, Buster—you'd better learn how to protect yourself. I had thrown my head back and laughed.

Veronica came out bearing coffee on a tray, and we slid in beside each other on the flowered double chaise. We passed the sugar, sipped the coffee, looked around. I could see Kate stepping around in the cold surf, running toward the smooth-backed waves, running back. Her body was as white as a statue's. Veronica touched my hand with her cup. I said Ow.

"You're so happy," she said. "You just love being the director."

"I do?"

"You just love it."

"I like the spotlight turned off me."

"You never noticed it was on you."

"You're so smart."

She sipped her coffee, making a slurping sound.

"I wish you wouldn't make that noise," I said.

"I've been making it all my life."

"You sound like you come from the country."

"I do come from the country."

"You come from the rich Hollywood ranchero life."

"It was in the country."

"Why do you say I'm being a director?"

"Because you are. You've got your little beauty out there dancing in the surf. You've brought her cleanly along."

"You ought to listen to yourself sometime. You sound like you make everything up before you say it."

"Some of us think before we speak."

"You're so jealous."

"I'm not jealous."

"Yes you are. You can't stand it that Kate came out of nowhere . . ."

". . . out of everywhere . . ."

"See—you can't stand that she came out of nowhere and in two years has climbed right up the movie mountain and taken the prize. I see you, girl. It just burns your ass."

She ran her tongue around her lips, plucked a hair out of the corner of her mouth. "Now whose is this?"—looking at it. "I'm not jealous. I got over being jealous ten years ago." She sighed. "I am a little tired, though."

Her first husband had been a bandleader; the traveling broke her spirit and she left him. Her second had been a still photographer who became a producer, using a good bit of her money. When it looked as if he wasn't going to get any more, he left her, in the wake of a guitar-playing actress who had a brief vogue as a singing horror goddess in drive-in pictures. She'd been by herself now for the last four years, something of a sadness for her, but if the truth were known, an easement for me.

"What have you got to be weary about?" I said. "You're the best-known woman in Hollywood. Restaurant mogul, everybody's friend."

"That'll tire you out."

"You love it. Everybody tells you their secrets. You're like a priest. The Hollywood confessor."

"I know. And I don't like it anymore. I'm tired of hearing about everyone's sleazy little peccadilloes."

"Well, I'll keep my mouth shut from now on."

"I wish you would."

She snuggled against me, pulled my face down, and kissed me on the lips.

"Get away from me, girl."

She pulled back. "You tease."

I grinned at her. "You got a little something between your teeth. An ant, I think."

"Get away from me." But she checked.

I lay back. The day soared over our heads chasing dark. We would go home soon, turn the phones off, get into bed, and sleep until dusk.

Veronica pushed up on an elbow. "Kate didn't take a towel with her."

"So?"

"I don't see her."

I didn't see her either. The wave line chopped lightly at the sand. The water was gray-green, coming on under clear sky to blue. A plank raft a couple hundred yards out bobbed slowly, empty. I got up and went to the rail. The rail was dry, no dew. A morning glory vine, a few of the flowers open already like tissue bugles, wound around the posts, trailing along the top of the rail. The beach was empty coming and going.

"She's not out there, is she?" Veronica said.

I looked around at her. She had tied her long hair back with a bright red scarf. "Have you two conspired?"

"Never happen, amigo."

"Then where is she?"

"Maybe she took a walk?"

"Why did you say she didn't take a towel?"

"I don't know."

"Where is she?"

"Maybe she trotted up to Jennie's."

"At six-thirty in the morning? She doesn't go to Jennie's by herself."

"She's a free spirit."

"Jesus, Veronica."

I ran down the steps. The sand was crusted, soft underneath. Half a dozen pigeons bobbed along near the rocks. The beach was empty, even the joggers disappeared. For a second the whole world seemed empty; I had come back from a sleep to find everyone gone. Northward, the beach curved in toward the ochre cliffs; beyond the thrust of land there was more beach, but the terrain was too rough for her to have gone that way. Southward, the strand sank into mist, but there was no one down there either. My heart began to beat hard. I waded into the surf and called her name. A black-and-white tern sank and rose, veering along the tide line. I was frightened, as if something I had feared was about to arrive. But I had been through this before. There were many nights when she didn't come home, and there was the movie world that took her away, took us both away; she had run off into the mountains the time I took her into the Sierras, come back only after I stopped looking. But still I was afraid. The water dashing at my ankles was cold. Even in summer the cold stabbed through to the bone.

I came out of the water, headed down the beach toward town. I wasn't going far, but I wanted to do something. I remembered the time as a child, six years old, I had walked away from my mother's beach house and disappeared. I wasn't going anywhere, one thing just led to another. I found leafy ropes of kelp, an abalone shell, a dead skate. I walked all the way to town, two miles, came up through the park under the big oaks to the post office where Jimmy Moran, a famous comedy actor, found me and drove me home. He told jokes the whole way, jokes in which the names of things were twisted to make them sound funny. This is what I do, he said, and made a funny face. I do it all day long, he said, sometimes by the time I get home, my face is stuck. That scared me; I didn't want my face to get stuck. He saw I was scared and patted my head and squeezed my thigh and said, That's all right, kid, don't worry, it's just a joke. We didn't really like each other much. When I got home my mother gave me a small whipping that I ran away from, around and around the breakfast room table, until she stopped, laughing with tears running down her cheeks.

Now I thought it was the same story with Kate; she had wandered off, following a line of seaweed, a figment in her brain. I didn't want to think anything else, though what I didn't want to think came on anyway. I am telling this so much later but I can remember it, remember the smell of salt in my nose, the jagged lines of kelp, brassy on the gray sand, the way my heart beat in my chest like angina. The distance stayed the distance, the ocean flopping stupidly in. The thing about the ocean is you can make anything you want come out of it. You can make maidens sliding along on silver chariots, you can make magnificent war horses riding in on the waves, you can make golden airplanes rise out of the surf, their propellers whirring. But I couldn't make my wife come up out of it.

Then I saw a guy out on his porch, this snappy house up the way, I noticed him. I angled up there; he was naked, taking a leak over the white deck rail. He hailed me, waving, and went on pissing. I had never seen him before. I asked if he'd noticed a woman come along there. He answered in an English accent, a Midlands accent I think, that no he hadn't seen a woman, but earlier he had seen two people in black suits running. No, I said, she would be a woman alone, a naked woman. I would certainly remember that, he said. He was skinny, he had narrow shoulders, he pressed his belly forward like a boy, shaking the last drops off his ropey cod. I can help you look for her, he said congenially. He looked down at himself. Actually, I believe I'm dressed for it.

How long have you been out here?

Just long enough to do this. He shook his hand, a little had gotten on him, I guess. I'm just visiting, he said. Flew in from Hong Kong two weeks ago for the Awards. It was marvelous, though our picture turned up a loser. He cocked his head at me. Would you like to come up for some breakfast? I could tell he knew who I was. Maybe he had seen Kate and stepped back to watch, as if we were a movie.

I thanked him and said no, continued up the beach. The houses, the open-faced mansions and fake plantation manors, the dovetailed soaring structures movie stars and the rich industry moguls of Beverly Hills had thrown up, looked shuttered and depressed, as if only action could give substance and pleasure. Each lifted on black, creosoted pilings, the houses seemed frail. When I came to my mother's, I stopped. A swooping Caribbean number with wide plank porch and louvered shutters, the house where Bobby died, it was closed for the night. In the freshening breeze, the row of potted palms on the second floor balcony trembled. As a young kid I would wake early and walk through the house. The stillness of it amazed me. The gray light in the halls, in the big room off the porch, seemed laden with knowledge and mystery. Through the glass walls I could hear the sea whispering to itself, or to me, I couldn't tell. I would get a piece of fruit from the refrigerator, pull a chair up to the glass, and sit looking out at the blue-and-gray world wondering what grand adventure was about to come crashing out of the surf.

The sand at the bottom of the beach steps had been disturbed. Small, narrow footprints led up to the porch. I followed them, wondering what she had in mind coming up here. The porch, back from the steps, was uncovered, a few white metal chairs set around a large glass table; the other part, where there was a mahogany-and-brass bar, was covered with a striped green awning.

Kate was there, lying on a sofa in a white robe thick as a polar bear suit; my mother was with her, sitting in a blue armchair.

"Well," I said, "it's a pleasure to find you two ladies out so early in the morning." My mother looked at me with strain in her eyes. She was wearing a blue nightgown, hunched forward, elbows on knees, like a workman. Kate, plush, fatigued, smiled at me. She wore dark glasses from under which leaked two glistening tear lines. "How you doing, girl?" I said.

My mother rose. "It's time to take your wife home, I think," she said flatly. There was anger in her voice.

"What's going on?"

Jennie made a small smacking sound. "It's too early in the morning to go into it," she said.

I sat down on the sofa, took Kate's bare feet in my hands. They were as cold as ice. "I thought you were lost."

She drew her feet away. "You don't always have to follow me."

"I don't know," I said, "maybe I do."

"It wears me out."

"Veronica just said she was worn out too."

My mother leaned back against the ebony bar rail. "This is what occurs," she said, "after you win big prizes."

I smiled at her—beautiful she was, her long black hair streaming over her thin shoulders. "All-night revels."

"Griefs and emptiness," she said, "this exhaustion. You want to fly forever, but you can't."

I wondered for the hundredth time, what it had been like for my mother, that moment in the year my brother Bobby died, when she realized she had crossed over into the downhill world, nothing much ahead but the dark woods and memories. Had she noticed it, tried to shake it off?

"You ready to go, girl?"

Kate rubbed her eyes under the glasses. "I might as well."

I helped her to her feet, and as I did so my mother rose too. Breeze caught in her gown so that it fluttered out around her like a cape. I saw the shape of her body, and I remembered how Bobby used to like to watch her coming down the stairs with the light behind her, how he would stand at the bottom, a look of foolish delight on his face, watching as her body, neatly outlined, floated down toward him. The gown blew back and I could see the corroded shape of her that still under only one thinness of cloth looked supple and fetching. She saw me looking, and the same old look of hauteur and appeal came into her eyes. "There are some things," she said, looking past me at Kate, "that no matter how many prizes you win you can't have. You can't have them even if you get them locked into your own arms. Even if you get them away, out into some desert a thousand miles from everything else; even then you can't have them."

Kate cocked her glasses down with one finger. Her wet crystal blue eyes gleamed. She smiled. The smile was predatory, triumphant. But Jennie, star that she was, did not crumple under it. Her full mouth trembled, and she touched the place under her jaw that she had touched a hundred times in movies, and her skin seemed to shimmer with vulnerability, but her eyes were hard with disdain, with the simple, direct, unbreakable will she had brought to the cameras and so to the world for twenty-five years of her working life, a look hammered out in the sooty streets of

Glasgow, the look I am sure she had given my father when, after the almost-divorce broke him, he had crawled on his knees in front of her sobbing, begging her to let him into her bed one more time.

Kate bared her teeth. "Only a god could stop me," she said, spun, and bounded down the steps. Her bruised leg buckled as she hit the sand, but she caught herself on the rail, ran out into the lifting sunlight. I kissed my mother lightly on her dry cheek, marveling, and followed behind. "Thank you, Jennie," Kate called, "I'll bring the robe back as soon as I can."

My mother's voice seemed to come from far away, from another era. "Keep it," she said.

"What was that all about?" I asked as we made our way up the beach. Kate limped away from me, moving faster wounded than I moved whole.

"Something—that look she gave me, Clement told me to watch out for that look."

"I've seen it a hundred times. She acts through it, but she means it."

"He said it could split me open, he said it could break me, but it wasn't so bad."

"Depends, I guess sometimes, on what's called it forth."

"Couldn't be worse for her."

The strand was still empty, but now music played somewhere among the spindly houses, there was a slamming of doors. From the hills, among myrtle bushes and yucca flares, came the morning cry of doves.

She began to run, limping. I let her go. She drifted to the waterline, stopped, bent at the waist, and pressed her hands flat into the slurry surf. I caught up. "What was it you wanted to tell her?"

Still bent, she patted her cheeks with salt. She ran her hands through the water. "No matter how bold it's been, how big and muscular, it winds up like this—this geezering. This whisper."

"Are you talking about Jennie or the ocean?"

"The ocean." She danced away on her good leg. "Even if it comes in strong, even if it rides a storm in a hundred feet high—tidal wave—all you have to do is step back a little, and it falls at your feet whimpering."

"It's strong enough where it lives."

She winked at me. "That's the problem, ain't it? That's where the trouble we get into comes from. If we go out on it. If there's something there we want bad enough to go out on it for."

"How did you get Jennie upset?"

"I told her—among other things—to come off the baloney. The old ruined actress bit. She's gotten so good at it she's forgotten it's an act."

I laughed. "I'll bet she liked hearing that."

"I believe she wanted to punch me." She blew her breath out, pressed her wide hand flat on her chest. Her nails were bright red. "She's a tough woman. The way you boys play the game it's a wonder she's alive at all."

I looked at her, at the vivid, bony face, the wild, shorn, white hair, the body almost tamed by the capacious robe as thick as a bearskin, and at that moment I would have followed her even if she was on her way to the bottom of the ocean.

"Maybe," I said, "it's how she keeps her spirits up."

"You can't keep your spirits up by sitting around thinking about yourself."

"You believe she does that?"

"She came downstairs with her Oscar in her hand."

"She probably wanted to give it to you."

"She was already up. I just caught her on the way out. She said she was going to throw it in the ocean."

"She'd still have one to spare." I looked at the ocean, coming on into blue. "She just wants someone to be kind to her and someone to be kind to."

"That's your job, isn't it?"

"Yours too, girl. If it's anybody's *job*."

She bent, skeeted water at me. "Here's some kindness," she said, grinning.

But there was something steely in her, something outraged. I could see it. It was in her muscled back, in the faint, razory lines around her eyes, in the way her mouth, the lips set straight one on the other, thinned and hardened. It was only later I understood that this had to do with Clement. He was off in Africa making a picture for the Italians, beating up black men for recreation, seducing and threatening actors, reducing his crew to mutiny or to slavery—it didn't matter to him—and though just the day before I had stood at the edge of my driveway watching men shovel poppies and roses into the back of a truck, I did not see the heavy shape of him rising like a juggernaut from out of the smelly blooms, I did not hear his coarse shouts of passion, and I did not suspect that Jennie White, on the sea deck of the cottage my brother had launched himself out of into the starry heavens, had just now received the first faint prologue to a story that would explode like a bomb at the center of our lives, that this woman, who made my skin crawl with desire, had explained to her, in a manner no one later could call her to account for, that it was not now the son, or only the son she wanted, but the father.

"Why don't I carry you to the house?" I said.

She pulled away. "I don't guess I want you to. This is the night I want to go all the way by myself. Until I fall down. I want to go on until I fall down."

"You look like you're close to it."

"Not yet, Bosco."

She whirled and raced away, running cleanly, as if her bruised leg had healed. I watched her run away from me, and I thought, watching, that no matter how fast I moved I couldn't gain ground on her. It was two years and I knew already that something in me was growing tired, was wearing out. That's the way it is when you get near the bold, flashing ones. They bring light into the room, but after a while you want the dark again. I felt a meanness entering me. I wondered where it came from. Whether it came from the world or was something of my own manufacture. Why was it so familiar? And why was it so strong? And why are we born with the knowledge—fitfully, slowly recognized—that it is our job here on this grubby planet to keep hatred and despair from taking over our hearts? In a world where anything goes?

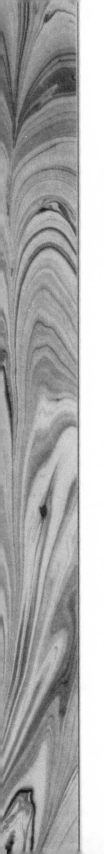

BOOK
THREE

THERE WERE LONG periods after that when I didn't see Kate. Her rocket took off and it carried her to distant worlds. We talked on the phone, calling from South America or Texas or Aix-en-Provence, speaking dramatically and fervently to each other as we watched Greek priests leading a funeral procession, or a family of redheaded girls file by toward the rocky beach outside Dubrovnik, or flat on our backs in hotel rooms in South Dakota or Manila, made promises and plans as makeup artists transformed our faces into the demented or the aged, as directors wheedled script changes out of tired writers, as assistants ran by carrying costumes and cups of coffee.

Standing under an umbrella in the rain in Madagascar, talking to me, so she said, as government soldiers frisked and beat a boy whose crime appeared to be that he wore American glasses, she swore eternal love to me, and I swore it back to her. From the Hotel Montana in Paris, as a rock band pounded its beat against the walls, we discussed patio furniture; from a pay phone outside a truck stop in Cherokee, Oklahoma, speaking to her as she painted her toenails orange on a balcony overlooking the Truk lagoon, where even now, so she said, oil slicks from the hundred Japanese ships sunk there during World War II shone like paint on the water, we discussed tax problems, and what to do with the dogs she'd collected, and who it was thought up banana pudding, and how it had happened that we were always so far from each other, and how far love seemed to reach when there was no other way to live it.

She began to make videos and send them to me. They were, at first, only simple recitations, barely moving pictures of her sitting on a bed talking, but soon they became more elaborate, soon they became productions she worked at, episodes in which she played parts that grew more involved and strange as time went on. For some of us, the dark will always have strange shapes in it, and our lives become our response to these shapes. We run

197

from them, or we learn to talk to them, or we pray to them, or we try to become like them, or we pretend they aren't there; Kate and I were among those who waked from fitful sleep into dark rooms to see odd, cavorting forms moving about, who saw great shapes standing in darkness watching us. For me, I guess, there was always a kind of protection that came from family and position, from the continuity of generations lived out in a familiar world, but for Kate, who had cut herself loose from her past, this was not the case. In her videos she began to explore what lived at the rims of her life; she began to describe the shapes, the odd characters that stepped forth into the circle of her looking. I know how some days the rain looks tragic, or how in every face you can see the death to come; I know how even sunshine can carry disaster, but for Kate it seemed that these were not just points of view or fleeting moods, but acts of perception, of accurate seeing. The worlds she described, the fears and desires she ticked off her fingers like errands she intended to run, became parts she played.

Now, instead of phone calls, there were scenes acted, passages in which cameras, held by men I didn't know, recorded her sitting in a sling atop a schooner mast in the Bay of Biscay, planting rice in Thailand, swimming naked under a waterfall in Ponape. In some she was in costume, in others, dressed in jeans and a T-shirt, she played parts that appeared to be elaborate fabrications devised to shock. She told me of her past, adding bright chips to the pile that had already begun to totter; she spoke the words of crushed and bedraggled women, of princesses, of gallant souls standing up for what they believed in. The parts revealed and concealed her at the same time. She had, as my mother had, the ability to inhabit creations distant from her own self, but through which her own electric living presence shined. As each creation became more elaborate and strange, she began to show more of what was behind it. She seemed to want to show herself entirely, but she wanted the self she showed to contain everything in the world. From behind paint, buried in layered costume, in vivid landscapes through which light poured like lava, her gaze peered out at me, and her voice, rising and falling like some flood in the body, chanted and trilled, telling stories that seemed to erase themselves as they were told, like a series of lights coming on and going off in a series of rooms, the light, chased by its own dark, racing to keep up with itself, to fill in the nooks and decorations of each room, before the pursuing tide of dark caught up.

For me, as I watched her leap like a sleek white dolphin through the hoops of her creation, the old tug of nostalgia and longing began. Into her haunted, predatory eyes came looks, glances that seemed to be the same as those I had discovered years ago in my own house, looks that had appeared like signs on the faces of my parents and my brother. From my own dreams then peered faces that were the doubles of the faces she showed me in her videos. I waked hearing her words in my ears, but they were words spoken by Bobby, or by my mother as she entered the Malibu house after a day's filming. I heard my father's troubled rumblings, my grandfather's whinnying laughter, Veronica's gravelly, anarchic wit; and there were times, evenings after a day's work, when I lay on a sofa in some hotel room in Memphis or Seattle, as outside my window a salty rain pelted the earth, or a dry wind creaked and keened in bent pines, that I heard my own voice speaking, telling a story of betrayal and disaster so terrible, so real, that I had to get up and walk out into the lighted places where others of my kind cavorted and whirled, placating the rubbery demons of their own lives, packing a few more sacks of sand against the attacks that raged around them in the dark night that we all wished day would soon rise out of.

How quickly we reverse ourselves; how quickly what we once threw from us we turn to embrace like a lover. The focal drift sharpened, shunted in tightly. What had been fatigue turned to longing. Surfeit, as it will, transformed itself into desire. Our apartness became our means. Our means became our lives. And our lives became scenes played at a distance, across which our voices grew fainter.

One day I lay down on a sofa on Veronica's side porch and watched all afternoon as blue jays pecked the fruit of a loquat bush. The jays' gray shit stained the leaves and the round orange fruit. The air smelled of cinnamon and plumeria blossoms. I could hear the ocean off in the distance, slapping the shore. Inside the house, Kate's taped voice droned. Upstairs, Veronica prepared for the evening shift. I had lain on sofas like this for years, dreaming, but now the dream was gone. The drift was gone, and the easy float of days. I watched the jays. They pecked at the fruit as if they wanted to kill it. Their harsh cries filled the air. Then I saw my life, I saw it roll in the yard like a dog. I saw the coarse hair, the dark, pleading eyes, the stained belly. I saw what it wanted.

THE PHONE RINGS. It's not Kate, it's not my brother calling from the grave, it's not my father begging for forgiveness. It's Kwilecki, the detective, calling on Kate's private line. The green clock face says 6:00 A.M. Out over the basin, day is putting on its yellow clothes. "Yes," I say, "how did you get this number?"

"We're the police," he says. "I thought you might be awake."

Why did he think that? "What is it, my friend?"

"We found your woman."

A cold blade touches my heart. "What woman?"

"You got another one? The one we been talking about. You remember?"

"Oh. How is she?"

"Somebody burned her up."

"Oh no."

"Yeah."

"Can you hold on a minute?"

"Sure."

I get up and open the French doors. I breathe deeply, trying to loosen the constriction in my chest. There is a tight band of metal around my head. The morning air smells of magnolias. I thought he meant Kate. A coyote barks, a snatched, strangled sound. I take deep breaths, stretch. All right.

Then: "Okay," I say into the white receiver, "what happened?"

"We found her, her and the car, too—black Corvette; that's how we know it's her—both of them burned up."

"Who was she?"

"We don't know. She's a Jane Doe in a black Corvette, but she fits your description—or the setup does. We won't know any more until forensics gets off their ass. She's a toasted muffin."

"Jesus."

He whistles, speaks to someone else. "Hey," he says, coming back on, "you ever seen somebody fried?"

"Not outside the movies."

"Why don't you come on down here?"

"Where did you find her?"

"Off Mulholland—the old part, one of those little dirt roads down into Santa Monica Rec. You know that area?"

"Sure. That's out of your jurisdiction, isn't it?"

"Yeah, but we're cooperating. Come on down here. She's at Sprucewood, at the morgue. You know where that is?"

"I know." I look around; my throat is dry, nothing to drink in sight. "I know that place." I had worked there, twice actually, on two different pictures. In one, in a movie rage, I had thrown a man's body off a slab, dragged the corpse out by its heels. The actor playing the detective had said, grinning at me: "Once they're dead you like to hurt 'em, don't you." To Kwilecki I say, "Is this a ploy? Do you think I'm connected to this?"

"Right now you're the only person in the world who's seen this woman with her face on."

"You're a coarse guy, Detective."

"Like I say, she's a cinder. But there's something else."

"What is it?"

"She's got something of yours."

"Of mine? How could that be? What is it?"

"You tell me."

"Ah. I see."

"We just need to clear this up."

"I'll get some coffee and come on down."

"Okay. Soon as you can. I'll be here."

THROUGH THE DARK house and out, into oceanic day. Clouds raise what they can of the Pacific into the sky, to bring it to us, little conflicted beings beginning to scurry, but soon the maneuver will falter and fade, the hot sun coming up over my shoulder will sweep them into nothing. There are places on this road, which seems to fall to its knees under the trees, where you could think you were driving through the original world. A bend where two huge eucalyptus lean above a rocky outcropping, a stand of cane, a swirl of myrtle bushes, and for a second, if your mind tends this way, you can see the world of this mountain range and basin as it was two hundred years ago, the dry stillness of it under the canopy that is cut by the hard sunlight as if by a gold knife; smell of dust and eucalyptus and pine. But there, now, contemporaneous with this moment, at the end of a white cement driveway, a minor movie star, a man with the look of urban violence in his face, sits on the trunk of a red Mercedes sports car holding his bare feet in his hands. Mexican maids, dressed in starched white uniforms, get off minibuses, swinging handbags colored like rainbows. At the bottom of the hill, in a white robe, still on his feet, Buster the Black Christ totes his cross made of oak branches wrapped in Christmas lights. I wave and he waves back, the grin of forgiveness and mercy lighting his face, ready to offer me the good news.

At the corner of Fairfax and Sunset lost boys pass a cup of red liquid among themselves, stamping their feet in the cool morning, for all the world, skinned versions of their factory worker, their good lawyer fathers, waiting for the bus. The sun is rising into their faces, it will shine robustly through the curtainless windows into the dusty, reeking rooms they sleep the world away in this afternoon, and they will rise into its smoky, leathered light, stretching, testing their corroded, already worn-out bones, hearing, as if from another room, the little chirps death makes as it moves about the house. Later they will go out on the shaky porches and lean into the breeze that is bringing the odors of rancid garbage and flowers up like ruined plunder out of the barrio, and like old men fighting off disease, they will try to remember what it was that brought them here, who it was they spoke so earnestly to last night in the cornered darkness of an anonymous club, that one who pulled them brusquely aside so that for a second they felt their hearts almost give way, someone they had hurt maybe, stolen from or lied to, but who, as recognition bobbed like a dead fish in their minds, became—clattering, sweating—only another version of themselves, some cramped, destroyed child, gasping for air, crying out for breath as he went under, drowning.

And there at the bus stop on Sunset and Collegio, in front of a new denim and leather outlet, where the old Paradise Hotel used to be, where as teenagers we danced to the music of Maurice Williams and the Zodiacs, and Bettina Levitz, a girl with hair the color of Gene Autry's horse, slapped Veronica for speaking to her boyfriend, and then slapped me for interfering, there, risen from the dead, I guess, this fine late spring morning, is Miss Lucy Porterfield, my kindergarten teacher.

I pull over, shoot the window down, and call to her. Huge in a gray tent dress patterned with green and purple triangles, gray headed—perhaps there are single kinked hairs on her chin, a sourness on her lips pressed like a knife cut into the meal of her face—she leans toward the car, blinking the sunlight off her lids, ready to straighten this *Schiesskopf* out. "Miss Lucy," I say, delighted, "it's Will Blake. Can I give you a lift?"

She places a fat, liverish hand on the windowsill, grasping it firmly, as if she might tear the door off. Her bright, black eyes that seemed to me the year I was five years old to be the eyes of a benevolent goddess, the eyes of a queen, glare defiantly at me, shining like coals on white cloth. "What is it you want?" she says.

"It's Will Blake, Miss Lucy. I'm on my way downtown—do you need a ride?"

She slaps the side of the car, bares her mossy teeth. "I'll tell you," she says loudly, "you people better quit pestering me. I've said it and I'll say it again—I hadn't got to go anywhere with you."

I put on the hand brake, get out of the car so she can see me. "Miss Lucy, I was in your kindergarten class. It's me, Will Blake." Maybe I'm only one of thousands, one of the nameless mass of wet-assed kids who passed through the flowery studio where we cut animals out of construction paper and played blocks and cymbals in the rhythm band. She told us fairies lived in the tops of the live oaks beyond the front porch. Maybe it was a dream I had. "See," I say, "I've grown up."

She glares at me without recognition. There are others here at the bus stop, however, who know me; they've seen my pictures. Miss Lucy steps back from the car. She dismisses me with an upright wave of her hand, a gesture I am sure I remember from thirty-three years ago. Why would I expect she would remember? "Go on along," she says wearily, her voice gusting up out of the tent of her body as if it is being squeezed from her. She is old, and the bitter lines around her narrow mouth are permanent. I can picture her in her darkened living room, her meaty forearms on her knees, talking back sourly to the television. It makes me want to weep. I take out a pen, tear a scrap of paper from my notebook, and scribble my name and phone number. I swing around the end of the car and offer it to her.

"This is my name and home phone number. See—Will Blake, your old student. You can call me if you need anything."

She accepts the paper from me, looks at it in her cupped palm. Her creased, fat brow furrows briefly. She brings the paper close to her mouth, spits on it, and tosses it away. Spit-weighted, the paper twirls to the ground. "Go on, boy," she says, making the same dismissive gesture.

And then in this place, vaguely but accurately, under the spindly Washington palms, near a hibiscus bush that is pushing out masses of bright red blossoms, I come a ways toward myself, only a step, but as through ground fog, I see myself, this selfish, gallant, hapless helper of the afflicted. In my eyes, without explanation, is my one-legged woman amorata, I see her on the beach, the bent pink prosthetic leg tossed down, see her standing balanced on the yellow sand. The picture sharpens, then fades. Shortly after Kate won her big award, my father began to call. He began to call Kate, begging her—he had no pride in these matters—to do a picture with him.

I bend down, pick up the piece of paper. Not quite sure of the etiquette, I offer it to Miss Lucy again. A smile crosses her thin lips like a zipper slowly pulled. Miss Lucy shakes her head. "You're still as dumb and useless, Will Blake," she says, "as you were when you were five years old." Her black eyes fix me like a specimen. "I'm doing fine. Run on along, boy."

And so, chastened, put accurately into my place, I slide into my sleek, plushy vehicle and roll on down the street. In the mirror before I turn on Consuela, I see the bus pull up, and catch a glimpse of Miss Lucy lifting her grand bulk up the silver steps.

It is still early, the light is introducing itself humbly to the silver-and-white buildings, it rises in the leaves of oak and palm, glides along the floor of the basin, gathering color from the patchy yards and from the torn sides of hills. A bank of magenta paradise flowers drizzles down the side of an embankment on top of which three stucco houses that look like defeated castles seem to raise themselves into the sunlight. Their fronts are as bright and washed as the faces of schoolchildren. Palms on the ridgeline look like tethered flares. The road slides downhill, sinking toward the railyards, dips below an underpass where when a hard rain comes the water is two feet deep and turns black within hours.

My wife rides my back like a white parrot, chattering, but I don't listen to what she says. We were happy for a time, or if we were not happy, we were excited. It is so easy to confuse excitement and fear. They feel the same. Both penetrate against the will, against the direction of your life. They whack you, hitting you as you come around the corner, like the flat of a sword. Sometimes I can't tell one from the other. I parry, I lunge, I feel the shock in my wrist as the blade enters and strikes bone, I see the dark shape fall: was it one come to kill, or to embrace me—I can't tell.

The morgue is a big green well-lit room, as big as a church basement, and it's in the basement, down a ramp, if you walk, that vehicles negotiate with their dead cargo. Kwilecki meets me in the hall. He looks skinny and tired; there is a tiny crust of white on his chin. He smiles to see me, shakes my hand, introduces his partner, a squat fellow with a country accent whose name I don't quite catch, and then introduces another man, Harvey Madrid, a Hollywood detective, whom I have known for ten years. Harvey was a consultant on a picture I made, and there was a brief time, before we discovered we didn't like each other much, when we would eat dinner together and I would ride with him on his shift, tagging along like a reporter as he visited crime scenes. His hair is sandy like mine and cut short like mine, but his face is heavier, sun worn; his blue irises have a nakedness, and a kind of baffled forthrightness that doesn't go well with the yellowy whites, or with the sunken, scornful corner of his mouth that he works sometimes as if he's chewing gum. He's the city partner for his Ventura County country cousins. He deals with Hollywood types, of which, for the police, I am one. We begin to banter, as if we are friends, but it is halfhearted and a little sad. He doesn't look well.

"I'm surprised you haven't been fired, Harvey," I say.

"I'm surprised they still let you make pictures, Will."

He claps me on the shoulder, a little too hard.

Kwilecki wets his top lip with the lower, sweeps his arm out like a maître d' or a producer. "This way, gents."

Harvey gives him a look. It's his territory. Kwilecki's arm falls.

"Come on through, Will," Harvey says. "You know your way around here."

I follow the cops into the big room, which is bursting with light. The light, from upended neon troughs on the ceiling, spanks stainless steel tables and sinks, rebounds off the walls, shines like streaks of spit on the long silver handles of the corpse lockers. It's as if the light wants to make up for something, fill absence in. There are four or five bodies in the room, a couple undressed in clear plastic shrouds, two bare-assed and lumpy carcasses under the hands of the callow attendants. A Japanese guy with extremely narrow shoulders, sleeves rolled up on smooth forearms the color of ivory, lifts an organ group from the split trunk of a body and sets it on the edge of a sink. The organs are a streaked muddle. Only the heart, the size of a peach, is recognizable. The cut yellow flesh of the trunk is peeled back like the lids of an eye. The place is air-conditioned, frost-conditioned, and antiseptic, but there is a strong cheesy odor, and an odor of stale chemicals, hints of cold meat.

"Harvey," I say, walking beside him—we're the same height, though he has more bulk—"did these guys tell you what's going on?"

"I heard about your scrape." He glances at my hairline. "The scar is very becoming."

"I kind of like it myself. I think it'll give a new tone to my work."

"You pretty boys need a few scars."

"We're just human, Harvey, you know that. Shit and piss, and groan in the dark just like everybody else."

"They just pay you better."

That had been a large part of the prickliness that grew between us, when we worked together. They paid Harvey ten thousand dollars for his advisory work, a goodly sum for a working man. Me they'd paid two million and points. If you thought about it, it'd make you sick, or dangerously angry. Harvey and I would argue about it. He was oddly fraternal for a man who put rules first. He thought actors should be paid like teachers, certainly no more than teachers. Maybe everybody should be on that scale, I said. Yeah, he said, I think you're right. Lower salaries instead of raising them, use the leftover to clean up the world. But he couldn't forgive me for what I made. I could see his point.

He touches my arm, directs me left toward a table near the lockers. Kwilecki and his partner hover close behind. There is a glint in the partner's amber, doglike eye, and I have a second of uneasiness. He looks like a guy who wants to get you close to the swimming pool so he can push you in. I look around; I don't want to light anywhere. I don't want to touch anything. Harvey steers me, I see the table, waist-high, silvery, shining steel under the light weight of a body wrapped in pale green plastic. It's black under the plastic, the body's black. I look at Kwilecki; I am angry. I turn to him, but he has stepped away, retreating into himself though his chest is thrust out like a little last stand. An attendant at the head of the table fingers the shroud's nylon zipper. I am thinking of my grandmother who died in a hospital of old lady's cancer. I left her deathbed to step across the hall into a room where someone else, a skinny codger in blue pajamas, died as I watched. It was a fluke, my being there, but I caught the moment when death rose in his throat and choked him. He did not look peaceful, in fact he looked angry, disappointed, bitter to the end. No one was around; I slid up to him and placed my hand on his chest. It was as springy as an empty cardboard box. There was warmth, but no life. With my thumbs I raised his eyelids. He had dead brown eyes flecked with yellow. He wasn't in there. It was from that room that I heard my grandmother cry out against the end, cry like a hurt child. The cry was sharp and frail, and completely hopeless.

This comes to mind now as I shuffle toward the burned body. The spirit has fled, I am watching. For a moment this woman and I came together. How supple the universe is. It is not a dream, I think, to say the universe is filled with small doors, gates, and passageways we sometimes fall through. You kiss your wife, look out the window, and the man next door is slapping his child. As you drop a coin into a beggar's cup you see the face of a boy who beat you in the fifty-yard dash thirty-five years ago. You come downstairs to find your wife dancing the tango with your father. Surprise ebbs, the shallow fears of youth ebb, you stop expecting much, but then spring comes and the blue flowers of the jacarandas seem to shine with a light of their own making. The bark of a coyote is horribly familiar. You drive away, fleeing the facts of your life, and then, at a stoplight on an ordinary street, a beautiful woman steps from the oleanders and fires three shots into a building. She roars away in a Corvette and you follow, gone mad for a moment or simply curious, or compelled to offer aid, or whipped by instinct to track down the wounded. What is it, you think, that forces us to make order? In a world that can't sustain it? Yes, you think the universe is orderly, but then you walk close to the ocean and it is tattered and random. The sun burns wildly. The stars are rushing toward empty space. The woman you swore to love for the rest of your life leaps from your arms into the arms of another. But here—ah yes—there is a trail of clear reason you might follow. This can be traced back to its source. So you think, so you tell yourself. She confesses her infidelity and you feel the shame of it like bright fires biting your body, but the shame is a clue. You burn with rage, with guilt, with despair, but these are all clues. You yourself have been unfaithful, you have schemed, lied. Was the weld unstable from the beginning? In the dark, confused, sweating, you get down on your hands and knees and feel for the trail. It was here, you recognized it once before, the bare earth track winding away from this fiery place; you strain to find it. But you are not used to this work. You are one who has preferred another approach, or, to put it another way, no approach at all. You, as you have claimed, are a gentleman rider, a drifter, or less grandiloquently, as your wife would have it, a lazybones. You are a local boy; life in this wild, flashing place is familiar to you. Skip it, you say, let it go. But there is a voice calling you, urging you on. A face appears in the window and looks at you with such clarity that you are changed. You rise from the familiar rumpled bed and go out. The face, her face, is gone, fled in the murmuring darkness, but you follow, unable to stop yourself. The path narrows, fades. You call out. There is no answer. You stand in the difficult darkness. Something huge and ravenous begins to touch you everywhere.

Now we sidle up, like drunks afraid they won't be served. The attendant, a boy who looks as if he finished high school just yesterday, greets us with a slender smile. Harvey nods. The attendant, good at this, deftly, indifferently, unzips the bag and draws the panels back.

She lies on her side, crouched into herself, clasping with her whole being whatever's left of her humanness. There's not much. Crusts of blackened skin stick to her shoulders and back, to her thin buttocks, in hunks, like shingles of pine bark. Her hair is burned away, the skin of her skull blackened and split, blistered in places down to the gray, seamed bone. The hands are clutched and clawed, praying under her throat; the skin on the knuckles is darkly translucent. There is the odor of ashes, dead fires, of soot, faint sweetness of roasted flesh. The pot of her burst belly contains the cooked organs.

I step back, something fist-sized going dead in my chest, something else rushing through me to cover it. An immense pain, an animal pain, dog pain, streaks through my body, screaming, accusing. My knees slip and I totter, but this may only be in my mind, because no one catches me, no one seems to notice. The policemen peer at the body with the professional detachment they have sadly earned. They have had their first shocks, they have already walked them, cried them, raged them off.

Harvey pats my shoulder. "They go quick," he says, "in a fire like that. Gasoline."

It is as if her body is a tar pit my eyes suck out of. "How the fuck do you know, Harvey?"

"It's true," he says. "They breathe the fire in and it takes them out"—he snaps his fingers—"like that."

I lean over her—it is all I can do to keep from climbing onto the table with her—and touch a smooth, polished place at her temple. The skin is as silky as fine leather. I once saw, in an exhibit at the UN, a book the Nazis had bound in the cured skin of a murdered Jew. The skin was ivory colored, fine grained, soft and luxurious. In the glass case, among photographs of Buchenwald and Auschwitz, it shone with its own light. The man beside me, a small man in a stained gray suit, leaning against the case, wept copious tears. I thought, There is no limit to what we will do. Nothing is beyond us. Here is a small example: I was curious to know which book it was they had bound so elegantly. I leaned close to see. It was Goethe: *Faust*.

Clowns peering out of smeared, grinning faces, we look and draw back. Inside ourselves we make the sign of the cross, send up small prayers like flares. The Ventura detectives are laughing about something. I turn. "What did you bring me down here for, Detective?"

Kwilecki looks at me. His face is the face of a man who knows the answer to the joke. "Do you recognize her?" he says.

"No."

"She must be your lady."

"How can you know? Because it was a Corvette? There must be ten thousand Corvettes in LA."

"Seventeen thousand seven hundred and eighty-two," Kwilecki's partner says. He licks his fat lips.

"Because of this," Kwilecki says. He reaches into his pocket, pulls out something, opens his hand. It's a small silver nugget in a plastic bag, polished on two sides, that Kate gave me after we finished the picture we made together. On one side is written in ornate script "For Wonder Willie Blake from Katie." On the other, two words, "Extra Love." There is a loop for a chain but it never had one; I carried it in my pocket like a boy carries a lucky buckeye. But she couldn't have taken it; it was still in my pocket—I patted it as I fell—when I climbed the front steps of my father's house.

"Where did you get that?"

"She had it in her mouth."

"I didn't know it was gone. If she took it, she took it when I was laid out."

"Probably. But it indicates something."

"What exactly?"

"That the two of you were likely together."

"Likely? I don't doubt she took it after she shot me, but who knows? Maybe she broke into my house. Maybe I left it somewhere. Maybe it fell out of my pocket." Could that have happened, could I have been mistaken? No. I never lost track of the nugget; it was a talisman; I touched it often. My mind slurs, darkens, but I can remember . . . I think I could remember touching it through my pocket as I came up the steps as my muddy, teeth-baring father loomed above me. I remember, but I don't say anything.

"It's about all we have to go on until we can identify this woman," the detective says.

"Shit—you guys. You're just jokers."

The partner, whose name I still don't know, swells. "This is serious business, Mr. Blake. Harvey here will tell you that."

I glance at Harvey. His face is blank.

"So what do you want? Is it time for me to get a lawyer? You think I'm responsible for this?"

"Look here," Kwilecki says.

He takes a milky plastic glove from the table, pulls it on, and touches the body. "Right here," he says.

He indicates a spot, a small hole just under the shoulder blade. He flicks me a sideways glance. "Look."

"What is it?"

"It's a bullet hole. Somebody shot this woman before he burned her."

"Murder," his partner says, grimacing. "Murder in the first degree."

"Ah," I say, "another ghoulish Hollywood mystery. You guys are going to be on TV."

Kwilecki strips the glove, his mouth twisting with distaste. "There are a number of connections here," he says, "and every one we get an answer to just makes the whole thing dirtier."

"And who am I?" I say. "The mystery perpetrator?"

The partner, the one with pale lips that look like bits of cut sponge, lips that can soak up liquid, says, "Maybe this has some connection to your wife. To her disappearance."

I push away from the table, I tear my eyes away from this reduced, humiliated body. I look him in the face. "What do you know about my wife?"

"She took off, didn't she?"

"That has nothing to do with this."

"Maybe there's some problem. These things happen, people's lives get tangled—love affairs and what all."

"Love affairs? And what all? *Harvey*—Jesus, man, take this goon out of here." Sometimes I feel as if I am tumbling out of my own life, like someone falling from a slow-moving car. I get up, brush myself off, and look around. Where is this? I think. What is going on here? But my impulse is not really to explore. It is to sit and wait.

Harvey gestures to the attendant, who carefully raises the plastic and zips the body up. "This is a serious investigation here," he says, "but maybe we need to take a little break from it." He grins at me. "Why don't we go get some breakfast."

The country boys decline; they've got work to do. They're going, they say, to check out the car, see what they can find. "I don't want to come on too strong, Mr. Blake," Kwilecki says, "but you're in here somewhere with all this. We'd appreciate it if you stayed in town awhile. Until this clears up." Like weather.

"I'll do what I can," I say.

They spin out ahead as Harvey and I come along.

Outside, the big blue day smells of the ocean. It is still early. A slight breeze lifts the upper fronds of some palm trees across the street, lifts them as gently as a lover might. A low rider decorated with tassels and hubcaps in which rhinestones glitter throbs by trailing grainy Mexican music. Toward the south, beyond the metal buildings, beyond Watts, beyond Long Beach and the Queen Mary and the Spruce Goose moldering in its vast hanger, beyond the pier and the breakwaters and San Pedro Bay, the piles of tufted cumulus look like a vast white city, a city that through effort, perseverance, and only a little magic, you might visit. My body creaks from lack of sleep, but it is a living body, capable of lifting and running, capable of lovemaking, of dance steps in the hall, of sight, of shivering at the taste of love. Out of humiliation and failure, out of loss, joy comes, I am sure of it, because at this moment, breathing the fragile, brassy air, I feel life crackle and swell in my body. Poor, poor girl, I think, but the phrase runs in my head—poor, poor girl—like a song, and I am almost happy.

"Harvey," I say, "are you still in pictures?"

"All the time. I got a part in a new one. I might even be leaving the force."

"Jeez, you too."

"Can't let guys like you have all the fun."

"Nor all the money either, eh?"

"You don't forget, do you?"

"You were pretty stubborn about it."

He claps his hands, shivers as if he's cold. A boy on a motor-scooter rushes by, his blue shirt streaming behind. "Let's go get something to eat," he says. "There are a couple of things I need to tell you."

We go up to Jizzy's, an old-time hash house off La Brea. When the studios were still in Hollywood, you would find the place in early morning packed with disheveled movie players, washed up into the light from the night sea of parties and arsenical glamor. Now kids come here, and the local neighborhood wounded, a few working men, a hooker or two. It's still open all night, and if you come late, in the cool morning hours after the store windows have begun to look like dioramas for the dead, you will see a selection of lonely characters, salesmen from Des Moines baffled by the intransigence of the city, a shift worker mourning the breakdown of his marriage, a hooker turning in her hands the key to a Porsche she lifted off a drunk, a kid writing in a notebook, telling the story of his brokenhearted life to the page, earnestly, furiously writing it down as if it is the last story in the world and he has been assigned to tell it.

We slide into a cracked booth and order, full breakfast for me, milk and toast for Harvey. He has an ulcer, he says, and taps his chest high up. "Everything I eat feels like a bomb going off. The first time it hit me I thought I was having a heart attack."

I shake my head with mock seriousness. "How did we know life was going to be so difficult?"

"It's better they didn't tell us."

"If we'd known, the world would have been full of child suicides."

Through the glass front doors I watch a man scraping something off the bottom of his shoe with a stick. "What was it you wanted to tell me?"

He takes out a small foil packet, tears it open, and chews down the two white pills it contains. There's a graininess in my mind, a small tickling at the back of my head. It's as if Kate's back there, tapping a blind message. Clement's plan ticks on, and I do nothing. Harvey looks worn out, the patches of dark skin under his eyes are as large as thumbprints. I notice, for the first time, that the tips of his fingers are fat and squared off, like frog pads. He presses his hand flat against his chest.

"I hate these things," he says chewing, "but they do me some good."

My mind has flown to the beach. I see Kate walking fast down the strand, a rich red scarf blowing around her neck. She told me I wanted to slow her down because I was afraid of where we were going. Because I was afraid. It was true, though I denied it. After her big success, after her shiny gold award, she sped up, making pictures one after the other. My father wouldn't let up; he begged her to make a picture for him.

Harvey raps my hand lightly with a spoon. "Where are you, Willie?" he says.

I come back abruptly. "Right here."

"You looked like a drunk off on an argument in his head."

"This shit's got me."

"Yeah, it's a messy business."

The waitress slides our breakfasts onto the speckled Formica. She's young, golden haired, hopeful, unburned. As she turns to leave I touch her hand. "Something else?" she says. "No, sorry, it was nothing." I just want to touch human flesh, a woman's flesh. She smiles, retreats, pushing strands of soft hair off her thin neck. A sadness, dark as anguish, specific, bolted to the platform of my body, lifts in me. I have seen many movie fires. I have stood at the edge of a set and watched the stuntman reel out of a burning building, watched him throw himself out of a burning car, rolling on the ground, his hands, his head burning in the fire suit, and I have watched the firemen, after the director called cut, sweep in with their big extinguishers, watched the man emerge grinning from a white cloud, seen him later sitting at a table off the set, his blackened suit stripped to his waist, eating a sandwich, laughing at the script girl's joke.

Harvey munches his toast, sips his milk. He watches with distaste as I eat. "You shouldn't eat all that crap," he says.

"I'm not the one who made you nervous," I say. Kate is gone now, she's gone for good. Everything now is extra.

"Times have changed," Harvey says. "We can't get away with all that grease and cholesterol. You ought to see a picture of your heart. I'll bet it's wrapped in glue."

"Well, if I don't think about it, it doesn't bother me."

"You live like that?"

"I do."

Harvey nods at someone across the room. I look up to see a couple, someone else, watching me. They recognize me. I am a reference, a cornerstone, a marker for them to orient themselves by. They want to see how I eat, they want to see me do something characteristic, that is to say, something they have seen me do in a movie. I am a moment in the rhythm of their lives. They are old; and what they don't know is that I can see down the corridor of their gray-headed lives to the end, to the shabby funerals, the slow Methodist music, the plastic flowers on the grave. I swear I can see this. Harvey says, "Those guys we just left are going to try to make you think about something."

"That's what I figure."

"They've got their eyes on the big case. They want to be stars."

"Just like you and me."

"It's serious, Will. They're going to try to make you eat this."

"Did you read about me in the paper?"

"Yeah, I did. Which time?"

"Did you see where I punched Bill Lenz?"

"I saw that. I liked it. That buzzard needed it."

"There's evidence that I've gone haywire. Did you read about my wife?"

"About Kate?" He shakes his head. The question is a way of letting me off the hook, a way of giving himself a moment to think of what to say. "I saw something about it."

"You read the tabloids, huh?"

"Don't you?"

"Sure."

"They're crazy."

"It's true."

"What's true?"

"Their story."

The blond waitress, descending from heaven, floats by, pours a thick stream of coffee into my white restaurant mug. I want to rise lightly, grab her in my arms, and dance around the room. I want to take her aside, to a fragrant place near the sea, and convince her that we will never die.

Harvey eyes the coffee, but he doesn't ask for a cup. We get older so that we can learn discipline. We strap ourselves in, check the gauges, we become convinced that the world is a terrible place, a dangerous, terrible place. A slag heap, as Kate put it. If we step out of line they trap us in our car, shoot us, and burn the bodies. I think of that hank of white back skin the Nazis covered their book in, think of the hands of the man who stitched it to the boards. Who was he? A Nazi? A young apprentice? A Jew? Kate, you were right: I lost you.

Harvey lifts his eyes as if they are heavy, lays his gaze on my face. "It's true, Harvey," I say. "The papers had it right. As a matter of fact they were circumspect."

"They said it was all in the family."

"Witty fellows. It is all in the family though."

"Kate?"

"And Clement."

"Your dad? Jesus, Will."

I want to try this out, I want to say this scandalous secret, this shameful fact out loud, see what happens. Will he turn aside? Veronica says let it go and move on, but she says this because she thinks I am angry. She doesn't want me to do anything—out of rage—that I'll live to regret. But it isn't rage that drives me. No, not rage.

"It gives me the willies," I say. "I had no idea life was so odd." And why didn't I know?

Harvey laughs. "I'm sorry, man. Willie with the willies. It would drive me crazy. What are you going to do—kill him? Kill them both?"

"That's a fine thing for a cop to say."

"Like I told you, I'm getting out of the business. God. This is the truth—you know it's the truth?"

"I saw it with my own eyes—in Mexico."

"She ran away, huh?"

"Yes."

"Damn, man, this is as bad as police work."

"It's pretty terrible, you think?"

"Hell, yes, Will. It'd put me in the asylum. Or else I'd kill somebody."

"I don't know. Maybe it's not that unusual."

He turns his head aside. He looks for a second as if he's about to spit. His neck is flushed. "I can't believe you're saying that."

"You're right—it's a lie."

"What is?"

"All that business. The papers just want to make copy. None of it's true."

For a second he's stopped. It's a moment of transition, that second when the world, pitched to the end of a phase, pauses before the next jerks it onward. Time is not seamless. And then, in his watery blue eyes, yellowed with disease, anger flashes. It is so quick I can hardly catch it, but it's there—outrage, the human terror behind it, the urge to strike, the decision to let it go. His breath, smelling of milk, whistles out. He shakes his head. "What the fuck, Will?" There is hurt in his eyes now. I took him partway and then I left him. I called him in and then I turned him out. But I am only acting. I look at his broad sandy head, at the skin that is dark brown at the temples, deep red across the flat cheek-bones as if he's just been punched, the narrow lips turned down

216

slightly to the left. Can you feel it when your brains begin to boil? "Damn, Will," he says, shaking his head.

"I'm sorry," I say, meaning it, wanting things to go smoothly. Beyond the plate-glass window three or four dwarf firs look like red wigs draped over sticks. We would enter Mexico through Mexicali, crossing the squat steel bridge, painted white that year, in the red Jaguar. She would tell stories as we traveled, stories of arcane sexual practices, rituals carried out under the light of kerosene lanterns, stories in which the low sounds of weeping drifted across a courtyard. There was a stretch of road along the coast, north of Guaymas, where the road sank down out of the pine woods, down through mesquite and ghostly sage, to a cove, an amphitheater carved by the sea out of white rock. There was a shelf of sandy beach, a canted board shack. We would stop there for the night, lie under sheets beside a small fire, just off the slanted porch. The stars sprawled thickly across the sky. "We are stars too," she would say, "living in our own heaven . . ." I would try to listen, try to believe her, but somehow we had passed each other by. . . .

Harvey catches my eye with his, a police look, releases me. "There's a lot of meanness around," he says. "It'll creep out of any damn place."

"This I know."

"So all that shit, the papers are just making it up?"

"It's just the stuff that collects around the Awards. They want to flash everything up."

"Yeah, yeah—I know. It must drive you crazy sometimes."

"It's not so bad. They're thinking about me. And it's interesting to see what another imagination can make of my life. I mean, it's what we're up to all the time. We just don't notice it."

"How so?"

"Maybe everybody's nothing more than what we make up about them."

"Shoot. You ride with me for a while you wouldn't think that."

"I have ridden with you."

"Not long enough, obviously."

I think this is an idea of what happens to actors. This is part of the drift. We're slick vehicles others gas up and point down the track. You want me to be a killer, a lover, a rumpus room proprietor—just show me my mark. It's life on the drift. I was ready when the paychecks started coming, when they brought me in and began to pay me for this. What you want I'll be. What I want Kate'll be. What Kate wants I'll be. She said tear her clothes off, I tore her clothes off. Weep for me, she said, I wept. I was born in Nebraska, she said, I'm a child of the plains; no, she said, I was born in New York, in Paris, in a white cottage on the banks of the Snake River. My mother, at this moment, is pirouetting in a room of muted light, flouncing the skirts of a dress she wore to play Queen Isabella. Her hand reaches through the brassy Southern California air, and it is the hand of Anna Karenina, reaching to touch Vronsky a last time before he abandons her for the life of a soldier. You accept a part and then you think, What is it about this man I'm playing that makes him different from others? You decide he has a sore on the inside of his mouth that he worries constantly with his tongue, you remember for him that his first child died in infancy, that his wife's breath smells of gas, that he hates the church. He dreams of swimming in a cold dark river, of lying naked in the grass as the sun dries his body. He's embarrassed about the size of his feet. Or you have done this so many times, you have slipped through the curtain, pulled on the vestments and begun to play, that you don't think about it anymore. You know what to do, and you do it.

Kate and I fill and empty each other, again and again passing the fuel between us. One knows nothing about the other.

"So," I say, "what about these Ventura County boys?"

He takes a sip of milk, grimaces as if it is sour. "They're as serious as they can be."

"How serious is that?"

"They'd probably like to put a gun in your hand. At the least they want you as an accessory."

"I'm the guy who got shot."

"You're the guy with the marquee value."

"What about this other guy, or whoever it was, the one she shot at, the one who shot her and burned her up. I mean it seems we got a rogue out there."

"It's just one of these crappy underbelly deals, man—drugs, love gone sour, some fool driven crazy by the Santa Annas. It's not a detective story; it probably doesn't mean anything, just some craziness. There's never any big reason."

I sighed. "Well, shit. I guess I'll have Earl call Sammy. Maybe he can put his foot on them."

"Your lawyer?"

"Yeah."

"Maybe he can. But it might not be a good idea to try to come down on the cops. And shit, you shouldn't tell me. We're not asshole buddies."

"No, we're not."

We stare at each other, each taking the other in. In our minds we leap over the table, grapple, tear, gouge and claw, throw punches hard as stones, drive the other down. He kicks me, I drive my knuckles into his teeth. Neither will quit until the other can't get up.

"Mr. Blake," a soft voice says. It is a tourist gent, the older fellow I noticed before, sliding his napkin in front of me. He offers a pen. "Would you?" he says. Mother hangs back, the shy one; in her face is the history of the sad town she comes from. The guy steps to the side, giving me space.

"Sure," I say, and sign my name with a flourish. I nod at Harvey. "You want his autograph, too. He's an actor."

"Oh, yes, of course," the gentleman says, blinking his small gray eyes. His eyelashes are colorless.

I push the paper toward Harvey. Harvey gets up. He pulls three bucks from his pocket, casts them down on the Formica. "I got to go," he says. "Excuse me," he says to the tourists. The old man, slightly baffled, steps back to let him out. Harvey looks at me. His eyes are tired, lanterns shining over the diseased body. "Take care of yourself, Will," he says. "Be sure you watch out."

I rise slightly, bend at the waist. "Thank you, Harvey," I say, and for a second I mean it. For one second the joke of it all slides away and I mean it. "I'll take good care."

A little while later, after I've invited the seniors to sit with me, after I've told them a story about the time Garland Stone and I took turns pushing each other into King Vidor's swimming pool, after they've explained to me that this is their fourteenth trip across the country in their recreation vehicle, after, for a dazzling moment, I think the angel of the lord has swum down out of the

219

heavens and touched their faces with celestial light, after the woman has promised me that if she was still of child-bearing age she would name a son after me, after the old man offers to become my permanent houseguest, after they reveal to me that they too cultivate secret dreams of stardom, shopworn and depleted now, but still alive like ringworm burrowed under their pasty skin, after they buy my breakfast and the waitress has me sign the dollar bills they pay with, after all that, and after my sauntering walk out of the restaurant, the famous movie walk in which I bounce on my toes, gliding forward as if I am related to big, dangerous cats, after I soar out into the bright, bristling LA day, after I notice an ocotillo bush in full red flower and think how strange it is to see an ocotillo this near the coast, and notice the three hummingbirds, which I think are actually angels, hovering over the spiky stalks, after I notice down the street, parked under a pepper tree, what I take to be a police car, a gray sedan with two men inside it watching me and I think, wild as a mongoose, *Roll camera, baby, let it roll,* after the thought comes to me for perhaps the one hundredth time that there is no way on this earth to penetrate deeply enough into the body and soul of another human being to know the first thing about them, think, for the one hundredth time, that everything on this planet is on its own, that brotherly love and kiss-ass are only two sides of the same coin, why is it, after my stomach catches, rises like a hot fist, and I vomit breakfast into a small haggardly blossoming oleander, why is it that the thought, winging in on the mind's silver platter, comes to me that we must love those around us, and, no matter what, do for them what we can?

SHE WAS WILD for success, eaten by it. She wanted more and more. She would go anywhere, take any risk, make any picture. For Paramount she fought the forest lords in Brazil. In *Dangerous,* she tracked a killer through the streets of Saigon. *The Windmill* opened with her lying naked in a field, the camera soaring in from space to pick her out. For Anton Mazaluk, the Polish director, she masturbated on camera, her feet propped on the huge shorn steel head of a woman, ten feet across, set like a trophy on the streaked marble floor of a palazzo in Venice. The camera caressed her pale body like the hands of love, and she opened herself to it, begging it—no, not begging, demanding—demanding that it reach into her, expose everything. One morning she drove away in a white Alfa Romeo and returned in the evening in a black limo, the Alfa forgotten somewhere on a lot in Burbank. She made up songs, sang them in the shower, recorded what she sang, in the shower, gave the tape to a producer and then six months later listened to the songs play on the radio—insane novelty tunes—as she was ferried to work. Like the queen of England, she lent her name to worthy causes, but only her name—*later,* she said, *later,* to requests for her presence, *I will do that later when I am old and those are the only parts I can get.* In her first few pictures she established herself as a beautiful woman, an actress capable of deep emotion; the camera idolized her, it followed her like a whipped dog, begging her to forgive it. She played in a consistent style, her white blondness poised in a rapt vulnerability, but always moving, able as she raced along to transfer the emotion of the moment from herself to the viewer. She was like a gunslinger who rolls on the ground firing accurately. Or like someone falling who explains the function of the beta ray spectrograph cogently as she falls. She was not an actor of repose, or stasis; she hummed. And amid it was her laughter, the tropical, sugary, crackling, hooting seal laugh she gave back to adversity, to whatever ridiculous suffering and useless traduction life magicked her way. She made you think she could never get enough, that the world was only a small party, that it'd never fill her up, that she was ready for the leap into space, into darkness, into destruction or light.

At home, for a while, she wanted pets, so she bought dogs, twenty of them maybe, all different breeds, and cats and a goat, a raccoon, a cow some farmer from the San Joaquin brought in the back of a truck and which she tethered out on the lawn, a black-and-white Holstein with a milky eye, which the city made her get rid of. The pets passed, trucked away to the pound or maybe, I don't know, stuffed into sacks and tossed into the ocean, and then it was parties, forays into the nightlife where she danced wildly, amazing the attendees as if she were Dr. Frankenstein making dangerous new life. Someone no one had ever seen before would appear on the set, driving a Jeep pickup or a rusted-out convertible, a redheaded guy with frozen blue eyes, he might be, or a small, sleek Mexican man, or a white-haired gent in a frayed black suit, once a three-hundred-pound guy with tufts of gray hair that stuck out between the buttons of his aloha shirt, another time a boy in a Cincinnati Reds baseball cap, and she would get into the truck or convertible, she would wave to the crew and to the gawkers behind the security line, and roar away.

At industry parties she told her stories, her tales of intricate flight and devilment, explaining with a kind of rapid patience the breathing procedure she used the time she had descended into White Angel Springs in western Brazil looking for her lover's body. She described the hay fields of Argentina and sunset over the pack ice at Point Barrow in the Beaufort Sea. She spoke of riding elephants in Thailand, of eating the goodun fruit, large as a channel mine and spiked, smelling like hog shit, so she said, an odor so pungent that if you were locked in a room with it you would beg to be let out, but which when eaten tasted of the sugary lips of heaven, of the sweetness of a morning dream; a taste, so she said, you would remember all your life.

She told these stories in public places, at parties with the host hovering off her elbow like a fireboat; she told them in the car on the way to the studio, and in her trailer on the set sipping a fruit punch made of guavas and limes; she told them wearing a gold brocade dress with flounces that weighed ten pounds apiece; and she told them to me, by long-distance telephone as I roasted in the Sahara sands of Morocco waiting for my call, told them to me as I lay on a teak bed in a damp hotel room in Milan smelling the rotted breath of the last person to use the phone; told them to me as I stood in a darkened room behind a wisteria trellis on Cat Island, Louisiana, wearing a Confederate uniform from which the left sleeve had been burned away, and she told them in my bedroom in the Hollywood Hills, creeping into the room late at night, sliding into the bed in a soft rustle of silk or flannel, naked, her skin shining in the moonlight, smelling of delicate florals. She told them in her array of voices, in the accents she tried on and discarded like resort clothes, told them as Teutonic maiden, colleen, Spanish waif, Arcadian princess, Murray Hill heiress, Georgia peach, Indiana cornheart, Italian coloratura, Valley Girl, death-row murderess, sweetheart of the Sigma Chi; she told them sweetly, harshly, flatly; told them as one politician might tell another, whispering in the halls of government; told them in a high-pitched scream that I begged her to leave off; told them in tears, laughing, cringing; told them in a voice rosy with lying, earnestly, viciously, with cold fury in her voice; told them in an accent filled with clicks and barks; told them in the voice of a child, sardonically, superciliously; told them impudently, abjectly, contemptuously, fretfully, mockingly, skittishly, with psychopathic intensity; told them in a voice that said this is the last thing on earth you will ever hear.

They say actors are people without a self, without the bedrock core of personality and being normal folk have. I don't think this is so. A long time ago there were only a few of us humans on earth; in the beginning there was only one. They say now there was an original mother, an Eve, from whose genetic pool all the rest of us have sprung. She lived a few million years ago, an African woman, an upright rock-and-roll lady of the forest edge, whose first step, whose bright glance out over the grasslands, was our first step and our first glance too. Where she walked and what she saw have been packed into our genetic memory, folded and tucked in like a used bus ticket for a journey out of which memory flashes like lights in a distant town that is receding from us, but in which strange and unnerving events occurred that trouble us in sleep. All the rest is layering, one veneer of life and event after another, years and lives lacquering on generation by generation, through wars and loves on to the present day. The reincarnationists believe they can stir into life memories of former lives, and all of us, peering out on a fresh scene, have the sense sometimes that it is familiar; I think these are the experiences, flashes, of the older layers, of the skins all of us once wore, the lives we walked around inside in the wooden cities of the Holy Roman Empire or on the stone docks of Rhodes or on some vague and tangled shore in Africa. The hand that rises to touch the loved face rises through a million years of love and loss, and the face it touches has felt on its cheeks the dry winds of the Sahara, the cool splash of a forest pool in Asia. In her eyes I see the running herds, the fires burning on the plains of Troy, I see the sad suppers of the bereaved, the turning of a glance toward the intimate pleading of a rejected suitor, the sleek sails lifting into a morning wind. For some, perhaps for all of us in extraordinary times, the layers peel back easily, or they are able to sink down through them like divers drifting toward the bottom, and what they see there—which is only what we all have seen—is raised up to us, grinning or grieving, some old suit of shabby splendor, some kingly cloak or beggar's trousers we once shambled around in, that we, bound in the chain of our days, recognize. Kate was such a one. What had brought this about happened long ago. It loosed her into the layers. Long ago, on an afternoon in Florida, or on the backsteps of a frame house in Nebraska—somewhere or somewhere—she had seen too much—as Bobby had, as I had—and what she saw—the core's rattling bones—had knocked her free from the loose weave of logic and agreement the rest of us lived within; she became a diver, a treasure hunter, a retriever spinning through the layers of the enormous past, and what she brought up she spread at our feet, these gold cups and rotted corpses we ourselves had sunk there only yesterday.

Then, what, eighteen months ago, I saw her on television, on CNN's "Hollywood Minute," explaining how she had dived a hundred and fifty-seven feet from a cliff into an Indonesian pool. They showed the clip, and there she was wearing the ruffled white dress of a conquistadoress, tossing an open umbrella from the mossy rim in a gesture so purely heartbreaking that I thought I would weep. The umbrella fluttered like a broken bird, falling as prophecy for her dive in elegant sarabande—a brilliant touch that I have no doubt she thought of herself—and then as the camera returned to her lifted face and began its slow retreat, she stepped forward into blue space, falling as one would fall from the edge of the world, life done, the end of the planet reached, tumbling like a white flower, head over heels. In the slow motion we will begin to move in after death, she fell, silently, as the camera pulled back exposing the vast bowl of the falls and the froth of treetops and beyond, the gold and tan plain stretching away for miles. The white dress merged with the blue pool, the splash of her body formed wide white skirts, and she went under.

I sat there in my linen chair high above Hollywood with my heart beating loudly. We live in a world that's trying to survive by hurting everything around it, but here was some beauty in death, in this white splashdown. For a second I lost my place. It had been years, I knew it had been years, since any star had done a stunt like that, if anyone had ever done a stunt like that. Johnny Weismuller dived off cliffs in Metro's backlot but never cliffs that high, never in a dress.

I called Able Cutter at Universal and asked him what the hell was going on. He said he didn't know, he said as far as he knew there was no stunt like that in the script, he said it must have been something they made up out on location. I said, I don't want my wife diving from heights—you guys must be crazy. I can understand that, Able said in his plain Oklahoma voice—I could see him doing rope tricks as we talked, his speciality—but Kate's got a mind of her own and they're nine thousand miles from home. SAG doesn't reach that far? I said. Yeah well, he said, of course; I'll check on it immediately and get back to you. He called me back that night, said it was something she made up on her own, something she convinced the second-unit crew to shoot on a day off. He said she promised to do it twice, once clothed and once naked. He said people were going to be fired. Good, I said, that's good, and I hung up.

This is all about powerlessness, I thought: I am being introduced, at thirty-seven, to one of the major truths of life. Ha, I thought, you can't fool me, you can't jar me with such foolishness as this: powerlessness is a truth I already know about. Long ago, the year my brother died, the year my mother took my best friend as a lover, that year in the hills above the Pima Valley, I learned about powerlessness. Thus, as I have said before, the drift. But this was another lesson, and I didn't like it.

I didn't call Kate. I didn't have to, since she called me, as she had called every night since she went on location. She hadn't mentioned a fall.

What did you think you were doing? I said. Have you lost your mind?

Didn't you think it was pretty? she asked.

It was gorgeous, but it scared me to death.

Me too, she said. If it hadn't been for all the kava we drank I'd never have done it.

You did it drunk?

Not drunk; you don't get exactly drunk on kava.

Just exactly crazy?

I think it was the first time anybody jumped off that cliff. You couldn't see them, but there were fifty or sixty local people on the bank at the bottom. They whistled as I flew through the air. It was stupendous.

Kate, I said, you're driving me crazy.

There was a silence on the line through which I could hear a ghostly voice arguing in an English accent about what sounded like an oil deal. "Drill or not, you have to guarantee . . ." the voice said. I pictured some fellow at a restaurant table in Kowloon, hair slicked back, seersucker suit chafing his crotch, crinkles of desperation around his eyes, arguing for the deal that would save his life. Are you there? I said.

I'm somewhere, she answered, and her voice was ghostly too.

What are you wearing?

Jeans, a white T-shirt, sandals.

I am terribly in love with you, I said, I am out of my head with love for you.

I know, she said.

What about you?

Is this love, she said, is that what I feel?

Love's a willingness, I said. I think that's what it is.

I have that.

I called Able Cutter, he said he was going to fire the idiots who let you do that dive.

Don't do that, Willie.

I've already done it.

Son of a bitch, she said softly. I wish you hadn't done that. These are good guys, and it was my idea.

You could have been killed.

What—they were usurping your prerogative?

I felt a chill. What are you talking about?

You, Willie.

I just can't stand the thought of you diving headfirst off some fucking Balinese cliff.

You could stand it if it was your idea.

I'd never have an idea like that.

The silence drifted through again, but it was brief.

You'll have the idea, Willie, she said. It'll come to you all by itself.

Then she hung up.

I sat back in the chair and thought about this. Where did this wild surmise come from? What was she saying here? I only wanted her to go into the danger I devised? I wanted to what—kill her? Nah, I thought, not death but desire. I desired her.

I was missing it all then, I was missing all but the ribbony rims of it, but I couldn't see. I didn't know then how easy it was to slip off the track of . . . sympathy—is that the word?—into another kind of being, an arrangement without a common purpose, one in which your job became defense and assault, and, before you could turn around, you were in there fighting for your life. I think what's terrible often begins softly, in a whisper. It is as simple as the smell of apples at six-thirty on a fall morning. It is as quiet as the radio in a room where two lovers are sleeping. It is as innocuous as the fingerprint a six-year-old girl pressed into the fresh shellac on a banister sixty years ago. We don't see it, we don't catch it, but in it, glowing like phosphorus, is the whole disaster to come.

The next night, from Indonesia, she said, Inclement keeps calling me.

He wants you to make a picture for him.

He's promising me everything.

Points, script control, your own cook.

He says he can make me a star.

He says you're going to be bigger than Marilyn, bigger than Bette Davis, bigger than Garbo.

He says he's my father-in-law and it's my duty.

He says it will break his heart if you don't work for him.

She barked her scratchy laugh. What am I going to do?

You can do what you want. I've already told you what I think.

Tell me again.

He'll kiss you, and then he'll break your back.

My sweet little back?

The very one. Listen, almost nobody out here looks like a killer, and the truth is there haven't been very many—most of these boys fold up when they hear the wheels of the cash wagon turning out of their driveway—but Clement looks like one and he *is* one. He's not joking when he says he'll do whatever he has to to make the picture.

That's not such a bad way to go about things.

I guess if you're in a war.

She honked her baby seal laugh. Well, what else is going on here?

You should like working with Clement then.

I think I'm game.

You—you're game for anything, but you don't know what you're getting into here. This is the Angel of Death we're talking about.

Willie, you're crazy.

I know, I know, but that's not the point.

She laughed again, and I could feel her laughter as if it were a finger poking me from nine thousand miles away, a sportive finger tickling me. But what it touched in me was hard as rock. I said, Imagine I am there with you in that hotel room in Bali, imagine I am sitting in front of you looking into your eyes. I am so much in earnest, it's frightening; if you could see me you would see it in my face and there would be no doubt. Kate, this is one of those moments like when a mother rushes across the lawn screaming that her baby has fallen into the pool; you don't question her, you know. I'm telling you, girl, you don't want to do business with Clement Blake.

How long have you felt like this?

I don't know—since I can remember. Since Bobby died, I guess.

You blame him for your brother?

She didn't say death; I wondered if she could say it.

No, not exactly, it's not like that. It's just that when Bobby was gone . . . I began to be able to see.

Maybe that's how everyone thinks when their brother kills himself.

Maybe.

Maybe she was right. Outside my window a stealing wind banged the eucalyptus trees, worrying them like a monkey trying its cage. The Pacific was a thin blue lens, the horizon sharp as a ruled line, nothing beyond it but the voice I was listening to. My mind wanted to go, wanted to flee to lost places. I said, They talk about blood ties, they talk about family, people wrestle and complain, but they can't—they won't—break the family tie, they feel connected no matter what happens to them—it's not always like that.

That's what I know, she said.

I can't tell. I don't know what you know.

I don't either anymore. I have so many versions.

This is one you don't want.

Don't tell me that, Will. Was there a note of pleading in her voice? She was the girl attached to nothing, now attached.

I promise you don't need this, I said. If you let it go by, you won't miss it.

Her voice came faintly, as if she had stepped back another thousand miles. You don't know what I miss.

And why was it then that I saw myself as if I were standing at the end of a path in childhood, holding a plastic shovel and a broken blue bird, a dead bird I was about to go into the woods and bury? My brother is a white angel living on my shoulder. He doesn't speak to me, he doesn't direct, he only lives there, nestled against my collar bone, watching. Why did they not tell us earlier that in this life no one would come forward to advise us? Why did they not tell us that everything is a mystery? I want to take Kate in my arms, I want to protect her, not man to woman, but human to human, as one would reach for the stranger falling over a cliff. Was this just some conjugal fantasy, some other blown-out portion I had scooped for myself, some itch of greed and desire I couldn't stop or control? I wanted to save her, I wanted to break her, I wanted to direct her life, I wanted to fall back and watch her sweep through Hollywood leaving specks of gold in her wake. Well, Kate, I said, still talking, if I could, I would tell you don't do this—don't do this.

You can't tell me what to do, she said, and she was right.

So I called my father and got his heavy, crackling voice on the phone. There was liquid in his mouth. Are you in the swimming pool? I said.

No, I'm eating soup. Venison stew actually. It's right good.

Kate says you're bothering her about doing a picture.

That's right. It's come to me that I can't live without her.

Learn.

You're talking to the wrong guy for that. I'm unteachable.

I don't want her making a picture with you.

It's terrible isn't it? I can't control myself. I've got this idea—she's the only one who could do it. She's the best new actress I've seen in fifteen years. She's a once-in-a-generation actress.

I know that.

Don't you want to help your old dad?

No, I don't.

You're an ungrateful son.

How would a psychopath know?

You ought to let me tell you about this picture. You would approve if you knew what it was about.

I wouldn't approve if it was *Gone With the Wind.*

That's what it is, *Gone With the Wind.*

Not just unteachable—unreachable.

I can't hear you.

Is there any way to call the cops on you?

Did I tell you about the time Archibald Evans tried that? Do you know who he was?

That bald character actor in the fifties? The one who used to play parts where he got cheated out of whatever he owned?

Yeah, that's him. He was a weakling on the screen and he was a weakling in life. Only in life, he was a mean weakling. A sneak. The time I'm talking about he tried to come back on me on a deal I'd shoved him out of. It was a part he thought I'd promised him—I never had—and he went around town saying I'd cheated him. I said, Okay, fine. I didn't defend myself. But one night I drove over to his house—he lived off Laurel Canyon, just a regular suburban guy—and I walked up these long redwood steps to his front door—it was like climbing one of those Swiss tram lines—and when he answered the door, I broke his nose. And I broke his wife's nose too—when she jumped me with a lamp, trying to defend him. I told him if he ever said another word about me I'd come back and kill him. He knew I meant it.

Did he ever say anything?

Not a goddamn word.

The Ape of Hollywood.

But here's the thing—I put him in three pictures after that, little smirking sleazy parts, and he never said a word. Never complained.

There was the sound of chewing.

Now isn't that something? he said.

Yes, we just don't quite know what.

I always do the necessary thing, always. I'm one guy who loves his work, who loves it better than he likes to eat, better than he likes to fuck. That's my secret. Nobody loves doing this more than I love it. I get everything I want because I love it so much. That's the secret of life. Did you know that? That's the secret. It's love, just like the shitasses say. You got to love something so much you'd do anything for it. You've got to love like there's no tomorrow, like there's nothing else in the world for you. You love and hold on, like a goddamn bulldog you hold on. (I saw his eyes flashing, his teeth snapping, the big head shaking.) You know this world's a pussy, it can't help itself. It *has* to give in. That's another secret. Everybody thinks it's so hard to live, so hard to make it in this world. Well, let me tell you, they're just pussies, the ones who think that. They got lemonade for blood. You want to make it in this world, you just squeeze the heart— give more, love more. (His voice shifted, became softer, confidential. I was the reluctant operative he was convincing.) The truth is, Willie, and I've told you this a thousand times, we're servants. Nobody seems to be able to get that straight. We all want to manage, we want to run things. But we're really servants. Our job is to serve what we love. We have to give everything to it. We give everything and then we give some more. Give beyond giving—that's the only way. Listen here, he said, the words snapping and clattering like rocks, we go into action every morning. It's an assault. We storm the fucking beaches. We do whatever we have to do. We play for keeps.

Right-o, Pop, I said. It's a story often told. Thinking, Why aren't there more ways to explain how we live? Hard work, luck, the inevitability of death, war, surrender, the promise of joy, fear or grief—we make the same claims over and over. I was a man who lay back in the sunny front seat of an old car, watching a cat climb among the tender branches of a Japanese plum some afternoon in June behind a house in Malibu. I could feel the sun on my arm, the taste of oranges in my mouth—I wanted nothing more than that soft, generous afternoon repeated again and again.

My father made a noise like a growl, the ape clearing his throat. And here's the thing, Willie. You're more like me than you can admit. Because you know what I'm talking about. You can understand a guy who wants to make a good picture.

My father once fired his own father off a picture. It was the only time they worked together. He didn't like the way GP interpreted a character, a rough old mule skinner in a cowboy epic, and so he fired him, face to face in front of the crew. My grandfather was so angry that for the last five years of his life he wouldn't let my father in his house.

Pop, I said, you have a vivid dream life.

Doesn't make any difference. That's where people get fucked up. They think there's a rational way to live they've got to find out about and apply to their lives. They drive themselves crazy because they keep falling short. Heart attack snaps them out, cancer eats their bowels. They go to therapy so some guy in an expensive suit can tell them—slowly, repetitively—how to live, how to integrate themselves into reality. Well, fuck reality. There's no such thing. The world can't say a thing about what we do to it. Neither can anybody else. We make our own way, we make up our own lives as we go along.

Actually, I'm calling to tell you to leave Kate alone.

Like I say, I can't help it. I'm one hog you can't keep away from the trough.

Maybe we can keep the trough away from you.

No. It's too bloody a job.

I didn't say anything. Hidden in the word—*bloody*—was a blow.

Yeah, he said, too much blood turns the stomach shy. You know how that is.

A fist clenched inside me. Watch out, Pop, I said.

Chewing noises.

I got my eyes peeled, he said.

I put the phone down.

The day I quit hunting there was blood. It was up in the White Mountains, the Sierra foothills; I shot a goat, but the goat didn't die. I was shooting a .410, loaded with slugs, and in a clearing under some oaks I hit a goat in the body, and it went down. But the goat didn't die. It thrashed on the ground, back broken, trying to lift itself. I shot it in the head and it flopped more wildly; I reloaded and shot it again, but it didn't die. It lay back on the ground blinking its eyes and coughing. It was a ram, with a short brown beard. My father and brother came up behind me as I shot it the third time. The goat stretched its neck and tried to bleat. I fell to my knees sobbing. Something broke; I began, frantically, to pat the goat, to stroke it. Bobby told me later I wasn't caressing it, I was hitting it, pounding its head and flank. It wouldn't die; it wouldn't get up. My father pushed me aside, knelt, grabbed the goat in his two hands, lifted it, and bit through its throat. Blood spurted over him. He threw the goat down, turned, and, eyes blazing, spit a mouthful of blood into my face. Bobby leveled his gun on him, a .410 too, the same gun that in less than a year he would turn on himself. They stared at each other, father and son. I could taste the goat's blood on my lips. It was sour, hot. And then my father grinned. His teeth were bloody. He tore his shirt open, bared his matted chest. *There,* he said, grinding the words through his grin, *do what you will.* My brother did not flinch. He pulled the trigger. The hammer snapped against the empty chamber. For a second they stared at each other. They were both entirely still. And then Bobby threw the gun down and walked away. He walked out from under the trees and crossed the field, upon which the sun blazed. My father got up and walked to the edge of the clearing. He looked out at Bobby striding away into the sunshine. He grasped the trunk of a sapling with one hand, shook it, but he didn't say anything, didn't step out. From the back, with the sun blazing before him, he looked like the dark king of the woods gazing out into the sunny country he was forever banished from. But he was not a king, he was only the murderous, indestructible creature my brother and I were heir to.

IN THE QUIET of my empty house, in the quiet helped along by the worried breeze telling its troubles to the eucalyptus trees, I don't try to understand my hatred. It is bone deep, endless, indecipherable, but I don't try to understand it. So much of life is simply prophylactic. We arm ourselves against the dangers. We know the enemy is out there, we can almost see him creeping among the trees. We set the alarm and lie down in the cold sheets and we try to rub up a little good feeling about things. But in our hearts we know that the danger the alarms warn us of comes outside any channel we have access to, that it's not on the screens we carefully monitor every day of our lives, that the early warning systems culture and training have rigged don't pick it up— it's the poison bug in the cup of coffee we absently lift to our lips while our eyes scan the horizon for the approaching armies; it's behind the voice of the one we love calling to us from the sunny yard; it's in back of the music that we hear inside our heads as we take the loved other fully into our arms. You go out into the wilderness—I know you've done this a time or two—you go out to the big swamp or to the desert or into the mountains, into someplace where the world is still wild, and you stand there, you stand there with the yellow jasmine and the solomon's seal curling around your ankles, or you stand there among the famished, point-blank rocks, or you stand knee-deep in water where bits of leaf matter and animal flesh float on the inky surface, and you let the quiet have its way with you, you let it come on until all you hear is the ancient silence of the natural world, the silence that stretches back beyond the generations of man, beyond woolly mammoths and the creaky dinosaurs into that time when the first rocks were laid down at the foundation of the world—you listen, in the pearly silence, you listen, until . . . until you hear something, something behind the silence, something that has been there all along. You strain to catch it—it isn't a song, it isn't a voice—you strain until every molecule of your body is standing on its toes, strain until you catch—what is it? Is it a plea, is it a reproach, is it a cry of love? Or is it a warning?

———

A FEW MONTHS LATER, a few months after I talked to Clement, Kate had come and gone. There was nothing I could do to stop her. She packed a bag—"I love how little you have to carry to make a movie," she said—got in the car sent for her, and disappeared down the drive to meet Clement in Italy. I walked around the house cringing, as if I were ashamed of something. At every window the world blazed. Then—I had timed it to the day, timed it to the minute—I got in the car and drove out to Veronica's. I stopped twice—once on a rocky curve where my brother had once leapt from the car to escape Clement's blows, and once on a stretch of beach, now built up, where my father had saved my life when I was ten. He'd seen a shark as I was swimming fifty yards out, thrashed his way to me, grabbed me under his arm, and pulled me in. He had never looked back at the shark. I walked between a dive shop and a small restaurant advertising a bonito special down to the water and stood there a minute, trying to recapture something, to find a place to start from, someplace I could push off from, but I couldn't get it; I couldn't get back the old feeling of excitement and power. There was only the dull concoction of ocean and sky, clouds pinned like tattered white feathers at the rims, nothing behind but the crooked houses and behind them the thorny chapparal: it all seemed familiar and permanent, a world without variation, without the possibility of change, for better or worse, but still, I had to shake myself to stop staring at it, to take my eyes off the wide stage of it, to pull back from the mesmerizing endless emptiness of it. My father wasn't out there in the water, I wasn't out there, maybe even the shark, silently running, was gone. I turned away, got back in the car, and whizzed on to Veronica's, where without a word I took her into my arms as if I believed along with Mr. Walt Whitman that a kelson of the creation was love, and crushed her body to me. She, rinsed and worn, sported the green flight suit my mother wore in one of her postwar movies, a strange, dark-angled number in which she wore her dead husband's clothes as she let herself be destroyed somewhere out in Indochina, a nurse gone bad, gone to guns, gone to a belief in justice and the triumph of good over evil. "Let the slick flesh slide," I said, making caresses out of the air; "Let the sporting times come," I said, as she pressed her face against my face, as my teeth bit lightly at her, grinning. I seemed to be hovering in a dream. What I had feared had come to pass, and locked-in, logical positivist homeboy, I was unable to adjust. Kate was gone to Italy making my father's picture. Making the picture and my father, and my father was making the picture and making her.

Beyond the wide, salt-filmed window, the Pacific blustered away at the land, its old enemy. The National Anthem of Night played in my head, but it played softly. I watched as out of a dream the Proprietor of Darkness stepped forth into the big room. Veronica's tongue licked between the buttons of my shirt. I touched her breasts, weighed their small softness. Gently I unzipped the front of the suit. She was naked underneath it. Her body smelled of roses. Her hand fluttered downward, trapped me. I sank my head toward the core, kissing my way. The fruity odor of her rose.

Somewhere else, a prostitute dressed as my wife stepped into an Italian street. A man in dark clothes approached; she asked him for a light. In the flare of the match she saw the Devil's face. He smiled. His cold fingers touched her cheek. "Let us go tonight," he said, "and make love among the poor." You could hear the whirr of the Panaflex, the small flacking sound of palm trees, you could look down the street, and each rounded cobble was clearly defined, as were the low houses on either side and the shops strung with flowers and at the bottom of the street the sea carrying the white handkerchiefs of the stars on its back. You could look the other way, merely turn your head, you could follow the black cables snaking, the tracks laid down on boards over the cobblestones, you could let your eyes step through cameramen, assistants, electricians, the script super saying the lines in her head, you could see my father, Clement Blake, standing with the cinematographer next to the camera operator, his black eyes gleaming, his mouth slightly open, a man trekked across famished miles to the feast, you could look past the trucks, the vans, the trailers, the limousine parked on the sidewalk, past the other cars and the three pedestrians stopped after midnight to watch this, past the *carabinieri*, the shopkeeper leaning from a window describing the scene to his wife, who lay in bed behind him kneading her swollen ankles, you could follow the street to the center of the small coastal city and on through the old ghetto now converted to shops and galleries, along the rain-slick arterial road through the suburbs, past the warehouses where coffee and spices and American bicycles racked like swords were stored, past the printing plant and the villa now used as an armory, to the airport where you could catch a plane to Rome and there catch another plane to New York and then another to Los Angeles, California, where it is four P.M. on a cool, smoky fall day, and so up the Pacific Coast Highway, California One, through the beach trash and pastel cottages of Santa Monica, along the Palisades past Topanga and Las Tunas, take a left at the stoplight in Malibu and then a right along the beach and so come, still looking, to the gull-winged house festooned with bougainvillea and wild beach vine, where if you looked up into the blue sky hazy with sea spray you could see the moon, fully exposed, nakedly and garishly white, smeared slightly at the edges, and you could pass through the warped front door, painted red like the door of an Episcopal church, into the huge sea room where a selection of hats was pinned to the walls and the wind chimes of shell and bone rustled and clattered faintly like the noisemakers that will be left over after the end of the world, and there come upon a woman and a man wearing the clothes of a movie star who was speaking, at this moment on an afternoon of salt sea spray and distinguished, pontifical light, the words of the script he had memorized: "Let us go tonight," he says, "and make love among the poor . . ."

M Y MOTHER SAID, said as we walked together in the nature preserve off Topanga, that in the beginning of her life she ran from whatever would leave a trace in her, a scar. Now, she said, pressing her glossy, dyed hair, I run from whatever won't. She said when you get old you want anything life will give you. The senses begin to fade, the ability to believe fades, hope fades. All you're left with is desire, she said. These days, she told me, I would stick my hand in a fire, I would be delighted to. Any time the world pokes me hard enough to feel something, I'm grateful.

I said, That's a sad place to come to.

No, she said, it's not either sad or happy; it's just life. It just happens.

It's a little against the grain of the direction I've traveled in heretofore, I said.

Don't talk so preciously, she said, her Lowland burr catching lightly in the syllables.

I haven't wanted to pay attention much, I said, I haven't really wanted to do anything.

You'll finish by wishing you had.

There is something I want to do. I want to cause pain.

That's possible too, she said, but sometimes difficult. It's a way to feel something, especially a way for the weak and the lost to feel something.

I'm not really thinking of the future; I'm not worried about the old man I will become.

I think, she said, we would like to look back on riches.

You don't mean money.

No, I mean a rich life. I think that's the main thing.

She leaned against a large oak, strummed her fingers along the trunk's corrugated side. Old age is a desert, she said, it gets emptier as you go along. Her corroded, square, strong Celtic peasant's hand played the trunk, plucking at it as if she could make sound, music, spring out. We want to play all our lives, she said; I thought the time would come when I wanted to be serious, when some kind of studiousness and belief would fill me, a solemnity like the gravity my father carried inside him as he walked down McLaren Street in Glasgow—thought I would become like him and looked forward to it in a horrified way; but that hasn't happened. I am sixty-five years old, not really an old woman yet, I'll admit, but I see no signs of seriousness, not of the sort my father maintained. I am the same girl who danced in the bracken on a spring morning sixty years ago. All I want to do is run in the dew. I want to open my mouth and feel the sun on my teeth. That's what makes old age hard.

I said, Maybe I'm more like you than you realize.

She turned her back to the tree and looked at me with her worn blue eyes. She was a woman who had enchanted a generation. When she won her first Oscar, the president called her up. She said his voice trembled as he congratulated her. The story was he asked her what she loved most about acting. *Making men writhe,* is what she was said to have told him. Now she arched her back, looked at me with her sad, ironic eyes. Maybe that is true, she said. I thought Bobby was like me, but maybe you are too. But maybe the idea that we are like other people, maybe the way we continue to see connections is just the need we have to tie things together, the godly part of us.

Is that what God does?

Yes, I think, or at least tries to; God tries to tie things together. He wants the world to work out.

I still have an urge to cause pain.

You believe that until you see someone step into traffic and you reach out, despite your resentment, to pull them back.

Who? I said.

Anyone.

I can only think of Kate.

Yes, she said, but Kate is out of reach.

I know, I said; I look at her, and it's as if there is a ghost walking around behind her eyes. She's one who got hurt early. Everything after is her way of dealing with that.

She said, I don't really believe in all that business about early trauma, one's bad parents, or childhood's terrible accidents ruining all the rest of life.

Some things stick with us.

Perhaps. I don't think so, though. I don't think even the worst, even the worst repeated, stays. The power that shoves around inside us shoves on. It is not a thinking power, and it doesn't build memorials. These ornery pasts are like paint on our fingers that we fling at the real beast rushing by. It's what's in us that wants to live that we are afraid of.

Beyond the trees we lingered under, beyond the yellowed grass, low, bushy hills rose into a clear sky. The bushes under bright sun looked faded, bristly at the tops.

I made myself up, she said—not from something but into something.

And a beautiful production it was.

Yes. I saw a beautiful, capable girl walking in sunshine, and I became that girl. She wanted to touch everything, and taste everything, and she has. Everything I have wanted to bring to my lips I have. I have tasted it, or licked it, or kissed it.

You sound like Kate. Or you sound like Jennie White doing a famous scene.

I am Jennie White.

Like Kate is Zebra Dunn.

No. Kate is still Kate yet. It's what makes her rage.

I feel like a condemned man. Somebody lurking about at the edge of a chase, watching his pursuers go over the hill following their dogs.

You just make these things up.

Maybe I am making Kate up, but I don't think I am making up Clement.

Kate thinks she is.

She is what?

She thinks she is making up this wild, hairy man in love with her. She came after the Oscars to tell me about him. She wanted me to believe he had become her creature.

Something inside me coldly uncoiled. I felt it like an ache, like a falling.

Jennie said, We dream of becoming something different without having to change: unchanging change; change unchanging. Clement has become Clement without ever not being Clement. It's fascinating to people like Kate Dunn.

And to Jennie White, I thought. And to Will Blake. Small internal birds rose, settled, and scattered in a shower. Pieces of me were flaking off—revealing what?

A yellow, exfoliate light tangled in the tops of bushes. The bushes, the bleached rock outcroppings, the dusty hills themselves, rising into slow rolls toward the west, seemed composed of fragments, of pieces broken off from something larger, something that if I could get a look at it entire would be a thing unlike any part of it showing here. My love for Kate was like a gold bracelet shining on an arm waved out a passing car window. I had made a dream and a way of life from a moment. But it was all like that; this face my mother turned toward me, corroded and beautiful, was only a flicker plucked from a burning field, from a fire raging in a country no one had ever taken me to, that no one, but God maybe, had ever seen. And so Kate's life, too. And everyone's. No wonder Clement stamped so hard. To feel the ungiving, actual ground under his feet. And no wonder I loved them all.

———

TOMMY SHOLEEN AND I are out on the deck throwing darts at the ripe oranges in the tree beside the swimming pool when Hannah Jell calls. Veronica's inside the house on Kate's phone giving orders to her staff at the restaurant. "No," she says, "don't throw the chowder out, just mix it with the gumbo." She wastes nothing, no matter how old it's getting. Hannah is chief gossip writer for *Entertainment Magazine*, and she's heard the news. The police are out there, somewhere under the brown sky, gathering evidence. "What are those fucks trying to do to you?" Hannah says.

"Do you know Harvey Madrid?" I say. Tommy's leaning over the rail trying to get a good angle for a toss. A red-feathered dart hangs from the side of an orange near the top of the tree.

"Sure," she says, "I know him."

"He's got the facts."

"I'll call him. But what about you—what are you doing?"

"I'm waiting for Clement to come back from Mexico so I can start work on his picture."

"You're really going to do it?"

"Why not?

I've known Hannah for years. She wanted to be an actress once; we worked on a picture together. I didn't know her well at the time, but when two weeks into shooting her father caught the stroke that killed him as he was getting into his car in Franklin, Illinois, I was the one who sat up with her all night and the one who drove her to the plane the next morning. It was odd, maybe it was because the shock was too great, maybe it was because she didn't know me, but she grinned and joked the whole time. As we stood at the gate, she grinned and shrugged, as if she was embarrassed that this had happened, and then she kissed me hard on the mouth, whirled, and ran for the plane. We had a short affair after that in which we were both very gentle; not long after that she quit pictures, and not long after that she went to work in the trades. Our paths cross from time to time; we don't speak about ancient times, but we seem to trust each other.

"And Will," she says, "what about Kate? Where is she?"

"In Mexico."

"Is someone there with you? Can you talk?"

"It's just Tommy—and Veronica."

"Tommy Sho?"

"Yeah, you want to talk to him? He's throwing darts into the yard. In a second he's going to be throwing them over the wall, trying to hit those fools down below."

"You still arguing with the neighbors?"

"It makes me feel alive."

"And now this woman's dead."

"Are you going to write something about this?"

"Well, what do you want me to do?"

"Nothing."

"It won't stay a secret very long."

"When it's not a secret you can write something."

Tommy looks at me cross-eyed. He smacks his lips. "What?" Hannah says. "Why are you laughing?"

"Tommy is showing me how he's going to make his leap from character parts to leading roles. I think he's got the knack."

"Forget Tommy. I don't see how I can't write about this."

"I'll tell Veronica to talk to you about it. She knows everything."

"How is Veronica? I saw her last week—she seems so sad."

"She needs to go on a vacation."

"I wish she would. She's been hanging around you and the terrible Blakes too long."

"*I've* been hanging around them too long."

"Billy's paying for Clement's picture, right? The one you're doing with him?"

"It amazes me too."

"Billy must think he's invincible."

"Billy was always invincible."

"Not like you."

"Oh, Hannah, now everybody will know my secret."

"I won't tell. They won't learn from me that Will Blake isn't the tough guy he pretends to be."

"That's good."

It could just go on and on, this talk. Not just this day, but every day, from this moment on into eternity. I am thinking of the desert, of the levels of austerity, of the salt pond at the bottom of Death Valley. Long-legged flies hover and spin above the acre of clear water that is too bitter for any animal to drink. I wonder not how they got there, but why they stay. I am thinking about Kate's list of the things she loved. She wrote it down, gave it to me as we crossed the border into Mexico. What did I do with it?

"Willie," Hannah says, and this is in confidence, "I'll back off if you want me to."

"Maybe we could have just this slow, distant rumble of publicity," I say. "Like heat lightning."

"It'll probably be more like a tidal wave."

I am wondering why we will do anything to get a little love. Or why some will. And why we get mixed up, why it takes us so long to figure out that the only thing available is the giving part. Whatever section of ourselves we want to keep intact, that's the one we have to shovel like a madman into the hopper. "Hannah," I say, "you can write what you want. As long as there are locked gates and limousine services, I can still have a quiet life."

Tommy Sholeen is winging darts full force as high and hard as he can toward the houses down below my compound. They arc through the air like speedo hummingbirds.

"I don't want to be the one who causes you trouble, Will."

"That's fine, Hannah."

Hannah thinks she loves me, but that won't stop her from

being the first on the street with the news. Inside the house Veronica talks loudly into the phone. I can see her walking back and forth behind Kate's white curtains. What was Bobby thinking when he killed himself? Could it have been a surprise? Even if he meant it, was it a surprise? And why even when we know exactly what's coming, does it still shock the shit out of us?

"Why don't you come over sometime and I'll tell you everything. It's a terrible story. It'll fill you with terror and pity."

"Oh, Will. How did you get in all this?"

"The fruits of clean living I guess."

And I am thinking, Maybe I only wanted, for once, to be loyal to something outside myself. But could that be true? Had things gotten that bad?

Veronica steps out through the French doors. The curtains billow around her. She is wearing a white sundress. Her skin, white, palely freckled, looks polished.

"Do you really want me to come out there?" Hannah says.

"Sure. Any time you want. I don't have to go to work for a while." How did Hannah find out about this? Harvey said they were keeping it quiet. "Who told you about this, Hannah?"

"A picture guy."

"Who—Billy?"

"No. Max Stein."

So it was Clement. So it is Clement. He spins the top. The truth that I have known for a while stares me hard in the face. I look blankly back. Even now, as the noose tightens, as I feel it scratching my neck, I do nothing. I see my brother leveling a shotgun at my father's hairy chest. I see him pull the trigger. I taste the blood in my mouth.

Veronica is watching me. Her eyes are stern, worn, grief-stricken. She touches the skin under her jaw, pressing a little at her mortality. I say, "Hannah, I have to go."

"I'll come out this week if it's all right."

"Fine."

I hang up, say to Tommy, who is leaning out over the rail to see where the darts fell, "That was Hannah."

"You going to get her out here and tell her everything."

"Yep."

"Then you crush her like a bug, right?"

"Yep."

I am thinking that it was as if the earth rose under my feet so gradually that I didn't notice, or if I noticed, so gradually that I was not frightened. Veronica is angry, she barks harshly into the phone; her face is mottled, patches of white stand out on her skin like leprosy, and I wonder who she is talking to, what it is between them that causes her so much pain, and though I know this Hollywood crew around me, my friends and the watchers from the periphery, could not produce the evidence necessary to accuse me of anything, I feel accused. The sky curves like the inside of a barrel. Above the murky smog it is a deep, velvety blue. In the south, far in the distance, smoke rises from unseen fires. At its rims, the world burns. If I were only a little higher, I could see beyond the fires and the rough, stricken mountains into Mexico. It was there, in what is now already another age, I met my enemy. It was there we fought, hand to hand, to the death.

FROM TELEPHONE TO telephone, Kate approached me. From Italy, calling late at night, whispering stories that chilled me, speaking to me of the rough hand that caressed her flesh, of the lips that kissed her, of the body pressing her down into a feather bed as deep as a nest. Her evening was my morning. The ringing waked me in the dawns. I sat on the edge of the bed in the ashen light whispering into the phone, keeping my voice low as if I were surrounded by malevolent strangers.

I am torn open, she said, *everything inside me has been pulled up into the air. I wear the inside on the outside. Nothing is hidden.*

I spoke back to her, my voice rising through a hollowness, through bones filled with air. *It is a dream,* I said, *it's gorgeous and full, it has many colors to it, it has depth and it resonates like some old song you're hearing again that breaks your heart, but it is only a dream.*

I know the dream, she said, *I know this . . . dream, but I don't know the life.*

The life is anything he's not in, I said.

But he's in everything.

I want you to go away with me.

I am away.

Not with me.

Take me to Mexico.

I did not throw the phone down then, I did not rip it from the wall; I called no lawyers or friends; I said, *Yes, all right, I will.*

To Mexico?

Yes. Anywhere.

It was the last call from Italy. She called from London, called from New York, called from the airplane as it passed seven miles above Nebraska. *I can see my house,* she said, *it's in the center of everything.*

Now you are.

Yes. And will be.

I do not believe there is always a way out. Or if there is a way, I do not believe we can always take it. The door cracks, the light of new life shines through, but we cannot rise, we cannot lift even our eyes toward it. A paralysis enters us, settles, and takes root. The one simple gesture—and we know it is simple, and only a gesture—the hand lifted, the glance, evades us. From across the valley of our lives the bugles of warning call to us. They call to us to flee. But we, who know everything, do not hear them, or, if we hear them, we can no longer listen or heed.

WE CROSSED INTO Mexico under a great arch constructed of red and yellow flowers. In a merciless sunlight the flowers shined like a band of burning. In her body she carried a pregnancy, another body sprouting inside her. She had told me of it first thing. It made my skin crawl. She said, *I wake up with a volcano inside me. I vomit as if everything in my being wants to expel this creature.*

It's a cracked mutant thing, I said, *that's why.*

No, she said, *everyone goes through it. I read a book about it. The book didn't say, but what it is is a new spirit entering us—that's what it's about: a new spirit that we can't control or own, that we have to carry, that we have to bring forth alive, in its own right, into the world. I'm amazed.*

You have to cut it out of you.

I can't. I wouldn't.

I won't have him, I won't have any piece of him alive inside you.

It isn't him. He's not the movie, he's just the usher.

I don't feel metaphysical about it. It's flesh, it's a thing—I want it out. The answer to this one, I think, is acceptance.

She grinned at me then, her lips wet from the drink she had

just sipped. We were high on a balcony in a hotel in the mountains above San Diego, poised for the plunge into Mexico. We
had stopped there because I wanted to go into Mexico with her
smell on me, I wanted to make love to her in an alien American
place and wipe her stink onto my body, to smear her grease into
my hair and onto my face, to taste it in my mouth. She was
accommodating, she was wild, she banged at my flesh with her
closed hands, beating a way for the energy to run through. Afterwards, wrapped in white sheets, we stood on the balcony looking eastward toward more mountains. She grinned at me and
there was nothing like triumph, nothing like pride, nothing like
mastery in the grin, there was only simple joy. *I can't believe this
has happened to me,* she said.

I think that's what I am supposed to say.

Is it? What are you supposed to say? What is it like for you?

Clement had called. He had come to the front door in Hollywood, but I wouldn't let him in. He had cried up to her, like
an ape Romeo, crying out to her as if I wasn't there.

We are leaving, I had yelled through the door. *We are on the way
to Mexico.*

He pounded on the door. I watched it shake and shudder. It
didn't give. He said, *I want to bring this out in the open. I want to get
it on the table.* The words ejected through sobs and croaks. They
sounded as if he were banging them together out of rocks. *Yell
all you want,* I cried. *Say anything you want—you can't get in.*

I made Carol call the cops. They came and got him, as quickly
as if they had been waiting at the bottom of the drive. Clement
fought; through the window I saw him rage, reeling, rising from
among them like a whale fighting the harpoon, but they subdued
him. I saw the nightstick rise, I saw it fall. I saw them lift him
like a trophy and carry him to the car. I flung the door open. *Oh,
policemen of Los Angeles,* I cried, laughing like a madman, *set me
free.*

Upstairs, when I arrived there shuddering under explosions of
terror and rage, I found her sitting naked in the center of her
stripped bed watching a video of herself. In the video she lay
naked on a black marble floor as men in evening dress stood in a
ring around her. Under their gaze she writhed. Her flesh was so
white it looked painted. The stab of hair at the center of her was
black, split by red. I threw a chair through the TV. It popped like

a glass bubble; it wheezed and spit like something alive. I whirled on her, but it was as if there was nothing there. Her face was blank.

Clement came by, I said, *but he couldn't stay. He said to say hello.*

Fine, she said. *I hope he's doing well.*

She stared into the smoking, shattered box as if it were the eye of God.

From the balcony I let my gaze rake the headlands, the battered dusty scrub, revolving until it came to her. An inch beyond her skin the world reeled. And she, her compact frame, the eyes hard as blue rocks, drew me. *It's funny,* I said; *what it's like for me is something so natural I'm not even thinking about it. Bobby used to say that everything we were supposed to do we knew how to do. He said it wasn't just that we knew how to do it, but that it didn't matter how we did it: we couldn't get it wrong.*

He did.

Yes. So I guess what he did—no, not what he did last, but what happened, what he did before the last was what he wasn't supposed to do.

What was that?

What you've done.

What?

Give in to the dark.

What dark?

Mr. C. R. Blake is, I believe, its local representative.

I'll keep the child.

The wind pressed the sheet against her body. Below us it snapped in the tops of palm trees, and beyond the trees down the rough, thorny slope, it rippled in the tops of bushes. It was hot and dry, without life, and everything seemed caught in it.

I WAS NOT running from my enemy, I was leading my enemy on. We dream of clean motives, succinct action, of resolution, but our lives continue on in their invariable, clumsy way. Yet we go to the movies, we fall in love, we bear children, as if we believe the good end, the golden bounty, is just over the next hill. I have lived my life as a gentleman rider, as one who, if not absolved from this mad hope, was not tainted by it, one for whom the conniptions and the frets of the world were alarms raised for others. I would, so I thought, instead of rousing myself, drift on, living my own form of grace, indifferent to storms and battles, nonaligned, the Switzerland of my household. But then I changed my mind. This woman, her ways, the accumulation of years, Clement's shenanigans, the wound my brother tore so neatly in my side, my mother's retreat, even Veronica spinning in her sadness, brought me to it, but they were not the cause. The cause was other. In this lifelong dialogue we conduct with the force that drives us, there are moments when the talking stops, when what we speak to—this god or ancient indivisible—falls silent and we are left alone on the field of our lives. In this moment, which as we endure it, seems to last forever, we can wait or we can act. I had seen myself as one capable of waiting, of living a patience that in its conception promised the riches of peace and joy, but when my moment came, I was not able to. In that trembling night of anticipation, when the wind that touches only the present seems to speak of the past and of the future just beyond the walls, that seems to whisper of disaster behind and disaster ahead, I did not rely on some kind of faith, on willingness, on the quietude resting at the core, to get me through. I made my plan, and I acted. I knew some things, I had seen the patterns form; I, who as a child had watched the mountain quail pick their repetitive way through underbrush, who had watched in the fall as the ducks came up the western flyways, who had lived in a world that despite appearances moved with an orderliness, a linked quickstep of money and glamor, who had lived among people whose reactions I thought I could predict, decided to bet on what he knew. So I made my error.

Into Mexico we roved, followed by the bear of my hatred and my longing. Under the burning arch into Mexicali, past the rusty houses and the houses the color of airplanes, through towns neon couldn't save, we sank southward. I had claimed a plan—a visit to my friend Pedro Manglona's ranch on the sea cliffs north of Mazatlán—but I did not have a place in mind, or any neat procedure devised; I wanted only to clear a space, to push aside the clamors of work and friends, so I could get down to the wrestle.

It rained on the outskirts of Mexicali, a bitter, harsh, clattering rain, falling so hard that we retreated from it into a hotel for the night. The next morning, in fresh sunshine, the desert began to bloom, throwing up magical flowers on the creosote and saltbush, tricking out purple blossoms on the vergo trees, bringing the smell of bananas and oranges into the courtyards. A small boy, his skin glistening under his white suit as if he had been dipped in oil, brought us fruit on a tray. Kate kissed him on the lips and sent him on his way.

The new fetal life grew between us, and it seemed to me that we each carried it. I could feel it under my heart, like a hot acorn, burning and whirling, as she, leaning back naked in the bed, pressing her long toes hard against the carved footboard, could too—I could see it in her eyes—but we did not speak of it. The jostle and terror, its small, atomic radiance—*its meaning*—was too much. In dreams, in a dream I had in the carved, expensive bed, under the rough-beamed ceiling that stood like bars above my closed eyes, it hung before me in a middle distance, a shape approaching out of a sunny field like the field my brother Bobby crossed on the afternoon he leveled the gun on my father, a furred, biting thing, a body like a grimace. I retreated from it, but the air behind me, the space, was thick as a wall, and I couldn't run. In the dream, sweating, drained of blood, unable to run, I knelt before it and begged it not to harm me.

During three days of travel, a slow arc turning toward the coast, we spoke to each other with our bodies. We made love furiously, in the car, in sand dunes, in bushes, in a stream in which the thin water ran over white rocks as smooth as paving stones, on the hood of the car parked beside the road as trucks carrying agricultural workers rumbled by. From a ditch filled to the rim with shattered colored glass—the place where cathedrals must have dumped their ruined windows—a man in white clothes rose and applauded us, as Kate, wearing only a red scarf around her neck, rode me like a cowgirl, like a barrel racer, grunting. With his crooked staff he tapped her on the head, in benediction or disgust, he didn't say, and toddled down the road. One night, cocooned in sheets beside a stream, we watched women in white dresses set fires in a bamboo grove, spilling fire from cans onto the bases of the tall feathery cane, until the world across the stream leapt in firelight. A man in Guaymas selling paper flowers outside the hotel spoke my name, but when I turned to him to see what he wanted, he became confused.

In corners, just beyond the peeling posters for rock and roll bands, outside restaurants in small villages where half-naked boys chased goats down alleyways that opened into white, shorn fields,

I looked for the follower, for the one coming on behind, but I did not see him. I knew Kate was looking too. Sipping a tall drink, she touched her throat with a movie star gesture and turned her head to scan the square where under blossoming poincianas old women in black dresses rolled balls of dark yarn in their hands. Twenty miles from any town, we passed a line of men in red shirts, marching somewhere. They didn't look at us as we passed, but their faces, dark and smooth, looked like the faces of men returned from terrible battles, and their eyes were dazed. On a street corner in a village in the state of Sinaloa a short man dressed in crumpled purple clothes opened a Tampa Nugget cigar box to show us a collection of poker chips, each lettered with the first initial of names he spoke in an oracular voice—Gabriela, Xavier, Fortunato, William, Katherine. A shaman gone bad, the idea was that you paid him money to stop, which I understood, saying my own name to him and Kate's, bowing as he pressed a finger to his lips, dropping dollar bills into the open box. The poker chips were streaked with mud.

In Tela, sitting on the library steps eating shrimp from a small woven basket, she asked me to tell her the next thing to do, and when I asked what she meant, she said "Anything—any next thing I will do."

"You're mocking me," I said.

Beyond her a flock of children shepherded by nuns in white, sail-winged cowls passed. The square was ringed with colonnades hung with colored paper streamers. Soldiers in jeeps slowly circled, their machine guns cradled in their laps.

"Sometimes," she said, "I want to be completely dominated. I want to let all the controls go, let anything happen."

"When you go down to the lobby by yourself, when you take your walks in the evenings—do you call Clement?"

"I have once or twice."

"Where is he?"

"Down here."

"He's following us?"

"It's more like we're pulling him along behind us."

"It makes me want to kill you."

"I know. I don't see why you don't."

"I have another plan."

A couple wearing evening clothes passed by. The woman's pale dress rustled. They glanced at us; I saw the flinch of recognition, the surprise, the face quickly setting behind the surprise, the whispers.

"Make me do something," Kate said.

"All right. Get up right now and go strike that woman."

"The woman in the party dress?"

"Hit her."

"All right."

She sprang up, ran to the couple, and as they turned, in slight surprise and pleasure—they knew who she was, this Zebra Dunn—she struck the woman across the face with her half-closed fist. The woman staggered, cringing; the man raised his arm, stepped back. Kate swung to strike again, and stopped. The man spluttered something. Kate stared at him. She stared for a long moment, turned, and walked back to me. Her face was flushed, filled with pain.

"I hit her," she said, rubbing her knuckles.

"Yes. You harmed the harmless. It hurts, doesn't it?"

"Yes. I hit her, and then I instantly . . . wanted to kiss her."

"Clement," I said, "would only want to go on hitting her."

She sat down beside me. Above us the moon had dissolved all the stars around it. From distant streets came the pop of gunfire. She said, "Do you know where Chimney Rock is?"

"I've heard of it."

"It's in Nebraska, it's near my house, the house I say I grew up in."

"But we don't really know where you grew up."

"No. Maybe there, maybe somewhere else. But near my house—my real or imaginary childhood house—this formation, this big stalagmite called Chimney Rock, rises out of the prairie. There used to be prairie for a thousand miles in every direction—now there's not, it's crowded like anywhere, but they've made a park and keep the rock inside it, and kept the ground clear around it, so you can still experience the effect. It's tall, like a monument God dribbled onto the prairie, it was the landmark the pioneers looked for on their way west. It was a sign, a proof, that they were traveling correctly, the first sign on the prairie of something other than grass seas forever. A kind of island, or introduction to the true West. You could see it from my house. It's thin, like a compass needle. Time has worn it away, worn what was around it away. It's a spire."

"Aspire."

"Yes. I think about it now. It's like a compass point for me. I think back on it; I picture it, and it rights me."

"Aspire."

"Yes."

"To what?"

"The way."

"What is that?"

"Who knows?"

We seemed to be falling down a long, painted tunnel. We spoke our private languages, but they were so similar that we thought each could understand the other. She could say, as she did standing naked in sunlight at our hotel room window, that I had a sweetness in me, and I would agree and tell her a story about swimming with Bobby in a cattle tank in Texas when we were children visiting one of my father's movie sets. The story would bounce up between us bright shining, but she did not seem to hear the anger and the accusation underneath it, and perhaps I misunderstood her willingness to go along with me, perhaps my idea that somehow guilt and shame had touched her at last was mistaken. All the time, every minute, I was waiting for Clement to arrive, to push through Mexico into our presence. I had told Jennie that I wanted to cause pain, that I wanted to get my own back, but it was not pain I wanted, or my own. I wanted to cause a death, bring an end.

In Mexico, in the Mexico we traveled through, the trees were filled with birds. Maybe the rain drove them down close to the earth. In early mornings, at the outskirts of villages, a camphor tree, or a mango, would be filled with thousands of birds, black-bodied, green-tailed birds, or larks, or sparrows, or finches. In the evening as we followed the road through grain fields and fields of poppies that burned red in the sunset, in a distance near the mountains, the birds would wheel in huge gray clouds into the trees. Our car scared up vultures off the highway. In village markets birds in twig cages sang all day. At night owls hooted from the trees near our hotel. The last night before he found us, it was a bird that waked me.

252

That night I came up out of sleep, swimming hard, like a man rising from his own drowning. She called to me, or a bird called to me in her voice, and I waked. A silvery light touched the chairs and tables, lay like paint on the windowsills. In the room next door a voice insistently pleaded in Spanish. I lay on my side listening to it, listening to the sad, urgent words. The bird, some bird, called from the dark, but it was no longer Kate. She slept beside me. The voice next door broke off, there was a small, weak cry, and then silence. Kate slept on her side, her arm crossed over her face as if to fend off a blow. The whispering began again through the wall, a man's voice pleading. He pleaded with someone who was crying. I put my ear to the wall; it was cold and slick against my face. In Kate's face turned toward me, even asleep, I could see everything. Her expression was one of guileless stupidity and abandonment, the sleep face we wear that exposes our origins, like a trip back through the layered brain to the ancient knot of neurons we started with—in her sleep face, more than any other, I could see the primitive, instinctual nature, the stubborn reptilian core that squatted, still alive, still active, in all of us. She had once told me that in my sleep I looked demented, but it was not dementia she saw, only the sullen, unwavering purpose that ran me, that runs us all, the intention, as pure as the first fire, to grasp and hold life. I had watched her on many nights, had watched the dreams ebb and flow across her face, her eyes twitching under their soft lids, but when the dreams faded, what appeared was this, what I looked at now, this pure devouring purpose, dumb and relentless and irresistible. It was what my father, through gift or some whacked training, was able to bring forth into the living day. It was what both of them had access to, what any actor, in some way, could occasionally touch and bring out signs of, but something that, in them, rushed forth unchecked, roving about stomping and dancing into wakeful life. Arrived from Italy in a white dress stamped with a pattern of small blue flowers, she had told me simply about Clement, about my father as lover, standing before me in her bedroom, her arms at her sides, looking straight at me as she spoke. Her voice was soft and steady. I had raised my hand to strike, but I could not do it. She told me what I knew already, but in some way it seemed as if the facts did not exist before she said them. I had thought that I would cringe, that I would fall, that something in me, the thing that held my sustained sense of who I was, would crack, that I would break down before her, and before myself, that the messy pleading that runs like the ground noise of life itself through each of us eternally, would rise up now, as it had in the man next door, and take over my life. But this did not happen. Something fierce, something harsh and sure, rose instead. I did not know yet that this rough energy, this resistance or capability, was only the other side of the same pleading face I feared. I was no timid, angst-bound soul afraid to say what he wanted, afraid to live. My drift was no pose, my life was not a rehearsal for a better part to come. Then, the words spoken, cast out into the air between us, she took a step toward me in that room. Sun flooded the walls, we seemed sunk in a well of sunlight. The air smelled of charred wood and sweet flowers. I stepped toward her, stepping from a shore so ancient there was no language, no knowledge, to describe or explain it. We rushed at each other. We threw each other down on the floor, tearing at each other's clothes. We tore through shirt and dress, ripping cloth, down to skin. And did not stop there. We ripped on, pounding, grabbing, tearing at each other's flesh. Her nails raked my chest, I bit her, we drew blood. Our tattered clothes, the pale floor, floor as yellow as a starlet's hair, our bodies, became slick with blood. We rolled in it. I thrust myself into her, through blood, through the tear at the center of her, into the crevice in which—this too admitted—the new being, my father's child, my brother, sucked life. I rammed myself in, I pounded myself into her body, into all their bodies, like a stake driven into the heart of the world.

No chill now—the whispery Latin voice subsided, something in there surrendered—but fever in waves splashing up through me. She slept in the black world underneath dreams. To reach her I would have to wake her, but for the moment I could not. I got up, pulled on my clothes, and went out. The village slept in its history. All but the filling station where I stopped for gas. There, men, Indians in loose gray clothes, rolled dice against the front wheel of a tractor trailer. The heavy arc lights above them threw a frayed radiance into the humid night. The rain had not returned, but the air was still moist. I wanted a little distance, a little space, preparation for consequences to come, trailer for the outfall of my plan that was drawing Clement to me; I wanted to see what would rush to fill the small gap, some idea of what would pour in after the main event. He was nearby, I knew he was, but I couldn't see him anywhere. He was not behind the derelict cars or the toppled fruit stall, nor was he in the café I looked into, where the thick, grainy music of late-night disasters played.

I drove as far as the heights above the town before I turned around. I stayed up there in the dusty toplands for a long time, sitting on one rock or another, letting a little tenderness, letting a little soft feeling come back into me. What I liked about sitting in driveways and lying on sofas, what I liked about loitering on the floor of my trailer on some movie set through an endless afternoon, was that it let a little quietness, a little sweetness enter you. Like a peach on a windowsill—the juices turned sugary. Bobby's life showed me the need for it.

The moon was up, a sorry, bitten piece of moon, and its light made the stony landscape glitter and tremble. The town was in a valley; it was a collection of colored lights that wound along a dry river like a thin jeweled snake. I stood in the wind looking down at it. I could imagine a life there, some fractious and simple Mexican life of family arguments and difficult labor, of church and feast days, and always something more needed that no one could quite get to, and it didn't seem very different from the life I lived. The wind pushed at the mountains, at me, and subsided, leaving a silence that was as clear as a bell. The life of the visible earth, the rock hills and the still and spiny desert floor, even the distant town whose tiny lights winked on their way through time, seemed poised in an ancient and perpetual balance.

Then a man came out of the shadows and spoke to me. He was an old man, an Indian, very short, with white whiskers bristling around his mouth, and he was leading a burro on whose back was stacked two bundles of sticks.

How goes it, old-timer, I said, or something like it, in Spanish, and he grinned at me and said it was a fine night but dangerous, as he had found out, to be traveling in the dark. I asked him what he meant, because it seemed to me the dark was safe and comforting, and then without prologue he told me a story about his daughter stepping on a snake in the dark, and I thought here we have another apocryphal raconteur, some member of Kate's family, because I had never heard of anyone stepping on a snake in the dark.

It's true, the old man said, she stepped on a snake and her leg swelled up black and huge and there was no remedy for it. In a matter of hours, *horas,* she began to cry out for breath, and then she couldn't catch her breath and then she died.

The grin stayed on his face the whole time he told me this. It was one of those grief grins. You see them at funerals and in hospitals.

I said, Listen, I once imagined that I wanted to live in hotels. It was my dream—to live in a hotel and order room service and stay up there high above the city in a clean place where the maid came in and changed the sheets every day and a guy in a suit gave you your mail. I used to carry this dream around like a talisman. It was a great dream, I thought, but then I became famous and I got my wish and I lived in hotels, big ones in big cities, and what happened was I would open the drapes and stand there looking out at all the lights, imagining the lives of the people behind them, the businessmen down on their knees before some bitter women, and the cleaning ladies buffing the floors of some stupid office, or some kid who was afraid, kneeling by the window saying his prayers, and all I could think was how I wanted to be at home where all the smells were familiar and even the people I didn't like recognized me.

Hearing my voice, I thought how callow I was, but then it seemed I was speaking to something behind what he said.

He continued to grin and then he went back to the burro, pulled a long machete from among the sticks, and said, Give me your money.

I didn't answer and he said it again. Give me your money.

You don't look like a robber, I said.

I am not a robber, he said, I am a poor man.

If you pull a machete and demand money, you're a robber.

No, I am only making life more equal.

Damn, I said. The machete blade shone in the moonlight. It had figures etched on it. An old guy like you, I said, a guy with a dead daughter, ought to know better than that. Isn't anybody content with their lot? I mean, how did this world get so fucked up that even peasants—no offense—are running around holding people up? I mean, I can understand guys like me doing it, we're agitated and selfish, but you guys—hasn't life proved to you that you aren't getting anything anyway; I mean, haven't you accepted that?

No, I haven't, he said.

Then I feel sorry for you.

You can feel sorry, amigo, but you also must give me your money.

Okay, I said.

So I pulled my wallet out, slapped him in the face with it, and took the machete away from him.

See, I said, now you're in real trouble.

I pushed him against the car with the point of the blade. Lightly.

I was mistaken, amigo. I'm sorry.

Now you want to apologize.

What else is there for me to do? I took you for someone else.

I held him with my forearm, reached past him and tossed the machete into the backseat. Kate's scent was in the car.

Okay, I said, you're free to go.

He drew back, an old man slightly wobbly, and looked at me with disdain.

You don't want to kill me?

I don't even know you. Why would I want to kill you?

Americans are stupid.

Ah yeah, I know, everybody says that. We call it generosity.

You should seek revenge.

Don't worry. I am one of the hard Americans.

So you will kill me?

No, not you. I have bigger game in mind.

I am not important enough for you.

Actually—I'm sorry, old-timer—that's true.

You have prejudice against Mexicans.

Not just Mexicans. I'm prejudiced against everybody.

I think you should kill me.

What's the matter with you? Are you a crazy guy or what?

I live in the world the way it is.

Ugh, you sound like my wife.

I wanted to break into a church and plunge my face into the font of holy water. And I wanted to raise my dripping head and watch the water slowly clear until I could see my face in it. I wanted to see my face staring back at me from holiness.

I said, Sometimes I wonder if there isn't something wrong with me.

There is something.

You don't know. I mean, no matter what happens, I still seem to be optimistic. I can't decide whether I am on to something or whether I am just looney.

Looney.

You're pissed because I won't do things your way.

Would you return my machete?

No, I can't do that.

You are the robber.

I'll pay you for it.

I pulled a ten out, looked at it, pulled out thirty or forty more bucks, and gave them to him.

This is American money, he said.

They'll change it.

You don't have pesos?

Come on, man, I could cut your head off if I wanted to.

You are afraid to do that. An American coward.

What a world. I'm being insulted by a damn bandit I just took a knife away from.

If I were a younger man you would be lying dead now.

I've heard that kind of business before.

He cocked his head, tapped the point of his chin with one finger. You will suffer, he said, uselessly.

Tough luck, old man, words are cumulative; they won't do this kind of *immediate* work.

I am telling the truth.

Maybe you're only being frank.

I am no liar.

And then a terrible violence rose in me, or it descended on me, like a black wing dropping out of the sky. I picked the old man up, carried him to the burro, threw him across the animal's neck, and kicked the burro in the ass. It started, broke into a trot, then slowed, shuffled down the hill. I lunged toward it, carried by a wind, but then I stopped. A powerful, murderous being lurched inside me, straining against my body, urging my body to carry it forward, but I resisted. It seemed to want to come out of my face. There was great pressure. My lips twisted, my eyes widened, my skin swelled. I shook. I shook and cried out.

The old man's voice drifted up to me. *Uselessly,* he said. And then whatever it was, the violence, the energy, nuclear and snapping, rushed away from me. I thought how all of us will soon leave this planet, all of us alive now, and drift out on dark wings into the emptiness of space. I fell to my knees. What had been looking for me found me. It took me in its arms, and it was cold and dark and wet. It held me. It held me in a silence that was the same as talk, because I understood every word. It said soon there will be silence forever. It said soon you will be alone forever. It said this is what is behind everything you are afraid of and it is true. Stupid prayers jabbered in my mouth, and they were no help. I pressed my face against the ground, pressed until I could feel my skull going into the earth. The silence roared on. Everything it said was true. Everything it said was going to happen would happen. There was nothing I could do about it. From the dark we lurch fitfully through our moment of light and back into the dark. Into the dark. Into the fucking shitty inevitable endless imperishable goddamn dark.

I HAD TOLD no one that we were going to Mexico, but Veronica figured it out. *I know what you are doing,* she said, *and it won't work.* We were up at the head of Sunset, or just off it, in Chinatown, at a blazing red restaurant, eating boiled eels. We peeled the black skin off the greasy white flesh with our fingers, arguing as we ate, arguing as we had begun to so often, and I listened to her tell me, as she had been telling me all my life, what I was up to and how bad an idea it was, and how I was not going to get anywhere with it. *Why should I listen to you,* I said, *you've never liked anything I've come up with.*

She said, *It's amazing isn't it.*

It only shows how little you know about how things work in this world. I'm as successful and competent a person as you know. Anybody would want to have what I have.

You're a numbskull. It only goes to show how slowly—and inevitably—the world works its processes out.

Don't use that word. Processes. There's no juice in it. Words like that, when you use them with someone you love, are gaps that let loneliness blow in.

Loneliness was already there. So you don't have to talk about it. It's your juiceless word.

That looks like a foreskin you're shucking.

259

Don't talk dirty.
I don't want to talk about what I am up to.
Stop acting.
I'm not acting.

And I wasn't. Maybe it was the first time in my life, I don't know, I didn't think, but I didn't want her to know what I was doing. I didn't want to know myself. I had believed all my life in fate, in things adding up and becoming inevitable, in the feather that tips the elephant, and it seemed to me now, as I watched her slide the black skin off the rubbery chunks of fish, that there was something with its feet anchored in a place so far down in my life that I could not, even if I had the best equipment in the world, dive down and touch it. The only way to get to it was to go forward, to complete the circle of it, if it was a circle, to push on to the next disastrous, or the last disastrous, occasion, and so to find, in the myth that haunts us all, the place I started from. Kate, I knew, had plans of her own, but when I saw her face, when she twirled into the house in her white dress carrying a bunch of lilies, there was as much exhaustion as energy in her eyes, and when I took her into my arms she sagged against me, giving me the whole weight of her body, and the weight, it seemed to me, of much more, of passion and consequence, and amazingly, of helplessness. It was in that moment, a moment I didn't describe to Veronica, that I decided what I would do, decided not on a plan, but on a resolution that I knew, if I set the bait, would step forth to me like a bear coming out of the woods at night to rummage and thieve among the goods of the visiting world, a world that had already—unknown to bears—won everything.

But when he found us, I almost missed him.

We had come up out of a valley, past a creamy white lake that looked as if laundry powder had been dissolved in it, through the mango orchards of an estate that had been planted in grass around the hacienda, grass so well watered that it looked painted into the range of mountains that divided the plateau from the ocean. We were running fast down the mountain road, coming on each rocky curve into glimpses of the ocean dark blue like a baby's eyes, when he passed us in a yellow T–Bird. The car was past, slipping in a gravelly spray around the turn ahead, when I realized, or thought I did, that the driver was Clement. My heart kicked. He wore a white cap jammed down on his head; he did not look at us.

"That was Clement," I said.

"I don't think so."

"Why?"

"I don't think it could be, not here, not in this empty place."

"You expect him farther down the line?"

"Different circumstances."

"I don't think he cares about the circumstances. It's all instinct with him anyway. If he waits, it's just for the opening."

But he had told her—I could see it—had told her where he would meet her, maybe had already met her, maybe when she went out on her evening walks through the pastel villages, maybe then, from a café table under the lemon trees, he had hailed her and they had sat talking, their hands clasped across the table, brushed by the light of a candle—or maybe last night as I climbed to my rendezvous with the old Indian in the hills, he had come to her bed, had fit his heavy body into the shallow scoop mine had left, obliterating it. Fine, I thought, fine—it's not magic you're working here, Pop, it's only greed, and its minion lust, and those boys might be clever, but they're dumb.

She leaned in a white dress against the door; her feet were propped on the dash. The wind blew her dress up, exposing her strong, tanned legs. She pulled the skirt to her waist. The world, everything outside the car, the saltbushes and the yucca and the ferny thorned bushes with no names, the red rocks and the pines cranked into angles and twists as if they had been tortured all their lives, seemed tied together, all of a piece, gathered by design, like the props on a movie set, and the road, angling down toward the sea, seemed a funnel through which flowed the river of our fate, upon which we rode now, in summer clothes, the wind bursting past us snapping and cawing.

I placed my hand on her thigh, ran my knuckles upstream to the edge of her white underpants.

She lifted her feet, laid them gently in my lap. From her bag she took a peach and bit softly into it. "You want some?"

"Not now."

She drew a thin strip of red skin from between her teeth. She wet her lips on the bitten peach, looking at me. There was a terrible tenderness in her eyes. I thought of a dream I had in which people I knew gathered around me to make accusations about my life. They accused me of looking at my mother naked, of seducing Veronica, of dishonoring my father. *You should be ashamed of yourself,* they said. Their eyes, too, were filled with tenderness, a soft morning light of kindness and concern, and under their gaze I had felt myself willing, as my body fell through itself, to sink to my knees before them and ask for forgiveness, even as my mind, which remained clean and apart from it all, said no, said no there is nothing to be ashamed of, said any move toward another, no matter how clumsy and terrible, is a move toward love. This was what I wanted to explain to her, and to Clement, how I understood what they were doing, explain with hand signals, with clubs and blows, with blood and murder.

She said, her voice gentle, "What is Earl doing now? What is Veronica doing?"

"They're ducking and covering, I think."

She laughed. "Veronica's so sad."

"She has a right to be. She's had a sad life."

"I'm sorry about how it gets to her. She takes it to her as if it's her baby she has to protect and coddle."

"It's her way of feeling things."

"Sometimes there's too much of that."

The mesas reached like stone fingers for the coast, bony and crumbling. We came around a last wide curve, past shattered red rocks that lay in piles against the cliffside. The road swung in gradual descent through a stand of willows. Beyond the willows it snapped left and down toward the shore, where beyond a flat sand race the Pacific opened sparkling and bustling. In the apex of the sharp curve the wooden road barrier had been broken through. Churned-up mica shined in the car tracks, a glittering road for leaping off of, and dust hung in the air.

"Oh my God," Kate cried. "Oh no."

There was terror in her face. It was love's terror, it was the truth, and I saw it like a blade coming at me.

"Stop, stop," she cried, "stop and get him, stop."

I pulled over into the dust cloud. It swirled around us like a magician's smoke. Sunlight bristled at its edges; through a gap I could see the ocean, and in a farther distance came sounds of music, brassy horn sounds and the sound of drums.

Kate sprang from the car and bounded down the brushy slope. I called to her, but my voice was thick in my throat and the dust blinded me. I followed her down, through bushes sprinkled with tiny purple flowers. The flowers smelled rank and rotten, as if they were rooted in the bodies of dead animals. The T-Bird had cut a path for itself, a patch that swirled with dust. The sun shined through the dust, slapping my face like a flat hand. I couldn't see her, couldn't see the car, and then I could, but I couldn't see Clement. And then she cried out happily.

"He's here."

I came up to the car. Clement lay on the hood, on his back. Kate had jumped up beside him; she squatted next to him, bending over him: she kissed him on the mouth. I put my hand on her back. Her flesh was wet under the dress, and it was soft, as if it were dissolving. She turned, grasped my hand, pulled it to her, pulled me to Clement, who lay on his back, his head propped against the windshield. "Here," she said, "feel. He's okay."

She placed my hand on my father's chest. Coarse, heavy breaths ran through, breath enough for two or more. He looked at me out of dazed black eyes. His lips were bloody, but there didn't seem to be any other wounds. He leaned toward Kate, pressed his face and chest against her hip. She caressed him, stroked his arm, his side, slipped her hand into his shirt, clasped my hand under hers and held it hard against his chest. "Nothing can hurt him bad. It's incredible."

My father looked at me and his eyes seemed filled with dust. He grimaced, grinned. "What a ride," he said.

We were a hundred feet down the slope. The car had come to rest in a flat place among bushes. Farther down, a sand track disappeared among pine trees. The surf boomed in the distance, a crumpling sound with a faint, hollow hiss at the end of it.

Clement grasped Kate's hand, grasped my hand under hers. There was power, the same old power in his grip. The hatred I felt for him, the jealousy and the envy, roared in me, but the love was there too, like a church on a battlefield, and as he turned and his other arm lifted and his hand grasped my neck and pulled me down to him, down into the sweaty, bloody well of him, as he drew my face to him and kissed me with his bloody lips, as the revulsion and terror sprang up howling in me, still there was the sturdy angel of my love, this white, shell-scarred structure standing inside me. I tore myself from it. I lurched backward, tripped and fell. He grinned at me.

"I was coming around that curve," he said, "so fast—I was almost flying . . ." He coughed. Kate patted him. "No, I'm all right," he said. "I just got the wind knocked out of me—but I was coming around the curve, and there, right . . . for an instant, it was like I snapped right off the earth, just cracked right off it—it was like, let me tell you, this came to me you know, it was like every part of the earth, and time and our bodies and all that shit, are snugged right up against a whole other world, like it's right there, just a finger snap away, not even that far, like any minute, like, you know, the way you feel out in the desert, out there in the Mohave—you know, Will, what I'm talking about— like the next thing after these rocks is eternity—Jesus, I'm talking like a teenager . . ."

"Take your time," Kate said.

"I'm okay, I'm gasping and I'm bruised, but I can tell I'm okay—but thank you, sweetheart."

He cleared his throat, spat a gob of bloody phlegm. I got up off the ground.

"I mean," he said, "I mean one minute I was flying, you know, and then the next I was *flying*. I was somewhere else entirely that was nothing like this place. And you know what I was thinking?"

"You were thinking about the movies," Kate said.

"Yes. You wonderful girl. That's exactly right. I was thinking about the movies. I was thinking about Renoir, Renoir *fils*—his son, Renoir *petit-fils*, is an artist too, did you know that? He's a sculptor, makes these clear plastic sculptures filled with dry-cleaning fluid— what is that stuff? Carbon tetrachloride?—yeah, Renoir—you just can't keep that art shit out of the blood once it gets in there—I was thinking about him, the *fils*, about what it was like for him after he finished *Rules of the Game*. I was thinking he probably brought the reels home and showed the picture to his family."

He pushed up on an elbow. There was a long scratch running like the edge of flame along his thick forearm. He leaned his head against the windshield for a moment and looked up into the sky. It was a deep, soft blue and curved like a shell. We were caught under it, looking up into it, and it was beautiful. If there wasn't anything beyond it, maybe it didn't matter, as long as the beauty of it went on knocking us out.

"It was probably the greatest picture ever made," he said, "so I think of him spooling the film into the home projector, sitting there with his wife and son, wartime bursting through Paris like a snowstorm, showing the picture to his loved ones. We got to make a picture together, son."

"Maybe not in this lifetime, Pop."

"Don't welsh on me, boy."

I didn't know what he meant, but I started to wade in when Kate raised herself and waved. "Cowboys," she said.

There were half a dozen men on horseback out on the path below us. They looked up at us, not doing anything, just looking. Kate called to them in Spanish and a couple stepped their horses up.

"We've had an accident," she said. "We need your help."

The men were on their way to a festival. They spoke to us without getting down.

"It's in a little village over on the beach," she said, translating. The men sat back on their horses, their straw hats pushed up on their heads. They wore loose white clothes tricked out with jeweled belts and colored woven sashes.

"They say the festival is spectacular," she said. "They say there are roast pigs and dances and drunken speeches and terrible dramas, and saints come alive and even—I think they said—a car race."

"A car race?" I said.

"That's what he told me."

"I don't see how we can miss that," Clement said.

"Yes," I said. "I think that's the place for us."

One extravaganza was as good as the next. And why not, in a village by the sea, under colored lanterns on a night of festival, why not come to grips in such a place with what gigged and slapped at me?

"We need someone to haul the old man and this car," I said.

"I'll go get them," Kate said.

She jumped down from the car, her skirt flaring like an open flower, and ran to the cowboys. One of them pulled her up behind him. Her face shined with sunlight. There was so much energy and quickness in her that you wouldn't think anything was calculated, but it had begun to seem to me, stranded now in bush with my supine father, that everything was—that the whole venture, from its first snappy moments at a party in someone's show house in Malibu, through the films and the awards and the arms of the man snorting like a buffalo beside me, was nothing more than a strict, intricate plan Kate was putting into action. But if that was true, I thought as I got into the T-Bird and began to fiddle with the ignition, it was no less incredible a feat, for who could come up with such a plan, and who with such a plan spinning in her guts could make it come alive and work in this world, where even the simplest gesture falls awry? It didn't seem to matter to her how everything was sliding like an old house down a muddy hill, it didn't seem to matter to her that everything broke, that love turned to hatred or indifference, that the old myths were reduced to logos, that any minute now the world—the sleek or dusty corner of it she inhabited—was about to spin out of control; it didn't seem to matter to her that we were dying here, falling in necrotic spin into the chaotic dark at the bottom of the world; it didn't bother her at all.

I watched through the bug-dusty windshield as she disappeared among the pines, and I was choking with love for her; it swelled in my throat and sent harsh disputative kicks through my body. Clement was watching her too, I could see his avid eye, see the infection and the delight; he lifted his head, swallowing, a shudder passed through him, and he began to slap lightly at his arms as if he were being bitten. I pressed my hand against the windshield, where his head rested, pushing my palm flat against the glass. Without turning, he said, "It's a miracle. That's all it is. You don't have to believe in a thing in this world, and it'll still turn around on you so fancy and gorgeous it knocks you right on your bohunkus."

He turned and pressed against the glass, looking in at me. Sweat, maybe tears, too, cut tracks through the dust on his face. The blood gleamed on his mouth like lipstick. "That ride rattled me," he said, "but it didn't knock anything out of me."

"I don't expect so," I said.

"I figured you would wonder."

"You taught me to expect the unexpected."

"But you never do—that's the thing. You're like your mother: anything that ever happened, she said, *I knew that was coming*. It used to anger the piss out of me."

He rolled off the hood, pushed upright, and shook himself.

He raised his face, stuck his tongue out hard, took big gulps of air. "I hate this long retreat," he said, "this joke and idiot concoction of a body that falls to pieces around your mind like peach flesh rotting around the pit." He crooked his elbow to his face, sniffed. "It stinks, my body stinks. I wake up at night and I can smell it rotting, putrefying, turning into sewage. Look at that," he said, holding his arm out to me. "The hair on my arms is falling off, and where did these fucking spots come from, and how come I got to sit on the edge of the bed concentrating like some mongrel over his shit just to get myself onto my feet?" He stamped his foot, kicking the pale dirt with his heel. Then he grinned. His teeth were bloody. He touched them with his forefinger, looked at the blood. The old hunting memory was there, where it always was, right out on the surface of his skin. "I can see things with my whole body," he said, "you know, like works of art, like statues do, like some animals do, deep swimming fish and, I don't know, hyenas"—he chuckled—"yeah, art and animals, like they do—you remember when Bobby shot me?"

"He didn't shoot you. There wasn't a shell in the gun."

"He shot me. You better believe it. For him, there was a shell in that gun. For him, he pulled the trigger. For him, he shot me."

"I know."

"You were there."

"Yes, I was."

He grimaced, hawked, and spat. He slapped his chest with the flat of his hand. It made a thick, stuffed sound. He twisted his head back and forth. "You hear my neck pop? I'm amazing. Fall, what, two hundred feet, and here I am, upright, ready to smash and gouge." Then he leaned against the car, sagged. "Bobby killed me," he said, "and that's what killed him, but you aren't that way. I've never had to worry about you. You're not a man to kill his father. You see too far ahead; you see what it'd do to you, how it'd take you straight on to dying, and you couldn't stand that; you're scared to death of it."

The rage lifted in my throat; there were bloody chunks of it inside of me. I said, my voice shaking, "I don't plan anything anymore. I don't say what I'm going to do even to myself. Kate's taught me some things."

"You won't catch up to Kate," he said.

"I don't want to hear about Kate from you."

"I don't expect so."

I turned the ignition. The car fired, choked, and caught.

"Jesus buddy," he said. "Couldn't even knock my car out. Isn't that something."

"Get in," I said.

I could have killed him right there, maybe I could. Maybe he was winded enough for me to choke the rest of the breath out of him, but I let the prey go. I thought I did. I wanted Kate to see what was coming. I wanted her to see it happen. Whatever I did, I wanted to do it in front of her, to spread it before her feet as another man would spread treasures of gold and silver. I wanted to dazzle her.

THE VILLAGE WAS hung with flowers. Hibiscus and poppies, swags of bougainvillea, frangipani and fat purple orchids, tufted bromeliads with their red throats open were strung on the walls of houses and in arcs over the dirt streets in which children frolicked in elaborate bushy white-and-red costumes. The houses fronted the ocean, stepping out of poppy fields that were all in thick, wild yellow and orange flower. We came through the fields, the car creaking over ruts and down into draws filled with snarled brush and tumbleweed. Birds flew up out of the brush in scattered flocks, blackbirds and white birds with red-streaked wings and small birds flittering, jewel birds like hummingbirds. There were yellow finches in a small stand of olive trees beside a broken-down corral.

Kate and one of the cowboys, a slim fellow with a sharp nose and long, slicked-back hair, got out of a Jeep and directed us to a parking place near the edge of a deep gully that ran along the edge of one of the poppy fields. A few children clustered around the car, but the village was busy and enthralled with its festival life. Plank tables on trestles were set out under trees near the beach and the planks sagged with food, with sugar-dusted cakes and stacks of tortillas and plastic bowls filled with puddings and beans and platters heaped with sausages and fist-sized hunks of beef and pork. The village, so the cowboy, Manolito, said, had once been a resort, but a hurricane had blown it down forty years before. He showed us the concrete hotel foundations, and the sky blue lobby floor that was now the village square and the swimming pool so thick with carp that their silver-and-gold backs flashed on the top of the water—"You could fall in and drown in fish," Kate said—and the stands of coconut and date palms planted by the owners. After the hurricane smashed everything, and after the surviving guests and the owners had gone away, the villagers, men and women who had worked as servants in the hotel, began to drift down here from the scrubby hill village they lived in, coming down the river that ran on the other side of the present village, to build their own versions of domicile, peasants sneaked onto the ruined royal ground, throwing up their thatch-roofed, adobe-wattle houses, half-walled, as long as they lasted, with pieces of cracked red sandstone the hotel was built from, until, in time, the old village was deserted, and the resort became their own.

The ocean out front was not a fishing ocean or a road, but a barrier, a constant boom of surf that accompanied life there, like echoes from a canyon, an emptiness like a badlands that no one went out into but only lived beside, backs to the emptiness and the vast brilliance of it. On the far side of the village the shallow river flowed out of the hills and crossed the wide yellow strand. Beyond the river was a racecourse, a narrow oval track ringed with hay bales. On the near side, between the track and the river, a rickety set of bleachers perched, empty now, but soon, so Manolito said, the place where the village would gather for the car race that was to be run later in the afternoon. The cars, rusted jalopies, old Chevies and Buicks, were parked in a row beside the bleachers. A few mechanics worked on them, at a distance looking like climbers of some sort as they crawled about the open bonnets with wrenches shining in their hands. They would be delighted, so Manolito said, to have us participate in the race; they would give us good cars, he said.

"You have to see the doctor first," Kate said to Clement, who except for his bloody mouth did not seem hurt at all.

I asked one of the cowboys to go get our car off the highway. He ran off to do it.

"I don't think a place like this has a doctor," Clement said. He flexed his arms, lifted onto his toes as he walked, preening.

"But they do. I've already talked to him. He knows you."

Her voice was exuberant, lilting. She had washed her face, dunked her head; her pale skin shined and water beads glistened in her bristly hair, which she had cut short for the Italian movie. A coarse, twanging music, drum-backed, had been playing all the time we walked through the village. Around a corner, in an open place, we came on the band, men in white clothes sitting on crates under lemon trees playing guitars and fat, long drums that sat between their knees. Before them on the hard yellow ground that looked beaten and swept, children danced in rows, waving palm branches. It was the introduction of the saint, Manolito said, the bringing forth of Berenita, the patron and goddess of seaside desert life, a woman with green frog skin and long yellow hair, who led the procession in a rustling yellow dress, capering before the children, who trailed after her waving their fronds and chanting. This went on as around them adults drank from coconut-shell cups, standing in groups, indifferently it looked to me, with sad eyes and faces from which all the energy had been drained, men in black suits and women in white dresses with a fringe of blue beadwork at the hems, who seemed almost embarrassed by the enthusiasm of the children, almost loitering, or stranded maybe. They made me think of the Mexican folk I saw in the barrio in Los Angeles, men and women standing on street corners or in the parking lots before restaurants around twilight, people talking to each other softly in the soft brown light, whispering, nodding their heads to each other like people afraid to go home, or sad about going home, as if nothing there could satisfy or help them. And as we stood in the stiff sunshine while Manolito went off to get the doctor, I thought of the visits Veronica and I had made into the barrio, the world beyond Echo Park and Silver Lake, which had once both been fashionable addresses, to eat, or just to wander around, a place where in the dusty twilight you could stand on the sidewalk and look across the patchy yards into houses in which women in pale, shapeless dresses moved about setting tables for dinner. On front steps, in shadows made from squat columns and frothy trellises of Japanese honeysuckle where, perhaps, forty or fifty years ago Alan Ladd or Barbara Stanwyck had stepped from the house into the filmed dream they were bringing to life—one dead of drink now, the other dead of loneliness and chagrin, but saints themselves nonetheless—children called sharply to us. The silvery, piercing, incomprehensible words drifted out to us from the shadows like warnings or claims made on occurrences we could know nothing of; and it would seem to us as we stood hand in hand that there was something in the words, something behind them maybe in the lives lived out in the crumbling cottages on streets that ran like pale gray thoughts toward some hilly bend beyond which there was nothing but empty sky, something we should know about, something terribly delicate and elusive that was going out of the world as we dumbly watched.

Now men in suits approached us, men in dusty suits with jeweled belts and wearing cowboy boots, who offered us cups filled with a brown, muddy drink. It was a liquor they twisted out of roots for festival. Kate and Clement gulped theirs down, and Clement licked the inside of the shallow cup, grinning. The men grinned back at him. He clapped them on the shoulder. "Things are going to get loose and free here," he said. "You fellows don't have a thing to worry about. Mad frolic is one muscle I know how to ride."

He threw his arm around me and squeezed me to him. "I got hold of you now," he said. "We're going to smash right through into the heart of things."

His eyes caught mine, and I saw the fierce desire and menace under the laughter, but I didn't respond, took no bait just yet. I disengaged, patting his arm, letting my fingers linger on the stiff hairs, my thumb brush his wrist. "Kindly, kindly," I said. "Let's go kindly."

The children chanted and waved their way out of the clearing, which was an open space between houses beyond which the river flashed in the sunlight. Down on the beach near the water, between the river and the houses, a large fire had been built, a fire as big as a house that men tended, pushing logs they upended and rolled onto the flames. Near the bonfire were smoldering pits where, Manolito said, whole pigs were being roasted. The children, caught in the spell of the goddess, wound their way down the street. One of them, a tiny boy with red cloth strips tied around his waist, flicked me with his palm branch. I caught at it, but he danced away laughing. We followed them out and met the doctor in the street.

He was a spry, slender, white-haired man in his seventies, a former actor who had known Clement when he was young and known my grandfather Willard in the old days. He introduced himself—Beryl James—and it came back to my father. "Christ goodness," Clement said, "I haven't thought of you in twenty-five years."

The doctor hadn't thought of him either. He'd quit acting, gone to med school, and retired down here fifteen years ago. He lived in a villa in the hills, near the old village, and administered to the local population. "It's a good life," he said, "It brings a natural peace to the spirit, which I am grateful for."

"I wouldn't know peace," Clement said, "if it stuck its dick down my throat."

A young woman, slender like the doctor, with a scar running from her right eye to the corner of her mouth, trailed along behind. He introduced her as Elpidia Reyes, his companion. The scar pulled her lower eyelid down so that one side of her face carried a look of manic surprise, but the smile she gave us was gentle, like the smiles of people who have surrendered to their own suffering. The children marched ahead of us up the street, scattering chickens and curly-tailed dogs. In groups, the adults watched them, shouting to them, one or two of the women stepping into the procession to straighten the deportment of an unruly reveler. Kate, walking beside me to the café where the doctor wanted to examine Clement, breathed in short, harsh breaths. She walked on the balls of her feet, springing up on them as she walked—locomotion that had become a signature in the movies but which was only her natural way—bouncing on her toes, bobbing beside me. She gripped my hand so hard that it hurt. "Don't worry," I said to her, "I think there's going to be plenty of wildness here."

"It's jumping around inside me," she said. She thrust out one hand, shook it. "Any minute fire will spurt from my fingers." She swooped low and sprang up, imitating the children; she whooped. She had taken off her sandals; her bare legs were dusted yellow to the knees. She bumped against me, knocking me with her shoulder as we drifted behind the others, and it became dreamy for a moment, the colors and the movement ahead a shifting and indecipherable agitation, the children snaking in a line down the street toward the piles of party food, toward the groves of palm trees that the wind ruffled the tops of and toward the ocean, which banged steadily against the blank strand, the sandstone-and-wattle houses hardly distinguishable from the rubble they had been heaped out of, men on horseback stepping their mounts through the crowds, the distant poppy fields over which vultures and gulls turned in high broad circles, a stack of Borden milk cans on a table outside a white house, a scattering of red berries on a doorstep—all shifting, rearranging, resettling themselves as we approached, like actors pulling on fresh costumes, merging and dissolving so that vision became a blindness, flashes of color lifting like blows from the mass. She bumped my shoulder, and her thick, natural perfume filled my nostrils, overpowering me. She was talking, flicking words, making them dance as she danced, saying: "There was a moment, in the picture . . ."

"What picture?"

"The Italian picture—we were out in a marsh, in a river, a kind of cove, where I was diving for the body of my drowned lover . . ."

"Who?"

"You already know—this poet I loved; it was nighttime, and so cold; everyone but me was bundled up in loden coats and sheepskin, and there I was all by myself in this rowboat diving off the side into this dark water that might as well have had ice cubes floating in it, doing it again and again, going in and climbing out, drying off, and getting up again on the gunwale and diving in, each time the director shouting at me from his platform to try it one more time, and everyone getting a little nervous about how long it was taking to get the shot, and worried about me, the masseuse rubbing me down, and one of the girls giving me bouillon to drink, wrapping me up between takes in this big raccoon coat—"

"And you calling me up at night," I said, "waking me at dawn to tell me what it felt like to have his hands rubbing the heat into your back—"

"—yes, and there was a moment there, with all that swirling around me and this huge black grassy marsh spread out, an empty place where the princes used to hunt ducks in the old days when there were princes—

"—and ducks—"

"—yes, empty all the way to the steel mills ten miles away, where you could see the glow of the fires, open hearth fires—"

"—like hell—"

"—yes, and every once and a while a mullet jumping, and me going down into the water, going down deep, so deep my ears hurt, right down to the bottom, grabbing the bottom with my two hands, feeling the mud and the litter of mussel shells—"

"—him going down into you, rummaging around in there, all that erotic, sweaty euphoria, tying a little sprig of life together inside you—"

"That's good—yes—half wanting, even as cold as it was, to stay down there in the dark, just sit down there, take up residence like an underwater princess and live there breathing water forever—"

"—and the crew and the director and all the actors amazed—"

"—yes, and there was a moment when everything about me, everything inside me and outside me was all of a piece, like my whole life, everything past and to come, was something I meant to happen, as if I had gotten down on my knees out in space when I was just a speck in the eye of God, and planned it all—"

"—it was five in the morning when you told me. Your voice was happy. I started screaming and you sat there on the other end of the line, not saying a word, listening to me scream—"

"—yes—"

We could have been in a cold, empty chamber somewhere, some anteroom off the court where a terrible sentence was about to be passed. We were whispering, in Mexico.

I staggered. Kate threw her arm around me. She drew me close, hard against her, like a man would, buddies. She kissed me on the cheek. "I have passed right through everything, Will," she said, "I have passed through it and come out on the other side."

"I wish you wouldn't talk so much," I said, my voice thick. "I don't really want to know these things."

"I don't think that's true. People who don't want to know things like this don't stay in one place as long as you do."

"I think I'm going to vomit."

"I've had practice at that; I can help you."

"It's not that hilarious, Katie."

But then the bristle and nudge of my future came up to me, rose like a shooting gallery duck in my mind, and I wrenched myself back into place. I had come down here to cut through, to uproot. But I wondered again, as I had wondered a thousand times in my life, what you could believe in, what it was that would get you through the blur and disaster of being alive on earth, and all I could come up with was the same thing, the same idea that somehow we had to get attached to each other, one sufferer attached to another sufferer, somehow bang through the lies and warning systems into the heart's homeplace, each squatted in, and squat down there with him, play the other's little game in the sand, give yourself to it. But what made this idea crazy to me was how it actually played itself out here among us, how no matter the way we turned ourselves, each gesture contained not only a caress but a slap, and each smile held up the grimace behind it, and each loved face, smiling above you, was the same face that stared out of dreams hating life, and how you had to live with both.

I said, "My age is coming on me. I am getting older, growing up despite myself."

"You were one who was bound to."

"Jennie says she doesn't care anymore what happens to her, just so something happens."

"That's what trying to stay still will do to you."

"I don't understand why we're walking here; I don't understand why we're even talking to each other, it seems to me that some explosion should have been set off long before now that just obliterated us both."

"Picked up, tossed around, smashed in the face, given a taste of our heart's desire just so we'll nearly kill ourselves trying to get more, shook silly, dragged through nights when we'd rather die than have to take another breath, days when the only thing we can do about our lives is get up and go to some backbreaking job they wouldn't make mules do, old guys exhausted in armchairs staring at the wall, women with their hair falling out, weeping over springtime, children shouting at nothing—and all I can think about is the next wild thing I'm about to do. It's a joke, and I'm just laughing and laughing."

"Now you're lying to me."

"I don't know, Will. Right now I am so full of life I can't stand it. I want to touch everything that is, I want to rub every leaf and rock and hair and germ and boot against my face; I want to feel all of it on me."

Clement and the doctor, followed by the gentle woman, turned in at the café. It was café and store, and bar, tables in back beyond shelves of dry goods and cans stacked in dusty rows. The doctor had Clement sit on a table.

Clement took his shirt off, bared his chest, which swelled. The doctor looked at him in admiration. "You're a specimen," he said. "You must be, what, seventy years old, and you don't look a day over forty-five."

"That would make him my brother," I said.

Clement cocked his head and winked at me. "I'm all of it," he said, "every configuration you can come up with."

James took Clement's head in his hands and gently turned it side to side. "How does your head feel, on your neck?"

"I got a little hot walnut in the back of it, down where it hooks on."

James touched the top of his spine. "It's nothing serious."

"Hey," Clement said to the large woman behind the counter, "tequila *por favor*, and glasses." He made drinking motions.

"Maybe you should rest awhile, take it easy."

"Impossible to do."

"Let me look at your mouth."

"My teeth are a little loose—tequila's good for loose teeth."

He began to tell a story about how he had once knocked another producer's teeth down his throat. "Actually down his throat," he said. "You hear about that, but you don't see it much. I hit him so hard he gulped and swallowed his own teeth."

"We don't know what's true about you, sweetie," Kate said, taking the bottle from the storekeeper and bringing it to him. The woman came along behind her wiping glasses on her dress. Elpidia, the gentle woman, watched us with her wild eye. She sat in a straight-backed chair against the wall, in a shadow that filled one side of the store. Outside, bright barooms of sound rose and fell, trumpets blared, and cries rose from the beach. Manolito, who had followed us in, said, "The runners are passing through."

"What runners are that?" Clement said, taking the bottle from Kate. He snatched the top off, slopped the clear liquid into the three glasses Kate held out to him.

"The Indian marathon," Manolito said.

"Indians?" Clement said.

"We—all of us," he said, touching his chest, "we're all Indians."

I went to the window. Down near the big fire, men in shorts and black tennis shoes ran through the crowd. There were several of them, running easily, waving at the crowd as they went by.

"What are Indians doing running?" Clement said.

"It's the *aniversario*, the anniversary, of the great battle. Long ago, many years ago, we rose up against the Spanish and fought them. The call went out and Indians had to come from great distances to help. They ran the whole way, for six days, running. Now we celebrate that."

With two fingers the doctor probed Clement's teeth. Clement opened his mouth wide, grimaced, his face for an instant taking on a devilish, animal look, and then he bit down, hard, on the doctor's fingers. A look of pain and surprise flashed in the doctor's face; he tried to pull his fingers out, but for a second Clement held on. His head shook with the doctor's pulling. "Let me . . ." the doctor cried.

Clement let him go. He slid off the table. "I like to taste that human flesh," he said and laughed. The laugh was coarse and hard, as if it was made to slap. Kate handed him his shirt. "I don't need that," he said. He rubbed his palms fast up and down on his chest. "Any flesh I touch, even mine—especially mine—makes me feel good. It makes me feel like I'm going to live a thousand years. Let's go see those running Indians."

"Let's go run with them," Kate said. She whirled, saw me. "Come on," she said, "let's go."

"I'm going to stay here where it's cool and quiet."

"You need the sunshine."

"There'll be sunshine soon enough on all of this."

She looked at me oddly, and there was a fleeting sadness in her eyes, but she didn't stop. She grabbed me in her arms, squeezed me hard. I could smell her hair, thick, wooly, rank as animal fur. She pinched me lightly as her fingers raced down my body. She whirled away, spinning out into the bright sunshine.

Clement ran after her. The breath woofed out of him as he passed. He slapped at my shoulder as he went by, a jolly hard slap that missed my shoulder and caught me against the neck and jaw. I clenched my fist and spun toward him, but he was past, and this wasn't the time for blows, not yet. "You can race on after us," he said, "catch up with us when you can. We'll be out there where everybody can see us."

I went to the counter and let the storekeeper pour me a glass of tequila. I took a swallow and then I sipped at it. The doctor and Elpidia sat side by side in straight-backed chairs at the table Clement had jumped down from. Their faces were calm and ravaged in a way that made them look very old. The doctor slowly turned his watch on his wrist, turning the band as if it were a socket he was carefully unscrewing. Elpidia looked at the wall where pictures from magazines had been tacked to the rough adobe. The pictures were of Mexican actresses, a couple of whom I knew. I thought of Jennie's Mexican conquistadoress movies, a dead-end direction she had taken in the fifties, in which she had dressed in cucaracha costume and twirled slick curls at her ears and worn slim red shoes with taps in the heels. We'll do anything, I thought, to stay in the game, anything at all.

An Indian man came in carrying a small girl on his shoulders. He was small himself, wore shapeless tattered clothes; a woman in a dress the washed-out gray of his shirt trailed him. They bought a sack of cornmeal, a tin of coffee, a small tin of cooking oil, and a whip of licorice for the little girl. They were too poor, I guessed, even to come to the festival. The man and woman were young, but their faces were toughened by sun and work. I could see them rising in the morning dark, see the woman pounding tortillas, the man washing in a basin out back, hear the little girl crying on a mat inside the dark house. In the morning down here, no matter how hard your life was, the sun was a magician bringing color and light to the fields, and the dew hanging on the flowers, and the spiderweb in the eaves just catching the light shined like gifts from a kind god, and the world, no matter how old and beaten it was, smelled like a new creation, and you got up on your feet into it, a creaking bit of flesh and bone without a future beyond one more day of backbreaking work, and you pulled on the old trousers and the frayed shirt and you went outside and splashed a little water on to your face and you looked at the chickens coming to life on their roosts in the lemon tree and at the pigs squealing in the pen and at the thick green leaves of yams and tomatoes, and you could feel in your body, through all of it, every day you'd been alive on earth, and you knew that each day to come was only going to add to the weight that already was more than you could carry, and you looked out into the fields that began like an ocean at the edge of the yard, the work that you dived into each day, the scurry of weeds you had to chop in the rows that ran straight as paths toward the mountains, and you knew it was never going to be any different, all days the same, and the end of the day coming like your life coming to an end, the slow, muddying twilight filling the fields like the pain filling your body, the dark coming on as you turned on your hoe to look back down the long way you had come at the lights of your house shining under the trees, and no government around strong enough or interested enough to change it, and no god either, and you swinging the hoe up onto your shoulder and beginning the long walk through the poppies that maybe the wind picked at the blossoms of, playfully almost, the breeze dry on your cheek, chilling you a little as it dried the sweat, and so you return home to the field edge, to the yard you left at daybreak, and you stand there for a second, facing the house this time, the field behind you fallen away like a dream, and you standing there, a fellow without importance, barely differentiated from the weeds and the shabby trees and the bundle of cane thatch propped against the house, and you draw water again and wash your face and you step into the house, out of another day.

The store seemed to float in a sea. Outside, the festival churned and threw up noise. In the dimness of the back room the doctor, ex-actor, and his companion sipped tequila. I pulled myself up on the table. A narrow back door opened on to a pig yard where a couple of muddy shoats butted at each other. Beyond the yard, the river, down its short slope, gleamed, and beyond the river the bleachers stood up like a frail monument. I lay back on the table. The pink tin ceiling was crusted with rosettes like scabs. Streaks of rust looked like rotted veins. The peasant couple shouldered their supplies, bowed to the proprietress, and went out. They paused in the street, looking toward the crowds near the beach. The little girl reached for something down that way, but her father turned away. The woman made no sign that anything beyond her own dumb following was of any interest to her. They disappeared beyond the doorway.

The doctor was saying something. He was telling me that I was in danger.

"How would you know about that?" I said.

He leaned back in the chair, flexing his long, thin thigh muscles. Elpidia stared at the wall as if a movie were playing on it.

"I've read the magazines," he said, "I've followed your story, all your stories. Now that I see you I can tell the things they say are true."

"You knew my father when he was young."

"I didn't know him, but I saw him. He was like something on fire."

Every move Kate made, every grace and awkwardness was familiar to me. I knew how she sat after a bath, one leg cocked over the other, rubbing the crown of her big toe; I knew how she licked her forefinger and cleaned behind her ears; knew how she opened her mouth to the wind to taste the breeze on her tongue; I had sat in the sun out at Veronica's as she wrapped wax strips on her thighs and pulled them off as she moaned and growled like a woman surprised by pain. In bed she would cock her white ass into the air and tell me to bite her, and I would, I would bite her until she screamed, until she bled. And there were times—there had been times—when we lay back in a big bed, out in a desert hotel maybe, where the wind is constant and the pale dust blows over everything, blows up into the sky in great sheets and sails, and we lay on the bed in a long afternoon, in the cool, tiled room, and she would tell me stories of her childhood that she made up as she told them, stories that were as beautiful in their clarity and balance as any stories I had heard in my life, and it would come to me as I listened to her changeling voice that it was possible to watch a civilization die out in the voice of a single woman, that you could lean back beside her in the cool, rumpled sheets and hear the voice of your time and place disappearing and not want to do anything or say anything about it.

The doctor spoke to me of Clement, and the man he described was familiar to me. All the stories were the same, and they had been the same for years. It was not hard to imagine him, a boy coming down a piney hill in Arkansas, swinging his arms, hands already fists. Any life aimed at a rainbow, no matter how hard it was, was easy to imagine. There's nothing mysterious about someone who thinks he is going to get somewhere. It was these others, like my brother Bobby, these characters and fools, these antic, idiot souls, who were going nowhere, who made their splashy useless displays, who spent their energies hoisting flags for dumb creeds nobody wanted to pledge allegiance to, who fascinated me. The doctor himself was one, though he spoke now of Clement—who was not one at all—as if he admired him.

"Tell me how you came here," I said.

"It's a simple story: I didn't have what it took to be an actor, but I had what it took to go to med school, and then I grew tired of practicing in a suburb, and I retired and came down here, where there is no other place to get to."

"How do you spend your day?"

"Idly."

"It's odd to find you down here, an old actor—it's like some kind of connivance, yours or the world's cunning, or Clement's."

"There's an inevitability about things, I've found."

"Maybe a place like this makes someone think that way—or maybe someone who thinks like that comes to places like this." I wondered if I had been the one lured here, if my plan, made as I went, was only a figment without substance before the practiced cunning of my father and Kate. But I didn't believe their way included cunning. I had looked into my father's face and the cleverness there was simple: it was clumsy, unsubtle. And Kate, for all her waywardness, was not dishonest. She had told me what she had done, had told me about Clement, told me as if describing a stain on her hands, straightforwardly, with pain in the words, and fear and the dumb energy of one who had never said no to anything in the world and wouldn't now.

The doctor said, "The world's a clamorous place. I think everyone in it needs an occasional sense of fatedness, of destiny. We want to know once in a while what's coming."

"For a long time," I said, "I wanted to know all the time. I did know—at least I thought I did. But then it began to seem as if everything was dying out around me."

"This is a beautiful place," he said, "as rough and poor as it is. Each day here is the same as every other, the life is the same, mostly, but it's like that only if you are passing through. It's like the ocean for tourists, the way it always seems the same—when you live beside it, you notice that it's different every day, there's always some new wrinkle you hadn't quite prepared yourself for, and you realize there's no way to make yourself happy unless you just give in to that."

"You're a real philosopher."

"I have a lot of time on my hands."

It was hot in the store, though breeze trickled through open doors, but it was dim and I liked that; I could bear sweating a long time if there was enough shade. I was one whose work came forth in the dark, a midnight peddler.

"I am very tired," the doctor said. And then he coughed once lightly, blinked his eyes, and slumped against Elpidia. I jumped up, but she was ahead of me. Without change of expression, she tapped his cheeks, took a vial from her dress pocket, shook a pill out, and forced it between the doctor's lips. She poured a little tequila into his mouth, tipped his head back. The doctor coughed again, shook himself, and straightened up. Elpidia fanned him with her palm.

I looked around—everything was the same. The doctor's face was blank, white; it slowly filled with color. The proprietress clucked behind her counter.

The doctor took a deep breath, leaned against his companion. "Angina," he said. Sweat stood on his forehead. He looked slowly around the room. A gray, almost blue cat sneaked toward the back door. "A sudden decompression of the body," he said, "as if I have appeared suddenly—too suddenly—in another world."

I could see it then in his face, the death that had hidden itself but now shined forth. It was in the white patches on his cheekbones and in the creases under his eyes and in the eyes themselves, in the blankness that was not really blankness but absence. It was in his arm, and in his shoulder, which he rubbed against Elpidia, and in his feet and legs, everywhere. It was near, it was almost touching me; I wanted to punch at it. I wanted to run, for a second I wanted to fight it, or I wanted to pretend I didn't see what I saw, but I did nothing; I made myself sit back down. I blushed, embarrassed to be frightened. The doctor chuckled.

"It's all right," he said. "Death is scary. Many in the village won't come near me anymore. I have no patients. They are afraid death will rub off my hands on to them. It's a common phenomenon. You see it with cancer patients, with those who have AIDS—people back away; they're afraid death will stretch its hand out of the suffering bodies and grab them."

"I'm sorry," I said.

"I don't mind. I did at first, it frightened me at first. If it hadn't been for dear Elpidia, who has experienced her own shunning, I would have failed. But she sustained me. And so I was able to withstand this eerie fate. It is strange to be set apart. First there's terror, then there's loneliness, then there's depression—this chained anger—then exhaustion, pleading maybe, weeping, and then there is a quiet, a peace. The peace is ample and rich. You begin to realize there is nothing to fear. You begin to realize you were born for this, this dying, and you are at home in the house of death."

"Does it make you believe in God?"

"Not in any thematic way. There is an appropriateness, a rightness about it, an integration—I can't describe it—it's as if you have been wandering around in the woods and realize suddenly and quietly that they are familiar woods, that you are not lost. God doesn't enter into it in any conceptual way, not as a force or being—there is nothing about righteousness or dogma. We live our lives fearing loss, trying to get, and the God we have devised is created to deal with these. He soothes us when we lose, he allows us to experience humility when we overreach ourselves, but in this place—not a place—in this state, these effects do not apply. There is no loss or gain, and so there is no need for any sort of god, or any sort of god we have heretofore conceived."

Elpidia stroked his arm and lightly pushed at him. "Yes," he said. "Could you?" he said to me, indicating a bench. I pushed the bench near. He lay down on it. "Ah," he said, "I feel as if I am floating."

"Shouldn't we take you home?"

"It's better to rest a little first."

He stretched his thin hand out to me. I took it; it was clammy, death-filled. I squeezed it. "See," he said, "it's there, but it's in me, not in you, or not so soon in you."

"We—myself, and those of my party—move too fast for it. Though I am one, personally, for the relaxed life."

"You look as if you are in pain. What are these people to you—besides the obvious relation?"

"I have become a kind of wife to them both."

"Married to the storm."

"Yes."

"It's terrible," he said, "when we come to believe we have problems."

"Who doesn't have them?"

"I don't think anymore anyone does. What we are afraid of is not really frightening. What comes to get us we are prepared for."

Easy for you to say, I thought, death junkie. Not easy for me.

"Your father," he said, "was a man who never understood himself, never understood anyone around him, never understood anything that happened to him—but he was game. He was a man prepared to be unstoppable."

"Not was—he isn't dead yet."

He ignored me. "And your wife, Zebra Dunn"—he pronounced it *Zehbra,* with a short *e,* English style—"is a woman of dramatic grace. She is so supple, so fluid, graceful, that the world, its slow, recessive nature, is a horror to her. I have read about her in the magazines—she is even featured in Mexican publications, though few of them reach this village—and it is very exciting to meet her."

Elpidia murmured something I didn't catch.

"Ellie says her skin has no pores—I don't know, I didn't look that closely—but she means that she is a woman who doesn't breathe air. That at least is the conclusion that follows."

"I think of her as breathing more deeply than others."

"Yes, of course. You live together. You see her smirking and belching. You see her on the days she cries and whines about things."

"She rarely whines."

"No, I guess not. She and your father—they are lovers, yes?"

"She is pregnant with his child."

"I thought so. It's a horrible, maddening thing, isn't it?"

"I've come down here, I've lured him down here, to kill him."

Elpidia whispered again, bending over him as if she were spitting into his ear. He stroked her face, let his finger linger a second on the scar. "Ellie says there is nothing here that can kill him, not here, not yet."

"Maybe I can slow him up a little."

He chuckled again, a hoarse, rasping sound. He looked at me. His eyes were pale gray. "You think that to resolve things you have to go through them, I can see you think that. No one could accuse you of living that way—it's your affectation, this laziness—but you believe it with all your heart."

"My life has brought me to a certain pitch, a willingness."

"That apparently, now, demands dramatic action."

"I have never really been lazy."

"No. You are very like them both. Maybe that's what torments you."

"There's more."

"Yes. Conclusions, especially conclusions reached without all the evidence, never quite seem to catch the essence. I don't usually draw conclusions, but I am old and dying, and now even the worst mistakes don't seem to matter much. What more?"

I thought of Bobby, of his pale face, his body shrunk to fit a casket; I thought of him, and it was as if in that dusty, dim place, that store or bar reeking of spices and tequila, he were singing to me, singing softly and insistently, as if he were standing near me watching me as he sang, waiting to see what I would do. Beyond the doors, the brilliant day flared so bright it seemed to be burning. I felt very cold, and then, in the center of the cold, something gripped inside me, a hand or a claw that closed around something precious. I felt a grief in me, a sudden cracking of my spirit, as if what I loved most in the world were being torn apart in front of my eyes. I did not know who I was, I did not know what to do next. An emptiness spread in my body and I could hear my brother's voice begin to scream, and I could see him holding the gun in his hands, raising it, see him bend down to it as a man would bend down to drink water from a clear pool, and I could hear the scream, the cry that did not come from his mouth but from his soul, the cry that had rung in my ears all my life.

I lurched forward, fell against the table. Elpidia stretched her hand out to me, but she could not stop me from going to my knees. I hit hard on the concrete floor and continued falling, it seemed to me a long way. Above me a voice whispered steadily. *Doucement, doucement,* it said, sweetly, sweetly, but now I could not tell whose voice it was.

MY FATHER USED to tell a story about a time he went coon hunting as a boy in Arkansas. He said it was his first or second time out. There were a dozen men, maybe two dozen dogs, wild nighttime woods, mountains all around. They let the dogs go and settled into a clearing to wait. The procedure was to sit by a fire sipping whiskey while the dogs ran; only after they raised, ran, and treed the coon would the action begin. You could tell by the calls, he said, what was happening, and each man could tell the call of his own dogs, the way someone would know the voice of a good friend. He said that after they sat there for a while, one of them heard birds singing, faint and then louder, off in the woods from the clearing. It was unusual—there were few night-singing birds in that part of the country—and it was louder than birdsong the men had heard at night before. Someone got up to investigate. He came back a few minutes later to say there was a tree a little ways away that was filled with singing birds. *Night warblers,* my father said they were, a common name for any bird besides a whippoorwill that sang at night. A couple of men went to see and they too came back amazed at the tree filled with singing birds. The other men got up to look at the phenomenon, and Clement went with them.

They came on the tree, a large oak in a small clearing, and it was as the first man had described: a tree filled with birds, all singing.

They sang like no birds I had ever heard before, my father said, *a whole tree filled with them, from the low branches to the top, where you could see them bobbing up among the wispiest twigs, singing away. They made a beautiful, wild song,* he said, *a song like mockingbirds make, of many parts and complicated, fluttery and sustained at the same time, and all of it a piece of the same song, like an orchestra or a chorus, as if there was one beautiful song the birds knew and they were all riffing and harmonizing on it.*

He said the men stood under the tree listening, transfixed. A couple took their hats off. Above them the night sky was filled with stars, and in the far distance the hounds bayed, a lonely, lonely sound, he said, like cries from the other world, the world they had come from, that they were free of now. One of the men touched the tree; *he stroked it,* my father said, *petted it like you would a puppy,* but the others just stood there with their faces lifted, listening.

We could have stood there all night, he said, *I think I could have stood there. We were poor people—some of those men lived in houses with no indoor water and no plumbing at all, and what were hard times, what had been hard times for two generations, were turning into the Great Depression, bad going to worse, and there was not a man there who could do the first thing about it, and all the worst meanness and horror of the century was out there beyond even the Depression, gathering force, about to crash over our heads, and here these men were in the middle of the night, holding their hats in their hands, listening to some birds sing. It was a miracle. Such a prettiness, like I had never heard.*

And then, he said, a man, standing a little off from the others, a bitter man maybe, who couldn't be reached even by a miracle, raised his gun and fired into the tree. A couple of birds fell, and the rest, the mass of them, rose, whirling up into the air. They scattered, he said, in a clamor, and the tree was empty. After the shot and the clamor, a silence fell, and my father said it was in that moment, in the silence, that a terrible violence came into him. *I had my gun with me, a little single-shot .20 gauge, loaded with a slug, and I raised that gun—I didn't even think what I was doing, I was so mad—and I shot that man. I aimed and fired and I hit him, shot him in the shoulder. He fell screaming,* my father said, *and he writhed on the ground like a man possessed. But I was the one possessed, I saw it. And I didn't mind. The other men came back to themselves and they were angry, but it didn't make me back down. I walked out of those woods and I walked down the road to my house, and I left them all there.*

It was shortly after that, he said, after the anger and the feud started between the shot man's family and his own, that his own father decided to take the family out of that country. The sheriff was poking around, and maybe there were going to be charges filed, but after they loaded the truck and closed the door on the old house and headed west, nothing came of it. *Nothing happened,* my father said, *but a whole new life. A miracle on one side and a miracle on the other. In between them a shooting.*

He would look hard at me then; maybe we were out in a car on the farm, maybe we were sitting out on the deck at Jennie's Malibu house, maybe we were lying on the back steps in Beverly Hills watching the hummingbirds drink from the honeysuckle flowers, maybe it was afternoon or early evening, maybe the day was hot, smelling of smoke and flowers, maybe I had just turned thirteen, maybe it was the spring after Bobby died, maybe my father was trying to tell me what kind of man he was, and how long he had been that way, but he would look at me with his hard black country eyes and it would come to me, with a shudder that my brother must have felt too when he was told this story, a shudder that reverberated to the bottom of his heart, that, come the right moment, there was no limit to what my father might do, and no love or power that could stop him.

I GOT UP from the bench where they had left me to rest, got up from a dream in which a rain was falling on a field of daisies, a dream in which I thought, even in the dream, of how important it was for someone to imagine a field of white daisies the rain was falling on, and thought, rising through the dream, through the rain lightly falling, that I was glad to be in a world—the general world, and my own—that lent itself so amply to the works of imagination and the flights of fancy. I remember sitting on the steps of the library at Columbia when I was twenty years old arguing with Lucian Debreck about whether the real world was the world of imagination or only this cocked concreteness risen around us, and how easy it was to believe and argue that the only world we cared about, really, was the world we imagined, and how angry Lucian became to hear this, a boy who was on his way to law school and a career as a famous professor of law, and as I got up, or as I prepared to get up, thinking too of Kate, of her white muscular arms and of her smile that was an act of imagination too, it came to me that I had not changed my mind about any of it, that in the eighteen years since, during which I had taken my rightful place as heir to and practitioner of the hard-working Hollywood life, I had continued to believe that what was best of us was what we imagined, what we brought into the light from heart and mind trained on the world just beyond sight, and how energetically everyone I knew participated in this, how my mother did, and how Kate did and my brother Bobby, and Veronica, everyone, even Clement, who stank of the real earth, if anyone did, and so what was the difference between us, among us, what was the difference that called me so relentlessly to this moment when I would crack the life and being gathered around me—what was I up to, I wondered, what was I doing?

I got up from under the shade of a banyan tree, crossed the river, and got into one of the rusted, dilapidated, revved-up automobiles the mechanics had parked in a row at the racecourse starting line, and Clement, wearing a torn straw hat that he pulled down low on his brow like a gangster, got in another. There were a dozen of us out there in the late afternoon sunshine, ten Indians and my father and me. Clement had suggested it, or he had said he was going to do it, going to ride the circuit that hung out there in the salt haze lined with hay bales, and I had said yes, I'll ride too. It was as close as we'd come to figuring what to do about this conundrum. Kate hadn't liked it at all. Clement, arrived by way of root wine and bonfires and slabs of pork meat whose grease he wiped off his lips with the back of his wrist, from the jostling and storytelling, the two miles he had run with the marathoners who flitted through like lean migrating birds, had not suggested we race but that he get in a car and drive, see what this was about, this circling at speed in the sand, why not. I had jerked myself up off the riverbank and said, Yes, that's a good idea—I'll drive too.

Kate—Clement went on ahead—had followed me, and she spit at me as we walked. She jumped around in front of me, her white dress twirling, her hair gleaming from a pomade someone had given her, and she spit at me. She missed the first time; the second time she hit me on the cheek. I wiped it off and licked my fingers. She spit again.

"You can't keep that up for long," I said. "You'll run out."

Her face contorted with rage. She hawked and spit; flit sprayed my chest. We crossed the river, wading. The bottom, where it wasn't sandy, was a white floor of rock, grainy and scoured, like the shell of the earth exposed. It was cool under my bare feet. Kate bent down, scooted water at me. I didn't fight back, not that way. "It's foolish," I said, "to try to stop someone when you don't have the firepower."

"This is not the thing for you," she said. "I'm trying to get that across."

"It's the thing that's available."

"And *you* don't have the firepower. You never did—not this kind."

"You nut. What do you think is going to happen?"

"You're going to try to hurt him."

"I'm going to do more than try."

"I'll kill you, Will. I swear I'll kill you."

I stopped then, stopped just the other side of the water, under the shadow of the grandstand, which was already filled with celebrants. They waved down at us, shaking scarves and hats, urging us on. Past them, past the circuit and the downshelve of beach, the sun had set the ocean on fire. Men silhouetted by the light danced at the edge of the sea, black figures raised by gods or powers I knew nothing about. I looked Kate in the face and there was nothing I recognized there. Anger streaked her skin. "It's amazing," I said. "Everything you show me—this conniption, this jumping-bean bit—just ties me to you stronger."

"You haven't rehearsed," she said. "You can't play a part you haven't rehearsed."

"You're better at talking than that, and what do you mean anyway, trying to talk me out of something? What has come over you? You don't have an opinion on what people do."

I spoke to her as if this were some work decision I was making, some movie part she was urging me not to take. But I knew what this was, knew everything about it. It was as if I had some terrible disease, as if all of us had it, this disease that terrorized our bodies and minds, cracked our spirits and made us into something we had never been before.

She skipped around in front of me like a photographer. "This doesn't have anything to do with love," she said, "that's what's so terrible about it. This has to do with what's dark and destructive, and it breaks my heart to see you give in to such a thing. You frighten me."

"Not enough."

"But why are you trying to outmuscle this? You think I don't know you're strong? You think I need some kind of impressive display?"

"It's not really for you, Kate. It's not a demo."

But the truth was I didn't have a thing to say about it. You lie down in shit, my grandfather used to say, you get up smelling like shit, but I was beyond such wisdom, if wisdom it was.

Under the bleachers small boys perched on the supports, hung from them by their hands, squawking and laughing. A clump of young girls in dresses that were cut-down imitations of their mothers' party frocks stood eating slices of green mango dipped in salt. They bent their heads like birds to lick the pale green fruit. Manolito and a couple of the mechanics, men I had said yes to when they urged me to take a place with Clement in the racing field, waved me toward a car. As I crossed the sand, Kate kept up her chatter, cursing me, dancing in front of me like some bird trying to excite the raptor to come after it—to ignore its chicks—but I kept on.

Behind us the village was nearly abandoned, everyone in it, and those come down from the hills, gathered on this side of the river. Except for a few, like the peasant families who couldn't break off their suffering even to celebrate a goddess, and the doctor, Beryl James, and Elpidia, whose cut black eye had stared into my face as if with her gaze she could peel layers off me. She had pushed one of the pills into my mouth before the doctor could stop her. The nitro went off inside me in a hot, thin explosion that sent a curtain of sparks blowing through my body. For a second my arms and legs had seemed two feet longer. The charge rebounded back into me, and things sped up. Now they watched us, a couple somehow absolved from this devilment—or maybe not somehow, maybe simply through death's approach, the calm and smoothing out of rough places that death sometimes pushes ahead of it—maybe they had bigger things in mind and didn't need to cross the river to cry and caper. They stood between two houses whose red sandstone sides looked like portals opening into a brightness, but the brightness was only the light of the faltering sun that was laying its long shadows across the poppy fields and against the ochre and maroon sides of the hills; in the gaps between hills, and under the mango trees, the shadows hung like the eviscerated skins of large animals. On this side the terrain was still bright, and everything had a naked, hazy look, and it was simplified too, cut back from jungle and variations of terrain: wide shelf of sand curving like a breast into the torn, chromatic surge of ocean, the racecourse and grandstand, the cars, even the big fire that burned like the fires built for getting rid of a terrible past, all the human rigging only temporary, collapsible equipment that tomorrow would be gathered up and hauled away.

I got into the car that had once been a snappy pale green Buick but was now only a rusted lump with no doors and a hood tied down with wire, and I started the machine up. Kate sprang onto the hood, pressed her face against the windshield. She hooted at me, flapped her arms. Her lips turned inside out against the glass. Clement, in the next car over, jabbered with the Indian buckeroo in the jalopy beside him. Snatches of his monologue drifted by. He was telling a story about a rattlesnake getting into the car, a story I had heard him tell on a movie set when I was a boy. It was a good, terrifying story that had given me bad dreams when I was ten, and even as Kate slapped the windshield and reached around it for my face like a monkey reaching for a piece of fruit, I half wished I could lean back and listen to it again, hear about how the snake had struck into the car's open door and landed on him as he sat out in the desert eating a pimento cheese sandwich. "This is a closed circuit, Katie," I said, grinning at her. "Everything that can possibly happen, everything that is going to happen, has to happen here, inside this circle."

"You're making something up, Will," she said. "You're trying to play in a game that's already over. None of this concerns you, it doesn't concern any of us, it doesn't matter."

"I don't know what you are talking about. You're not backing down from anything."

"The snake landed right in my lap," Clement said, throwing up his arms to show the Indian how scary it was. He shook his head, laughing.

"I'm not the wizard you think I am," Kate said. "I haven't devised any way to deal with things, I haven't made a drama out of this, I am just leaping from rock to rock, trying to keep my feet under me."

She slid down off the hood, pressed her side against the door frame. "I had to grab him," Clement said, "like you'd grab your cock—can you believe it, this fat rattler, he must have been six feet long, stretched out across the seat, his head, big as a tomahawk, poked up out of my lap . . ."

"What is it you are pleading for?" I said.

"I'm not pleading, I'm just trying to divert you."

"Maybe there are limits to that."

"No," she said, "there can't be. You don't get it at all, Willie. You think there are limits, but there aren't."

"This seems like something extra to me—something over beyond what's happened before."

"I screwed the head right off that fucking snake," Clement crowed, raising his fist and twisting it, "And you know what?" The Indian, a smooth-faced young man in a cowboy hat, nodded his head . . .

"No," Kate said, "this is just another little Willie ranchero you're trying to get everything corralled into. You want some end and resolution to things, some crop you can harvest and haul to the house and stack up in the silo for market . . ."

". . . for a second there," Clement said, "for one damn second there, I thought I had wrenched my own cock off. It was strange—I once knew this guy who could grab a snake by the tail, back in Arkansas, and snap its head off like popping a bull-whip—holding that big head, blood in my lap, and that white mouth open, those fangs like little needles . . ."

"You think that's the way to go," Kate said banging her fist against the roof, "you think if you can grab it and stop it, come to an end of it, you'll be free, but I have been telling you for the last five years of your life—I have been showing it to you—that the end of things is where we die, that's the death call. The only pen you can't get out of is the one you die in . . ."

She turned away from me as she spoke, half-listening to Clement, who had turned too and was looking at us. It was clear by the grin on the Indian's face that he hadn't understood a word Clement was saying. But I understood it; I understood the raised fist and the head of the memory-snake clasped in it, the thick shaft and the glittering beaded head—and Kate, who had touched everything in her life, and brought it to her lips and tasted of it, understood too: I could see it, not in her face, which turned away from me, though it was there, but in the slightest patch of her skin, in the ripple of the cloth across her back, in the smeared creases of her white skirt, in the hollow behind her ankle, and in the slick pearl of pomade gumming a tuft of her hair.

From behind, I reached around her hip and raised her skirt.

"Don't," she said, but she didn't stop me. Clement was look-ing straight at us. I lifted the skirt, bunched it to the side, pulled her closer to me. She pressed her back against the roof edge; her heels were sunk into the sand as if she were planted there. With my other hand, I reached between her legs and grasped her sex. I forced my hand under the band of her underpants, clutched the springy hair. She trembled, turned slightly toward me, but I held her up. I tightened my grip, working my fingers in, thrusting. She looked down at me with surprise and anger in her face, but she did not try to pull away. I pushed my fingers deeper. She groaned, and it was the heavy, secret groan of night sex, the involuntary animal groan only a lover hears. Clement could hear it too. The groan was in his face, as if my hand was going into him. He bared his teeth and his head drew back. The groan, the sound, my fingers entered him, tearing. He twisted, and for a second he looked as if he was going to come out of the car, but something in her face must have stopped him. He turned away from us and leaned his head back on the seat. He closed his eyes. He didn't look at us again.

Which of us is not being dragged down forever?

Kate reached into the car and touched my head. She stroked my hair, let her fingers caress my face. She said, "I picture you as a little boy, and I can see you, and see your sweetness, and how you loved everything around you."

"I'm still that boy."

"You're not, but you wish you were. You remember him, and it kills you that you can't hold on to him, that you can't get back to him."

I licked the tips of her fingers. They tasted of sweat and mud, of salt, like a sediment, the slightest, thinnest, the what-we-don't-notice veneer that like a wall made of rock separates us from every other living thing. I could have reached up inside her and pulled her guts out, but I couldn't get to her. And my father, the clump of bones and blood in the next car, the bruiser, the snake killer, grinned at me. He had tipped his hat back, and he leaned back in the seat and he was grinning at me, a grin of such ferocity and happiness that I thought I would fall out of the car shrieking. Kate pressed her hand over mine and pressed it hard against her pubis. I pulled away.

"Ah," she said, "like a hawk I fly."

"I can't even slow you down."

"Oh, Willie, if I was standing still you couldn't stop me."

And then out of nowhere, out of space, or out of the jumpy magic at the bottom of my own heart, joy flooded me. It surged through me in a sweet, clear wave. It brought everything, every possibility and every hope and every twist that turns to delight. I was beside myself. I wanted to get out of the car and dance. I pumped the accelerator, banged the steering wheel. "Jesus Christ," I said, laughing, "I feel so good I want to kill somebody."

She stepped away from me. There was surprise in her eyes, and some fear.

"It's all right," I said. "I want all this to happen. I want it to get as wild as it can get. I wish I had dynamite."

"You'd blow your hand off." She spoke boldly, but there was a shiver in her voice. She stepped off and stood there between the two cars.

"What are you going to do now, darling?" I said.

She was the best of them all, Kate was.

She pressed her hand against her chest, fluttered it over her heart. Her smile, the one she had lifted into the movies, the one that shined on her face some nights when we made love, ignited. It erased everything else in her face. "I want to see what happens, too," she said. "I want to see all of it."

She was a fire set at the center of my life, devouring me, lighting everything around me.

SO THE FLAG dropped, and I banged the decrepit car into gear, slammed the accelerator to the floor. The race was ten circuits, and I drove them, hitting the highest speed I could. The cars roared, reeled, sped along the hard sand. On the corners we bumped and jostled. The Mexican men, the Indian men I should say, for that is what they were, wore straw cowboy hats and bandannas tied around their necks. The crowd screamed in a language I couldn't understand, but I could understand what they wanted. My father's yellow T-Bird, sprung by its flight over the cliff, hung on its chassis at an odd angle, but it made its speed. He was ahead of me, slurring through the turns, banging against the slab sides of the old Buicks and Chevrolets, cars that in the States workers drove into the fields and abandoned to the crows and the rains.

The circuits unrolled as the cars sped down to the ocean, careened toward the waves, and then swept a left turn along the beach and around the hay bales and inland toward the shaggy sea grapes and the cliff behind, rattled past the grandstand, past the screams, the hanks of cloth waved in the deepening twilight. The torches burned like fierce yellow heads on fire. I was back in the pack, figuring the car out, letting it go and drawing it back, accelerating, braking, downshifting through the soupy gears. A guy with a dark hawk face pulled alongside, flashed me a look of maniacal glee and eased past. He pulled in tightly in front, so smoothly that I had to brake. A car behind bumped me and wobbled away, veering toward the hay bales, righting itself finally, like an addled fish, and swam on. The problem with beauty, as I could have told the old doctor, was it popped up in such odd places. In the west the sun bled all over the sky; saffrons and apricots, deep bold reds and a streak of purple like a scarf unfurled lay on top of each other. In the center the sun burned gold. The waves crashed the shore, shooting spray against the cars; I had to use the windshield wipers to see as I came around the ocean turn.

Slowly I began to gain on the leaders, on my father, who ran with them. I could see him ahead, rolling the wheel like a body he was turning over. He shook his fist out the window at a sport who passed him. Kate seemed to have disappeared into the shadows. Then I thought I saw her standing across the river in front of the houses, a child in her arms. But then the woman didn't seem to be her. And then she was by the cooking fires, her white dress changed for jeans, bending over a large pot stirring something. And then I saw her on the highest tier of the bleachers, waving two dark scarves, her face lit by torches. But it wasn't her. And then she was the woman walking by herself down the beach, stopping, turning to look back at the spectacle. But it wasn't. And then she was under the trees, and then she was perched on an outcrop of ragged stone behind the village, and then she was sitting among a crowd of women by the river telling a story with her hands.

I gunned the car toward my father, crawling up the track, banging my way. He was three cars ahead, then two cars, and then there was only a single car between us. It was the dark hawk-faced guy, driving a green Chevrolet. He swung the car from side to side, holding me back. I tried the horn, which worked. He glanced in his rearview mirror and grinned. I waved at him. He let the car drift back, bumped me, and then accelerated. We swung into the upside curve and he drifted wide. I rattled up beside him. He grinned at me again and waved, started to come in across my bow. I held him off. The straightaway opened and I held the car in second, inching past him. He dropped back and I waved, grinning into the mirror. Now there was only my father ahead, cruising, driving with one hand like a gent out for a Sunday ramble. But I knew the man, I knew this guy. I knew that studied nonchalance, that appearance of effortlessness. Underneath he was as wild as a jackal.

His car seemed to pull me up on a rope. Steadily, stamping the accelerator as if it were a snake, I gained on him. I couldn't see Kate anymore, or I couldn't see the figment, the shapeshifter she had become, but I didn't mind; I knew she could see me. If she had become a bird, or a bristly bush, or a child sucking a cloth teat dipped in coconut milk, still I knew she could see me. I eased up behind Clement, tapped his bumper. He glanced back, grinned. His black head looked as big as a basketball. I bumped him, swung left; he swung with me, holding me back. He decelerated; I could feel the weight of his car against my own. Then the hawky guy began to pull alongside, and Clement and I both sped up, pushing out beyond him into the open space behind the leaders, who were running steadily and uncatchable in identical Pontiac GTOs. The cliffs twirled by, night-dark and tall as ships, holding the earth back. I edged into the turn and came up along the inside. I couldn't tell whether he was allowing me to come up or I was outmuscling him; I bumped him; the flanks of our battered cars clanked and massaged each other, rubbing as if they wanted to nestle together.

We rolled past the bleachers that were filled with a festive crowd. Men in white clothes stood yelling. Their language was the old one, Indian language, and as far as I knew they were yelling the words they had yelled as Moctezuma went down before Cortés. The women, separated, standing in the heights of the bleachers, yelled too, waving cloth streamers. As we flashed past, I thought I saw Kate, saw her white head above the dark heads of the women, and I remembered the morning after our first night together, the night we didn't make love, when she came in naked off the porch and woke me. She had touched me as if I was precious to her, or as if, and I thought this then, anything that wasn't her was precious to her. Love flapped up in me like a flock of sparrows and I wanted to touch her then more than I had wanted to touch anyone I ever knew. And I wanted to see—I remember this—how she went about living this affection for the world's creatures. And now I had seen it.

I inched my bow past my father's car, but I couldn't pass him. He shot me a look, holding the wheel with hands pushing at it, and the look was something I had seen before, a look of determination, of the will's fire, desperate, almost invincible, terrified, ruthless, goaty, purely bestial. I had seen it as a child, this look. I knew what my father would do to get what he wanted. I knew what he was famous for, what had made his reputation. It was no figment. It wasn't a posture. It wasn't a manner. Ha ha, he would say, they don't think I mean it, but I do. Ah, you young disputavos, you clamorers and whiners, all you filled up to your eyeteeth with longing. Here is the way to go about things, he would say. You have to mean it. You have to mean it more than you mean anything in your life. If you won't give your life for it, my father said, then it doesn't matter.

We spun down the straightaway, straight on toward the battering ocean. The waves lifted their white flags toward us, tall as cavalry. Clement was outside, I was inside; I held the bow of my car-boat heavily against his prow, matching speed for speed. He wouldn't let me by, and because he wouldn't, I knew I had him. I didn't want to get by. Clement had said to me—or was it Kate?— *I want to live a life that peels skin off the faces of the people around me.* Or did I say that? Was it a movie line I spoke and surrendered to the meaning of? No, my thing was the drift, I don't want to forget that. I don't take sides, I don't fight back, I let things go.

I held the wheel to the right, pinning him. I wouldn't let him make the turn. It came on us ferociously, enlarging as it came, this wall of ocean. Farther to the right were the fires of the roasting ovens, men tending them. Clement swung the wheel hard at me, but I had the bow in front and wouldn't give. He shook his fist, bared his teeth. Then he looked to the right, looked for a way out off the track through the cooking area. He couldn't make it. He looked back at me and there was a look of such silly bafflement, such wonder on his broad face, that I almost laughed out loud. He glanced at the ocean and his lips pulled back from his teeth and his eyes narrowed and he pulled himself up toward the wheel.

We hit the water at sixty, and we were lucky at first because a big wave had just busted down to nothing—we hit the surf planing for a second—even this impact throwing me against the wheel—and then the rough stuff came, a large gray wave streaked with white like flung paint: we hit, me first, then him, and I was flung against the doorpost and knocked senseless. But not before I saw his car slur, rip sideways, and soar roof-first into the wave that crashed over it in a cloud of spray, obliterating it.

I came to almost immediately. There was seawater in my nose, in my chest. I coughed and retched, underwater, whirling in a fragmented green-and-gray place, the sandy water like pulverized concrete bashing and soughing. The car was submerged to the roof. I pulled myself out, climbed up top, held on as a wave crashed over me, and looked around. Clement's car was thirty feet farther on, upside down.

I dived off the roof, swam to the T-Bird, ducked under, and found him. He was alive, conscious and disoriented, pushing at the front windshield. The salt stung my eyes as it rolled in clouds around us, scattering billows of sand.

I grabbed him by the throat and began to choke him. His skin was slippery and he fought me, but I had a good strong grip. I dragged him by the throat out of the car, kicked to the surface, and shoved him against the side of the car. A wave caught me by the shoulders and spun me away, but I dived under the next one, thrashed back, and grabbed him again. He struck me above the ear, caught me with overhand punches. I sputtered words that made no sense, I didn't know what I was saying. The bump on his forehead was now a cut; it gleamed whitely, the edges neat and thin. I punched him in the face. He fell back against the car, a wave caught him and dragged him under. I dived, gulping air as I went, found him cartwheeled against the side of the car. I don't know why, but I began to tear his clothes off. I dragged him to the surface, scrabbling at his shirt, ripping it. It came off in split patches, and then I pulled at his trousers and dragged them down his hairy thighs, and then, him banging the top of my head with his heavy fists, I pulled his boxers off, surged to the surface, and flung them away. I screamed at him as I came up, screamed the words of betrayal that are the trademarks of this sort of business.

There were people around now, men waded into the surf behind us. I looked back at them, and to me it seemed as if bandits were approaching, or a murderous army. The men carried cane poles, one guy pushed a black inner tube ahead of him as he came. I thought they wanted to do something to me, something foul.

What I wanted was to hear my father cry out; I wanted to hear him beg for mercy. But he didn't. Even as I lunged at him, turning his thick body in my arms, cracking him across the back with my forearm, he didn't cry out. He fought me, grimly, out of the memory of an old man's strength, he fought me with his whole body, and as I slammed my fists against him, slammed my body against his naked, furry body, I could feel the kinship, the inestimable connection that lived between us, that would go on living no matter what happened, and I hated it, I hated being who

I was and hated the stupid world as it was and my father as he was and Kate soaring like a white bird through the skies of my life, and I hated the next breath and the breath after that and all the breaths that had come before—something in me began to sob and I hated this, I forced it back down like a beast into a hole and I hit harder, my punches more desperate, and it seemed to me, as I rose from the surf, hauling my father up by the scruff of the neck, that the red, swollen sky in the west was mired in its own battle with the earth, with the sea that reared beneath it, and it seemed to me that this battle had been going on forever and would go on forever, and it seemed there was to be no end to it ever and this was the way it was on earth and maybe the way it had to be, maybe there was no question of any other way to live a life and no possibility of another.

Something rose through my body like a piece of shrapnel burning and tearing through me, and I began to scream; I let go, let everything go, screaming so that when the village men grabbed me, pulling me away from my father who, fine man that he was, punched on steadily, just another hardworking dumb Arkie mule, I screamed in their frightened, slick faces, crying inexplicable sounds so that they had to manhandle me, roughly drag me away kicking like a lunatic, raving, flinging my arms wildly, half a dozen of them pinching holds like crabs about the body, dragging me out of the teeming surf, up onto the dry land, onto the footings of the continent and the sand that they pressed me down into and held me down on, that I rose up off of thrashing, wailing like a demon. I almost made it to my feet again, I almost got upright, I could see openings appearing in front of me, avenues down which wide roads rolled away, I could feel the strength coming back, the power, the drive to break free, to triumph, but as I strained against them, as I gathered myself for the first step away from them, someone, some cowboy I hadn't noticed, swung a club, caught me against the side of the head, and sent me out.

Ah, muchachos, look up. In the fake heaven above, fake angels are crying fake tears.

FOR THE SECOND time that day I came to on my back. It was in a shed, a small, square tin room with a concrete floor. They'd left a bowl of chopped pineapple, half a bottle of tequila, and a lantern on the floor beside me. The lantern threw a thick orange radiance on the corrugated walls. There were two windows, they were small, no glass in them, only chicken wire. There were small round holes in the walls, as if someone had taken a gun to the place. I tried the door. It was held with a piece of wire, and outside it—I could see through a crack—a man with a machete guarded me. I didn't know how late it was, but the sky was fully dark.

I banged on the door. The man put his face to the crack. I asked him what was going on and he told me that I had been put there for safekeeping, for my own good. You scared everyone, he said, you frightened the whole village.

Nobody ever saw a fight before? I said.

You tried to kill your father. This is too bad.

Where is he?

Celebrating.

The guard was a stout man, very dark; a thin fringe of hair fell over his eyes.

I said, How long are you going to keep me here?

Until morning.

Then what?

Then you must leave.

What is that throbbing, humming sound?

The generators—for electricity.

It was steady, low, almost earthy. Around it came the soft crack of surf. The generator must have been close by, because I could only barely hear the sounds of festival, a few shouts, the pop of firecrackers.

I stood up, looked out the window. Nearby were small houses, a section of street that led downhill. Beyond them the glow of the bonfire flickered. My head hurt. I vaguely remembered being brought here, remembered the doctor leaning over me, shooting something into my arm. I said, Have I been asleep?

For hours. The doctor made you sleep.

Maybe I'll try some of that again. Do you know any stories?

What stores?

Any stories—legends, terrible tales, bloody accidents, doomed romances, rough stuff. I like to hear a story before I go to sleep.

Outside, shouts. I looked out the window. Men in white clothes, wearing masks, ran by in the street, a group of them.

Other men followed brandishing whips. The whips cracked in the air like pistol shots. Behind them came children running. They disappeared past the houses.

What is the name of this festival? I said.

The Day of the Dead.

It's not like any Day of the Dead festival I've seen. Where are the sugar skulls and the procession and the body of Christ and all that?

They came and went.

Where and when? I thought. It was like a radio just barely picking up a distant station. I couldn't tune it in clearly enough to find out what it was. You had to work really hard to find out anything. About anyone, about any part of the world. You think it is easy, you think you are getting it, but then your lover shows you the scar on her ankle and tells you the story of the boy who put it there and you look into her eyes, totally baffled, and you have no idea who she is. You wake up early and you go to the window and something has happened, you don't know what any of this is, what those bushes are for, or those horses cropping grass or that sky that looks as if it goes on forever, and you turn back to the room that is filled with sunshine and you look into the face of the one you have lived with for years, look at her sleeping, at her face turned toward you on the pillow, and you have no idea who she is or what she is doing here, you don't know if she is to be loved or feared, if she is a saviour or an assassin, and you look down at your own hands and you know them as yours because they are attached to the ends of your arms, but you know nothing about them, you don't know what they have done, what they have grasped, and you have no idea, no idea at all, how they got so veined and worn, how age and time have torn them so.

I thought of Jennie White sitting on her ocean deck staring at the banging sea, and I wondered what stories played in her mind, if she rolled the old movies through, playing the parts she played in the long ago, if in her easy chair in the shade safe from sun under umbrella and vast hat she saw herself walking into the ball-room she had walked into like a queen in *Isabella,* forty years ago, and I wondered what it would be for me when I sat on a deck in the sunshine and thought about the past, what it would mean to me, and what I would think about it when everything but the last few breaths were behind me, if I would curse my life or stroke it like the back of a kitten—and I thought of Veronica, who might at that moment be lying beside Jennie, lying in the big bed in the high room overlooking the ocean, and wondered what it was for her, what she had felt in those arms that had first taken her when she was thirteen years old, and if she even noticed the change in flesh that had occurred, noticed the slackening, the drift in the body, if for her there was no change, or no change that mattered, and if it—this not noticing—was the glory of life, or one of its glories, the thing that love was for, this suspension of time that carried us through the years of our lives unappalled by the corrosion and decay that was everywhere around us, if it was that simple, as simple as looking into the face of the aging, spotted creature you had married or fallen in love with fifty years before, and seeing only the gleaming glorious beauty itself that shined there, the sweet spirit under it all, that endured forever.

The man outside my door, the jailer, was talking. He had remembered a story and he was telling it to me. Shouts, another pod of celebrants whirled by. I thought I saw Clement, changed into white clothes, waving a burning branch, but I couldn't be sure. The man was telling a story about a mad girl, a young girl born mad, he said, and how she drove an old man crazy. I didn't get it at first; he seemed to be speaking of my own life, or the lives of my loved ones, but then he said the girl was his sister and the old man was his father, and it wasn't a story about a love affair, but about family, and it was terrible.

I got the tequila bottle and a handful of pineapple and stood at the window eating and drinking, listening to him. The girl got madder as she grew older, the man said, until she was so mad she would not live in the house but wandered in the bush and in the fields, staying out like a cat in the woods. It drove his father crazy, he said.

More people passed by in the street. Dancers and runners, men carrying torches, women whirling in dance, went by. Each group was costumed more strangely than the one preceding it. The masks got more terrible, red eyed, golden, dripping blood. Arms and hands were painted white. I said, I was wrong; it looks like everything is showing up in this festival.

We display the dark, the man said.

I think you're right on the money, I said. What happened to the girl?

My sister.

That makes it more terrible.

Yes, always.

Three boys on horses went by. They were painted black and the horses were black. They rode bareback, with their arms raised. One of them leaned down from the horse and grabbed the leaves of a banana tree growing beside the street. He grasped the leaves to tear them off, it seemed, but the leaves held and he was pulled from his horse. The others hooted but they didn't stop for him. And his horse, shying, didn't stop either, it pranced on without him.

The guard said, My sister slept in the woods, she lived with the animals. Sometimes she would come to the kitchen and my mother would feed her, with tears in her eyes. My sister wouldn't come in the house. She squatted in the yard, eating from a plate on the ground. She would eat on her hands and knees like an animal. If my father was around he would rush out and run her away, beat her away with a piece of rope. My mother would scream at him, she would try to protect my sister from the blows, but my father would not stop. My sister would run into the field, she would grab up rocks and throw them at my father. She would scream like an animal, like one who had never known human speech.

And then it came back to me how I was dragged up out of the surf and carried on the shoulders of the men like a slaughtered animal to this place, this Sears Roebuck shed beside a banana grove, and how roughly they had handled me, cuffing me and pinching me, and how the doctor and Kate had protected me, had prevented them from throwing me in the fire as some of the men wanted to do, and I wished I had been more awake so I could understand exactly the experience of being excluded from the human circle, of becoming one for whom no attachments held—I wanted to know if I was terrified or relieved, I wanted to know if I fought back or argued, but I couldn't remember.

The man continued talking, telling his story like someone stupidly, uselessly breaking rocks in the dark. He said his sister became some kind of wailing schizo highwayman, attacking people on the road, grabbing not for money, but for glittering things, buttons or belt buckles, pieces of fruit, and how most people became used to it, but some were frightened, especially the children and the animals, and some of the women, and how people began carrying sticks when they traveled in the area to beat her away if she attacked. She would rise up naked from the fields, he said, and throw stones. They were big stones and they hurt if they hit you.

Wasn't there anything you could do for her?

Nothing that would work. The doctor had pills, but who could make her take them? And there was no place to put her. We couldn't even catch her.

A clamorous, striking music sounded, and then, from around a corner, the band appeared. They had stripped down and wore loincloths made of palm fronds. Their bodies were oiled and they pranced in the light of torches borne by children. They looked like figures from a dark and ancient past, prancing and capering, but the instruments, the horns and the piccolos and the accordion worked by a tall man with a belly that looked pumped up for the occasion, were modern; and the tune they played was only a popular song we had already heard chuffing out of boom boxes on street corners in towns we had passed through. They played it badly, off key, but then I thought it must be intentional because there was a grating, tearing motif grinding through that must have been intentional, as if some other music, something that lived on its own, were pushing up through the sugary melody, but it was not clear, and I couldn't be sure. The guard banged the machete handle on the ground, keeping an awkward time.

What happened to your sister? I said.

She came to a bad end.

I expect so, but what happened?

My father.

What did he do?

My teeth were clenched, and my body was rigid. Out on the street, Kate, riding in a gold-painted chair lifted high, was going by. She wore the same white dress, but now it was torn and threaded with flowers. She wore a flower garland on her head. Her arms were red streaked, by blood or paint I couldn't tell. She waved a palm branch.

I pressed my face against the wire, pressed until the wire bit my skin. What did your father do? I said.

The guard was on his feet, waving. The street was a rocking sea.

He lost his mind, the guard said. The shame was too great for him.

The chair was held aloft by half a dozen men, probably the same men who had carried me on their shoulders to this place. Not all the same, because one of them was Clement. With one arm he held a chair rocker, with the other he held Kate. She swayed in the air, leaning from side to side, drawing the branch across the air above her as if she were painting the sky with it.

What did he do? I said.

He went after her. He hunted her like a deer.

Did you go too?

Yes.

I banged on the window frame, but Kate did not look my way.

What happened? I said.

For three days my father stalked her through the woods. I followed him, stalking her too.

Clement's big face was wild, smeared with grease. He shouted. Kate placed her hand on his head, lifted herself. She seemed about to leap into the air.

Did you find her? I said.

Yes. We found her early one morning. She had come out into the fields, as the deer do, to eat the corn.

I banged on the window frame, I cried out. The guard looked at me, crossed the machete over his chest. His face was slick with sweat. His head bobbed as he spoke, as if he were bumping the words with his lips as they came out of him.

She was squatting in a row, he said, gnawing an ear of corn. She was entirely naked and covered with dirt, even her face . . .

His voice caught in his throat, trailed away in soupy swallows.

What happened?

I do not want to say.

Tell me.

The din was enormous. Kate cried out, shouted, screeched. She waved her arms. Children danced around the procession, leaping to touch her. The torches shed sparks. The instruments flashed.

I know about this, I said. I was shouting.

How could you know? He was shouting too, lifting on his toes as he spoke.

I know from my own life.

Not like this.

My head ached, and a hazy dimming shadow seemed to be moving in from the front, a cloud like smoke, obscuring everything. I heard cries, and the cries seemed to come from children, from children who were crying out in great pain. They were crying for someone to help them, to save them. The cries were thin and heartbroken and they were all around me, not only out in the street but in the empty yard before us, and coming from the houses through the broken walls of which light poured, and from behind the shed, and from inside the shed too. They were close, but they were small, as if I were hearing not the present but a past that lingered in this place.

What happened? I shouted.

She tried to run away, he said.

He shouted, but the words seemed whispered.

He said, She leapt up and threw the ear of corn at us. Her eyes were white in her face. She was like a demon. Her hair was torn and ragged. She ran at us. And my father raised his gun. He raised his gun and he shot her.

I held on to the window for dear life. The screaming was everywhere; the cries, the children's cries, whispery and insistent, cut through everything. The air blazed. And I saw Kate, the blond unbreakable one, the woman I loved, lean down and take my father's head in her hands, ram her face into his, and kiss him full on the lips.

Was she dead? I said.

She was dead. She never rose up again. We buried her there in the field among the corn.

He turned his face away, crying.

The procession disappeared around the corner and what was left of the night flowed back over us, but I did not watch the revelers go and did not watch the night come back. I sank away from the window. The room had extra shadows in it, shadows the lantern couldn't chase, but I didn't mind. The world might be upside down, I might be a shade, killed out there in the surf and only dreaming this now, but it didn't bother me. Beyond this room, beyond this cool concrete floor in Mexico, where in daylight I saw houses propped up by sticks, and fields of poppies fluttering and a desert strung together with thorny brush and a village come to madness, there might be nothing at all, there might be only ashes and a black landscape burned to the roots—it might be only something I had dreamed, and everything beyond it a dream: Hollywood, and my life in the movies, and Veronica, and long afternoons listening to the radio, and my quiet white house in the hills—they all might be only figments passing in a dream, but I did not care. Somewhere among them, somewhere among the rubble or among the tissue of dream, my father squatted over Kate, somewhere, on some bit of ground, his brute face and body pressed against hers; wherever that place was, on earth, or in dream, or in heaven or hell, I would find it and kill them both.

TIME PASSED, THE guard slept. I undid the baling wire fastening the door, took his machete, and slipped away.

I climbed into the hills, like Moses, to get a little strength, to get the next scene straight. The desert was alive with movement. Animals scurried in the brush, insects flittered, and great dark birds, flying blind, hung in soaring, dihedral drift in the clear sky. I wanted to stand away, apart from human life for a time, to see if there was some other word I might hear, some other notion this particular arrangement of space and time might come up with, hear what the dirt and the opossums and the squaw bush and the oldest rocks had to say about all this, but they didn't have anything new to offer. I had been on my knees in a desert more than once, I had walked out among the sage and the creosote more than one time, walking away and walking toward, and I had seen how big and strange the world gets in the places where human life hadn't made a dent in it yet, and I knew something about what space and distance and solitude have to teach us, and I knew how we were all connected and bound together, and how one thing was a part of another thing, but the desert this night didn't say anything I hadn't heard before, and the sky and the wind gnawing at the bushes and the mice and the rabbits looking up from their chores didn't cast any fresh light on anything. God didn't come down out of heaven and speak to me, and no white deer enticed me, and the goddesses had all been called off on other jobs, and no unctuous golem muttered in my ear. I couldn't even hear Bobby, couldn't hear the soft singing that had haunted me all my life, couldn't feel his smoky weight pressed against my back. I was on my own.

And maybe, I thought, crouching with my face pressed into the perfume of a lavender bush, this is the way it always is when you have crossed over into the death ramble, maybe in all those parts I'd played, those killers and avengers I had run myself through, maybe I had missed something, maybe the secret story told in the basement rooms by men who have come to the last terrible moment had not reached me; and then, thinking this, squatted close enough to the desert floor to smell the bitter odors of bugs and roots, I felt the slight shiver and thrill of discovery, the quick leap inside as something new, some fresh turn of the wheel, showed itself to me, and there, the cords of my life tensed in my hand as if they held up a bridge over roiling disaster, I thought yes, even the biggest things are small things, and no matter what we do there is still this moment coming when we squat in the corner listening to our breathing, smelling in our nostrils the freshly baked bread in the house next door, and I wondered, as I had hardly wondered before in my life, where I would be tomorrow, in what world I would be rising, and what I would see, and what sort of man I would have become. For a moment I wanted to stay there and ponder these things, to see what fresh scenario might shape itself out of the dust and the dry odors of scrub, but there was no time left, the night was turning on the gimbal of time, and I had things to do.

I slipped around the hills, came down through a stand of sugar cane into a small grove of orange trees. The ground crackled underfoot, springy with leaves. I paused at the edge of the grove, hidden in shadow, squatted in the leaves, and looked around. The houses radiated off a central square, not a square really but a meeting place of tamped earth and dusty tile that had been the lobby of the resort hotel. I was afraid the village dogs might find me, but the breeze was blowing off the ocean and maybe at party time they too were sated; none barked. I wanted to leap up whooping and yelling, but I restrained myself.

I was thinking about Johnny Weismuller. Thinking of him slim and limber soaring through the jungle in his Tarzan movies. As a kid I watched him on TV, fat and wise, playing Jungle Jim. And then later as a young man I saw him at a party and he was an angry, self-important man, flaccid and agitated. And then my father, who visited him in the actor's home, told me he had lost his mind, that he stood on a table in the dayroom beating his chest and yelling like Tarzan. Hollywood was a great place for getting a look at what beauty and vigor could turn into. We all get to see the stars in their glory, in their moment when the kiss of heaven shines in their faces, but unless you live where they grow old, you don't get to see what happens next. You don't get to see the glamor queen pushing her cart at the liquor store tricked out in green makeup, scarves knotted around the crepuscular neck, twitching a wad of bills into the clerk's face with a hand as wizened as a mummy's. You don't get to see the formerly robust, rock-jawed idol listing into the arms of his paid companion as he staggers bald and drunk down the sea walk at Newport Beach. You don't get to see the sweet-faced child star who is now the liquor store clerk the ruined actress thrusts her money toward, grinning his bitter and supercilious grin, laughing in her face. You don't get to see the great character actor on his deathbed calling damnation down on the heads of his enemies, begging for someone to come and kill him so he can get off this murderous planet. It is powerful because we know them so well when they are beautiful. Even as they shuffle down the corridors of retirement homes or lean back in their wheelchairs as a nurse wipes spittle from their lips, we can look up at the screen, where they are still beautifully, wildly playing. The images they created, the faces they brought forth into the darkened rooms of our desire, move yet in fact and life, even as the leathery claw reaches from the stinking bed and the cracked voice begs for a cookie.

Under the orange trees that smelled like the trees at my father's farm, I touched my face, probed it lightly with my fingers. All the emotions—or all the emotions I could come up with—had moved through my face into a camera and out into the world. A twitch here, a twitch there, some memory that widened my eyes, my lip protruded, I had made the gestures. In movies you play close in, like a boxer or a lover, the face on the screen is huge; it doesn't have to move much. But it has to move. The director says, Take two steps forward, stop on the mark, look down and to the left. What am I looking at? you ask. You are looking at your wife in the arms of your father. Yes, well, is that anger, horror, glee—what? Let's try terror. I don't know if I can do terror; I'm a little placid for that. Then think about—what in your past scared you? I don't know. What about the time you watched your mother lick your best friend's pussy? Maybe. What about the time your parents divorced? I suppose. What about the morning your father came into your room crying, his clothes torn, to tell you Bobby was dead? Yes. What about your wife's face when she got out of the car after her flight from Italy, when she stepped into the white sunshine carrying a wicker jug of homemade wine and looked up at you as you waited just outside her bedroom doors—what about the look in her eyes? Yes, I see. Do you have it? Yes, I have it. Two steps forward, stop, look down and to the left. Yes. But what am I looking at?

I ran across an open space and flopped down beside a small thatched house. The village houses were mostly small and square, roofed with pandanus and coconut thatch. There was a central street, but the houses seemed randomly tossed down among the banyan trees and the coconut palms. Bananas sprouted behind each one in big tufts. A baby cried. I sprang up and ran to another house, slid in behind a stack of torn baskets. Inside the house men laughed. I started to get up, but they came outside. They were drinking. There were four of them passing a bottle around. The moon glinted in the dark glass as they raised it. I squinted across an open space; there was a faint light coming from a shack over there, I thought I heard Kate's voice. One of the men squatted down near me. I was just behind the corner. The bottle reached him, he raised it, and as he did, a centipede dropped from the thatch onto his shoulder. It was as large as my hand. I started to speak, to touch him in warning, started before I thought, but I caught myself. The man didn't notice the centipede. Something in me twisted, kicked. If I warned him I would give myself away. The centipede lay quietly on his shoulder, the tapered multiple legs that in daylight would be reddish purple, lying flat, a deadly brooch. Something inside me shrunk back gasping, but I didn't move. I wanted to call out, I wanted to brush the poison thing off his shoulder—a centipede that size could paralyze you for years—but if I did I would give myself away. I waited for someone to see it, for the man to sense it perched there, but no one moved except the man himself, who raised his arm to pass the bottle on.

And then the centipede moved. It slid closer to the collar of his shirt and stopped, then moved again, slightly closer. I could feel it moving on my own skin, the light, spiky legs creeping. And then the man felt it himself. But he felt it as one might feel a feather or a leaf. He raised his right hand without looking, to brush the touch away, or to investigate it; he grasped the centipede. For a moment it was in his hand and he held it out to look at it—*what is this?*—and then he saw what it was, but it was too late. As he flung it from him, it bit him. Screaming, he shook it off him, flinging it at the feet of the other men. They cried out, springing back. The bitten man lurched to his feet, lunged sideways, and fell holding his wrist. He screamed again—*Madre Dios*—and his hurt hand clutched spasmodically. I slipped back along the side of the house as the men cried out and from huts across the way faces began to appear.

It was a bad sign, proof of something I didn't want proven. Even in the dim light I had seen the look of surprise and horror on the man's face.

Crouching, I ran along a row of huts, dodging from darkness into darkness. It was late; the feast had twirled on through its ceremonies and drifted now toward the dawn. There were more shouts from the place I'd fled, but along the row I passed, near the river, the houses were dark. Here and there I heard someone talking, soft night murmurs, the startled cries of babies. I paused at each house, listened, and moved on.

Then I came to a small square house with canvas flaps covering sides made of sticks. The canvas had been rolled partway up along two sides. I knelt against the cloth—I heard Kate's voice.

She was talking to someone. I lay flat against the side of the house. "Death's come around," she said.

"Somebody stepped on a nail," my father said.

I was home.

The ground I lay on was hard, tamped down; it smelled of old rain and piss, of woody rot. Above my head in the thatch that hung over the eaves like matted hair, birds rustled, birds or spirits. I could see the river, striped lightly by moonlight, and see part of the bleachers where the crowd had roared. Now there were only these two voices. Through thin gaps in the wall thicket I could see a lamp burning. I pressed my eye close, made out their bodies, the dark mass of them, lying together on a pallet against the far wall.

Maybe in a minute I would rush in and confront them, but for now, I thought, it's better to lie here and listen. Their voices slipped and drifted, talking of their lives. The rage twirled away and I was filled with a coldness and a fascination. I came on a place in myself I hadn't been before. Knotted bits, like hammered pieces of myself, broke free and drifted through my body. They were like pieces of memory, something heard and transformed; they fell through me like gravel through water. I could hardly hear, or could hear only partially, as if the voices spoke only certain words fully. It was not the clamorous night that prevented me. The wind had died. The shouts had faded. Kate was talking, inventing, building her strapping world. She said, or I heard her say, something about what lasted, what would go on forever. I pressed my face against the wattles. I wanted to press through and hang there like a sculpted mask on the wall. Clement answered in his slow, corroded bass, asking questions. No, she said, not that. He asked again, curiosity in his voice. Yes, she said, the sounds, whatever we say. It seemed the talk in my head was being spoken in the shadowed room. Speaking inside my head, I said, *No, it's a little different than that, darling.* She had once told me a story about shooting a man. It was out in the desert—the desert of which country she didn't say—she had stopped to help a driver beside the road and he had attacked her. She said, I shot him. I shot him in the legs, got back in my car, and drove on. Now her voice drifted up, like a bird flying closer. She said, "Out in space all these sounds we make are collected somewhere, in a cloud maybe off the shoulder of a star. I imagine myself, or the spirit or ghost I'm going to be, floating out there, sorting through them, trying to locate some important, lost statement."

"What would you like to hear again?" Clement said.

"I want to hear my brother talking to me just before he died."

"Just before?"

"Yes."

Clement was silent, then he said, "I would like to hear my boy Bobby's voice again. I would do anything to hear his voice."

She coughed, and, speaking, her voice thinned, faded. I heard a murmur, distant shouts. A ways off, someone waded noisily across the river: a black form strode up the bank, disappeared between the houses.

". . . a kind of angel," Kate said.

"Yes. I believe in that, too."

"The way the truck seemed to slowly stretch the bus apart."

"It's horrible. To have to watch that."

"I see it every night."

"I know. I see Bobby."

"I see the face of the truck, and it was like a face, and I see the pole, that silver pole next to the door in buses . . ."

"Yes."

"Like a thin silver beam we pull ourselves aboard on . . ."

"Yes."

"I see it bend and break, snap like a stalk of light. And I see us, as the big truck face pushes through, lean away from it, crouching against the seat, like kids in a fairy tale, and see the pole or heaven's beam swing down and level like a lance, and see us with no place to flee to, not another inch anywhere to squeeze ourselves into, and see the lance, as I hold my brother in my arms, see it press against steadily and then enter his chest, push straight through like a finger poking dough, and then the blood welling over us both, the blood suddenly there as if it had been there all the time and we just noticed, and David crying to me to save him, and David screaming, and the screams choking off, and the bus breaking in half, the big face moving by and carrying my brother away like a trophy."

There was silence. Then Clement spoke, and there were tears in his voice. "I don't know how you can stand living after that."

"For you it's the same."

"Yes. It is. I'll never get over losing Bobby."

"Here's what I see," she said. "I see us holding each other. I see me shrinking away from the lance, I see myself letting the lance or beam take my brother instead of me."

"You had no way out. It was God's choice."

"No. I moved. I twisted in the seat. I saw what was coming— it was all so slow, so elaborate, like an opera—and I gave my brother to the terrible face. I tricked them both."

"Oh, sweetie, we always blame ourselves."

"I don't blame myself. I only saw who I was."

"Anyone would have done the same thing. We do it without thinking about it."

"You are that way."

"Yes, I am, all the way to my toes. All the way down to my bones."

And so on, and so on, I thought, not listening anymore. There were tiers and levels, armies, vast shoals of lies here. She would say anything, she would do anything to make a vivid world. Who were these people? Even as they stepped into the new day, the sunny or rainy, the sweet-smelling or stinking day, they transformed it. It was a kind of hatred of the world, a sacrilege like the churches say, something devilish and awful, a grand, permanent, inclusive refusal. Or was it—me thinking this as I speak another lie, listening to a small bird begin to twitter in the thatch—was it love? Do you love something so much that you must bathe its body, perfume it, dress it in the finest clothes, and send it forth like some baby doge in elaborate Venice, into the world? Well, Kate would say—Clement would say—we give what we have, everything of what we have.

". . . broken, yes . . . how . . . ?" Kate speaking. A slight accent, something more English than American, more Scottish than English. My mother speaking, or my mother's younger sister, who died in childbirth in her lover's house in Edinburgh. ". . . some eternal idea . . ."

"Yes."

"You said . . ."

"Once, when I was a boy," my father said, "I chased a crook, a thief. He'd stolen money, robbed a store. It was out near Encino, on the other side of the mountains, where we lived when we first came to California."

"When did you get here?"

"There." (Coconut palms. Dust blown and fading against the sun, and beyond the dust, finally, after all those miles, the ocean, clean and blue, that none of them had ever seen before.) "We arrived in 1935, in a Ford truck. Pulled up under a big orange tree. A guy shouted at us when we tried to pick a few oranges. I was fifteen. I rode the last thousand miles in the open air, outside, in the back of the truck. It was all humiliating and wonderful, that time, those days. Everyone was shattered and hopeful at the same time. And they were ruined and the ruin was in them

like a disease. We were peasants, but peasants with a spark in us—
you know? If you could call it a spark. We stumbled on—nothing
else to do. The drought, the banks, all that merciless crap that
nearly killed us, was like one of the great plagues. It swept over
the land . . ."

"Swept over the land. Like you come from the time of
legends."

"We do. Everyone from back then does. Now it seems so.
Medieval. Ancient. Biblical, my mother called it. And grubby and
terrifying and ridiculous; your body burning because you couldn't
wash it; shitting in the bushes; eating mush. Moving about was
like walking through a goddamn concentration camp. The whole
world, for two thousand miles, was the color of dust and it was
made of dust. And what you arrived into, what we found, was
just another kind of feudal madness, overlords and gangsters,
primped Hollywood fucks and growers who hated you. The only
thing we had going for us was that we were too tough to kill.
We just wouldn't die."

"What happened with the robber?"

"I chased him down. A woman came out of the store and
yelled. It was a summer day, hot. A village store. The man ran
down the street, dashed into an alley. He had a fistful of bills,
those big old bills from the thirties that are gone now."

"Did you catch him?"

"That's what I want to tell you about. I didn't think, I just
ran after him. Down the alley. There were two big trees at the
end—sycamores, yeah, sycamores, shadows under them. He ran
toward the shadows. Coming out of the bright light—it was as
if he were running toward a gate of darkness . . ."

"You sound like Willie."

"He sounds like me . . . I chased him down, caught him in the
shadow. We both plunged into it. I leapt, I tackled the fucker, I
had him. Then all of a sudden there were all these voices around.
People shouting. And the guy I had tackled, a wiry little guy,
started cursing me and cursing things in general. He threw the
bills down and told me to get off him. I knew something was
wrong. There were voices shouting. I looked up—there were guys
on the roof. Guys and a camera."

"It was a movie."

"Yeah. They were filming. I had cut into the shot. Jesus. I was an Arkie ignoramus; I thought it was real. They'd been filming from the roof, a long take on tracks—along this flat roof that ran the length of the alley—following the guy as he ran from the store. I'd caught him, I had him down, I'd saved the day except there wasn't any day to save."

"But then there was."

"Yes—handsomely. I let him up and he began yelling, cursing the director, ranting, a real banshee, and so, with this thought in my mind—a quick thought I'd never had before: *jump for this*—I slugged him, knocked him down. He came up yelling at me. I yelled back and knocked him down again. A couple of guys came up and pulled me off. The director was watching this all the time. He was Lou Martin—you don't remember him, but he was something, he had a lot of power in those days—a big fat guy who looked like he should be carried around in a chair but who was in fact very agile, very light on his feet. Mentally too. He climbed down a ladder at the side of the building. His big butt swayed as he came down, like the old mare's ass. He was wearing white Mexican trousers that billowed like sails around his legs. He was a very big, handsome guy with delicate features, shiny little black eye lumps—he'd started as an actor—and this glistening mouth that was very mobile but at the same time very tough. He had an air as if, if he didn't like you, he could forget you in a second, and it was the truth. He came up to me and said he thought I could help him with his picture. Shit, I wasn't even twenty years old. He offered me a job. It wasn't much, but I took it—running errands, being the tough guy if I had to be, fixing sandwiches, anything he wanted, really—and that's how I got started. I got started and then I started my family. My father died cursing me, but the truth is, I was the one who got him in the movies. I got him a job working with the stock on one of Lou's horse operas. He went into acting from that."

I was drifting. Lying with my back to the earth, lost in Mexico, I drifted. I wanted to sleep, I wanted to dream vast dreams that carried out over the ocean on big white wings. Every day you learn something new. Every day the one you love gets out of the bed a new woman, reinvented, someone you have to fit yourself to again. And the same with you for her. All over the world strangers get out of bed with each other. We come and we go. We think we know and then we don't know anything.

These thoughts came to me as the talk swirled. She told him she believed him and asked him why he told the story, and he said it was what he always did, tell that story. For a moment there was something almost humble in his voice, almost childlike, and at the same time something very knowing. I wanted to kiss them and then kill them.

The stars were tiny white flowers scattered across the sky. The moon went down into the sea. The surf had faded, but it came up again, sending its muffled signal across the wide beach. The man with the bitten hand went by, crying among a clutch of men who held him up. His ruined hand floated above his head like a small, dead, swollen pet. Shouts and murmurs. Somewhere else battles were being fought. People were dying for what they believed in, and people were dying senselessly, begging for their lives. Somewhere else a woman walked out onto her patio and looked down the cliff at the ocean. She looked until she heard the voice inside her crying louder than the surf. Then she turned to the lighted room where just last night friends had laughed as they washed the dinner dishes. Now there was only emptiness, and it seemed to her that the emptiness would go on forever and it seemed to her that she was falling through it helplessly and she would fall forever. One day passes into the next and what it brings is so strange that we bite our knuckles in terror. I saw this woman, frail maybe, once strong, and she was a woman I had known and loved though I could not tell her name, and I saw her turn and stare back into the lighted house and I saw, and felt, the movement of her mind, the pain of her loss, and I saw what she would do next. Tears welled in my eyes. There is no end to suffering.

And then Kate's voice winging along, trickling through the wattles, her escapade voice. She said, "Sometimes do you picture a woman standing in a boat shouting into a house? Sometimes I do. Do you see a cherry orchard and a flock of young children in the trees picking cherries and singing into the wind? I see that. What about a sleek black car stranded in snow up a lonely mountain? Do you see yourself flying over the Grand Canyon? What about children, do you see them in white robes leaping off a cliff into the sea? I look over the prairie and I see flocks of blackbirds like a black carpet covering everything. I hear bells that are pealing the hours in a small chapel in Rome. I smell apples in the winter. A ghost shakes me awake to tell me he is the missing judge. I call long-distance and the woman on the other end of the line is me. We talk about our childhood and can't agree. I buy a pair of purple satin shoes, fill them with seeds, and leave them in the woods for the birds.

"Listen," she said, "someone is outside this house. Someone is watching us."

My father looked straight at the wall behind which I crouched. "It must be that doctor," he said. "I'll go talk to him."

"No, don't move. I don't want to stop what is going to happen from happening."

"Yes you do."

"No."

"You're strong enough?"

"No. I'll never get strong enough."

"Then I'd better go and see."

"No—here, put your hand on me instead."

"Ah—that's your hand on me."

"I used to go into department stores—when I was a child—to the women's clothing section, and I'd pluck threads from my own clothes and put them into the pockets or someway attach them to the new clothes. They were little gifts I gave, parts of me transferred to whomever bought them."

"That's nice."

"Yes"—she laughed—"you like this don't you?"

"Yes, I do."

"It gets better all the time."

"Yes, it does."

"We are over the edge now. We're headed for space."

"It's better than a courtesy car."

"It's better than fake weeping."

"Now I don't feel like such an old man. Oh—I'm getting younger all the time. I'm only half-old now."

"You have a rich body."

I drew away from the wall, began to inch around the side of the house. Out on the beach there was wailing: the bitten man crying and crying, sobs like child cries, animal moans. I slid along thinking of Johnny Weismuller and the desert fathers, of everyone who had gone off into the arid, rocky places or into the jungle, of what it was that drove them out of the glamorous world; thinking of Bobby again, at last, sure of his presence again, wondering what it would have taken for him not to kill himself, wondering what he thought of the child, the brother, the new version of him that lived inside Kate, and if he would survive this time, or if the circumstances, the crazy encroachment of Kate's body against Clement's, would destroy him again; and as I moved through dust and the tinny debris surrounding the house, picking my way toward the door through which a plank of light was thrust, a plank I might walk up into the heart of my love and hate, a bugle, some brass horn, began to call from far away, began to play some sad and mournful tune, some soft singularity of shame and loss. It was only one of the musicians, some guy drunk on tequila, some reveler wrenched into loneliness by the crowd, come to the last moments of a day too filled with life and death, who was letting the last waking breaths go into a horn out on the beach under the reckless stars, but it seemed to me the horn was playing the notes to the song that had been playing inside me all my life, and it seemed to me that this song, this clear and simple tune, was carrying me, that I rode on it, lifted and carried as a child is carried in the arms of its mother out into the sunshine of its first day, into the sunshine and the suffering of life on earth.

A sob rose in my throat. I let it come. It bulged in my throat, filling me. I had to move to breathe.

The path leading from the front door was lined with white stones. Set among the stones were poppies in tin cans. It was good to see the work of another hand intent on beautifying things. The door itself was a flap of cloth pulled halfway back, like a piece of skin half torn away. I could hear their movement, the rustle and slap of bodies, before I saw them. With the tip of the machete I pushed the curtain back.

They were naked. Clement rode her old style, heaving his hips into her. His body was thick, thickly haired, and under the hair, purely white, as Kate's body was, white and sweat-streaked, splayed under him. I had seen all this in the long ago, my father and not Kate but Jennie, and it was terrible and hilarious then, but now it was just terrible.

He held her arms above her head, clutched at the wrists. She strained against him, pushing upward. His teeth bit her neck. I felt a sharp pain all through me, as if something had crushed down on me, compressing my bones in on themselves. Kate's tongue was out, she was licking him. There was dirt and paint on their bodies, splashes of white and red, dark streaks up their legs. Their hands were dirty and rough-looking, as if they had become field workers' hands, stained and scratched, and they clutched at each other's bodies.

It killed me that the door was half-open, that they didn't care who saw them.

In two steps, with the machete raised, I was on them. I threw myself down onto their bodies, dived onto them, like a man throwing himself into the bed he'd walked a hundred miles to get to. Here was my prize, the reward of patience and perseverance.

I caught Clement on the downstroke and rode him into her. I forced his body down, pressing the machete against the back of his neck. He writhed under me, trying to get up, growling— "You shit," he cried—but the steel was sharp; the trap was sprung, I had him.

"I can cut right through you both," I whispered. "It's easy to do."

Clement swung his arm out, raised it, reaching back, but he didn't grab me. I kissed Kate on the lips, banged my face against hers. She blinked, and the surprise in her eyes turned to anger, turned to sadness. She gasped.

"You're crushing me," she said.

"Yes," I said. "It won't take long."

"Get up, Will," my father said.

Their stink was all around me; I was in a pit of it. There were a thousand smells between them, all of them familiar, even the grease and dirt of Mexico, and the salt sea smell, and the sex stink, and the bitter roach smell of fear, and the fire smell, the reek of flames and ashes, and the smell of Los Angeles and the father and wife smell—all of it. I rooted in the stench, pressed my face in, holding them down with my body and with the blade.

Clement's back tensed, he started to rise, then he let go. He turned his face to the side; he looked at me out of the side of his eye. I put my hand over him, covered the look.

"You will pay for this forever," he said.

"I have already been paying for it forever."

Forcing the blade against the back of my father's neck, I reached down, found the lock between them, unsocketed my father's cock. His body twitched, but I held him. "You like this?" I said.

"No."

"It doesn't matter one way or the other."

His cock was slippery with her juices. My heart pounded, but my mind was fully awake. Nothing hurt. Everything shined, throbbed. The hut was as big as a ballroom. The lamp threw yellow light on the walls. I rubbed the head of his cock against her pussy. My knuckles scraped the groove. Cupping my fingers around the shaft, I thrust us both into her, hand and cock. She moaned and her head fell to the side. Her hand lifted, slowly, as if pulled by string from the ceiling. I drew away, but she wasn't trying to hit me. Her fingers found my face, groped. She pressed her palm over my face, covering eyes and mouth. There was a shyness in the touch, an insistent tenderness, the smooth fingertips drifting, stalling on my skin, bringing me to life as they always had.

"Even now," she said, "I know the hour when . . ."

"Yes," I answered, pressing the blade against my father's neck, with my other hand thrusting deeply among the ridges and wet plains of her interior, "yes, but you don't know what will come."

"I can't resist," she said, "I try, but I can't."

"Me neither. It moves right through me." She groaned.

My father twitched through his hairy backskin. The nerves wimpled and shuddered. I pushed him into her. He groaned, made a small cry, a cheep. I pressed my whole body hard down onto them. My father's heart banged through his back. I closed my eyes, and then it seemed to me that another weight, something greater, something much larger, settled onto us, onto my back, enveloping us, and pressed us down. And then it seemed that the dirt room was littered with bodies; it seemed that I could open my eyes and see them, men and women sprawled on their backs or facedown in the dirt, and there seemed to be something religious about this as if all these people—the room had become vast—were sprawled in their attitudes praying or making homage to their god, and then I could hear their voices, which sounded distant, murmurous, like flies buzzing dumbly on a summer's day, and it seemed that the voices were saying the awful, brokenhearted, pent-up words that each had carried all his life, or all her life, and though I couldn't make out the words, I could understand the helplessness and the defeat and the inevitability in each voice so that the sounds, jumbled and various, seemed to make one sound and one voice, and I recognized it as my own voice, my own prayer, my own body sprawled in the dark praying, and it seemed to me that this was the way it had always been, that I myself and everyone else in the bloody world, everyone walking around or killing or making money or driving the kids to school—everyone breathing on the planet—was in fact not really doing these things or that these activities were only the dream they were having, that in fact each was sprawled in a dark room on a far coast, sprawled facedown or faceup praying, begging in fact, crying out, whispering, shouting, muttering, making the old human noise of groans and bleats, trying to remember something that continuously eluded them, trying to say something that they steadily forgot even as the words rose to their lips, trying to be, from the center heart to the far reaches of their toes and fingers, the simple, unwasted, electrified, and breathing conductors of the general current, the godly empowerment, and there was nothing else, and never had been anything else—not in this world—going on.

I opened my eyes and saw my wife's eyes. It was as if I had just woken naked in the rain. She looked at me and I could see through her eyes into her skull—as she could see into mine—see through bone and brain into the wash of thought. She did not know me, and I did not know her. She was alone as I was alone. And then, instead of penetrating deeper, I drew back and saw not some trembling, pilgrim core, but only her face, saw the fine, worn, damp eyes and the thicket of black lashes, the thick brows that nearly joined in the middle, saw the high cheekbones like knots under the fine skin, saw the two crescent lines like razor cuts on either side of the long mouth. I saw her age and her becoming and her being in her face, saw the unshakable humanness and frailty, the death lingering in the slightly pursed flesh under her ear, saw the bitterness she had fought off and the sadness she lived with, and the grief that she carried and that we all carry like the mark of Cain, saw her face filled with hours and days, saw the years of sleep and the years of walking about, the years of weeping and laughing.

I pressed the raw blade against my father's spine, and for a moment it seemed I must go on pressing in; it seemed inevitable that, fully weighted, driven, the blade must cut through skin, meat, and bone, into and through the strong throat from which my name was first spoken by a man, through and out the other side so I might then lift the heavy, brutish head off the shoulders and hold it aloft. It would not be difficult to do this. My left hand holding his cock, trapping it inside Kate's body, my right hand and forearm pressing the blade against his knobby spine, I did not shrink from murder. But then I looked in her face again. There was nothing in it of mystery or metaphysics. It was simply a face, a little awed, a little frightened, a little weary. Just a face. No god tapped on my skull, no saint rose up to bless me and lift me off. I looked at her face and I saw the sad humanness of it, the simple womanliness, the days and the years, the skin that rain and sunlight had touched, and it was enough.

I pulled my hand out of her and placed it on my father's back. He sighed, turned his head, and I saw his eye blink. The lashes fluttered. He was scared to death. I pressed my hand into the center of his back and got up off him. Kate was looking at me all the time. She was looking at me as if she was wondering what would happen next. I almost laughed out loud. My father stirred, his shoulder came up, but not far, because I turned the machete in my hand, grasped it by the blade, and cracked the handle across the back of his skull. His body twitched forward and went limp.

I straightened up. It was like climbing out of a well. I dragged his body off her, shoved it aside. The kerosene lamp threw its pale radiance across her shoulders, across her breasts and hips. She did not attempt to cover herself.

"Whose place is this?" I said.

"That old doctor's. Or his girlfriend's." Her blue eyes glittered. She looked at me as if she had never seen me before. It infuriated me that she knew more about the doctor—the actor—than I did.

"Make up a story about it," I said. "Tell me something strange and impertinent, something impossible that you make me believe because I am gullible and you are so good at telling stories."

"We are already in the middle of a story."

"But I don't like this one. It is too difficult."

She began to roll away, to cover herself. "No," I cried. I slashed at her with the machete, caught her across the thigh, opening a fat cut.

She threw up her arm, shrank back. And then she let the arm fall. "Are you going to kill me?"

"Would it change your attitude?"

"Probably not."

Blood welled slowly from the cut, steadily. I had not meant to strike, hadn't meant to draw blood. "Think about dying," I said. "Think about how close you are to it."

"I think about it all the time."

"If you talk that way I am going to stab you."

"How do you want me to talk?"

"Body language."

I tapped her ankle with the tip of the machete. She spread her legs. "Wider," I said. She drew her knees up slightly, opened her legs. The sooty business of her sex shone. It was the jewel at the end of the world, or it was only the sad display at the end of a Mexico night. A gravelly, sarcastic music played in my head. Bobby had flown back to heaven. In the party world, in Hollywood, in Newport Beach and Malibu, in Mexico City and Mazatlán, the retreats had begun, the sad routs and enfilades had begun to gather momentum. The hearts were breaking, the irretrievable accusations had been made, the awful truths told, the shameful practices had played out. "Spread your legs wider," I said.

She lifted her knees toward her chest, exposing the long crease, the puckered slit of her anus.

"Touch yourself."

"I'll do anything you want."

"Don't anticipate, don't acquiesce so easily; show a little pain and sorrow."

"I am in pain, I am sorrowful."

"Let me see it in your face. You're an actress, you can show how this maneuver, this set of actions is breaking your heart. It's ruining your life and the lives of everyone around you. You can show all that, can't you?"

"Ah, Will."

"Give me the tears, give me the surrender."

She ran the edge of her palm down her sex, raised the hand to her mouth and licked the juice off. "Good," I said. "More."

I unzipped, shucked my cock. It flopped out hardening.

"Say I'm Bobby," I said.

"You're Bobby."

"Say it again."

She said it again.

"Say you love me, say you're sorry for everything you've done to me."

"I love you. I am so sorry."

"Say you're Veronica."

"I'm Veronica."

"Say you're Jennie."

"I'm Jennie."

"Say you're Clement."

"I'm Clement."

"Say I'm your father, say you want me to fuck you."

"Ah."

"Say I'm your father. Say you want me to fuck you."

"You're my father. I want you to fuck me."

"Say Daddy, fuck me."

"Daddy, fuck me."

I stood between her legs. I kicked them out wider. "Show me your pussy. Show Daddy your pussy."

With the fingers of both hands, she spread herself.

"Do it like a man would. Let me see the strength in your hands."

She pulled herself apart. The flesh parted; she showed me the dark gap.

"Say Daddy, look at me: say Daddy, look at my pussy."

"Look at me, Daddy. Look at my pussy."

I jacked my cock. Each stroke piled one more burning stone into my body. Rocks of uranium, of atomic matter, hummed and banged inside me. I reached above my head, grasped the beam pole and held on, hanging over her. She was wide open, touching herself, and I saw the lust and the grief in her eyes.

"Are you going to fuck me?" she said.

"No."

A snake struck in my guts, a snake with fire in its mouth. I dropped down onto her, caught her between my knees. "Take it in your mouth."

She took it.

The hot stone burst out of me. I came through a knot of agony.

She caught it, all of it, in her mouth.

I held myself up on one arm.

326

"Hold it," I said, "hold it in your mouth."

I felt as if I were going blind, as if I were falling into a terrible hole. I fought to get the light back, fought to stay upright. There were only seconds to work in.

I grasped her by the neck, swung her up and over Clement's body. "Don't swallow it," I said, "spit it on him."

She resisted, but I forced her face down. Clement groaned beneath us, grinding in his dream. His features were slack, the skin sagged, a patch of white bristles beside his mouth gleamed with spittle. I forced her mouth against his, slapped the back of her head. She choked, coughed, she spit.

I kicked her aside.

The jism had spilled out of his mouth onto his cheeks. It ran down onto his neck. I smeared it on his face. Gusts of horror blew through me, dry and grasping. They stung, whipping. The world blazed, colors of red and orange shot through my eyes.

I pushed upright, got to my feet. Kate lay sprawled among the blankets they had pulled together to make a bed. There was blood spattered over her legs, on the white-and-black striped blankets.

I stood on the edge of emptiness. I swayed on my feet, looking at the blankness, more tired than I had ever been.

Kate got onto her knees. She rocked back and forth, holding herself in her arms. She bent down, pressed her face into the blankets, straightened up. Clement groaned again, twitched; buffeted. She glanced at him, and it seemed to me she looked at him as if she did not know him. Soft, wet breaths rustled in his mouth. I remembered him waking me once when we traveled up north, in Oregon. We were on the way by car to see Jennie on a movie set. He had reached over the seat and gently shaken me, telling me I was talking in my sleep. His big face shined like a friendly white moon above me. Foggy and lost, I had stared at him and the dear fond love in his face, the unremarkable happiness, was the world I lived in. I believed that wherever I was, he was, and I believed that whatever might hurt me, he could protect me from.

"Somewhere," I said, "under all this, under everything, I am as clean as a whistle. He is too."

"Me too," Kate said.

I looked at her, and I hated her then. Later I would feel the pity and the grief, later it would come to me that her sorrow and her separation from everything the rest of us held dear was a fate beyond any I could imagine, and my heart would break for her, but now I only hated her. She saw it in my face.

"There is nothing I can do," she said.

She got up and began to dress.

"What are you doing?"

"I'm coming with you."

"I don't want you with me."

"He won't let you live after this. I don't think he will let me live either."

"This won't make him kill me. He wouldn't kill me over you."

"Maybe not. But what you know about your brother will make him."

The place was strewn with flowers. Orchids and chrysanthemums and poppies. They were all crushed, tangled, as if they had been rolled over.

"What do I know about Bobby?"

"You know that Clement killed him."

"He wasn't there."

"He didn't have to be. Bobby knew everything, and Clement saw he knew, and he let it destroy him."

"That's just in your mind."

"He tried to kill Clement too, and he couldn't. Clement knew what would happen then. He told him to do it."

"Bobby did what he couldn't avoid doing."

"What he couldn't avoid was your father."

Maybe, maybe. Maybe everything she said was true, maybe I knew it already, maybe everything had lined up for murder and destruction, maybe death was the only next step possible, maybe this man, snorting on the floor, would rise up from this place and kill me—it was so, I knew it was—but whatever blow I was supposed to strike next I couldn't strike.

"Even this," she said, "even this mess, him naked and cold cocked—it's just part of the power to him. He's still got it. You see that, don't you? This is just one more round for him. This looks terrible, but he's right at home in it. This is just fuel to him."

I was cold; I began to shiver. My mind went blank, or not blank, it slid through pictures, scenes, terrible moments of grip-

ping and strangling, like the final rank fumes of a dream, someone, some shape staggering through a thorny dark, exhausted.

"I've got to go," I said. My voice was small and hollow.

"Yes."

She picked up the lantern, put her arm around me, and she led
me out. I stopped at the door. "You go on."

I went back in and knelt down beside my father. I put my
hands around his throat and pressed, lightly. He began to waken.
I wiped the fluid from around his mouth, leaned down, and kissed
him on the lips. It was flesh against flesh, only that, all I had left
to give him.

Outside, I walked past her where she stood in the empty street,
in the middle of the sleeping village. The houses rocked back into
a darkness so deep they might never wake up. I turned to look at
her, but I didn't stop. She swung the lantern back and forth at
her knees. Above us the stars rushed on, unstoppable. The faint,
dry scent of the fields blew over us. I walked down the long street
toward the car, but I turned once as I walked, and as I did so I
saw her raise the lantern, swing it around her head, and fling it.
It tumbled end over end, flaring, and burst against the hut's
thatched roof. It burst against the roof, spilling flame across the
straw, and it burst inside my heart. I did not turn back, I did not
rush back to save him. Perhaps I could have. Perhaps it is only
then, in the moment beyond exhaustion, when the next, the un-
prophecied horror occurs, that we see ourselves for what we really are. Love's only meaning is forgiveness. Perhaps I could have
turned back as the flames leapt across the roof, perhaps I could
have . . . but I didn't.

She ran by me, limping a little on the leg blood streamed from,
and I followed her. I say I followed her, followed her through
the village dreaming toward an emergency, but she was too far
out ahead of me to follow. When she turned a corner between
two houses and disappeared toward the car and I was alone for
two minutes there under the enfeebled, dissolving stars, alone
with the flowery breeze and the sound of the surf sweeping the
shore, it did not seem to me I was following her or anyone else.
No god or brother or lover called me on then. I was as alone as
I had ever been. This was so, yet as I walked away, my back to
the fire, everything around me, every thought in my head, seemed
familiar.

AND WHO COULD follow us close enough to see what happened then? Who could come along with us on the two cold, stony days we traveled as her leg got worse and she got sicker? Who could stand with me outside the monastery in Obregón, or the country museum that had once been a monastery, where I went into the ruined church and fell on my face to pray words that soaked into the crumbling walls like water? Who could have come with me when I returned at two in the afternoon through a garden planted by monks long dead, carrying a wand of red ocotillo flower to find her lying on her back on a bench under a pecan tree hemorrhaging? And who could have ridden with us over the mountain to the infirmary as blood splashed into the floor well, as she raved and raged, biting words, calling out for demons to take her, for all the dead to rise up and strike her? And who could have waited with me in the hallway where the hands of children had painted pictures of smiling blue and red animals on the walls and the scent of orange flowers blew in the open windows as the doctor vacuumed the last of him out of her? And what phantom shape could an observer have assumed to linger with me in the room made of curtains as nurses whispered soft words of sympathy and watched her sleep? And what brother, friend, or lover could have snuggled close enough to me during that long night to see what was in my heart and mind, to hear the old voices speaking to me from a past that had become my future—who could have loved us enough to watch me turn from the window, where in a house next door a girl in a pale blue dress shouted at a puppy and cuffed it across the face with an open hand, crying, and listened to me say to Kate as she slept her drugged and dreamless sleep, that I was leaving? And who could have walked with me then out into the gritty dawn? And who could have watched me get into the car and drive away? And who could tell what part of me it was I left behind that morning in Mexico, and what part I saved?

THREE DAYS IT took to get out, three days of dream. The thorny hills rose and fell like a sea. The sky was endless in every direction. One village replaced another like sets on a screen. I drank a lemon soda beside a river where women washed coarse brown sheets and hung them across bushes to dry. I watched a deaf girl talking with her hands to a baby in a sunny courtyard in Santa Victoria. I saw a drunken woman fall on her face in the road outside Sierra Depesto. I slept on a piney woods floor in the mountains. I talked back to the radio as if it were my best friend. I stood with my back to a door in a bar in Ponce de Leon while two men fought with knives over a silver chain. Someone pushed me against a wall, and for a moment I thought I must kill him to go on with my life, but the face above the shirt I grasped grinned at me as if he knew me and knew all about me, and I let the man go.

In Mexicali, with the whole barrage balloon of America tethered above my head, I sank myself into the streets, into crowds of revelers and desperate characters, and I saw there in the faces passing the news of my time and place, saw the exhortations and the lies, saw the twisted mouths of desire, and the alliances broken up and the feuds that would go on for generations; I saw the pale faces of longing, and the wet mouths, and I saw the griefs for whom the bearer was the only one to blame; and I saw the oppressed and the triumphant, the sycophants and the true believers, the caged and the careless, the sweet mockers and the frail children chewing sugar cane, saw the woman dancing with her skirts about her waist and the skinny man on his knees vomiting blood; and I saw in every face the terrible bafflement and estrangement from everything of value, and saw the knowledge and the memory working like worm lines through the foreheads of priests, saw the passions, the virtues, the horrible secrets and hopes, the estrangements and the wishful thinking, saw the shame and the pride and the terror and the last drink of the evening balanced on the bar like the holy grail—and each one, everything I saw, all of it, slamming at the night, fallen to its knees before me, each and all, was familiar, and I loved it.

Later I was home again in the big-winged house in the hills, later I lay myself down in the big bed alone and slept. For a while I could not hear her voice calling to me, but soon it would rise again, her voice and her face, rise before me to accuse and plead, but for a time I was alone. Soon enough the blow she struck would call its answer, the blow that was itself only response to another, that was itself . . .

It was not the lust, it was not the battering, it was not the woman stolen, it was not my dead brother that made my father decide to kill me, it was the fire. He thought I tried to burn him up. And I never said it wasn't so.

BOOK
FOUR

BELOW ME, BELOW all of us lifted into the hills, the city burns. The suffering have set fires to mark the places where suffering became unendurable. Time is no longer seamless: it jerks and stalls, falters, stands in the dark staring with wide open eyes. Days lie around my feet. Hannah Jell has come and gone. Sitting in this plush chair on my breezy deck, I listened to her tell me everything. Perhaps it is only the contemporary method, but it was strange to me that I—the subject of her interview—was not required to speak, only to listen raptly to her recitation of facts and dates, of reasons. She knew the story, or she knew *a* story that was filled with drama and desire, a tale of betrayal and loss, of rage and murder that moved me so I nearly wept. She told it with glee, with a naked human greed in her brown eyes, her thin voice hanging on the words. She spoke to me as if she were confessing. I denied nothing. I nodded, agreed, smiled fondly, gave her absolution.

To the south, tall black-streaked smoke spires rise above the basin. Sirens wail like beasts from the burning pits and blocked trails. The air smells of creosote, of burned rubber, oddly of cinnamon. My eyes move through the pampered yard, past the trained and delicate flowers, the imported glories of plumeria and bougainvillea, to the desert beyond the parapets. Even up here, among the fortresses and the million-dollar bungalows, the old desert, the original world, thrives. The wind shakes itself in a saltbush, the yellow roseate flower of prickly pear shines. The thorny, dangerous, ancient world stares back.

"For Ms. Dunn," the doctor wrote, "we feel great pain and sorrow, and a sadness that I know will be permanent." The words are in a letter I hold in my hands. I received it two months ago. Three weeks after I left her, Kate returned to the Indian village, stayed a week, and disappeared. She spent the week as a guest in the doctor's house up in the hills. She had sat each day, the doctor said, most of the day, in a large white wicker chair out on the balcony, looking out over the downsweep of mountain to the ocean. She ate only fruit, he said, and she barely spoke. He had asked her to stay as long as she liked, he wanted her to stay, he said, but one morning when Elpidia came to wake her, she was gone, her room empty—cleaned by her own hand, Elpidia said—and no message left.

"I cannot tell you," the doctor said, "how the knowledge of her, how her beauty and energy have fascinated me. I should have known better perhaps, having been myself one of the toilers in the movie trade, but I could not stop myself, and the fact is, I welcomed such beauty in my life. I do not think I could live without beauty. I do not think I would want to live if beauty were not in the world and if it were not a world in which one could pursue this beauty. We seek it as the deer seeks water. She was this to me, a kind of water . . ."

The *was,* then, reading the letter for the first time on the deck at Veronica's as she painted the living room for perhaps the one hundredth time—charging toward perfection—had made my skin crawl. I folded the letter against itself and brought the edge down one line at a time, so I could not see what was ahead. I wanted the day—pale blue, surf-drenched, booming—and my life, whirled round as it was, to stay the same, not to be further transformed.

"I have followed her career since the beginning," the doctor said, "since her picture first appeared in a magazine I ran across in Mexico City. I saw her films—only occasionally because my life is here—and even with her voice dubbed, her beauty and rough grace jumped off the screen into me. I saw in her face not the selfish, carpentered beauty of a movie star but the old-time swing of zest and perseverance, the sharp eye, the strong back, the willingness to endure, the power of wakefulness, the laughter, which must have been what the first pioneers brought across the country when they rolled their wagons through the desert. Feckless and violent and naïve and clever, and fearless—all this. She shocked and charmed me; she seduced me, as you can see, and when she walked into the village I thought my heart would burst. Forgive me for going on so, but what has happened to her has broken my heart, and I am an old man who believed his heart could never be broken again; she has unhorsed me."

It was as if the letter had been dipped in liquid oxygen; the cold chill seeped through my fingers into my body. I leaned back in my chair, listening to Veronica, listening to her sing some Broadway song she had heard on the radio. Ample and bright, I thought: so the day pours its perfection at my feet.

"I changed the bandages for her," he said, "and before she left I took the stitches out. The wound had healed cleanly, for that we can be grateful. She never complained, she never spoke a word of blame. But her eyes burned; they frightened me. I wanted to talk to her about it, to comfort her, to tell her—to tell her what I don't know, to say to her that this was not the end, but I could not; her eyes wouldn't let me. The stump . . ."

I had put my hand over the letter and closed my eyes. The sun burned through my lids, a red, shimmering fire. There was no breath in my body, no air around me. Slowly, my skin peeled, what protected me from the world peeled, and every hidden patch, every scar and soft place was revealed. I was afraid to move, terrified that if I moved an inch my body would explode. I tried to speak my brother's name, tried to speak a name, but there was no voice in my throat. I leaned over my knees and began to sob; tears, tears from the bottom rushed out of me.

I got to my feet—only seconds had passed—walked to the open glass door, and stood there looking at Veronica. Except for a red scarf tied around her head she was naked. Pale red paint—a color called desert sunset—streaked her arms and breast.

She swung the roller in an arc toward me, saw my face and stopped. "Will," she said and her voice was small and breathless and appalled.

I said, "Veronica, they have cut Kate's leg off."

"Oh, God," she said, and clutched the roller to her breast. Red-speckled white cloths covered the furniture, but except near the walls she had not covered the white stone floor. Her toenails were painted bright red. And the red paint, the desert sunset, spilled from the roller, ran down her chest and belly, dripped down her thighs. It was everywhere, everything was turning red.

This letter then, creased and hand-turned to pliability, lies in my lap beside the report submitted by my lawyer's detectives. When I came back from Mexico, after the week I spent inside this house groaning like a demented person, I called my lawyer, Sammy Spiegal, told him what had happened, told him what I knew was coming, and asked him to go to work on it. He put detectives on Clement. This morning Sammy has called to say the police want to charge me with murder. They may have an indictment by the end of the week, he said. He told me not to worry. I said I wouldn't. I called Earl and Earl has flown into a rage. *This cannot happen,* he screamed. *This cannot happen.* I held the phone away from me. I spoke to it at arm's length, said, Earl, you had better call Billy Dangelo. I don't know if he could hear me. *They'll pay,* he screamed, *every day of their lives from now on they will pay for this.* I carried the phone to the deck rail—it was cordless—and dropped it over the side. In the distance the smoke spires rose, their tops diffuse and glittering, into the sunlight.

Now I lean back in my stuffed deck chair, seigneur de Hollywood, to read again the first of the reports. There are a dozen of them, but this is the one I want to see. Behind me, in my bed, Veronica sleeps, in a blue silk nightgown my mother gave her. It is the gown Jennie wore in *The Possessed,* a movie she made in the fifties. Wearing the gown, star of a story in which no happiness could be found for doomed lovers, she threw herself into a circus water tank from the top of a diving platform. Unlike Kate in Indonesia, it was not Jennie who dived from the tower, but it was Jennie who lay faceup in the water, wide-eyed and drowned. Bobby, poor soul, was on the set that day. One more time, poor fool, he had to adjust himself to his mother, whose death by fall and drowning was only play. I believe, in the end, he was probably jealous, jealous of us all. But I don't want to think about it right now.

For the first time in my life I have my father's itinerary. It is a document any son would wish to have. For two months, until the Awards, until he had me shot, or if not shot, until he had the woman killed and fixed the blame on me, we did not talk. He had crawled out of the burning hut, wiped the jism off his face, helped put the fire out—shouting orders, so the doctor wrote, covered in soot—gotten in his car, and driven back to Los Angeles—straight into silence. In this silence, in this solitude of the self where the devil does his work, a man who believed his own son had set him on fire, he planned his murder of me.

During this time he returned to Mexico. Kate sent him videos. Panting, oppressed, dragging the trampled body of his desire, he searched for her, in the Indian village, then through Sinaloa and Sonora, finally to the hospital where they'd taken her leg off. He missed her on the coast, missed her in the mountains, missed her in the thorny desert, where he fell to his knees crying out her name, crying out in animal rage. He missed her everywhere until he came to Los Brecas, my friend Pedro Manglona's house on the sea cliffs north of Mazatlán. He found her there, recovering from her wounds, working in the studio that Pedro, a former director and now vice-chairman of the Mexican film board, had set up out in his barn. The detectives had spied on him, they'd paid one of the maids to give them information, and what she told them was in the report.

There wasn't much. Clement—Señor Toro, she called him—became white in the face when he saw Kate. She drew her skirt back, showed him the rosy stump, and the sight of it made him sick. He vomited into the shrubbery, the maid said, ran like a blind man into the yard, and fell on his face on the ground. He cried like a little boy. Kate, on crutches, followed him out and stood over him. She poked him in the side with the tip of a crutch. The maid said Clement curled up into a ball. He cried, he sobbed, he shrieked. And Señora Dunn, the maid said, never stopped laughing.

I am a man who prepares. I had this information before the Awards, I knew it when I walked into the Pavilion, it rang in my ears as I listened to him tell me of his movie project, of the film he wanted us to make together. He had told Kate that he planned to kill me. Where does responsibility begin? At what moment does our only hope become the admission of the truth about ourselves? My father rose from the ground, so the report said, from the dusty, rocky earth, in a place where bulls bellowed in corrals, where behind the stone house hewn from local rock the pastures faded into desert, and he lifted Kate into his arms. He carried her down a flight of cliff stairs to the beach. With her holding on to him, with her arms clasped around his neck, he waded out through the surf and swam straight out into the Pacific. They were out there a long time, the maid said, maybe an hour. Señor Manglona came out to the gazebo and watched them through binoculars. She said they were so far away and the swells were so big you could not see them with the naked eye. No one could understand what they were doing, the maid said. Even Señor Manglona could not understand.

But I could. Over and over, with her arms clasped around his neck, he had dived, pulling for the bottom.

Veronica stands in the doorway. She rises onto her toes,

stretching. The sun makes the blue gown shine. "It all looks like plane crashes out there," she says, speaking of the smoke plumes.

"If it wasn't for the movies," I say, "you wouldn't have any idea what a plane crash looks like."

"No, I've seen one, out in the Valley. I saw it when I was a girl."

She crosses to the table Carol has set with breakfast, selects a peach and bites into it. Juice swells around her mouth.

"When was there a plane crash out there?"

"When I was a girl. A crop duster went down in an orange grove. You were living in town, staying with Jennie at the St. Vick house"—St. Victoire Street, Beverly Hills—"and so you missed it. Those smoke columns look just like it. Someone else has reached the end of things."

"Different deal."

"Yes," she says absently, sits down in a wire chair and hoists her feet onto the rail. "I dreamed last night that people were slapping me in the street. I was out walking, and everyone who approached me slapped me. You were there, and Clement and Kate, and none of you raised a hand to stop it."

"It doesn't sound like us."

"No, it doesn't, does it? What are you reading?"

"Traffic reports."

"Hard to lose your place there."

"Were you ever angry at Jennie?"

"How so?"

"Because of her seducing you when you were a kid."

"Is that what she did? I thought she was loving me, initiating me."

"Did it ever make you angry?"

"No, not so far. Maybe if it had stopped, maybe if we had broken up—maybe then I would have gotten angry—maybe I would get angry—but it hasn't ever stopped. When I see her now, my heart gets peaceful. Instantly. The way I get agitated when I see you."

"I don't make you peaceful?"

"These days, sweetie, you wouldn't make a dead man peaceful." She draws her legs up to her chest, places the half-eaten peach in a napkin, tightly wraps it, and sets it on a plate. She leans back in the chair, raises her face, and closes her eyes.

Yesterday I drove out to Kerry Dunlop's animal ranch—she supplies dogs, chimps, rabbits, or whatever crawls and flies for the movies—and spent the afternoon petting living creatures, holding a wolf pup in my arms, lying down in the shade of the live oaks with the goats. I had never liked having animals around me, I didn't even want a dog, but yesterday, down on my knees in the straw, I wanted to pull every hairy living thing she had into my arms. Crying, stupid, a nut, licking the black rubbery tits of a she-chimp, speaking the idiot baby talk of the deranged, I unsettled Kerry, caused her to turn away. You ought to go talk to a psychiatrist, Will, she told me, but I said I didn't need that form of entertainment right now, thank you. Pass me another chimp, I said, grinning maniacally, but she wouldn't and finally shooed me off the property.

I say, "Sammy called to tell me they are going to charge me with murder."

She bounds up from the chair as if a switch has been tripped. "No, Will. They can't do that."

"I believe they can."

"Those squirts. Goddamn."

She kneels beside my chair and takes me in her arms. She smells of sleep, of faint, flowery perfume. "Oh, Will," she says, "it's mad."

"Strange world."

"How could they do this? It's total craziness." She draws away. There are tears in her eyes, gathered at the rims. Her face is flushed. "Sammy told you this?"

"Not half an hour ago."

"What did he say?"

"He said"—I imitated Sammy's growly, Chicago accent—"the bastards have played a rank hand, and we will make them pay."

"They're going to charge you with murder?"

"They say I burned that woman up."

"What can we do?"

"Anything we like. It's Hollywood."

"Don't joke. This is terrible."

"Are you going to Billy's tonight?"

"What? To Billy's? What are you talking about? To Billy's party? Who cares about that?"

"I think I would like to go."

341

"Oh, Will, Jesus, these rascals—they should be arrested. Have you told Jennie?"

"I just heard about it. You're the only one I've had time to inform. You and Earl."

"What did Earl say?"

"Like you, he impotently cursed."

"Goddamn, goddamn."

"Yes, like that."

I am watching the fires. The city burns toward the center. For months the fires have drawn closer. There are reports of houses burned in West Hollywood, of a store going up in Beverly Hills; last night there was a red glow in the sky just over the ridge from here, I stood on the deck watching it, and my heart leapt, a man chilled and rippling with desire, but it was only the moon, rising in the east, riding in its cool light, lifting over the mountain.

Veronica stands up. She is slender, beautiful, and worn, a fine woman who loves me and whom I love; her love has been a gift to me all my life, it encloses me like breath. I would know her anywhere, in any dark; and I have smelled, so many times, my mother's scent on her body, met my mother there, made love to Jennie, to my own mother through my best friend's body, become my own son and father, brother to myself, saved myself, saved my grief, brought my brother back to life through her and through myself loving her; through this love, this mother-daughter-sister-brother-lover taste, this smell in the loins, skin and sweat, these bones the spirit inhabits, this lankiness and fervor, nights in dampened sheets, through all this I discover who I am, who I have always been: a man who will do anything.

I say, "I want to be alone for a while. Do you mind?"

"Will you be all right?"

"No. But I want to think about a few things." My head, where I was shot, hurts, and my leg hurts.

"Maybe you can think of a way out of this. That's what I am going to do."

I laugh, grin at her. "You've never thought your way out of anything. Everything you were ever in, you're still in."

"What a crude, unwise thing to say, you, who have never been past the city limits except to make a movie."

"I'll call you this afternoon," I say, getting up. "I have some errands I want to run first. Are you going to be at Jennie's?"

"Yes. She's moved back to the St. Vick house. She says she's tired of the sun."

"Good."

She embraces me. For a second I can feel every bone in her body. And every bone in mine.

I DRIVE OUT to Imperial, not to see Billy, but on an errand of my own. Around the offices, among the white stucco buildings, poincianas are in bloom. Their red, fiery crowns shake in breeze. The smell of the fires is everywhere. In these days of trouble office workers go home early, the freeways are clogged by one. The detective's reports are stacked beside me. It is only lately I have received them. I had the first one early, but then I asked Sammy not to show them to me. Last week he said I had better take a look. The facts, or such facts as you can gather staring from a distance, are there. My father, in fits of busted energy, took women into the desert, made brutal love to them in resort bedrooms, hauled them back to town, and put them out on the street in front of their houses. He was seen in restaurants, in the mountains driving fast, at Jennie's Malibu house, at various studios, at his club in the Hills haranguing waiters, at a picnic table outside a taco stand in Venice shaking his finger at Causey Clark. The report informed me that the state trooper, Causey, an Arkie himself, was deeply in debt to Clement, had bought land from him, built a store, a bait and tackle shop, and now, close to retirement, was unable to pay the note. Clement had put him to work. And the woman, the black-haired gunslinger, the succubus, had been an actor, or had wanted to be an actor; Clement had met her, possibly he had met her, at a horse show out in the Pima, where she had apparently come on her own with intentions of catching his eye. She had caught it. So the clock ticks, and every tick speaks disaster. The theme is loss. What we have lost, what we will lose. And so we set our hearts against it, against loss, against life. We say this shall not happen to me, I will not let it. But it happens anyway. The truck pierces the bus's armor and stabs us with a silver pole. We are fourteen and unable to find a way to live. I cannot get to the place I must be, we say, I cannot be who I must, so I will lay me down now, and sleep.

It is all in here, in this report, in the fragile pages printed out by a computer. As it is in Kate's videos, produced, so I discovered, first in a studio at Pedro Manglona's, and then later on the road, outside towns she probably didn't ask the name of, with crews she paid from her Hollywood earnings, on sets she constructed with her own hands, on location, a camera whirring in the desert, catching the light and the place where she was the absence of light, catching the shape of her as she moved across a wild landscape, as she spoke words she wrote herself, the unscripted configurations she had practiced all her life to play.

There is a rock, Chimney Rock, she told me when I returned to Mexico, a mountain eroded to a spire, and it is permanent, it will last forever. It was the first of the West, and the last of the East. It bears the weight of joining, she said. It is the hinge. And it is unbreakable, the place of joining. So I will find this place, she said, so I have found this place, in my own life.

In these flickers, I saw, moving across a screen, what she had found. In my life she had found it, and in my father's life. Which Clement did not understand.

He returned to Los Angeles empty-handed. Maybe he had wanted to bring her back, to retrieve her, but I do not think this is so. Her breakdown was too much for him. The maid said that when he brought her up from the beach, carrying her, as if his strength could not fail him ever, he set her down in the gazebo and knelt before her. He lay his head in her lap, the maid said, and remained in that position for several minutes. Señora Dunn stroked his hair, which was matted by the sea salt, but she looked away from him, she stroked him as one would idly stroke a cat.

I know he felt the absence in her fingers. He looked up at her then and he could see how far away she was from him. Her face was thinner: the bones stood out in it as if they had nearly rubbed through the skin. He could see what she had become, and what she had become terrified him. He rose, leaned down, and kissed her on the top of the head, and then, without a word, walked to his car, got in, and drove away.

I park the car in the lot—I am welcome here—and walk down the street to Soundstage Three. I stop in the office just inside the door and speak to Bunnie Hoops, the old man who manages this cavern. I've known him all my life, since he was a location manager on one of my father's early epics. It was Bunnie who directed the building of the walls of Jericho, out in the desert, walls sixty feet high, made of plaster and wooden laths, that Alexander Cord, in the clothes of Joshua and blowing his horn, called down the destruction of the Lord upon. He wears a blue-striped shirt and red suspenders, and his white hair is plastered back. The skin around his eyes looks as if it has been put through a grinder, but the damage is from the sun shining on a smiling face. He greets me with a handshake through which I can feel bones. They have just finished filming a remake of *Deep Blue Sea*, the set is still intact, and I ask him if I might go take a look at it.

Anything you want, he says. In his breast pocket he carries Tampa cigars, rank stogies that he does not smoke himself but passes out to whoever at the moment offends him, with hopes they'll light up and be sickened. He says he's heard Clement's back in action, that we're set to make a picture together. It's another epic, Bunnie, I say. He slaps his leg, winces, and does a little half-step sideways dance. He looks as if he's falling, but he's not. Old Clement, he says, he just won't ever give up on it, will he? He winks at me, co-conspirator. What you planning? he says. You got something cooked up for this soundstage?

I want to look at things, I say. I have an arrangement in mind.

Go do what you like, he says. You need any help just yell out.

I thank him and enter the interior. The space, half as large as a football field, soars into darkness. In the heights, where you could hide a bomber squadron, are catwalks and steel grid plates swung on pulleys. Scaffolding climbs in tiers into the shadows. Along the concrete floor the camera tracks are still in place, but the lights have been gathered in bunches along the wall. Cyclopean, they stare blindly. At the far end is the place I am looking for: the water tank, fifty feet across, still full. At one end is the wave machine, a large wooden sweep operated electrically. The tank is only five feet deep, but it is deep enough and wide enough to play the part of the Pacific Ocean, when lit, an ocean on the back of which actors rode toward their thirsty cinematic deaths. At the far end is a scene painting of sea and distant beach, a blank blue sky over ruddy, desert mountains.

It is dark here, murky. The surface of the tank is black, the distant mountains gray smudges. I go to the intercom, punch up Bunnie, ask if I might fire things up back here. He says, a little reluctantly, I can if I want to. I'm in the wrong union to be pulling switches. I won't be long, I say, I want to get a look at the tank and the wave action. Don't break anything, he says.

I push a light stand around, flick switches, and then I turn on the sweep. The blaze of clear light is harsh, but it brings the place alive. The sweep pushes a low swell across the tank. I take off my clothes, pile them neatly in a chair, climb the six steps to the edge, and push out across the water. The water is cold; it smells of chlorine. I go under, swim toward the center. The painting, the arid beach, the rocky, dust-capped mountains, do not become the wild coast they are meant to represent. On film it would look as if I were swimming toward a vast undiscovered country. On film I would be a man reaching for a new continent, a man far out beyond civilization, drifted out past the final outposts, the flimsy final refuse of what his culture had built and learned to live with. On film this artifice would look like life.

I roll onto my back and float. Where the sky should be there are steel beams, a cargo net swung between grids. I look down my flung-out body at the mountains. With water in my eyes they look a little more real. They are brushy in the gaps, there are a few skinny trees near the beach. Wherever that place is, it is far away and inhospitable. But I am fine, for a second I am okay. On this stage there is a little silence, a little peace, a little enclosure. Outside this building, beyond the streets and the fires and the policemen who believe I am a murderer, there are actual mountains, desert brush, a few streams fanned over rocks; in the meadows above the Pima farm, poppies are in bloom and lupine and penstemon; at the beach, beyond the fabulous houses, the Pacific crashes relentlessly in. But out there, everywhere I turned my head, in any direction I looked, I would see, at the edges, a wavering, a breakdown, the world slipping away from me into haze and chaos. In here, in this tank, above which, just last week, the Panaflex caught the cadences and conniptions of actors, there is a succinct and comely order. It holds, it is sustained. I lie on my back at the center of it. For a second now, the accusations, Kate, my father planning his last maneuvers, the maneuvers I have planned, even Veronica, gallant and continuing, my mother, the city of my birth, the friends of my youth and age—all I know and live among—fades into the mist of dream. My gods are here, and my peace. In here are limits, walls, an end to vision. What occurs must take place inside the cage of finity. If there is safety, it is here. Only in such places is there hope, and life.

This is what I think as I float on my back, taking small sips of water from time to time to wet my throat. The chill that spun like a web across my skin since Sammy called, since I returned from Mexico, since I stood in the street watching Kate throw the lantern, since my brother died, since . . . has faded, for a second it is no longer there. I picture myself in a hotel room, sitting on the bed eating a cheeseburger. A television is softly playing, some silly, comforting family show; in the living room Veronica is calling everyone she knows. Outside, the day harshly flares, but in here, in this room, which is like every other room in the vast and well-appointed hotel, life is ordered and clean. I picture myself sitting on the bed, slowly eating. The burger tastes good, in a second I will wash it down with a swallow of Coke. I am sitting on the bed; I am eating. I am sitting—I hold this picture in my mind, carefully like a grail, until the lights go off, and I hear Bunnie's croupy voice behind me, calling me to come out of the water.

KATE SAID: *THEY say parallel lines never meet, but what about their shadows—do their shadows ever meet?*

Two days before the Awards, with the first report in my pocket, I flew to Mazatlán, rented a car, and drove to Pedro's house. He had called, on Kate's orders, to tell me she was there. The white house was built of stone, rough-hewn mountain stone, like something chopped out of the cliffs, and the flowers Pedro had set around it, the bougainvillea and the passion vine climbing walls and trellises, the red and yellow flowering hibiscus bushes my father had puked into crowding the veranda, did not hide the brutal nature of the structure. It was the place Pedro's grandfather, a revolutionary, a Panchoista-turned-rancher, had hacked for himself out of the rock scrub overlooking the sea. The house sat in a basin surrounded by low hills. Behind it were pastures and behind the pastures was the desert, unbroken yet, rough and thorny, rising toward the western cordillera. There were barns and corrals around the house, and in front of it a large yard that opened directly on to the cliffs, beyond which, a hundred feet down, the Pacific stretched away.

The bulls were bellowing. I could hear them before I got to the ranch. They were big lumpy animals, pale mostly, with out-size horns that looked like props, and they crowded around watering troughs near the fences. Young boys in white pants forked hay over the fence. One of them, a tall teenager with a narrow brown chest and a shock of bushy hair, turned and stared at me as I drove past. I nodded to him, and he grinned, exposing a toothless mouth. In front of the house two young girls and a boy skipped rope in a dry puddle, kicking up dust. The dust shined whitely on their legs and arms. I went in—Pedro wasn't there— and asked for Kate. The woman, his housekeeper, recognized me; she said Kate was down on the beach.

The kids followed me across the yard, talking about a wildcat someone had trapped in the hills. They said one of the ranch hands had set the dogs on it. The cat had killed two of the dogs before the dogs tore it apart. One of the girls was sad about it, but the other two children were delighted. It was nearly twilight now; lanterns had come on in the barns and in the house behind me. Someone called the children and they said good-bye and ran to the house. At the top of the cliff was a pavilion like a band-stand. Wicker chairs faced the ocean. I sat down in one of the chairs and looked out at the Pacific. Late sun glittered on the water. Up the beach, the glow from the town rose from behind massed cliffs. I thought maybe Kate would come up, but she didn't. Something fell away from me and I didn't know who I was. Everything around me, the worn board floor of the pavilion, the wicker chairs with their pads turned up to keep the salt off, the painted reed basket in a corner, were as vivid as if the world had been pumped with oxygen. A rachitic, muddling tenderness washed over me. I was lifted on it, taken up. Then it subsided and the world stepped back from me, rolled away, cameras film-ing all of it, dollying back into an endless distance. I was some-thing very tiny and frail, something distant and unrecognizable among all the other tiny, frail objects. I got up, found the beach stairs, and started down.

I wanted to ask her a question. I wanted to know why she threw the lantern. She was waiting for me, or she was simply waiting, expecting the next thing; I could see it in her face, which lifted to me as I approached. She was on crutches, wearing a fake leg padded with bandages. She was familiar and strange. I acted as if the missing leg didn't bother me, played the part of one not surprised or shocked, but I was stunned nearly; pain cut through me. We didn't embrace.

She looked at me, pressing her wild hair back with the flat of her hand. Let's be quick about this, she said.

I didn't know where you were.

You don't yet.

That doctor sent a letter—I got it last week—and then Pedro called.

There were cats all over the beach. Wild house cats come down from the hills to eat fish washed up by a red tide. They snarled and fought among themselves. They were all around her. They scattered as I came up.

She patted her chest. I feel every breath now. I feel every one as if it is the last breath.

I am about to start panting myself.

Say what you have to say.

We had not embraced; we did not touch.

It doesn't have to be dramatic, I said. We're married; we can take it easy.

The truth was, I had no real pity for her, even now.

She said, None of you, none of you protected people, you gifted sleek people, you users—none of you know a thing about me.

It was part of the charm, I think.

I have good days, days when the sunny world slides along and I slide with it. But other days I am hung up, caught, tangled among the thorns.

Why did you throw the lantern? Why did you try to kill him?

She smiled, the same old frank grin. But her face was older, the pain had aged it, cut lines in it. Her skin was dry, flaky. I don't think I could explain it to you, she said, not in a way you'd understand.

It's changed me. I'd like to know.

You are a selfish, blinded man.

Yes, I said, and angry.

An accomplice.

Perhaps.

She shifted her weight, leaned on her good leg. The cats snarled and whined. A large gray tabby streaked across the beach carrying a silver hunk of fish in its mouth. Out over the Pacific the sun was going down redly. The top of the cliffs caught the light. The brush along the edge, the spindly trees, shined bright gold.

She said, Look at the curve of my shoulder. Can you see it? She said, Look, let me drop the robe.

She pushed her dark robe off her shoulders. They were white, rounded, unmarked.

You see, she said, you see the curve? It is beautiful. There is the curve of my shoulder, and the curve of my breast, and the curve of my hip, and the curve of my ass, and they are all beautiful.

Yes, I said, they are.

A line swings away, from its starting point, swings back. And our hearts break. She ran her hand slowly along her shoulder, cupped it lightly. It is very simple. And it is enough to break our hearts.

Yes.

Can you find, she said, the beauty in a devilish thing?

I find it in you.

Yes. Do you remember the way the lantern flew through the air? The curve of its flight? It trailed fire.

My heart stopped.

It has to break.

That happened a long time ago.

Yes, so you say. When Bobby died.

Yes.

Find the beauty in a devilish thing. If you don't, what's devilish will kill you.

I don't understand you, I don't think I do; even now I don't.

It's not in your mind; it won't fix itself there.

Where then?

Anywhere else. Go on past the last thing and see.

I am already past it. I am where I have never been before.

Be careful, she said. Look closely.

At what?

The shape of things, the curve.

I don't understand you.

No, you don't. But don't make that your last excuse.

What?

That I didn't know her, and I didn't know what I was doing.

I knew what I was doing.

Have I told you the story about the man who wanted to commit suicide but was afraid so he hired an assassin to do it?

No.

It's a true story. He hired an assassin, and then became afraid of the assassin and ran for his life.

What happened.

He ran across the world fleeing his death. He lost everything, ruined himself, destroyed his life.

Did the assassin find him?

Yes. In the usual way. He befriended a child, traveled with him, crossed deserts and jungles with him, stole and murdered with him, and then one day he looked into the child's eyes and saw his death there.

The child was the assassin?

From beginning to end.

I said, Here's something I think about. The day will come when there is only one person still alive at this moment. That person is somewhere now on the earth. Maybe a little three-year-old girl sitting on a porch step looking out at an orchard. Maybe, a hundred and five years from now, as a wrinkled old lady wheezing her way into oblivion, maybe she will still be able to remember this day, maybe it will be a day called up by the neurons, maybe it will be one of the days flashing by in her mind, maybe she will remember sitting on the porch steps and remember how the sun filled the trees with light, and remember how happy she was, remember how for a second there was no difference between her and the grass and her and the trees and her and the light. What do you think of that?

You don't need my permission.

Who are you? I said.

Your brother.

Who are you?

Your mother.

Who are you?

The end of the story.

Who are you?

Fate.

Who are you? Who are you? Who are you?

When he was eight, my brother wore cap pistols all day long, every day. He wore them to keep order in the house. He wanted things to go smoothly. He wanted peace. What happened was, he couldn't make the world be still. So he died. The tender-hearted gunslinger. The idiot.

She had never stopped smiling. And she was smiling now. She said, What was inside is outside. What was unknown is known.

Who are you? I said.

Maybe the last thing you will ever see.

From the pocket of the robe she took a pistol, raised it, aimed it at my heart.

It was as if there were a groove in the space between us the size of a pistol and she fit the gun into it. It was the hinge between us, it locked us one to the other. Chills, then heat, then chills again went through me. I hadn't thought a thing about this, about this possibility, but it seemed to me then that it was what I had come for, to let her do this, to show up for it. We stood there a long time. Every minute was the last minute. And every minute I thought she was going to shoot me. But she didn't.

She said, Do you remember that rock I told you about, the spire in Nebraska?

Chimney Rock?

Yes. The marker, the gateway to the true West. It was where the New World began, the place where those who had come to the New World and found it old, found a newer world.

Yes. I would like to see it.

Look, she said. She turned her face to the west. The sun was going down into the sea; the last red curve of it, a fiery bulge, was slipping under. Cloud wisps, the moisture of the ocean, burned at the rim. There were bolts of red light, spires of fire burning. Look, she said.

I looked. The fires, torn up from the earth, torn from the surface of the sun, burned in space, hotter than any fire we could imagine. They burned steadily, trembling, pulsing, filling the western sky.

Fires of discovery, she said. Fires of heaven. One gate, one way.

There were tears in her eyes. She lowered the gun, put it back into her pocket.

I took a step toward her, but she waved me away. Go, she said.

All right.

I crossed the beach, climbed the stairs. At the top of the cliff I looked back. Darkness had slipped in behind me, but in the darkness I could still see her, still see the white-blond head, the white body from which the robe had fallen. Around her the cats snarled and capered, tearing at each other, fighting. She rose from among them like some terrible, primitive queen, queen of the beasts, or no, maybe only some outcast, some solitary sailor left to rot on a desolate shore, some adventurer, some Magellan, some last survivor of the tribe of those compelled by the itch of desire to move forward into the unexplored dark, some last twitch of the force that drives us all, nothing ahead at last, nothing more to come but water, and fire.

BUT IN THIS life there is no end.

From a telephone in Westwood I call Harvey Madrid. I ask him if he has received a copy of Sammy's investigative reports.

He says yes.

"Well?" I say.

"The prosecutor has one too," he says.

"What do you think?"

"I think you'll slide on out from under this one," he says.

I tell him I am glad to hear that, but what about the indictment, the charge?

"I think we can squash that," he says. His voice is croaky, diminished, there is a frailness in it.

"Will they charge me first, or drop it?" I say.

"It depends on how fast things move," he says. "I don't think you'll be charged; having to back off it the next day would be too embarrassing for everyone concerned. You're a lucky guy."

"How so?"

"Those shits from Ventura really wanted to nail you, and apparently they're not alone."

"Clement," I say.

"What is wrong with you people?"

"Some of us don't think there is anything wrong."

"That's it," he says, his hoarse voice bursting out of the phone. "That's it. You extra-special bastards, you fancy assholes."

"Only some of us," I say. "What's wrong with *you?*"

353

"Nothing's wrong with me. It's you guys."

"Harvey . . ." but he won't be stopped. His raked voice rails at me. "None of you guys," he says, "can even see what's wrong with you. You've got no humility. Every one of you thinks he has some extra privilege that exempts him from life in this world, some dispensation that excludes you from the fucking mayhem the rest of us have to live with. You don't believe in anything, none of you do, you don't believe in anything except the next patch of glory you're headed for, or the next pot of money, or the next triumph. You guys have no idea that the rest of us, all the rest of us, are down here on the ground, where it stinks, where nothing's going to come along and save our ass, where we're going to have to pay with our fucking lives for every breath we take. Hell, all these fires, all these people burning the city up— they make more sense to me, and I'm a cop, than you people do. They got a grievance, a real one. They got a lifetime of griev- ances. Nothing has ever worked out for them. And nothing's going to work out. You guys, you guys in the gold buttons, *everything* works out for you . . ."

"I don't think so, Harvey."

"Fuck it, man, it's true. You guys. But you better watch out. Reorganization's coming."

"And right on time, I expect."

"That's what I mean—nothing touches you. You people are impervious. There's no way to get through to you. There's no knife can wound you, there's no gun can put a bullet deep enough in you to stop you. Jesus. There's a woman dead here. Some- body—your fucking father, I guess—killed her. He burned her up . . ."

"I saw her . . ."

"He shot her in her own car, and then he burned her up. A life. A used-to-be-living woman. Like she was trash he was burn- ing. Doesn't he know he can't do that?"

"No," I say, "he doesn't."

"And you—your fucking wife, man. Sordid nonsense. You were telling me the truth about that."

"Yes, I was."

"It's not going to end, man. You're just jumping out of one fire right into another."

"I'm losing you. Or you're losing me."

"Man, I lost you a long time ago. I'm glad of it, too."

"How's your ulcer?"

He stops. There's a moment of silence.

"Fuck me, man," he says, and sighs. "The doctor says it's not an ulcer."

"What is it?"

"He says it's cancer. Can you believe it? Just when I'm about to join the elite, I get fucking cancer."

"Maybe he's mistaken."

"So what if he is? I can't get hired if they think I've got cancer. They won't hire me now because the word cancer has been spoken in the same room with me. You know how it works."

"The same for all of us."

He coughs into the phone, clears his throat. The sound is thin, frail. "Not the same," he says. "And when you're on the losing end, there's no way to make it look the same."

"I think this particular string of events has played itself out."

He sighs again. I hear his life in the sigh. "You don't understand at all," he says, "you no-humility guys, none of you understand, that's the thing about it. You can't learn."

"I'm sorry to hear about the cancer."

"Yeah. I wish you were sorry enough to change places with me."

"I bet you do."

AFTER THE FIRST time I left Kate in Mexico, but before I saw my life's work ahead of me, the work of slowly, carefully, one day at a time explaining to myself who Kate was, and who my father was, and what had happened to us—before the Awards, and before the woman, slapped crazy by Hollywood, by her yearning, had shot me, before I returned to Mexico following the dumb, terrible story that seemed to have been telling itself to me all my life, I worked three days on a picture my friend Robert Putnam was making. He wanted me to play the part of an executive who fires an employee and then, in turn, is shot by the employee, whose failed life has driven him crazy. It was a cameo, a boost for the picture, a quick in and out, a favor that paid me half a million dollars for four minutes in front of the camera. I had made a promise to Robert, who was directing his first picture, and I made good on the promise.

I said the lines, clearly with brisk malice, pausing between certain words to let the hard blade of silence do its dirty work, and after it was over I could see the admiration and the delight and the gratitude in Robert's face and in the faces of the other actors who had come onto the set to watch me work, but inside me there was a coldness that did not come from acting, an anger and hard despairing determination that was unlike any feeling I had had before; and it did not subside when I had changed out of my costume into the jeans and sweater I had arrived in, and it did not fade as I accepted the praise of my colleagues or as I spoke to Earl on the phone.

It was not mysterious, this anger and this despair—if that's what I could call it—but it was strange to me. I held it close as one would hold a small rattled child, wanting to take it somewhere and quiet it and look at it, but instead of doing that, I invited a script girl back to my room in a motel at the beach, where I had moved as if I no longer had a home, and there, conversing casually all the time, I undressed and took a bath with her in the room, making no comment on my nakedness or my swollen penis, making no move to touch her, even to get near her, and then, toweled dry, I lay on the bed and slowly, openly masturbated, talking all the time about Roman churches and the day my mother and Bobby and I tried to light candles in as many as we could.

The woman sat solemnly across the room from me, listening apparently, asking questions occasionally about Italian Renaissance sculpture, until I finished. Then she got up, thanked me for the conversation, and went out, pausing at the door to say only that she hoped my pain would pass. Was this kindness, was this understanding, or was this only the role one plays around a crazy person? I ran after her, pulling on clothes, caught up with her under a lime tree near the car, tried to take her in my arms, but she pushed me gently away. And was this a gesture on my part of understanding—yes, it's pain: what about you—or of dishonesty, a movie star raking a fledgling into his field of attention, waking up, oh, it's you darling, you're the one. I grabbed her arm, but she pulled away. She said, I can't, I'm with someone

356

else, I should have left sooner, and I said, Yes. I know, I understand about that, about not being able to leave quite on time. It's sweet, we want a little bit more, but then it's too late, things have gone too far. How did it happen?

We sat on the hood of her car and talked. On the other side of the road, below the corroded cliffs, the Pacific banged at the continent. Westward, stars fell toward the ocean. I said, Do you know my wife? She said, Yes, of course, everyone knows your wife. Well, listen to this, I said, and I told her the story, told her about the five years and Mexico, and the videos, the smacky parts Kate played. She listened, her head down, eyes avid, as if I were describing a movie.

That's really something, she said when I finished.

What about you? I said. Tell me something strange and secret.

There's nothing, she said.

There must be something.

No, she said, my life is very ordinary.

I jumped up from the car hood, began to pace. Wind spanked the upper leaves of the lime tree. The air smelled of rust. This is good, I said, frantic. Maybe I am coming on the truth here.

What truth?

I like to think everyone lives above a craziness—you know, like maybe they have a troll in the basement . . . of their lives— and they make do as best they can with this beast down there. But maybe this isn't true. You think this isn't true?

I don't know.

Or maybe you just don't want to say.

I think I had better go.

No, don't. Stay.

I'm frightened.

Do I frighten you?

Yes, some.

Why?

You're too intense.

Out here we call it energetic. Where are you from?

Wisconsin—Milwaukee.

I've never been there.

I have to go.

I said, Listen, I want to expose myself to you again. I want you to see me naked.

No, I'd better not.

It will only take a minute.

I would feel bad, I would feel guilty—you need to rest.

I've been resting all my life.

She shook her head. That—

What?

That—exposing yourself—it only stands for something . . .

You're a counselor?

No, but I think there's something else you want to do . . . that you're not doing.

I want to do something indelible but gratuitous.

Not this.

No, I guess not.

The wind cuffed the leaves and spun. Down on the highway cars swirled by at high speed. The woman slid off the hood, her dress rolling up, exposing her fine, pale legs. I began to take off my clothes.

I'm going, she said.

Go, I said, undressing.

I stripped naked. She started the car, looked at me. I said, There, you see?

Yes, she said, I see you.

Life is some kind of adventure, isn't it?

It sure is.

She roared away, gravel crunching like bones under the wheels of her little car. The sky was filled with bristly stars. Out over the Pacific huge clouds hung like white treasure piled on scales. I stood there in the parking lot naked, my cock shriveling in the cool sea air, my skin rippling with terror.

I EAT LUNCH in a Mexican café off Delgado. In front of the café are half a dozen shabby palm trees and a few concrete picnic tables. The house next door has been burned to the ground; piles of charred timbers still smoke. A burned mattress and its iron bedstead have been pulled out into the yard; around it are stacks of clothes and what look like kitchen utensils; a woman and two children sort through them. The acrid stink of watered ashes fills the café, and it seems everyone is talking about the fire, about the looting that has been going on for days. Everyone has been touched by it. No one speaks English or wants to; even the menu, written in pen on a sheet of waxy paper, is untranslatable, but they are willing to bring me food nonetheless. I order enchiladas with salsa verde. The man behind the counter, cook and owner, a large man wearing a hat made of butcher paper, serves me with a frown on his face.

Sometimes Kate and I would wake early, just at dawn. Maybe we both had studio work to do, but we would get up, go down to the kitchen, and eat breakfast together. In the early light that was just barely light, we would sit across the table from each other and eat fruit and cereal. I would look at her face; so early in the morning it was unprotected, untouched by the hard day coming. She was wise in the face, and this always surprised me, because I did not think of her as a wise person, but in the soft, pale light blown in from the yard, there was a look of what must have been wisdom in her. She would tell me of her travels, of her adventures in this or that odd place, of waking under stars on an Argentine cattle ranch, of making love on a houseboat on the Seine, of walking all afternoon along a stream in Africa while monkeys raced through the trees keeping her raucous company. I didn't believe a word of what she said, but I loved the stories. They were filled with life. In Argentina, so she said, there were little puffed blue flowers that made her sneeze, the Seine smelled of old galoshes, and the monkeys had mange.

When most people tell you a story, if it's a good story, you think they've picked up something in the experience, some knowledge or bit of wordly truth, and it's added to the life. Sometimes all this, this adding to, bears the teller down, and you can see it in each sometimes, the weight of experience, the accretion that is slowly becoming too much to carry. Most people know too much, see too much, and it hurts them. But this wasn't so with Kate. She had more stories than anyone I ever met, and she couldn't stop telling them. She had seen so much, and her mind moved so fast, that she couldn't keep her mouth shut. But what amazed me was that instead of experience and the world's hackneyed truths piling up on her, they were shed. In each of the places she described, in the glassy lagoon in Truk, in Madagascar, where the lemurs leapt like drunken cats through the trees, on the dark interior roads of America, where men stood beside their cars shaking with sobs, she had left parts of herself, dropped bits of this or that feeling or temper until there was only this clean, rinsed light in her face, this thing I call wisdom. She wasn't smart, really, I doubt she did well in school; what passed for intelligence was actually cleverness and a kind of intuitive cunning, but on those palely lit mornings when we'd sit at the glass table under the kitchen windows eating mangoes and peaches and she would tell me some story, some tale perhaps about picking flowers in a wheat field in Saskatchewan, I would marvel at what had been stripped away, at how much life had been cast off, like bits of fur snagged in thorny brush, and how beautiful the loss had made her.

I am thinking about this as my eye moves about the café, from the proprietor, who is scolding a teenage girl, his daughter I guess, behind the counter, to the customers who are beat Mexican men mostly, furtive, slight men without jobs, without even the means to participate in the looting and destruction that has been going on all year, to the big cleaned window and outside to the palm trees, the frothy tops of which are snapping in breeze. The wind, gusts of it, hits the trees hard, whipping the fronds; it pounds them, it snaps up clouds of smoke and ashes and whirls them into the air. Waving her arms, the ruined mother sends her children scurrying about, shouting at them to pick up this or that important article, to find this or that treasure that has disappeared in the fire, and as I watch her, I think of the limo driver whose name I have forgotten—no, I haven't: it was Arnold, Arnold Pescadoro—who spoke of his family burned up by marauders, by the current vandals and Visigoths that are taking over the city, that even now the local Caesars are negotiating with, piling promises and excuses into the brawny arms of those who would take their empire from them, but it is the palms, these tropical weeds wind-snapped and dusty, that take my attention. Why is it, I wonder, that the world around them seems to be rushing away at great speed? And why is it that they seem to have stepped forth from another world, like prophets come out of the desert, and why does it seem that even as the wind cracks the torn fronds they are unaffected by what is going on, by anything at all, and why are they like old men, standing in their shaggy beards all by themselves in a place where there is nothing but dirt and debris everywhere, a place it will take generations and a collapse of everything to make beautiful, and why is it that they seem to be impervious to everything, standing, though it is windy and there is a clamor around them, in a silence that nothing can break? I do not know what the world means. I do not know where the world is going. The palms are pale and stiff and they have been growing in the same place for maybe a hundred years, and if they are not burned up in a fire, they will be in this place for another hundred years perhaps, and everyone I know will soon be dead, soon enough, and the world we are trying to save, trying to find a means to live in, does not even notice we are here and doesn't care, and even if we burn it to a cinder, to rock, it will use the cinders and the rock to make of itself what it was about to become, and nothing we have done to it, and nothing we have said about it will matter, we who take ourselves and our earnestness so seriously; it will go on, making of itself what is next, rock or garden, wild bucking horse rolling through the heavens trailing screams and fire.

And now the proprietor is calling me. He is indicating the telephone on the counter. I get up, thank him, wondering what is going on, and take the receiver. Clement's voice comes through. "I'm looking at you," he says, "I'm looking straight at you."

"That's fine, Pop," I say. "I can't see you."

"I'm hidden; I'm out of sight."

The proprietor is speaking harshly to his daughter, if that's who the girl is; he is leaning toward her, gesturing roughly. The girl is maybe sixteen, she is wearing small gold beads in her ears; her hair is thick, bushy, her narrow face is like a brown, beautiful surprise beneath it. She lifts her face to the scolding.

"I have been following you all morning," my father says. "You certainly do a lot of traveling."

"It's a big city."

"You went from Hollywood to Beverly Hills, down to San Pedro, back through town and over the mountain to the studio, then you were in Glendale, and then Pasadena and San Marino, and now you're in El Sereno. You on a quest or something?"

"Where have you been? No one's heard from you in a while."

"I had to work off a little steam."

"Did Sammy send you the papers? Is that why you are following me?"

"Those papers don't mean shit. They don't prove a thing."

"I think they will mean enough to the LAPD."

"Why are you doing this to me?"

"What is it you think I am doing?"

"Getting me in trouble—ruining me."

The proprietor is getting angrier; this is something more than a routine work problem; a wormy vein stands in the center of his forehead, upright above the eyebrows; he is waving his fat arms. I step away from the counter. Outside, the scene is the same; there is no new area of struggle. I don't know if Clement can see me or not, but I am not really surprised that he has followed me, that he is now standing in some phone booth nearby, or sitting in his car whispering into the receiver.

"Why didn't you call me before this?" I say. "I have a phone in the car."

"I wanted to see you. I wanted to see what it felt like to sneak behind someone."

"How do you like it?"

"It makes me feel crude and desperate. It makes me feel ashamed. You must have been feeling like that for years. Do you know where I've come from?"

"Not if it's been in the last week. I had Sammy call the detectives off. I gave up on you."

"That's the thing about you, you and Bobby both—you were liable to falter, you were liable to let your scruples—that's another name for scaredness—get the best of you."

I think, no, we're like Amazons, the people in this family: we're strong, we take on anything, we fight back, we win every war, but we don't reproduce. We're dying out, time is turning into darkness all around us, filling in around us, until we're about to disappear into it. Suddenly I am full of grief, or suddenly the grief that is always in me comes to the surface. It is thick and leaden, horrible, but there is something almost comforting in it: it is real, it is life.

Behind me the ruckus has intensified. The man is shouting at his daughter. Another customer, a friend maybe, is on his feet; he too is shouting. Maybe the house next door belongs to the proprietor, maybe what has been happening here, the collapse of sense, of the ordinary concreteness of things, has busted something in this man. He raves at his daughter, swinging his arms. The girl cringes, but she doesn't step back.

I say, "Pop, I think the next thing coming for you will be very rough and too big for you to fight your way out of."

"That's where you always got me wrong," he says. "I wasn't fighting, I was just moving ahead. You have to move ahead, son."

Now the man has begun to strike his daughter. He raises his arms, swings awkwardly, openhanded, and hits her in the face. She staggers back, but she doesn't run. He raises his arm, strikes again. Her head jerks to one side with the blow.

"Hold the phone a second, Pop," I say, "there's something going on here."

I put the receiver down. Color has drained from the man's face, the life has drained from his face. There is a dumbness, a bleakness in his eyes, as if he is on the other side of exhaustion. He strikes the girl with a downward falling blow, the hand following the wrist down, flailing. The girl looks into his eyes. Her face is still, without emotion. She is receiving, as if it is simply the next inevitable moment, what is falling upon her.

I step to the counter, lean over it. I raise my arm, and it hangs in the air; I am unable to do anything. Even here there is a kind of beauty, something extraordinary being expressed in the way the man futilely swings at the girl, and in the way the girl stands there, as if this is her destiny, taking blows. Words are still chirping and growling in the receiver, but I can't understand them, I can't hear what Clement is saying.

I swing around and look out the window, just a glance. Out there the woman is still directing her children, and the palm trees are taking the wind into their arms, and the street, gray as a road of ashes, winds away downhill between the shabby houses. Beyond them, on a rise of ground, there is a stand of cedars, and beyond the cedars is the sky, which is a lovely coffee-muddled blue color, and maybe my father, who has found me again, is out there watching me, maybe he can see me in here anchored at this counter, where violence has stepped up to take over the negotiations, but if there is something out there, some message flown up from Mexico or from Malibu, or from the studios where men and women make movies, or from my past, or the future, which is setting itself on fire as I watch, I do not hear it, it is indecipherable, like the voice on this phone lying lonely on the counter, and I do not wait then, for things to clear up, don't wait any longer for the wise hand to touch my shoulder and direct me, I vault onto the counter, leap into the kitchen well, and catch this ruined, raging man against the cheekbone with my closed fist, a hard, straight-arm blow that drives him back. He shakes his head, stares at me as if I am the devil come for him, and for a second I see the despair gathered in his black eyes, and I see the bleakness and the terrible loss he is living with, and see how it isn't going to get any better, not this day or on any day he can imagine, and it is terrible, and I pity him, but terror and pity do not stop me this time, they do not even slow me down. I spring forward, swing my left arm this time, a hooking blow, and catch him in the temple, and send him down into the well of surprise and blankness waiting for him on the floor.

I stand over him gasping. Thin streams of colored light rush through my eyes. Around me the hubbub continues, it gets even louder. The girl is screaming and now there are other people screaming. The man who tried to help, a skinny man in a torn Panama hat, lashes a blow at me, but it bounces off my shoulder. The girl is screaming at me. Her mouth looks torn; her gums are red, bloody looking. I push the little man away, pick up the phone. A man and a woman at a table in the corner are shaking their fists at me and cursing me in Spanish. I understand what they are saying; I am the implacable representative of the implacable force that is tormenting them. I say, "Pop"—whispering; I say, "Pop, are you there?"—it has come to me that there is still a way out for my father, there is still a means by which he can reach the other side of the disaster that is overtaking him, and I want to tell him about it, I want to counsel with him a second here. I say his name again, I say *Clement,* I press the receiver to my ear, but the line is dead.

A YEAR AFTER we were married I took Kate to Arkansas, to see the place where my father and his father were born. I had not been there before, and now, married, my life unaccountably freshened by this brisk woman, I wanted to see the place my people came from, and to show it to her. We had a few relatives back in the hills, but we had not stayed in touch with them as far as I knew; when we cut loose in the thirties we put the past behind us, and no one but my grandfather, and then only in his old age, was sentimental about it.

There was a town with a redbrick courthouse that had clocks painted on the cupola, and a silver water tower, and a meat-packing plant with smelly stockyards around it filled with hogs, but there was no movie theater, and no one recognized us. I had directions to the home place I had never seen; it was up a county road that meandered through a valley that narrowed along a rocky stream as it climbed into wooded hills. The road was new; you could see the track of the old road running along the contours of the hills, following us like a ghost. There were apple orchards filled with green fruit and patches of summer wheat, and in the pastures the Queen Anne's lace was coming into bloom.

The house was up a dirt road fronted by a clutch of crooked mailboxes; the road wound between blackberry bushes past cut banks of yellow earth and past a couple of unpainted houses, the porches of which faded away from the road across a wide sprawl of field. The place was a small rectangular house set in a notch under pines. The side windows and part of the porch overlooked the valley and the road.

When we got there I at first didn't want to go up to it. The house was not run-down; it was freshly painted and there were gladiolas blossoming by the front steps, and in back a garden prospered above thick rolls of turned earth. Kate asked if my people still lived there and I said I thought so, some of them anyway, cousins I guessed. We sat in the car at the bottom of the drive.

After a while a woman and a little girl came out on the porch and looked at us. They seemed familiar. I asked Kate to wait while I went up to talk to them. There were red crepe paper streamers in the pine trees nearest the house. There was an old sofa on the porch, turned so it faced out over the valley. A little boy came out of the house and stood with the woman and the girl. The boy, maybe six, pointed at us. I got out of the car, walked up the drive. An old truck parked to one side had yellow splashes of pine sap on the hood and there were splashes of sap on the concrete front steps. I stopped at the head of the short walkway along which white-painted tires had been set in the ground. Geraniums were planted in the tires. I spoke to the woman, told her I was Will Blake, son of Clement Blake, grandson of Willard Blake, both of whom were born in the house. She stared at me without answering. I said my name again. "Who is that, Mama?" the little boy said.

The girl waved a hand at him, a slapping motion. "He told you his name, stupid," she said.

The woman clutched herself in her arms. She was narrow and tall; she had my father's strong, bony jaw, the black hair like fur, but she was much thinner than my father and grandfather. "I just want to take a look at the house," I said. "I've never seen it before. My wife and I have come from California."

Something—maybe the word *California*—caught the woman. Her face came to life. "My baby died yesterday," she said.

"I'm terribly sorry to hear that," I said. "Is there anything we can do?"

"My husband's out in the garden digging a grave for her."

The little girl, five maybe, made a half-spin away from her mother, her arms out. "Billy killed him," she said. She meant the little boy. The boy cringed, his face twisted. "I didn't mean to," he said.

"He killed him." the girl said. "He pushed him off the table."

"She was a girl," the woman said. She looked down at the girl as if she were a strange being, squinting as if she were far away.

"I didn't mean to do it," Billy said.

"But you did it," the little girl said. "He did it, Mama."

"Hush," the woman said.

I looked back at the car. Kate had gotten out; she leaned against the open door. She was wearing white clothes, loose pants, and a shirt with the sleeves rolled up. She had a red bandanna knotted around her head. Her stiff, pale hair stuck out of the bandanna. When I looked at her, she began to walk up the drive.

"Maybe we could come back another time," I said.

"It's all right," the woman said.

"Billy is a killer," the little girl said.

"Hush," her mother said again.

A man came around the side of the house carrying a shovel. He wore rubber boots splashed with yellow mud. He was thin, almost scrawny. His long chestnut hair was watered down onto his skull.

I introduced myself, but he ignored me. "The hole's dug," he said dully.

Kate came up to me. I told her what had happened. "Oh no,"

she said. Tears welled in her eyes. The tears startled me. They appeared so quickly.

"Maybe we had better leave," I said.

"No," she said. "We can't now."

She climbed the steps and embraced the woman. The woman stood stiffly in her arms. "The baby's in the house," she said over Kate's shoulder, speaking straight out into the air.

The little girl threw her arms up. "We're going to put the baby in the ground," she yelled, half in terror, half in glee. "We're going to plant the baby," she cried.

The little boy made a break for it. He ran down the steps, headed toward the stand of pines at the edge of the yard. "Billy," his father cried. The boy stopped at the edge of the woods, but he didn't come back. He was crying. "I didn't mean to do it," he said. "It was a accident."

The man stood in the yard with the shovel cradled in his arms like a rifle. He looked up at the woman. "Go get her, Hartie," he said.

The little girl jiggered and spun. "Don't do it," she cried. She grabbed at her mother, hit her on the leg. "Don't do it."

Her mother looked down at her, patted her head. "Come on, Odilene," she said. "Come help me."

"I don't want to," the girl said. "I don't want to plant the baby."

The woman looked at her again as if she didn't know her. Her face was filled with the eroded, blunt stupidity of grief. She flicked a strand of hair away from her face as if it were a fly, turned, and went into the house. The little girl looked confused; she hesitated, gulped tears, and followed her mother. The man walked over to the little boy, who stood under a pine tree turning a green twig in his hands. He jerked the boy up into his arms, hugged him tightly. The boy squirmed and then went limp.

"They're doing this all by themselves," I said.

"It's a good thing we came along."

"We're interrupting."

"No. We're witnesses. That's good for everyone concerned."

"The little boy knocked the baby off the table. I think that's what the woman said."

"Is she your relative?"

"The woman is, I think. She looks like us."

"It's scary," she said.

"I know—someone dying out here in the woods, nobody to help."

"No. Finding what you come out of is. And finding how close you are to it."

It had struck me too. Cousin I guess the woman was, we had come from the same close-by source. Only the slightest of twists separated us. I thought of Jennie, of the Lowland Scots workers she had come from, thought how hard she had worked to escape her origins, how she had hammered herself until every part of her was changed into something new, and how she had married, just the same, a man who stank of the rough ground he was born on, who was not so different from these people trudging about in this primitive place. A space opened inside me, a widening area that contained distances, life and events I knew nothing about.

The woman came out of the house carrying the baby wrapped in an olive blanket. She had tied a piece of blue Christmas ribbon around the bundle. The girl tagged at her heels chattering. She wanted to know what would happen to the baby after they put it in the ground, if it would sprout leaves and flowers. "Will it be a bush or a tree?" she said. "Will it be a rosebush?"

"It's dead," her mother said.

We followed them into the garden behind the house. The man had dug a hole at the end of a row of corn. The crumbled yellow earth beside the hole was streaked with blue clay. There were pea vines climbing the cornstalks, and a breeze moved over the corn, shaking the pale yellow tassels.

The woman set the bundle on the ground and she and her husband knelt down beside it. With her forefinger, delicately, as if she were lightly drawing something, the woman opened the blanket over the baby's face. The face was wrinkled, twisted, like something that had been screwed into a socket, very pale, and there was a cleaned open cut running down the forehead. The baby's hair was thick and glossy black.

"Kneel down here," the man said to the children. The boy and the girl were crying. The girl twisted her hands in the hem of her dress. The boy hunched his shoulders. The man pulled them down.

Kate and I, back a ways among tomato bushes that sagged

with yellowing fruit, knelt too. Brown, speckled bugs flexing colorless wings under hard curved shells crawled among the vines. A trail of black ants threaded its way down the row. There were a few starry yellow flowers among the tomato fruit. Kate was crying. The tears ran down her cheeks. She made no move to brush them away.

The man began to wail and cry out. He lifted his face, raised his arms. He cried words that were not words, a rapid gibberish broken by short barks and wails. The woman began to keen, a high, humming sound, and she rocked on her heels back and forth, dropping her face down to touch it against the baby's. The children sobbed. And then Kate began to cry out. She made thick coughing sounds and then her voice cleared and she began first to cry out and then to sing. Her voice came in low, as if she were drawing it up out of the ground; she sang the spiritual "Over Jordan," and the words fell from her mouth creased with pain and a hollow rising inflection that made her voice strange and coarse. She pressed her shoulder against me and her head swayed. There were tears in my eyes too, tears for the moment, for all of us kneeling there in the yellow dirt, and tears that I didn't know the origins of.

The man raised his voice higher, babbling, and he began to tear at his clothes, ripping at his shirt and banging his fists against his chest and against his neck. The woman pressed her face against the baby, pushed her face against its body as if she wanted to press it into the earth. The little girl fell onto her side crying; her brother, the convicted, cringed, drawing back, crying too but without any other excitations. The boy's eyes were wild and terrified. I walked on my knees over to him and took him in my arms. He writhed and then eased against me; he clutched my wrists. I drew him in, drew him to my body. He smelled of piss and bitter sweat and smelled of the rank earth and of sour human dirt, of stinking mortal life. There were bits of dirt in his hair and there was a glossy spot of pine sap on his cheek like a stuck-on tear.

I hugged him, held him as his father lifted the baby, cupped the dead bundle in his hands, and raised it over his head. The babbling became words, became the name of Jesus repeated over and over. "Jesus, oh Jesus, oh Jesus," the man cried.

"Oh my lovely baby Jesus," the woman shouted. She

wrenched herself half up and fell onto her side. She lifted her arms to the baby in the air above her. The man swayed back and forth calling Jesus' name.

The little girl sat up. "Don't go to the ground," she cried. "Baby, stay."

Kate pitched forward across the narrow grave, rolled off it onto her back, and scraped at the ground, tearing handfuls of yellow dirt. She slapped the dirt against her face, rubbed it in, rubbed it against her bare arms, thrust her slick fingers into her hair. She cried out, calling the name of Jesus, calling the name of the country Lord responsible for all of this. I began to shuffle backwards on my knees, carrying the boy with me. He didn't want to go, squirmed in my arms, and I caught a glimpse of his face and of the terror in it, and then his fingernails bit into my forearm and he surged forward, lunging like an animal, and I let him go.

The man held the baby above the grave, he held it high over the hole that was no deeper than the hole you might bury a dog in, and he swayed as if a wind were beating at him, as if he leaned over the edge of a high cliff and the wind were about to snatch this bundle from him. The woman dragged herself to the grave, and then on her belly she began to slither into it. The man shifted the baby into his left hand and grabbed his wife with his right. He grabbed her at the waist and began to pull her back. The woman was going headfirst into the grave. "Don't snatch me," the woman cried.

I got up then and walked back to the house. A screen porch sagged across the rear. Two lines of dried gourds had been hung across the screens and a gardenia bush next to the back steps was filled with brown, wadded blooms. I opened the back door and went in. The place smelled damp and leathery. This was the house—I was sure of it—where my father was born. The story was they had used a knife to rip him out of his mother's womb. He said it was the knife she used in the kitchen, a knife he remembered as a child. He said he would open the kitchen drawer and stare at it, the knife that sliced meat and bread, that lay on the counter at meals, disguised, so my father said, as a domestic utensil.

Out in the garden the cries rose into the heavens. The living whirled about the dead child. As I watched, fiddling with a small basket containing a few walnuts, the man raised the baby again as his wife clutched at him. She fought him for the baby. They sank, the man holding the baby, headfirst into the grave. Kate, grown calmer, leaned in after them. There was a struggle. Behind them the girl shrieked and the boy lay on his side saying nothing. And then they rose, without the baby. Somehow they'd cut it loose. Life had stepped in and snapped the attachment like a twig.

The woman leaned back into her husband's arms. He stood up, and drew her up. They looked into the grave. Kate was on her knees and she stared into the grave too. I went outside, walked into the yard. A flock of blackbirds, heading north toward the ridge, passed overhead. The birds made harsh, bony cries. Breeze shifted in a line of apple trees beyond the garden, a spectator wind, looking for a better view.

The family and Kate, now risen to her feet, stared into the grave. What was so lately a part of them was now a part of something else. I could feel it like a change of weather. The man stepped back, and his wife stepped back with him. He didn't seem to know what to do next, he seemed embarrassed. He shook his head. Kate smiled at him. Her smile was gentle, a smile of understanding. The man began to pray out loud. He thanked God for the child and asked God to bless her and take her into heaven. "We didn't know her much," he said, "but we will miss her, and we will think about her, and we will always love her. She was such a pretty baby."

"Such a pretty baby," the woman whispered. She stood straight now, her shoulders back. Tears streamed down her thin cheeks. With an awkward grace she let her arm swing toward the grave and drop. The man said, "She was sweet as sugar, pretty as a summer day." He was silent a moment, and then he repeated the sentence, "She was sweet as sugar . . ."

Crying, tears dripping from her jaw, spotting the front of her gray dress, the woman repeated the sentence after him. The words seemed to make her stronger. She touched her husband on the shoulder. At the touch his body sagged. She placed a hand on each shoulder and held him. He swayed forward, almost toppled into the grave, but she held him upright. He straightened up, raised his head. His face was young, but his neck was crepey and discolored. He said, "Let the sunlight shine on this place, dear Jesus, and let the rain fall that makes the grass grow. Shelter our baby under your strong wing. Protect her and keep her from being lonely. Make eternity sweet. Keep her safe until we come to join her."

The children huddled together, the girl crying softly. The boy stared into the garden, where small brown birds flitted about among the corn and the beans. Above a sprawl of squash vines white butterflies darted and drifted. My father came back to me, and my mother and my brother, and the day we buried Bobby in the cemetery down the road from the Pima farm came back to me. I saw my father's anger, which was really grief, and I saw my mother, who on that day let something pass out of her body that never came back, and I saw us all, and the friends gathered, and saw how hapless and insubstantial we were, and saw how hard it was for us to understand anything, saw how death was too big for all of us, how it confused and broke us, and how it put its mark on us and whispered its lessons in our ears, made its trade.

I took a step forward and then I crossed the yard to the yellow grave. I stepped around the hole and took Kate in my arms. She was streaked with clay. She cried against my shoulder as the man began to shovel dirt into the grave. The woman swayed and began to hum. We all stood there as the dirt covered the body, covered the green blanket it was swaddled in. It became a lump under the soil and then the soil covered the rise of it and the hole was only soil, added little by little. As it rose higher the man reached in and tamped it down with the flat of the shovel. He softly gasped each time the blade touched the earth. The baby was so small there was no dirt left over. Maybe only an inch or two above the original surface. The man tamped the yellow soil down. Then we all stood there and looked at where the hole had been, at where the baby lay, four feet down. Breeze stumbled through the pine trees at the edge of the woods. The breeze turned the needles over, exposing their silver undersides. Three or four white butterflies drifted among us, bobbling in the breeze. All around us there was a vast beauty and silence. Something huge and imperishable had moved out among us as we wailed and cried. It lay upon us and within us. Kate blew a kiss into the grave. Her eyes shined. For a second there, I could see what drove her, and drove my father too.

I LIE BACK on the big bed and punch buttons to bring up the video I lately received. I didn't watch it at first, waited. I have grown afraid of what might show up on the screen. Who knows what might be torn away next? A scent of smoke, a scent of oranges blows through the open windows. The newscasts caution citizens to stay close to home. I've been on to that all my life, I said back to it before I switched on the VCR.

A salt-and-pepper static converts to a pinkish yellow light. A band of blue appears, slowly spreads until it fills the screen. Then blackness. Then a burst of white light and a landscape appears, shot from above, a single tree overlooking a long sweep of what at first looks like grassland, but as the camera moves in I see is brushy desert. There are stony mountains in the distance, and far off, a tall, thin mountain, like a spire.

The camera closes on the tree. Under it there is someone sitting in a chair. It is Kate, in a white wicker armchair. She wears a long white dress. The camera closes, frames her.

She smiles. The smile is sweet, serene, potent. There is a long minute of silence. A breeze shakes the leaves around her, but she is very still.

There is a tight fist in my chest. I realize I need this distance, I realize I have always needed it.

She begins to speak, she says, "I wanted to love the story of my life, I wanted to love everything that happened, everything I thought about, everything I saw. When I was a little girl I decided that's what I wanted to do. I did everything I could think of, and I could think of a lot. Push further, I thought, see more. I loved the intensity, the punch in the heart, my breath coming quick. It's cost me almost everything, but not quite. I'm still alive.

"My life seems a miracle to me. A glorious miracle, dramatic and tangible, like the Bible miracles where men were turned into pigs and seas parted. It's been a miracle I could taste and feel, a miracle I could see. I know it is a child's version of life, I know I have no excuse for it, and I know it has ruined me, but somehow, even now, even like this, I do not mind. I didn't want only the joy."

Her face and body are very still. She looks straight at me. "I don't repent, and I don't want to be redeemed. I feel the dirt in the creases of my body, I feel the loss, every second of it, I see the shadows move—all my life I've wondered what I would do when the worst came, wondered if I would shake and cringe when the unavoidable showed up, and now I know. I shook, I cringed, I cried out; I hallucinated, I saw red kites in the trees and bottles flying through the air, and beds on fire, and I heard a bell ringing, and something cold and dirty tasted me in its mouth, and there was a voice in the wind—not your Bobby's voice—mumbling terrible things; and I couldn't stop the pain, couldn't stop the bones from being broken in front of me. I saw a little girl sitting on the summery steps and saw a black shape rising toward her—and she was unprotected and she couldn't see the shape, and it took her in its mouth and bit the blood out of her body . . ."

I lie stiffly on the bed, I am not relaxed. The bright spot of the TV screen is like a hole torn in the side of the house. A force more powerful than fire or earthquake has tunneled its way into my inner rooms. I would flee, but there is nowhere to go; I am already home; I am already at the center. Each frame, each word she says, burns. Pain caused, pain suffered—who knows which is worse? I have decided to see it through, to see all this . . . through. The decision is what I am holding on to—it is very important, I think, to do this. Let the phones ring, I will stay here and watch.

". . . and Willie," she says, "boy I know so well and don't know at all, as this was happening, as these visions streaked by, everything hurtling, I saw, as if it were in the corner of my eye, the road leading to my grandfather's farm. I don't know why. His farm in Nebraska. The road was white, dusty, and it led through bean fields along a white fence grown up in sassafras and plum bushes. The road turned in at the white gate and I saw the house that was tall and white and old. My grandfather was born there. And I could see the big oaks in front of the house, and the garden and the pigpen and the barns down the way. There were apple trees in front of the oaks and in the trees were little striped apples. I could remember the taste of the apples and remember climbing into the tree and eating them on a cool fall day, and remember leaning back on a big limb and looking up into the sky; and I could remember how the sun burned in a bath of fire, and how the light leaped, and how the sky itself seemed to be drawing me away, drawing me up into it. I stood there in this vision of myself, and it came to me, like a fragrance in a field, that no matter what happens, the good, the beauty here among us, will find us; it'll find us, like the little dog that comes home after weeks of wandering, it'll slip right through all the dirt and disaster of our lives, and if it doesn't change or reform what's terrible, still, it remains itself, it comes on anyway. Isn't that fine?

"You said to me, in one of the worst moments, when everything had broken into pieces, that underneath it all we were as clean as a whistle. I didn't believe you. And so I threw a fire into a fire. But the world and life are too big for them to be a dream. The fire was a real fire. When the sun is going down behind Chimney Rock, it looks as if the mountain is burning. But the rock is not on fire. It is only rock and the sun does not change it. What is a dream to you does not make your life a dream. I see myself standing in the dusty driveway of my grandfather's farm, and I can taste in my mouth the tartness of the apples, and I see the sun shining in the tree, and I think it isn't a dream, it is real, I am really there, I can taste the apple in my mouth, and I don't know . . ."

I switch the machine off. It is far too late for anything she could say. The room is dark, even though outside it is still light. I smell the fires. I cover my face, open my eyes behind my hands. Everything's black. Nothing moves. "It was a terrible mistake," I say, "to get caught up among folks like us." I begin to laugh. I laugh for a long time. And then I get up and begin to prepare for the evening.

ON THE SERVICE road just inside the wall that rings Billy Dangelo's estate like the wall of a medieval fortress, I wait. The drive curves uphill under mango trees. Billy, a fastidious man, has tagged each tree with small metal cards that state the variety, origin, and date of planting. A few of the cards catch light from the house and the floodlit yard, glitter like eyes among the leaves. There are guards at the gate and along the drive and guards around the house itself, there to protect the privileges of the few who are able to sustain a saucy life in this time of troubles, but down here, where servants walk their last mile before their long day begins, where delivery trucks rumble, there is no one. Down the mountain, wisps of smoke blow through the gates of Beverly Hills. Fires have been reported off Mulholland, there are rumors of an explosion outside—or was it inside—Sebastian Count's house— not half a mile from here—but they haven't been confirmed. To the south, from any high point, you can see flames. The revelers tonight have left their Ferraris and Lamborghinis at home. They arrive in limousines and Range Rovers, protected by armor plate and tinted, bulletproof glass. Their chauffeurs carry pistols.

Beyond the mangos, beyond a wide stretch of watered lawn, beyond a stand of slim cypresses, the big house glitters like an iceberg. There are sculptures on the lawn, here and there, contorted white shapes, cut from stone. The house itself, stacked in tiers to which boxy appendages adhere, looks like stone, but it is wood, cunningly fashioned, marbleized, a fabrication like a movie set, Billy's *faux* delight. Billy himself, who Sammy told me this afternoon will protect Clement from arrest, stands on the front steps in a black tuxedo, bathed in a creamy, expensive light, welcoming his guests. The reports we have, Sammy said, will pull us through, but Billy plans to save Clement; he wants to keep him from going down; he's the one—I'm sorry to say—Billy thinks can do him the most good. There's been too much in the paper about Kate, Sammy said, the rumors have congealed, word's gotten out about what happened—story's out you're the culprit.

Earl rang later to confirm. It's trouble, he said—I told you not to get into all this in the first place; you should have left the woman alone—they're going to strip you on this one . . .

When did you tell me, I asked, not to get into this?

A long time ago—I told you the first week you met Kate Dunn, I told you she was too wild and clever. And you know I've always told you to stay away from your dad.

Earl, I said, where are you calling me from?

From the garden. He had an English garden—hollyhocks and yew trees—watered and pampered behind his house, and in the early mornings, when even in the desert there is a hint of dew and damp, he liked to walk among his pansies and chrysanthemums, wearing bristly tweeds and humming "Rule Britannia."

You out there watering the roses?

I have an infestation of aphids. It's terrible. I've tried everything, but I can't overcome them.

Earl, I said, you're fired.

Who's fired?

You are, bro. I don't want to hear from you again.

Ah, Willie, I didn't mean . . .

It's okay, Earl. I don't want to hear anything more.

Okay, okay. I'll back off. You've got a worried mind—I understand.

Earl, you understand nothing. If we painted it red and shoved it up your ass, you wouldn't understand it.

He began to sputter, to explain, to wheedle, but I wasn't listening. I was thinking of Clement peeling an orange with his teeth, thinking of how he spit the rind onto the ground, of the white inner skin, of the simple, ravenous glee in his eyes as he bit the citrus flesh. I hung up the phone.

A guard truck, a Jeep filled with deadly hardware, manned by two men in uniforms, pulls up beside me. They flash a light into the car, recognize me. We chat a moment. One of them I know well. He's Ronald Kato, chief of the security force many Hollywoodans use. He worked a party of my mother's last fall. A stiff, formal man, he will, if you are on the wrong side of the money and offend, so it is said, attack you as if you were a snake. He has achieved the state so many here aspire to, the one in which the cultivation of mercy and tolerance is no longer necessary. He has the clean, static look of those for whom decorum is the highest virtue. He knows me, he includes me in the circle of the elect, and so offers a sleek humility, but he wants to know what I am doing here nonetheless. I tell him I am waiting to meet my father, who has a gift for Billy. It's traditional, I say; we're starting a picture together, it's time for gifts. He wants to know why I wait here, out on the service road under the mango trees. We're going to take it around to the back, I say. Can we help you? No, I say, I wish you could. Or yes, would you go on around and tell them to expect us.

Clement is at this moment getting out of a limo at the front steps. The steps roll toward him in white waves. Billy descends. I hope the guards don't turn around, don't glance that way. They don't. The chief wishes me a good evening—he mustn't press too far into the lives of his charges, and he knows the Blakes—and he and his deputy continue on around the drive.

When at Jennie's Beverly Hills house this afternoon I told Veronica that it looked as if I might get off, might escape a murder charge, she at first was angry.

Why did you say they were going to charge you if you turn right around and tell me they aren't?

Early it looked like they were; later it didn't. I talked to Harvey. He knows how things work. He said the info Sammy gave them would get me off.

So what's wrong with Sammy?

He doesn't know Harvey. I believe he thought the reports were enough to stop a conviction, but not the charge.

I was about to go crazy.

Me too.

We were on the back porch, sitting under a large avocado tree, waiting for Jennie. The big yard was filled with blossoming flowers, protected by a wall of bamboo. At the far end was a small swimming pool. Its interior walls were painted black. In lemon trees beside the pool wind chimes tinkled and clattered in a light breeze. Veronica wore a thick white robe.

Does Clement know about this? she asked.

Yes. He's been following me all day. He's probably out in the street now, sitting in his car.

Agh. Don't go on. It makes me shudder. He's probably planning something terrible.

There's a lot about this I haven't told you, but I will.

I want to hear it, but not today.

I don't want to hear it at all, Jennie said, coming out onto the porch.

She wore a white robe identical to Veronica's.

It's complicated, I said.

Not complicated enough.

She smiled. Seams and creases fretted the smile, but she was beautiful nonetheless.

I think everything's understandable, she said, in some way. It's a mystery too, of course, but what we need to know of it, enough to live, comes clear. Some people have to light a fire to see themselves. Sometimes the fire gets out of hand, and burns them up.

That's neatly spoken, Mother. I didn't know old ladies became philosophers.

Given enough time. And you're getting old too.

I feel ancient.

Well, you rest then, while we aging beauties take a swim.

I walked with them down to the pool and sat in a folding chair under the orange trees while they swam. They were naked under the robes. Each in her own way was aging, rounding out toward death. But they slipped the robes from their bodies and stood proudly in the sunlight. They did not mind my watching them, they did not mind the light. As they slipped into the pool, creatures without shame or fear, a faintness, a lightness entered me. As the water received them, as the sunlight shined on their slender bodies, in the midst of my rage and my future, I was blessed.

When the Jeep's taillights disappear beyond the trees I put the car in gear and ease on around the drive. Billy had embraced Clement, they were glad to see each other. Clement wore a white suit. Even at a distance I could see the bunch of red cloth, like a bouquet, he sported for a tie. His chauffeur pulled the car around to the head of the main drive. Good for a quick exit. Clement embraced Billy, stepped back, threw his arms out, ready to embrace everything else too. All afternoon, in the car, at the house, even at Jennie's, the phone rang. I didn't answer, didn't come to the phone when I was called. He left messages, threats, pleas. I grew stiff with resistance, and then the stiffness subsided and a tranquillity came over me, a quiet. I pushed through into another place, or something I had avoided finally reached me, and I was calm. I stopped at a camping gear shop, bought my supplies, and packed them in a suitcase.

I pull up behind the house. A wide deck overlooks a descent of lawn. The doors are thrown open. Light spills onto the concrete apron. A basketball goal is nailed to the front of a garage. Palms grow out of pots. Servants in purple jackets run across the drive, carrying food and trays of glasses from the guest house near the pool. In a pen under some crippled oaks peacocks cry.

I get out, open the trunk, and retrieve the suitcase. There is an entrance to the basement somewhere back here, I've seen it. I thought it was outside, but no, now I remember, it's off the kitchen. I climb the steps, nod at future movie stars and courtesans, who bow and try to catch my eye. Celebrity is like a wave, thinning as it runs up the beach. Here, far from the break, at the rear of the house, it is thin and oily, sinking into the sand.

I reach the porch, am about to enter the kitchen, when Billy steps out. His black tuxedo is immaculate, as is his smile and everything else about him.

"Willie boy," he says, "what are you doing back here?"

"Working," I say.

"Good, good. It's good to keep up the practice. What have you got there?"

"Billy," I say, "it's my combustibles. I'm going to burn the house down."

"Great. It'll save me the trouble. Here, let me help you."

I swing the suitcase away from him. I have not lied to him, I am not joking.

"These are special favors," I say, "I'd better handle them."

I am walking into the kitchen as I speak. Billy, behind his hatchet face, follows me. The kitchen glitters like a treasure room. It is as large as a tract house. Roasts, oysters, sculpted tofu, lobsters in ruddy piles, cauldrons of salad greens are set everywhere. Servants shoulder loads and head for the party rooms.

"Isn't this something?" Billy says. "It's like the rich during the Depression, like France before the revolution. Nothing affects us; we're shameless, we go right on generating illusion and piling up the riches, no matter who suffers."

"Art for the masters."

"Yes, yes." He tears a claw off a lobster, sucks it, smacks his lips. "It always amazes me how there is such yearning to believe the world moves in cycles; everyone's such a sucker for the idea that the era of extravagance is over, that the bubble has burst, the crooks have learned their lesson, we're going to shape up now, all that, go penitentially onward, in simple clothes, into the next era."

"They don't know Hollywood."

"They sure don't know me. You ought to try some of this, man—it's like eating gold."

I am looking around for the basement door. It must be . . . over there, in the pantry. A thought strikes me. "Is Lenz here?"

"Bill? Sure. I know I saw him. He's around somewhere, showing off."

Billy is puffed and powerful, but he has come out here to make sure I am not up to something. He's worried I might cause a scene with Clement. The hammer has fallen on this affair, and as far as Billy is concerned, I am the one who got crushed.

"I'd like to make amends to the guy," I say. "I'd like to clean things up between us."

"You're in a new mood."

"Yes. My wound has made me gentle."

He scrutinizes my face. "There's something different about you," he says. "You seem . . . collected."

"I'm tired of the fighting. I'm tired of all this ruckus."

"That's good. I was worried you might be, I don't know . . . rattled."

"I was. But now I'm all right."

"Clement will be glad to hear that. He's here too."

His eyes sparkle and shift. He's so narrow, if he turned sideways I couldn't see him. He presses the insides of his wrists against his chest, pushing the bones in toward the heart. It's a characteristic gesture, a checking of his armor before he strikes. He is perfectly willing to slice me to pieces right here in the kitchen, but he would rather have a larger audience. He likes to see the blood spatter onto as many faces as possible. His sharp nose bobs toward me. "Clement is looking for you," he says.

"Yes. I'm looking for him, too. But I need to catch my breath. Why don't you go out and find him? I want to get myself together here a minute, say a little prayer of thanks and supplication."

"You are an odd one, Will."

"Getting shot will make you slightly odd, Billy."

"I don't doubt it."

He is reluctant to leave me—a liar himself, he trusts no one—but his party calls. Servants, some eyeing us with disdain, whirl about us, passing under weights of silvery tureens and platters. Drinks sparkle on trays like amber and scarlet jewels.

"I'll go and get Clement," he says. "You come on around."

"Fine."

As soon as he is out of sight I slide into the pantry. The cellar door is in here, tucked in between shelves containing expensive canned foods. I push open the door and descend. Billy, originally a farm boy, has one of the few cellars in Los Angeles. The front part is another public room, done up in tweedy intimate style, but the back, the part I descend to, is raw. The walls are pale desert stone, the floor is stone. I find the light, switch it on. Piled around me are wooden crates containing old studio files, a large wall rack of wine bottles, kept for Billy's personal use, and the heavy wooden columns that hold the house up. It is the columns, a foot square, cut from the hearts of mountain pine, I am interested in. I kneel, open the suitcase, and take out the three cans of white gasoline I bought this afternoon. There is a pistol in the suitcase too, a black 9-millimeter Glock semiautomatic, and I take it out and slip it into the pocket of my jacket.

I set the gas cans on the floor, unscrew the caps, punch through the seals with the blade of the penknife my grandfather gave me after Bobby died. The knife is silver and flat, etched with my name. I lift the gas can and step with it to the base of the nearest column, start to tip it, and then I stop. I set the can down. The room has the quality of one of those abandoned adobe houses you come on out in the desert. The walls absorb light, absorb everything. In rooms like these, lives muffle down to silence, breath fades. I lift the can again and set it down. I am not weak, I am not chilled, but I am unable to do this. I screw the caps back on, return the cans to the suitcase, and close and lock it. I need some air. With the case under my arm, I switch out the light, climb the stairs, go out through the kitchen, down the back steps, and into the yard.

High smoke—maybe it is only clouds—obscures the stars. Only here and there, fleetingly, they poke through. The clouds or smoke are so dark that the stars seem to be igniting and extinguishing on their own, as if the power supply up there is failing. There is a smell of smoke and of orange blossoms and, over near the peacock cages, of bird shit. The peacocks cry out loudly; something has disturbed them.

I lie down on the grass. The ground is dry, but it smells of life. Something sharp, something hung deep inside, lets go, and passes out of me. I am filled with wonder. It turns out I am not who I thought I was. This is fine with me. You think something stirring, something incisive, some sweet word from the lips of a beautiful maid, even the soft perfume of a flowering bush, will appear to save you, but it is not like that, at least this is not like that. I am free, and I don't even know how I got free. I stretch my arms out, spread my legs; I feel the night, the torn and weary night, lean down and kiss me on the lips. I kiss back. I have been kissing back all my life—this thought comes to me. I am glad this is so. I didn't know what I was doing—I knew what I was doing. "Bobby," I say out loud, "it is better to be alive than dead. You were wrong there. No matter what, it is better to be alive."

"Who are you talking to?" It is my father's voice. He has come across the lawn to fetch me. I raise myself on an elbow, glad—

instantly, without thought—to see him. Then life comes back, knowledge comes back; they hit, but they don't penetrate. "I heard your voice and I couldn't see you and then I saw you," Clement says. "Billy said you were in the kitchen."

"I was. Then I was in the cellar, and now I'm out here."

"I've caught up with you at last."

He stands over me, fidgeting. His white suit glows. The red scarf knotted at his neck looks black.

"I was going to resolve things in a bright way, but I decided not to."

"You have been curiously active for the last few days. You were hard to keep up with."

His voice is coarse and there is a torn, glottal sound in it, as if other words, thorny sounds, are pressing against the words he says. He takes a step forward, stands with one foot between my ankles. He leans toward me, and his eyes under the thick brows take my measure. Beyond us, out on the lawn near the garage, forms move. I push up on an elbow. My father sways above me. The forms—servants, caterers men, I think—rush about.

"You shouldn't get into a fight with your father," Clement says.

"I didn't really want to do that," I say.

"A father can anticipate; a father can see his son's next move."

"I'm not sure that isn't an illusion sometimes."

"I know why you came here; I know what you have in that suitcase."

Several points of fire appear in the yard, fires struck and lit in the darkness. The fires bobble, waver, and then, one by one, they fly up into the night, soaring high-trailing fire, and smash into flame against the side of the house. One or two go through the open windows. Immediately there is the crack and pop of gunfire, and I see the forms, the figures of men racing toward the house. Clement half turns. He stares at the men, there must be a dozen of them, as they run. Some have guns, some are lighting fire-bombs as they run.

"Son of a bitch, it's an attack," he says.

A man runs by near us. He is wearing the short dark jacket of a house servant, snapping a lighter at the end of a rag-stuffed bottle as he goes. The lighter is like a firefly blinking in his hands. Clement yells at him, "Hey, you, bastard." The man turns, slows.

He continues to flick the lighter. Clement rushes at him. The man tries to dodge, but Clement has surprised him. He runs straight into him, as if he is a wall he has to break through. He lowers his shoulder at the last instant, lifts the man off his feet, and sends him sprawling. The bottle rolls away in the grass.

Clement grabs the man up by his shirt, lifts him off the ground. All around us are shouts, gunfire. Jeeps appear from under the trees; they speed toward the house, security men firing as they come. The house is in flames; the back wall and one side wall under the colonnade are burning. It is on fire inside, too. People are screaming inside and out; there is a tumult of voices from the front of the house. Clement pulls the man toward him, looks in his eyes, and then pushes him out to arm's length and strikes him in the face. The man's head snaps back; Clement drops him on the grass.

He jogs heavily back to where I am still lying on the grass. "It's the fucking employees," he says. "They're attacking the goddamn house."

"They look pretty well prepared."

"Not prepared enough."

"Pop," I say, getting up, "I've thought of a way out for you. I've been riding around all day thinking about it."

"I need that suitcase," he says. "You've got all your sleazy little reports in it and I need it."

"I was thinking—I know it's a simple and plain idea—that you need to confess. You need to admit. I think you ought to stand forth in front of people and say what you have done. You can get an audience—anybody will do really—and you can start at the latest point, say what you and Billy were up to tonight, and work your way back, all the way to Bobby, and on further if you need to, all the way back to Arkansas if that's what it takes. I think this would be a good idea—the best thing you could do."

People are running out of the house. The Jeeps have pulled up into the back turnaround; security men crouch beside the vehicles. They shoot occasionally—over there under the basketball goal, two men wrestle—but they mostly hold their fire; they can't afford to hit the guests. The back porch, a long gallery behind the kitchen, is lit with fires. The flames are dancing under the second-story windows. A ball of flame puffs up in the kitchen, flares in the open doorway, and subsides. In its light there is a form, a shape, someone standing just outside the doorway. It looks like Kate.

I am on my feet, but I nearly fall. My knees go loose, and something in my chest drops straight down. I stagger, I stumble. Clement snatches the suitcase.

"Pop," I say, "is Kate here?"

"Kate?" His voice falters. "Where would she be?"

"On the porch there, in a white dress. She was standing in the doorway." But she is gone now, whoever stood there is gone. My heart races. Inside it's like a line of trees, a forest blown down by hurricane. I can hear the blood in my ears, the rushing of wind. Still, now, so late in this passage through time, again, I want to run to her, want to find her. The fire flares against the back wall, but she is gone, whoever stood there is gone. A sadness, something heavy and crumbled inside me, falls. I throw my head back, I scream. A dizziness, a strange, startled, ripping sensation rushes through me; it seems to drag me with it, like a wind blowing, dragging me, tumbling me—and I am on my knees, and all at once it seems to me that Bobby is nearby again, and Jennie and Veronica, and friends of my youth, even Billy alive from the days when we strode across the blond hills of the Pima plinking pellet guns at the upland birds—and here, now, I can see again the boys tricked up in dresses and the bad men bending over them, and I can see the face of the boy who nearly escaped as he climbs the hill toward me, and I can see his eyes, which are terribly familiar to me, which are asking me, begging me to save him, and this I think, this I realize in a horror that burns like acid, is my brother begging me . . .

I get up from my knees, I take the pistol from my pocket, and I point it at my father. He has turned partly away from me, looking at the fire, looking for Kate. He holds the suitcase in his arms, cradling it against his chest.

"Clement."

He is watching the fire, basking in the spectacle. The fire roars and crackles. The flames eat at the house, leaping. There is a man on the roof. He shouts and waves his arms. Out on the big lawn people stand in groups. Security men herd them toward the gates. Sirens sound in the distance. Off under the trees, under a stand of pines near where the yard gives way to the desert, gunplay continues. Marauders, men from the downtown districts, the disaffected, fire pistols at the security officers. The forces of culture push them back, into the trees, into the scrub.

I say my father's name again. The gun is light in my hand. He turns, sees it, and smiles. The smile is a scar opening.

"Secretly," he says, "you work to destroy, to prevent. You are an inhibitor, a gall."

"Do you know Harvey Madrid?" I say.

"I've heard of him."

"He'll be here in a minute, if he's not here already. He wants to talk to you."

"I bring life to everything. Everything I touch rustles up and blooms, it becomes itself—I give it that."

"That woman off Topanga, the one you burned up—I don't think she'd agree."

"Death's part of it too. Death's the sound life makes. And you're one of those who keeps his ears stoppered—hides out, doesn't want to leave home."

"I don't mind, Pop, I don't mind anymore. There's a lot to learn close to home."

"Yeah. And I guess I have it now in this little case. Your research. All your sneaking around and looking in windows—it's in here I'm sure."

"You've always gotten in too close to me. To everyone. Nobody likes anyone standing that close, Pop."

"I wasn't getting close, I was running you over."

"Not this time."

He looks at the pistol; he laughs. The laugh is coarse, full of life. It is all there before me. You look someone in the face and everything, the whole past, every breath they've taken, is right there in front of you. But the present is where the power is. It's all here, right now, this flash of time is everything. "I like this moment," I say, "I love it. I love seeing you here, standing in front of me. You're my father, I know you better almost than I know anyone, better even than I know Kate or Veronica; I know the hairs on your legs and the scar under your beltline, and I know how you twist the side of your mouth when you're excited; I know the smell of your knees and how you squeeze your shoulders with your hands before you come into a room . . ."

He sees my face and something in him changes. There is a slight shift, a slide—so it seems—downward, like a man losing his footing at the edge of a ditch. "You're going to shoot me," he says.

"Yes."

"There're bullets in *that* gun."

"Yes."

He looks at the burning house. The flames are orange and yellow; they are full and blowing, meaty and glistening with life. Two men race by shouting. They look familiar, but maybe it is only the desperation in their faces, the urgency of their flight that is familiar. "I have had such a wonderful time here," my father says.

"Better than anyone could hope for."

"Yes, it's true. We were all of us, all of us travelers, us escapees, us Arkies, all of us were ruined, it was clear—you should have seen us, you should have seen what it was like on the roads in those days, nothing to do but sit on a rock and drink cornmeal soup." He sighs. "I don't know what it is keeps men moving, I don't know what it is'll make a man, even after he's ruined, pick up his feet and keep moving. I don't know what it is, but it fascinates me. It fascinates me that I am one of them. I wake up every day and I am amazed."

"We are all impressed."

"You mock me."

"No. You are right—you stir up life everywhere: in me, in everyone."

He shakes his head. "I don't know what God means by all of this. I've been curious all my life about what he is up to, about why he lets us run around the way we do. It makes me breathless to see the next thing happen."

"You sound like Kate."

"Yes. I never met anyone like her. Except myself, I mean."

I glance toward the house, a quick scan. She, the figment, dream, or reality, is gone.

"Pop," I say, "this is the best I can do for you."

His eyes flash, and he begins to growl. The sound is ancient, indecipherable, it rumbles in his throat, grinds. His body begins to shake, his arms tremble, he throws his head back and howls. The howl is piercing, fierce, untamable. It rises above the sound of the fire, above the shouts and the cries of the wounded. It is a pure, wild, desolate sound, and it is the sound I fire into.

I am twenty feet from him. The bullet hits the case, and I think I see the bullet hit him in the chest, see the surprise in his eyes, but I cannot be sure, because the case, the gasoline inside it, explodes in a black-and-red ball that obscures him and blows me onto my back. The fire touches me, strikes me, my shirt catches, I roll on the ground extinguishing it, and then I see him, farther off now, a shape in flame, see him rise from the ground in flames, see him push himself up off the grass screaming. Flames roll off him, leap from him; he revolves, staggering, in a roulade of fire. It is as if he is made of fire.

He stumbles toward me; his hands are raised, they jerk like a puppet's, he is screaming steadily, bellowing. He takes a step, two steps, and another, a last step, his leg twitching up, jerked down hard, and then, as behind us the house roars in flames and the fire trucks pull into the yard, and the security men shout, and the last of the attackers flee, as above us the stars roll on into eternity, he stands before me, a father consumed by fire. He lifts his melted, burning face to me, and I see the shape that is no longer recognizable; and the burning hands and the body burning I see, and what is burning inside the fire I see, Clement, my father, I see. He sways, leans slowly left, puts his arm out, and topples. He falls burning into the grass.

I stay with him, squatted near him, leaning forward with my palms on the grass, taking the heat on my face, until there is no heat, until there is nothing but the charred corpse.

I had wondered what might show itself at this moment, what might rise through the first breaths drawn in a world where he did not exist, but there is nothing. Later, perhaps later, the lurking truths will scurry forth, but now, high in these hills where the cool breezes have begun to blow in off the sea, no greater knowledge, no illuminating figuration appears. A dull, slow throbbing begins. I lift my head, I listen for my brother's voice, for the soft singing, but there is nothing. I look around. Even Kate, who could live anywhere, even in a house on fire, is gone.